NO OTHER CHOICE

Satan's Favorite Lie

James R. Milstead

Editorial Services: Karen Roberts, RQuest, LLC

Printed in the United States of America

ISBN-13: 9780692576083
ISBN-10: 0692576088

For permission to use material or arrange for a speaking engagement, contact:

James R. Milstead
1726 S. Mayberry Dr.
Frankfort, IN 46041
765-654-7749
Email jrmilstead@comcast.net

CONTENTS

PREFACE

This novel is an amalgam of fictional characters and documented historical events that shaped the lives of many baby boomers in the late 1960s and early 1970s. From my forty-plus year attempt to understand the role I played in those turbulent times as a B-52 tail gunner during the Vietnam War came the genesis of this book. Although the last year of the war figures prominently in the beginning of the adventure, some of the major social issues tearing at the fabric of society during that time gain momentum as the story unfolds.

A hidden gem in this novel is the compelling yet tragic, story of the Hmong tribesmen of Laos. The Hmong were courageous allies of the U.S., fighting a secret war in Laos for more than a decade. Our country owes them a tremendous debt for the sacrifices they made on our behalf.

PART I

Survival

CHAPTER ONE

S ome people say that when you die, a blinding white light surrounds you, and your whole life passes before your eyes. Tail gunner Jake Lemaster didn't know if it was true, but he felt sure he was about to find out.

But as quickly as it had come, the white light vanished. It was replaced by an oppressive darkness punctuated with searing flames, a deafening roar, and the pungent smell of burning sulfur scorching his nostrils. A blast of frigid air chilled him to the marrow. Spiraling downward, out of control, he fought to make sense of what was happening.

"We're hit!" copilot First Lieutenant Jim Sizemore called out to the crew on the intercom as he struggled to keep the damaged B-52 bomber in the air. The cockpit had fogged, and papers were flying through the air as the forward compartment lost pressurization. When his vision cleared, he looked to his left and saw the pilot slumped over, drenched in blood. In front of him, red fire warning lights for engines one and two on the left wing lit up the instrument panel, and the oil pressure gauges signaled a hydraulic leak.

The copilot quickly shut down the damaged engines and stood hard on the right rudder pedal to keep the nose of the aircraft straight. Next he pulled the power back on the engines on the right wing to compensate for the loss of power on the left side of the plane. After plummeting fifteen thousand feet in a matter of seconds, the aircraft eventually stabilized with the altimeter showing 18,000 feet.

"Crew, status check," the copilot said at last.

"EW's okay," said Major Cash, the crew's electronic warfare officer.

"Gunner's okay," said Jake, still reeling from the shock of the last few minutes. He looked down at his leg, which was beginning to throb from the shrapnel that'd shredded his compartment. Only then did he understand. The great, white light had come from the explosion of a lethal surface-to-air missile just beneath the bomber. Judgment day, at least for him, had been postponed. Not so for others. He listened for the rest of his crew's responses.

"Radar navigator, report in," ordered the copilot.

No response.

"Navigator, report in."

Again no response.

"EW, go down and check on the navigators."

The EW unstrapped from his seat and went down the ladder into the navigators' compartment. There he saw a gaping hole in the left side of the plane beside what remained of the radar navigator, Major Lassiter. The navigator, Captain Fallon, was slumped over his workstation, lifeless and bathed in blood. They never had a chance. The missile had exploded adjacent to their compartment.

Strapping back into his ejection seat upstairs, the EW reported the grim news. "Both navigators are dead."

"Roger," said the copilot. "The pilot's dead as well, so I'm in command. I'll keep us flying as long as possible. The heading indicator and altimeter are still functioning, but airspeed has dropped to under 300 knots. I'll fly a heading of 270 degrees for twenty minutes. That should get us out of North Vietnam. After that, we'll turn south over Laos and try to get back into Thailand. EW, start timing me now. Let me know when twenty minutes have gone by. I've got my hands full up here just keeping us straight and level."

"Roger. Starting stopwatch now."

"How do things look from the tail, guns?" the copilot asked.

"I don't see any fires now," Jake said.

"Roger that. We'll descend to 10,000 feet as we head west. Both of you, be prepared to bail out if I can't keep this thing in the air."

Jake tightened his parachute straps and rechecked the survival equipment. His .38 caliber pistol was fully loaded. With his flashlight, he examined his aching lower right leg. His flight suit was peppered with small holes, revealing several wounds oozing blood, but he didn't feel any broken bones. His thoughts turned to the fate of the pilot, his friend, Captain Morgan. For the moment, the news of his death stung him more intensely than his physical wounds. He fought hard to suppress his emotions. There would be plenty of time for grieving later if he survived.

"Crew, listen up," said the copilot. "I'm going to test the bailout light to make sure it's working in case we have to abandon the aircraft. This will just be a test. Check in and let me know you understand."

"EW copies."

"Gunner copies."

"Stand by for the bailout light, and let me know if yours is working. Ready, now."

Jake saw the red bailout light activate, illuminating the darkened gunner's compartment.

"EW's bailout light working."

"Gunner's bailout light working."

"Copilot copies. If we lose communication over the intercom, I'll activate the bailout light if we need to exit the aircraft. I'll fly as long as I can to be sure you're out, and then I'll eject."

To Jake it seemed the copilot had control of the aircraft and a coherent plan of action to get them out of the most immediate danger. If they went down in their present location, capture within North Vietnam would most likely be swift. If they made it to the border of Laos, maybe they would have a fighting chance of getting back to the base in Thailand alive.

He checked his watch and saw that it was 0030 hours. *Thirty minutes past midnight,* he said to himself as a reminder of that moment. *It's early morning on December 19, 1972.*

What would become the longest twenty minutes of his life crawled by as the badly damaged aircraft inched its way toward the first goal of reaching Laos. *At home in the States, twenty minutes would have flown by in the time it took to listen to "MacArthur Park" and "Bye, Bye, Miss American Pie" on WLS-AM radio station out of Chicago.*

Alone with his thoughts, Sergeant Jake Lemaster, tail gunner in one of America's most magnificent war machines, replayed in his mind the cataclysmic events of the last twenty-four hours that'd so dramatically altered the course of his life.

Until yesterday the fear of death had been a foreign concept to him. Although he and his crew had flown more than thirty combat missions since arriving in Southeast Asia nearly two months ago, never had he harbored any thought of not returning safely at the completion of a mission.

Then came the announcement from Eighth Air Force Headquarters that all B-52 crewmembers had best put their affairs in order because the next mission would be "extremely hazardous to your health." Colonel Smith, the 307th Bomb Wing Commander at U-Tapao, Thailand, had delivered the mission briefing that morning. "Gentlemen, your target for tonight is Hanoi," he said as he unveiled a wall-sized map of North Vietnam that displayed multiple targets surrounding the enemy's capital city. He went on to explain the specifics of this mission, including the dangers.

After the meeting, crewmembers had been allowed one five-minute overseas call to speak to their loved ones. They were prohibited, however, from divulging any details of what was to come for them. Jake expected his cryptic phone conversation would unnerve his wife, Donna, back at their home in Ohio. But instead, what she told him turned his world upside down.

"I'm pregnant," she said. "Jake, you're going to be a father."

Paul McCartney was right, he thought to himself—*yesterday all my troubles seemed so far away.*

That evening, the bus carrying the five officers on his crew arrived promptly at 1830 hours as he was finishing a smoke in front of the barracks. The last vestiges of sunlight had faded moments before, leaving him veiled in darkness. He flicked the spent Marlboro into the road and watched briefly as the burning tobacco missile cartwheeled across the asphalt. Grabbing his helmet bag, he jumped through the open door of the bus.

Captain Morgan, Jake's pilot, greeted him as he climbed aboard. "Ready to go, Sergeant Lemaster?"

"Yes, sir. Let's rock and roll," Jake said with as much of the usual bravado as he could muster.

Morgan was thirty-five years old, thirteen years Jake's senior. As the aircraft commander, he was the officer responsible for everything in Jake's life that could affect the rest of the crew, most especially the safe performance of his duties as the gunner in protecting the aircraft during a mission. Under normal circumstances, Jake already would have confided in Morgan the news that Donna had related to him. Morgan would have given him wise fatherly advice. But these were not normal times. "Hello, Jake," said the copilot, First Lieutenant Jim Sizemore, as Jake made his way to the back of the bus.

"Hello, sir," Jake called out in response.

Sizemore was twenty-six years old, the youngest and most athletic of the crew's five officers. Even though officers generally avoided socializing with enlisted crewmembers, he and Jake occasionally played basketball or racquetball together back in the States. Jake liked Jim's laid-back manner and his love of sports. He too had a beautiful young wife waiting for him at home and was not pleased to be 9,000 miles away from her. "Hi, guns." This time it was the navigator, Captain Roy Fallon, who spoke. "I have a feeling we're going to need you tonight."

"I'll be ready, sir," Jake said with confidence.

Fallon was twenty-nine years old and the nicest guy in the world, or so it seemed to Jake. He was a college grad who had grown up on a farm in Ohio before enlisting in the U.S. Air Force. He treated Jake like a younger brother and never pulled rank on him as some other officers did. Jake nodded to the other two officers, radar navigator Major Lassiter (bombardier) and electronic warfare officer (EW) Major Cash. The two were silent, staring off into the dark, tropical landscape outside. Jake took a seat beside them.

Major Lassiter was a cynical forty-year old Bostonian. In contrast, Major Cash was a laid-back thirty-eight year old Missourian who loved country music and Coca-Cola. Jake's relationship with them was congenial but distant, typical for officers and enlisted men such as Jake.

As the bus pulled away from the gunners' quarters on the base—located on the Gulf of Siam, a hundred miles southeast of Bangkok, Thailand—Jake wondered if he would see any of his gunner friends back there in the barracks again. They'd all made a pact before this mission to leave the keys to their lockers in the rooms for easy access so those who didn't return could have their personal items shipped to their families back home. The gravity of the upcoming battle could not be ignored. They were well aware that some unfortunate families might soon receive notice from an Air Force official, "We regret to inform you . . ."

As tail gunner of a B-52D, Jake's station was in the back of the mammoth bomber with a rear facing view. His job was to protect the rear of the plane with four computer-controlled fifty-caliber machine guns. The crew also relied on him to spot SAMs (Russian-made SA-2 surface-to-air missiles) and call for evasive action in the event the aircraft came under attack. The gravity of his role weighed heavily on him.

After their preflight mission briefing, Jake's crew picked up survival equipment and headed by bus to the aircraft to prepare for a 2100 hours takeoff time. *Sapphire Cell*, the official call sign for the three-aircraft formation in which Jake's crew would be flying, would be joining up with other B-52s over northern Laos in about two and a half hours in order to be over the target at midnight.

"Are you okay, Jake?" Captain Morgan asked as the crew stepped off the bus. The pilot had waited intentionally for a moment to speak to Jake personally.

"Yes, sir. Just anxious to get started, I guess."

"Did you call your young bride yesterday while you had the chance?"

"Yes, sir. But as you know, I really couldn't tell her much about what's going on here."

"Sometimes it's not as important what you say to a woman as it is just being there to listen to what she has to say."

"I'm finding that out, sir."

The truth was, Jake knew very little about how to be a husband. Although he and Donna had dated off and on for several years, the suddenness of their marriage took everyone by surprise—including him.

He proposed a few days after receiving orders for a six-month combat tour in Southeast Asia, assuming they'd be married when he returned. Donna, however, was insistent on having the wedding as soon as possible, much to the chagrin of her father. In retrospect, he was sure that's why she did so. Her father was not a big fan of Jake Lemaster.

Gear in hand, Jake walked to the back of the 159-foot long bomber as the pilot headed to the front. He threw his helmet bag and survival equipment onto the yellow maintenance stand directly below the open entrance to his "home" for the next five hours. From atop the stand, he hoisted himself up inside the small tunnel leading to the gunner's compartment. Packing his six foot two frame inside the cramped chamber was no easy task.

"Here's your equipment, Sarge," the maintenance crewman called out as he tossed the helmet bag and survival gear up to Jake after he was inside. "Good luck, man. I'll be praying for you."

"Right. Thanks," Jake said flatly as the maintenance crewman closed and latched the door beneath him.

At that moment, the routine boarding procedure he knew so well seemed different, as if he'd just been sealed inside a tomb. *I hope that guy has a direct link to God. Why is it that I always wait 'til I'm in a jam to pray?*

After an on-time takeoff, the three planes flying as *Sapphire Cell* entered Laotian airspace heading northeast to rendezvous with more B-52s coming from Andersen Air Force base on the tiny Pacific island of Guam, located some 3,000 miles away. The flight plan called for all aircraft to enter North Vietnamese airspace from the west and proceed northeast to a point north of Hanoi, very near the Chinese border. All planes, flying the same route, would then turn southeast on their bomb run over the city of Hanoi. After striking their targets, all aircraft would make a rapid and steep post-target turn and exit North Vietnam, heading west back into Laos.

The night was nearly pitch black with only a crescent moon to light the sky. Jake strained to see the Laotian landscape below as he peered through scattered clouds that outlined vague, jagged mountain peaks dotting the western horizon. He and his crew had flown many bombing missions in this area trying to impede the constant flow of NVA troops and supplies coming down the Ho Chi Minh Trail through Laos and Cambodia to their destination in South Vietnam. But that's about where his knowledge of Laos ended.

Maybe someday I'll have a chance to learn a little more about this place.

Without warning, emergency broadcasts over the Guard channel shattered the relative calm. Jake knew the Guard channel was reserved for aircrews under duress, and what he heard certainly confirmed that. "SAM, SAM, vicinity of Hanoi," called out a crewmember, presumably from one of the B-52s leading the strike force. That news meant the enemy was aware of the attack and had begun to fire deadly surface-to-air missiles at the bomber crews. *Sapphire Cell*, his cell, would be the tenth group of bombers dropping their payload over Hanoi.

Let's hope they've exhausted their whole arsenal before we get there.

The frightening sound of an emergency locator beacon blared over the Guard channel, signifying an airman had bailed out of an aircraft. More calls warned of SAM launches around Hanoi, and the ominous, warbling sound of more emergency beacons pierced the airwaves.

The war had suddenly become very real and personal to Jake, even from six miles above the earth. He sensed his heart rate quickening, and his hands felt clammy with perspiration. He was acutely aware of each breath he took beneath the hard rubber oxygen mask.

Alone in the tail, he focused his thoughts on the light from the radar screen in front of him, periodically shattering the darkness as the radar system swept through an arc behind the aircraft, searching for enemy fighters. All radar returns looked the same— a small white blip on the screen, as the radar painted it—whether from an enemy MiG fighter jet or from a friendly F-4 fighter providing protection. American fighter pilots knew better than to fly too close to a B-52, especially over Hanoi, where any radar returns would be considered hostile aircraft. Enemy pilots, however, would be more intent on their ultimate goal, rapidly closing in from behind and firing machine guns mounted in the nose of their aircraft. That's where Jake had an advantage. The effective firing range of his guns was greater than that of the enemy. He just hoped any MiG he might encounter was not armed with long-range, heat-seeking missiles.

As *Sapphire Cell's* three B-52s turned to the east and entered North Vietnam to begin the bomb run, the navigators and radar navigators began completing their checklists methodically and directing the course to the target. In the cockpit, the pilots and copilots could see brilliant explosions lighting up the sky ahead like fireworks on the fourth of July. All the while, the Guard channel rang out with repeated cries of "SAM launch, Hanoi."

"EW, we're almost in range of those SAM sites," Captain Morgan called out. "Are your jammers on?"

"Roger, pilot," said Major Cash.

The electronic warfare officer was responsible for monitoring enemy radar tracking the plane—primarily SAM sites—and countering a threat by jamming the enemy frequency. He was also responsible for dropping chaff and flares to protect the plane from a missile launched by an enemy fighter.

Jake constantly searched both sides of the aircraft from his rear-facing seat to detect any SAMs rocketing toward the aircraft. Their movement, at three times the speed of sound, was a challenge to detect. His view was limited to the back half of the plane, from the three o'clock to nine o'clock position. He had yet to see the menacing display of missile explosions the pilots were being treated to out front. He'd been told that a SAM looked like a telephone pole with fire on the bottom end until it detonated beneath a plane, spraying the aircraft with deadly shrapnel. He knew the Russian SA-2 surface-to-air missiles were effective up to 60,000 feet altitude. His plane was flying at slingshot range by comparison, making Sapphire 3 a much easier target.

"Pilot, come left three degrees," radar navigator Major Lassiter said.

"Roger, coming left three degrees."

Suddenly a target appeared on Jake's radar screen. "Crew, gunner. I have a bogey at eight o'clock low, range seven miles."

"Keep an eye on him," Captain Morgan replied.

"Roger."

As Jake watched the radar image, sweat dripped from beneath his helmet and stung his eyes. He pressed the action switches on the control panel, put the circle cursor over the bogey, and pressed the target acquisition button. Immediately the white rays of the radar strobed out on the dark screen, like the speed gun of a traffic cop, and acquired the target. The green light on the radar screen signified a lock-on. The radar system automatically would follow the target until it disappeared—one way or another.

Time seemed to stand still. He labored to breathe inside the tight-fitting oxygen mask, anxiously awaiting the inevitable attack. Every muscle in his body twitched with anticipation as the bogey moved rapidly into the six o'clock position, directly behind the B-52, and closed to within four miles.

After a momentary pause, the MiG accelerated toward the aircraft with amazing speed. The radar return grew steadily bigger as the enemy fighter closed the distance and began its attack run on Sapphire 3.

With his heart hammering in his chest, he called out, "EW, drop chaff and flares!"

When the MiG closed to within 2,000 yards, Jake reported his status. "Crew, gunner firing now!"

Depressing the action switches and squeezing the triggers, he fired three short bursts. In seconds, a thousand rounds of .50 caliber bullets, each the size of his hand, streaked out of the guns toward the enemy fighter. All of a sudden, the target on the radar screen ballooned to three times its normal intensity and then disappeared. It was a hit!

*This is no time to cele*brate, he thought to himself. *Keep your head in the game.*

"One minute to bomb release," said the radar navigator. "Pilot, come left two degrees."

"Roger, two degrees left."

"Crew, gunner. We're clear back here for now."

"Roger, guns," the pilot said. "Stay alert. There are SAMs everywhere up ahead."

No one else was in a position to see SAMs except the two pilots and the gunner, since only they had a view outside the aircraft. And since Jake was facing backward, only the pilots witnessed the initial SAM firings up ahead. Their chilling comments were not reassuring.

"I'm picking up SAM search radar," said the EW.

"Roger," said the pilot. "They're firing a lot of missiles at the guys in front of us."

"SAM coming up just off the nose on my side," said the copilot.

"Keep an eye on it," said the pilot.

"SAM detonation two o'clock high," said the copilot.

Jake was busy looking out both sides of the canopy, searching for SAMs and intermittently glancing at his radar screen. He could see none. That worried him. He'd been trained that the mostly deadly SAM was the one you never saw.

"Somebody just got hit," said the pilot as he witnessed a SAM destroy a bomber in the cell just ahead.

"Mayday, Mayday. *Diamond 3* going down!" cried out a crewmember from a dying B-52 over the Guard channel. The aircraft disappeared into the night.

An emergency locator beacon sent out its chilling signal over the Guard channel followed closely by two more warbling beacons.

"Fifteen seconds to bomb release," said radar navigator Major Lassiter. "Bomb doors coming open. Pilot, give me one degree left."

"Roger, one degree left."

"SAM at eleven o'clock, coming through the clouds," said the pilot.

"Coming up on ten seconds to release," said the radar navigator. "Ready, ready, now."

"Two SAMs, three o'clock low," said the copilot.

"Five, four, three, two, one. Bombs away!" said the radar navigator as *Sapphire 3's* payload was released into the darkness.

"Bomb doors coming closed," the radar navigator reported. "Turn right heading 270 degrees."

"Coming right to 270 degrees," said the pilot as he yanked the bomber into a tight, 60-degree bank to the right.

In an instant, a SAM streaked by the front of the left wing and vented its parcel of death harmlessly overhead. Then a second SAM exploded just off the nose of the aircraft, momentarily blinding both pilots but missing its target. Captain Morgan fought to keep the plane in a steep turn as the aircraft came up on the outbound heading, exiting the target area.

Just as *Sapphire 3* rolled out of the turn, Jake saw it—too late. A third SAM. It erupted beneath the left wing, spraying the left side of the aircraft with hundreds of molten metal projectiles. He was bathed in a sea of brilliant, blinding, white light.

"Twenty minutes are up, copilot."

The EW's strained voice shattered the silence and shocked Jake back into the present. The wait that had sent him into a review of the last twenty-four hours of his life was over, and he was pulled abruptly back into the present. Their damaged aircraft, now under the control of the copilot after the SAM had exploded and killed the pilot and the two navigators, had made it to its first goal. They were out of North Vietnam and above Laos.

"Roger. I'll start a slow left turn to a heading of 180 degrees," said the copilot. "We're level at 10,000 feet."

Relieved, Jake took off his mask and shut off the flow of oxygen to it from the control panel. Hurriedly he lit a cigarette and enjoyed a much-needed smoke. He didn't know when he'd get the chance again. Taking Donna's picture from the pocket of his flight suit, and using light from the flashlight, he fixed his eyes on the precious photo.

"You're going to be a father," she'd said. There was no way he wasn't going to make it home.

He finished the first cigarette and lit another. The fear of dying of cancer was not a major concern at that moment. After the second cigarette, he drank a bottle of water and then relieved himself with the urine bottle. Just for practice, he reached out with his left hand and grasped the yellow ejection handle. *Let's hope it works as advertised,* he thought to himself.

Just then he felt the aircraft buffeting and vibrating violently as pieces of the left wing began falling away from the still smoldering plane. All hope of making it back to the base ended. The red bailout light came to life as he heard the copilot say those dreaded words, "Bailout, bailout!"

Jake leaned forward and jerked the ejection handle outward and toward him, watching as the tail compartment of the aircraft shot backward into the inky night sky. *Like a spent rocket booster jettisoned from an Apollo spacecraft,* he thought.

As he grabbed the assist handles on each side of the gunner's compartment and prepared to lunge out through the opening, the aircraft pitched nose down. It would take all the strength he could muster to overcome the force of gravity as the plane continued its dive toward the earth. He struggled to complete the task he'd been trained to do but had hoped never to execute. Finally he wrenched himself free of the earthbound plane. As soon as he was clear, he pulled the metal ring on the parachute. The chute opened above him with a violent jerk. Silence surrounded him as he drifted toward the ground.

Looking below, he witnessed the huge fireball and heard the deafening roar of impact as his plane, *Sapphire 3*, crashed into the earth. He saw no other parachutes. Taking out his emergency radio, he attempted, without success, to reach someone on Guard channel. Again there was an eerie and yet peaceful silence, one that disguised the dangers waiting for him in the jungle beneath him.

The sky was dark, and he could not see the terrain below until seconds before impact. The trees enveloped him. His helmet cracked against a huge branch, and then everything went black.

CHAPTER TWO

Lo Chang was cloaked in midnight darkness, concealed in thick jungle on the side of a hill overlooking what the Americans called the Ho Chi Minh Trail. He simply knew it as home.

For more years than he could remember, he'd been fighting the Vietnamese enemy invading his land. He longed to return to his family and pursue a peaceful life as a rice farmer. Fate, however, had thrust him into a lifelong battle for the right to remain free.

His people, the Hmong, had inhabited the highlands of Laos for thousands of years. They were a people who treasured the concepts of honor, loyalty, and freedom. The advent of World War II had brought Japanese soldiers to Indochina, where they enslaved and brutalized his Hmong tribesmen. Thousands of his people had died fighting a guerrilla war for the Allies against the occupying force for more than five years. No sooner had the Japanese surrendered than a new threat emerged—the Viet Minh.

A Marxist revolutionary, Ho Chi Minh, had taken advantage of the power vacuum in postwar Indochina and created the

Democratic Republic of Vietnam. Lo Chang was only a child at the time. Ho's dream of spreading communism throughout the region led to a gradual buildup of North Vietnamese soldiers in neighboring Laos. The Viet Minh's victory over the French at Dien Bien Phu in 1954 occurred less than ten years later. The Communists were emboldened to conquer first Laos, and then the rest of Indochina. Pathet Lao forces, Laotian Communists sympathetic to the revolutionary cause, joined in the fighting alongside the Vietnamese against the Hmong.

Lo Chang had a burning hatred for such traitors. As a youth, he'd watched helplessly as Pathet Lao soldiers destroyed his village and ruthlessly killed his mother and father. He was imprisoned in a Communist indoctrination camp for several months before escaping and seeking refuge in the rugged mountains of central Laos. He soon joined a group of Hmong soldiers and began fighting the Communists throughout northeastern Laos.

It was another ten years before the Americans arrived—in the early 1960s. At the time, the Americans were in the first days of a massive ground war in South Vietnam. The CIA asked the Hmong leaders to help defeat the Communists. The Hmong told them to send weapons, and they'd fight to the death to protect their people and their way of life. Freedom eluded the Hmong, however, while death was an ever-present companion.

Now, nearly ten years later, Lo Chang was still battling for survival and freedom for his land against overwhelming odds. Age was a relative concept in his culture. He wasn't sure how many years he'd lived, but he knew his only son was now old enough to carry a gun and fight alongside him. It hurt him deep inside each time he thought about his wife and daughter. He hadn't seen them for more than a year. He wondered if they were even alive. He wondered too how long he and his son could survive.

The trail below where he had positioned himself suddenly sprang to life with the shouting of commands in Vietnamese and the noise of trucks starting their engines. For a long time, he watched from his secure vantage point. Too many enemy soldiers. He had to find a small, vulnerable target for a successful hit-and-run attack. Speed and surprise were needed to inflict maximum pain on the enemy. Fortunately, he knew the terrain better than anyone. This was his home.

The shrill whining sound of jet engines coming from somewhere north of his position caught his attention. He turned to see a massive plane, engulfed in flames, hurtling toward the ground like a shooting star passing through the heavens. The deafening explosion and the accompanying fireball surely signaled certain death for anyone aboard. He'd never seen a B-52 before, but he suspected he'd just witnessed the crash of one of the Americans' bombers.

Lo Na, his son, was rudely awakened by the plane's explosion. He stood close to his father and anxiously scanned the surroundings for an explanation. His father signaled for him to remain silent and then pointed in the direction of the crash.

Lo Chang had been working behind enemy lines most of his life. His job was to spy on the enemy and sabotage their efforts whenever and wherever he could. The information he provided to the Americans allowed them to bomb enemy targets with precision, something that gave him great satisfaction. Nothing so far, however, could compare to the pride he'd felt many times before after rescuing a downed American pilot.

Men like him called themselves by the Lao words *tahaan su tai*—"soldiers willing to die." The Americans called them *men of courage.* Many Hmong had died trying to rescue American pilots and crewmembers shot down over Laos.

The Communists knew the Hmong would make every effort to save their American allies, so they often hid near a crash site and ambushed them when they came near. The plane most likely was returning to a base in Thailand after a bombing mission in North Vietnam.

Lo Chang would not risk going to the crash site. He had no hopes of finding any survivors there from the fiery crash, but he wondered if some of the crew had bailed out of the plane prior to impact. He estimated the crash site to be five kilometers northwest of his present position. He determined to look farther to the north.

As he set out at a brisk pace with his son close behind, he formulated a plan in his mind. He was sure the enemy would reach the crash site first, since the Pathet Lao and their North Vietnamese comrades controlled that area of eastern Laos. He and his son would be near where the plane had gone down by the time the sun came up, and they could watch from a distance. Then they would head north and look for signs of American spotter planes searching for any downed airmen. If they found one, perhaps his son would earn the title *tahaan su tai* that day.

When Jake regained consciousness, his head was pounding as if someone had hit him with a crowbar. The luminescent dial on his Seiko wristwatch told him it was 0230 hours. As he stood up, a wave of dizziness and nausea swept over him like a tsunami. He retched and vomited until his stomach was empty.

Surveying the area, he saw that he had landed on the slope of a mountain, the top of it shrouded in a veil of fog. Traveling in the dark through the dense jungle vegetation that surrounded him would be futile. He had no sense of direction and no knowledge of the terrain or the people inhabiting the area. Only one thing was certain. The fiery crash of his B-52 would have awakened everyone in a ten-mile radius, including any Viet Cong or North Vietnamese troops nearby.

He gathered up his parachute, helmet, and survival equipment and then sought cover in a thicket of trees and tropical plants nearby. His plan was to remain hidden until daylight and then reevaluate his options when he could see more clearly. Hopefully, he'd be able to contact a rescue team on the emergency radio in the survival vest. Reaching for the radio, he realized it was gone. Only then did he remember he'd been holding it in his hand, attempting to radio for help, during the parachute landing.

Using his flashlight, he frantically searched the ground near the spot where he landed. No radio. His head was throbbing, and he was feeling so weak he thought he was going to pass out. He retreated to the relative safety of his hiding spot to wait for the first light of day.

He took stock of the contents of his survival equipment and was relieved to see that everything else was there—food, water, and a survival guide. He took a drink from the water bottle, lay back on the folded parachute, and tried to collect his thoughts. A quick examination of his injured right leg revealed only superficial wounds, which he quickly bandaged. Multiple areas of his bruised body ached, but he had somehow escaped major injuries. Daylight was four hours away. He knew he'd better get some rest while he could. The adrenaline had long since worn off from the traumatic events of the night, and he felt weary. Sleep, however, seemed impossible.

Taking Donna's picture from the pocket of his flight suit, he shined the pale beam from his flashlight onto his wife's image. Theirs was an improbable story, one that confirmed the truth that opposites do indeed attract.

Let's hope adversity strengthens the bond we have between us.

⊫⊣⊢⊨

It was the fall of 1968. Jake was beginning his freshmen year at Grantham College, a small private school in southern Illinois. At the time, the country was still reeling from the tragic assassinations of Martin Luther King and Bobby Kennedy, and antiwar protests had escalated after the Tet Offensive had dispelled the notion that the U.S. was winning the war in Vietnam.

When Donna Kingston walked into English class on the first day of classes, he was smitten immediately. Her long, wavy blonde hair framed a finely sculpted face that needed no makeup to enhance its China doll features. She sported a winsome smile and blue eyes that sparkled when she fixed her gaze upon him as she took the seat next to his.

"Hi," she said. "My name is Donna."

"Hi, Donna. I'm Jake."

"Where are you from, Jake?"

"A small town three hours north of here."

"Where's that?"

"Clarkston. How about you?"

"St. Louis."

"How'd you end up at Grantham?"

"My father is an alumnus," she said. "He wanted me to come here because Grantham has a strong business program. What are you majoring in?"

"Journalism, with a minor in football. I'm here on a football scholarship, but my passion is writing."

"Journalism. Great. Maybe you can help me get through this class. I have difficulty writing a sentence."

Jake had trouble believing she struggled with any academic endeavor, considering the ease with which she'd just communicated. She hadn't used the all-too-common *groovy* or *far out* a single time during their introduction.

"Anytime," he said as he wrote down his telephone number on a scrap of paper and handed it to her. "I'm living in Grover Hall with the other jocks."

"I'm in Bethany Woods," she said, taking the paper and stashing it inside her backpack. She was surprised by the strange attraction she felt as she took in her new acquaintance's ruggedly masculine features and easy-going manner. Although his dark brown hair and matching eyes were handsome, she determined she would treat him as she did all other admiring boys—keep him at a distance so as to avoid any romantic advances.

As he'd suspected, it was soon apparent she needed no help making it through freshman English class. They talked occasionally, but outside of the classroom, their paths seldom crossed. She was immersed in the school of business, while he was busy butting heads on the football field. His phone never rang.

The fall semester ended, and he did not see her again for several months. Then on a gorgeous spring day in early April, as he was heading back to his room after a class, he saw her sitting on a bench near the lake on campus. She was reading a textbook on accounting as he approached. The bright sunlight made her hair appear like strands of gold falling gently across her bare shoulders. The yellow halter-top she was wearing revealed delicate white skin, beginning to blush from the effects of the intense sunlight.

"Hey, stranger," he said as he sat down beside her on the bench.

"Hi. It's been a long time."

"I see you're doing a little light reading."

"I have a major exam coming up in my accounting class this week."

"I can't help you there. But if you need some pointers on throwing a football . . . "

"I'll keep that in mind. How did your team do in the fall?"

"You mean you weren't a loyal fan, living only for game day?" he said with mock surprise.

"Spare me," she said with a sardonic look. "That may be true for some of my more shallow friends who worship your type, but I have more important things to do with my time."

"Like what?"

"Like graduating at the top of my class in two more years."

"You're planning on graduating after three years? What's the rush?"

"I have my reasons. What about you? Are you still thinking of getting your degree in journalism? Or are you hoping to be a professional football player?"

"Football was just my ticket to attend college. Without the scholarship, I could never have afforded to go to any college, let alone Grantham."

"Wouldn't your parents have helped you pay the tuition and fees?"

"My dad died of a heart attack when I was ten. Money has been tight ever since."

"I'm sorry," she said, softening her voice.

"That's all right. It seems like a long time ago now."

"Did your mother remarry?"

"Yeah, she married a widower who owns a gas station back in Clarkston. Mike's a nice guy, but he has a daughter to support. So I took advantage of Grantham's offer to play quarterback in exchange for a scholarship."

"Do you have sisters or brothers?"

"Yes. My older brother, Greg, was killed in Vietnam in 1965. He was a paratrooper in the army."

"Oh, I'm sorry again. I'm going to stop asking you questions now. You've had a lot of loss in your life."

"It's okay. For some reason I'm comfortable talking to you."

When he saw her become fidgety after that comment, he decided to end the conversation on a high note. "I'll let you get back to your studies. It was good seeing you again. Take care."

As he stood to leave, she motioned for him to wait. To his surprise, she carefully wrote her phone number on a piece of paper and handed it to him. "Call me sometime. If you wait for me to call you, we'll both be old and gray."

He took the paper from her and put it in his pocket. "Message received."

After that chance encounter, he spent several anxious days waiting for the weekend to arrive. As he reflected on their conversation, he realized he knew very little about the girl who'd captured his affection. She'd said she was from St. Louis, and her father had gone to school at Grantham. She was certainly goal-oriented and determined to graduate from college in as short a time as possible. But why was she so different from other girls he knew? What was motivating her?

When Friday evening finally arrived, he hurriedly dialed her phone number.

"Hello."

"Hi, this is Jake."

"Hi, Jake. I'm glad you called."

"Listen, why don't we grab a bite to eat? There's a good Chinese restaurant nearby."

"That sounds great."

"Can you be ready by seven?"

"I'll be waiting in front of the dorm."

"See you soon."

As he stopped his 1965 Mustang convertible in front of Bethany Woods dorm, he saw her coming out of the door. She was wearing a white skirt that draped softly, revealing shapely legs and a blue short-sleeved top that matched the color of her eyes. She strode gracefully toward the car, and he got out and opened the passenger door for her.

"Nice car. I almost believed that story you gave me about having no money."

"It was my brother's," he said as he started the engine. "Greg bought it a few months before he went to 'Nam. When he didn't come back . . ."

"I keep putting my foot in my mouth, don't I?"

"Yes, but you do it so well. What are those, about size eight?" he asked as he glanced down at her feet.

"They're size six, thank you," she said with a laugh. "So I guess this beauty will always be more than just a car to you."

"Yeah. It's like a part of Greg is still with me. So how'd your accounting test go?"

"No problem. I was prepared for it."

They both enjoyed dinner and the casual conversation about their classes and college life. Jake had dated other girls, but never anyone like her. Most of them just wanted to talk about themselves. Donna seemed to prefer asking the questions. He couldn't help but notice how she skillfully deflected any probes of his into her life. Maybe it's what had piqued his interest in her in the first place. Or maybe it was that air of sophistication she possessed, something foreign to him. Whatever it was, he liked it.

"What does your fortune cookie say?" he asked as the waitress cleared the table.

"Family will be the most important thing in your life," she said as she rolled her eyes.

"Tell me about your family."

"It's all rather boring."

"Let me be the judge of that."

"Are you putting on your journalist hat now? How did a jock like you get interested in journalism anyway?"

"I'll answer that question after you answer mine."

She hesitated, and then in a serious tone said, "Jake, I like you. Whatever I say to you needs to be kept between the two of us. I don't want anyone else to know. Okay?"

"Sure," he said, not knowing what she could possibly say that required such secrecy.

"My mother's maiden name was Blanford."

"Isn't there a Blanford Hall on campus?"

"Yes. My father donated some money to Grantham several years ago for the construction of a new building for the School of Business, and the college graciously named it after my mother's family."

"Go on," he said.

"My mother's father started a pharmaceutical company before World War II. After my mother married and my grandfather aged to the point that he struggled with managing the company, my father took over the business. Now my father, Douglas Kingston, is president and CEO of Blanford Pharmaceuticals, a half billion dollar-a-year Fortune 500 corporation."

"I'm impressed. I would've never guessed you were rich and famous."

"Oh, please. I'm neither. But your response is exactly why I keep my life so private."

"So you feel people treat you differently when they know your background?"

"Absolutely. Some people try to take advantage of me, and others think I'm a rich snob. So I have very few friends—especially close friends."

"That sounds like a lonely way to go through life."

"I guess that's why I'm so focused on my studies and getting out into the business world."

"Do you have brothers and sisters?"

"No. I will be the sole heir to the family business when my father steps down. He's counting on me to get a good education and then come back to St. Louis so he can groom me to take over."

"I wondered what was motivating you."

"My father has told me for years that I'll have to work harder and be smarter than most men in order to be a CEO of a major corporation as a woman."

"That's what your father wants for you. What do *you* want out of life?"

"I've never really considered doing anything else."

The look on her face revealed otherwise to Jake, but he kept the thought to himself.

"Now it's your turn," she said deftly. "What inspired Jake Lemaster to want to be a journalist?"

He noticed once again that careful shift in conversation away from her but decided it was time for him to share something personal as well.

"We bought our first TV set when I was four years old, and that big black-and-white window into the world was like magic to me. I could hardly wait to watch my favorite programs like the *Mickey Mouse Club, Howdy Doody,* and *The Lone Ranger.* But for some reason, I was especially drawn to the people who did the news."

"I can't see you as an Edward R. Murrow worshipper."

"You might laugh, but I used to set up a small desk in front of the TV and shuffle some papers as I pretended to give the evening report right along with whoever was doing the news."

"That's hilarious," she said, laughing.

"You're a St. Louis girl, so you should love this part. When the baseball game of the week came on every Saturday afternoon, I would sing 'Wabash Cannonball' along with Dizzy Dean and Pee Wee Reese, the commentators. Dizzy used to pitch for the Cardinals, and he did a commercial for Falstaff beer."

"I remember, though I didn't spend much time watching sports. Tell me more."

"One time my dad's mother and father came for a visit during the game, and when the beer commercial came on, I shouted out, 'Daddy likes beer! Daddy likes beer!' Dad was not happy because Grandma and Grandpa didn't approve of alcohol."

"Those are great stories," she said, obviously enjoying herself. "I haven't laughed so much in a long time. So tell me something serious now. How difficult was your life after your father died?"

"I was in fifth grade at the time. What I noticed most was how sad and withdrawn my mom was after he died. She took it real hard, and it affected the relationship Greg and I had with her. As for Dad, he was a factory worker, so he wasn't around much. He worked hard and provided for his family, but I never got to know him well. I probably miss him more now than I did when I was younger."

"Thanks for sharing. It's difficult for me to imagine. So what will you do after college?"

"I haven't thought that far ahead yet. Right now I'm just trying to get through this semester and then enjoy the summer break."

"What are your plans?"

"First, I'm going to visit my cousins in Montana for a few weeks. I've gone hiking in the mountains with them every summer since my dad died. I enjoy getting away and doing a little trout fishing up in Blodgett Canyon. After that, I'll go back to Clarkston and help my stepfather at his gas station."

"Montana sounds exciting. I'll be here at summer school while you're out fishing."

"Someday I'll take you to Montana and show you the Bitterroot Valley."

"Promises, promises. I'll bet you say that to all the girls."

"There are no other girls," he said as he took her hand in his. "Come on. Let's get out of here."

They left the restaurant and drove back to Bethany Woods, where he parked the car. They were both quiet during the short trip.

"I had a nice time tonight," she said as she turned toward him. "I hope you have a good summer."

"Can we get together again before the semester's over?"

"I'm going to be very busy getting ready for finals."

"Then let's go out for dinner after exams are over."

She knew what she had to say next. "Jake, I like you. But I can't allow myself to become involved with anyone."

He put his arm around her and pulled her close to him. "It's too late for that. I'm already involved with you."

Before she could pull away, he kissed her lightly and felt her inhibitions melt away. For the first time since they'd met, he thought he'd gotten a glimpse of the true Donna Kingston. And he'd broken though the carefully constructed wall of defense she'd built over the years. He'd found the woman he wanted to love.

CHAPTER THREE

The constant buzzing of hungry mosquitoes swarming around Jake's face harassed him continuously throughout the early morning hours as he waited for the first light of day. His leg ached, his head throbbed, and the heat and humidity were oppressive. Exotic birdcalls and the shrill cry of monkeys frequently pierced the stillness of the jungle. He listened intently for any sound indicating the approach of someone searching for a downed American airman.

As the first rays of sunlight penetrated the jungle, he glanced at his watch and saw that it was 0600 hours. Time to move. Using only his hands as tools, he dug a hole, buried his helmet and parachute, and then covered the spot with branches and leaves. The effort was exhausting but it had to be done. After a brief rest, he eased stealthily out of his hiding place to where he could see the morning sun silhouetting a massive, purple-colored mountain directly ahead.

That direction must be west. If I can find my radio, I'll head for higher ground and try to reach someone on Guard channel to arrange a rescue mission.

Memories of escape and evasion techniques taught in survival training came racing into his mind as he alternately crept forward and then paused to look and listen for any enemy approaching his position. He spent several frustrating minutes searching the groundcover where he had landed hours before in vain. The radio was nowhere in sight.

The sound of voices nearby, coming in his direction, shocked him into action. As he turned to regain the shelter of his hiding place, his left foot struck something solid beneath a banana leaf. There it was! Quickly he snatched up the emergency radio and slid back into the thicket. He was able to conceal himself just before a small group of soldiers wearing black clothing and armed with AK-47 automatic weapons passed within ten yards of his position.

His heart was slamming his chest like a jackhammer. He wet his parched mouth with water from his canteen and waited silently for the threat to pass. After a full ten minutes went by with no further signs of the enemy, he once again left the sanctuary and ventured out into the open. This time he headed for the side of the mountain, now drenched in brilliant sunlight, inching slowly down toward the jungle.

⊷+ +⊶

The acrid smell of burning chemicals and the plume of black smoke emanating from the crash site led Lo Chang and his son to their destination as the sun was rising in the east. A horde of Communist soldiers was scouring the area for anything of value remaining after the impact. Lo Chang could see parts of the plane scattered over a large field scorched by the smoldering wreckage. He identified eight partially destroyed engines among the debris. The Americans had only one plane with eight engines—the B-52 bomber.

In the distance, set apart from the mass of wreckage, he saw the tail of the airplane. The black vertical stabilizer stood straight up in the air, so he could see the tail number 6688 in red numerals. He also noticed a gaping hole in the back of the tail before he and Lo Na skirted the perimeter of the enemy and hurried north down narrow trails through the dense jungle to a place of relative safety. That hole could mean one of two things. Either an airman had escaped, or the back of the plane had taken a direct hit.

He didn't know how many crewmembers flew on a B-52, but he knew their chance of survival would decline rapidly, even if they were able to parachute safely into the Laotian jungle. He had seen how the Communists tortured their prisoners. He needed to find the survivors, if there were any, before the enemy did.

The jungle teemed with Pathet Lao soldiers seeking to capture the coveted prize of an American airman. Lo Chang's progress was severely impeded by so much enemy activity, all the more so since he and Lo Na were traveling together. He decided to send his son on a safer path farther to the west. He would continue north while keeping himself between the enemy and his son's position. He instructed his son to meet him that night at a cave where they'd sheltered many times in the past and then watched as Lo Na disappeared down a separate trail.

An hour or so later, Lo Chang heard a gunshot followed by the sound of excited voices. He climbed the side of the mountain bordering the trail to get a better view of the commotion. What he saw filled him with horror. There in the middle of a rice paddy was an American airman being hacked to death by Pathet Lao soldiers savagely wielding machetes. A single Pathet Lao soldier lay dead nearby. The airman had shot one of his would-be captors before losing his life.

He watched as the soldiers loaded the mutilated airman's body onto a cart pulled by oxen and carried it away. The American had chosen an honorable death rather than being taken prisoner. That was something Lo Chang understood and respected.

⊷⊶

Jake eventually came to a small clearing with a good view up the mountain. He hid himself in the tall grass on the edge and watched for any sign of danger. It was 0730 hours. He was sure the bad guys would be scouring the jungle looking for him and any other survivors, if there were any.

I wonder if Lieutenant Sizemore and Major Cash made it out of the aircraft, he thought, remembering the horrific last minutes before the crash and his last communication with the copilot and the EW. *If they did, they may have already alerted rescue forces to come looking for us and get us out of here.* That thought was followed by an uneasy one. *They have no way of knowing I'm alive.*

Just then he spied enemy soldiers walking along a trail on the side of the mountain about a half-mile away from his location. A small cave had been carved out of the limestone, and they headed right for it. He watched as several of them ducked inside the cave while others stood guard at the entrance. After a few minutes, the soldiers inside exited the cave, and the entire group resumed their march down the trail.

The thought occurred to him that a recently searched cave might be a good place to hole up while he tried to use the emergency radio to reach friendly forces. With renewed enthusiasm, he lit out at a brisk pace in order to get to the cave. Thirty minutes later, he entered the mouth of the cave, took out the emergency radio, and turned the power switch on.

"Mayday. Mayday. Downed crewmember from *Sapphire 3* calling all aircraft, come in," he said over the Guard channel. No response. He repeated the call several times, all the while anxiously scanning the skies.

"*Sapphire 3* crewmember, this is *Raven*, over."

Raven was the call sign for a small OV-10 aircraft used as a forward air controller, or FAC as it was called. The FAC was often the first aircraft on the scene of a crash and initiated search and rescue efforts. *Help is on its way*, he thought.

"Roger, *Raven*. This is *Sapphire 3* gunner on the ground."

"Roger, gunner. Stay calm, and we'll get you out of there. First, you need to authenticate."

"Authenticating. Foxtrot, Romeo, Alpha, November."

"Authentication verified. Can you help me pinpoint your location?"

"I'm at the entrance of a cave about a third of the way up on the east side of a mountain. I bailed out several miles north of the crash site. That's the best I can do."

"*Raven* copies. I'm heading your way. Let me know when you have me in sight."

Relief flooded his body at the thought of rescue. After about a minute, he heard the humming of a small propeller-driven airplane coming toward him from the south. He spotted it flying 3,000 feet above him at his two o'clock position.

"*Raven*, I've got you in sight. I'm at your ten o'clock position."

"Roger. Can you signal me?"

"Standby," he said as he took the signal mirror out of his survival vest. He moved out into the sunlight and reflected the rising sun's rays in *Raven's* direction.

"I've got a fix on your position. Stay put while I take a look around."

As he waited for *Raven* to contact him again, he was filled with renewed hope. He allowed his mind to wander to thoughts of home.

Snap out of it, Jake. You have to stay focused if you want to get home alive. This thing isn't over yet.

"*Sapphire 3* gunner, you've got bad guys in your area. What's your condition? Can you travel?"

"Affirmative."

"I'm going to vector you to a safer area where we can get some friendly forces in."

"Copy. Where do you want me to go?"

"Head south from your present position, and I'll keep an eye on the bad guys."

"Roger, I'm heading south."

Somewhat reluctantly, he left the relative safety of the cave and started down the trail leading south.

There must be a lot of enemy soldiers nearby if it's too dangerous to land a helicopter full of Special Forces here, he thought to himself as he hurried down the trail.

Suddenly the repeated booming of antiaircraft guns filled the air. He looked up to see the sky around *Raven* peppered with deadly flak. His heart sank as he watched the small airplane disintegrate right before his eyes.

Lo Chang worked his way northward, being careful not to fall prey to the Communists himself. Another hour went by with no sign of any activity. As he stopped briefly to eat some fruit, he heard the faint droning of the small aircraft coming from behind and off to his left. Within minutes, a slow-moving American spotter plane passed overhead and turned to the northwest. He knew there must be airmen alive nearby, calling for help. It was the spotter's job to locate the airmen and then call a search-and-rescue team in to evacuate the crewmen by helicopter.

He navigated cautiously toward the sound of the plane as it circled somewhere around the bend of a mountain a few kilometers away. Suddenly thunderous bursts of antiaircraft artillery echoed through the valley. The spotter plane was like a sitting duck in the flak-filled sky.

Too many times he'd seen the Communists shoot down American pilots who were heroically trying to rescue their fellow soldiers. In his mind, he could visualize a distressed American airman now fleeing for his life in an unfamiliar and hostile environment, his hope for survival dashed. He'd seen the animal panic at first in the eyes of those he'd rescued in the past. He'd also seen the tears of joy pouring from those same eyes when they realized they'd been saved. The tears of joy were what motivated him.

Dazed and confused, Jake stood in the middle of the trail, looking up at the sky as the black vapor of the flak slowly dissipated. His hope of rescue dissipated as well. He had no way of knowing if the spotter plane had radioed his location before it went down.

Motion on the trail nearby caught his attention. He spied a young soldier carrying an automatic weapon approaching slowly. The soldier was saying words he couldn't understand. The two made eye contact. Jake raised the .38 caliber pistol and pointed it at the advancing young man. The young soldier then raised his automatic weapon into firing position. He pointed it directly at Jake.

Jake had no other choice. Instinctively he crouched and fired twice, putting two bullets in the soldier's chest. He watched the young man fall to the ground. Frothy blood gurgled from his mouth, but he remained motionless.

Before he could think what to do next, he felt the chilling sensation of cold steel from the muzzle of an AK-47 pressed against the back of his neck. A guerrilla soldier took his pistol and shoved him roughly so that he fell facedown onto the ground. His arms were pulled behind him, his hands were tied behind his back, and a rope was placed around his neck. A powerful yank of the ropes brought him to his feet.

Immediately six more guerrilla soldiers dressed in black crowded around him. One of them walked over to the young man Jake had shot and spit on his lifeless body as he confiscated the dead man's weapon. That move evoked a chorus of laughter from his comrades, who then began dragging Jake up the trail, heading north.

⊨⟨+ +⟩⊨

Lo Chang paused and listened as two gunshots rang out. They must have come from a pistol in the hands of an American soldier, he told himself. No automatic weapon answered in reply. He feared the worst. Had his son made it safely through the enemy territory?

The shots were a reminder to Lo Chang that he needed to exercise extreme caution. The area would be filled soon with enemy soldiers who'd heard the shots as well. The Pathet Lao Communist soldiers enjoyed only one thing more than capturing an American, and that was capturing and torturing a Hmong warrior.

He picked his way stealthily through the jungle. By this time it was near the middle of the day, and the heat was stifling. The only sound was staccato squawking from a pair of blue-and-gold Macaws perched in a palm tree high above him. He checked his American-made M-16 automatic weapon to make sure he had a full magazine loaded, and then he flipped the safety selector switch to fire as he emerged onto a narrow trail that skirted the mountain.

Hesitating for a moment, he turned to the right and followed the path northward, toward the sound of the shots just fired. He'd gone no more than two hundred meters when he saw the vague outline of a body. It was lying in the middle of the trail up ahead.

Shouldering his weapon, he crept forward slowly while continually scanning left and right for signs of the enemy. His mind raced to analyze the dangerous situation. The Pathet Lao would not abandon an American airman, even a dead one. Was this the corpse of a Pathet Lao soldier killed by an American?

As he approached within twenty meters, a chilling thought seized his mind. Heart pounding, he raced forward, no longer attentive to his personal safety. Each step drew him closer to the realization of his worst fears. There on the ground was his son's lifeless body.

Lo Na's eyes were wide open, glazed and fixed. His dilated pupils declared the horror of his death even as warm blood still oozed from his chest wounds. Lo Chang had seen the look of death so many times he'd almost become numb to it. At that moment, however, intense sorrow and grief overwhelmed him, spewing forth in cries like molten lava from an exploding volcano.

Falling to his knees, he cradled Lo Na's head in his lap and rocked back and forth, propelled by waves of sobbing that overtook him. Time seemed to stand still as the full weight of his grief oppressed him. No torture of the enemy could compare to the agony of losing his only son. He no longer cared whether he lived or died. An enemy bullet in his head would be a welcome relief from the unbearable pain he felt.

＝＋＋＝

Exhausted and demoralized by his plight, Jake tried to sort out what had happened. His captors were forcibly marching him through the jungle at a rapid pace, clearly intent on a plan of action for their prize. As he replayed the events of the last few minutes in his mind, a frightening thought struck him.

I must have just killed one of the friendly forces Raven *had said he would lead me to.* It all made sense now. The young man who'd approached him, who looked no older than a boy, was not dressed in black like his captors.

He was raising his weapon to kill the soldier behind me. He was trying to save my life. Instead I took his life and was captured by the real enemy.

His foot caught on a vine on the trail, and he fell hard on the ground, striking his head on a tree. In response, one of the captors jerked violently on the rope around his neck, causing him to gasp for air as he struggled to his feet without the use of his hands. From behind, he felt the prod of a gun poked into his back to propel him forward. And then on they went for nearly an hour without stopping. The heat was suffocating. He was becoming lightheaded from dehydration, and waves of nausea swept over him. He didn't think he could go much longer without rest and water.

When at last they came around a bend of the mountain, he could see that the trail descended sharply into a clearing where the guerrilla soldiers had established a base. His eyes quickly scanned the camp, but he saw no sign of Lieutenant Sizemore or Major Cash. There were, however, a handful of bamboo and thatch buildings scattered around the edge of the clearing with a small muddy brown river running nearby.

They reached the clearing within minutes, and the enemy soldiers stopped him in front of a thatch hut. One of them ducked inside. In a few seconds, an older soldier with a stern appearance came out of the hut and stood in front of him. He said something Jake couldn't understand and then sneered. By the man's demeanor, Jake guessed it must have been something like, "Welcome to hell."

A jagged scar distorted the man's face, making him look hideous. His eyes burned with anger. He began taking everything out of the pockets of Jake's flight suit and examining them one by one. His gaze lingered long over the photo of Donna. A cruel smile hinted that he'd found some important piece of information to use against his new prisoner. The Seiko watch was removed last.

The scar-faced man barked an order with a jerk of his head, and the soldiers around him scrambled to obey. Jake was led to a large, 10-foot deep hole located in the center of the camp. With his hands still tied behind his back, he was shoved head first into the pit. A thatch mat was thrown over the opening, leaving him in total darkness.

There was no changing how this life had ended for Lo Na, but Lo Chang believed with all of his heart that his only son's next life would be greatly affected by his adherence to the sacred burial rituals that must take place. He surmised that an evil spirit had avenged some wrong on him by taking his son's life. He tried to think of something he'd done to anger the spirits, but no answer was found. When he was finally able to return to his village, he would seek a shaman to intervene by communicating with the spirit world. For the time being, he was alone in enemy territory, and no such help could be found. He would do what he knew must be done now for the sake of his son's future life.

He reasoned that transporting Lo Na's corpse a long distance through dense jungle to a Hmong village was impossible. Burial preparations would have to be altered somewhat, considering the circumstances. According to custom, the burial site needed to be on the side of a mountain with the body facing west, the direction of death. Lo Chang decided to construct a litter to carry his son's body to the far side of the mountain, just ahead to the west. He would adhere to as much tradition as possible to ensure his son's soul would not roam for eternity but be guided back to heaven to ask for reincarnation.

Methodically he constructed a litter and placed his son's lifeless body on it. Dragging the litter along the trail was dangerous and difficult, but he felt he had no choice. As the final rays of sunlight faded away, Lo Chang reached his destination—a cave midway up the west side of the mountain. There he rested and played out in his mind what must happen next. The spirits would have to understand he could not celebrate the rebirth of his son with a typical Hmong feast lasting many days and attended by a multitude of family and tribesmen. Instead he would prepare the body as best as he could for burial in the morning when the sun rose again and find another way to celebrate. Tonight he would rest and reflect on the painful events of the day.

After making a small fire, he ate a meager portion of rice and raw fish. Although his hunger dissipated, he felt a profound emptiness inside. The emptiness was more intense than at any time since the Pathet Lao warriors had stolen his family from him when he was an innocent young boy. The atrocities committed against some of his family and other Hmong villagers were so vicious that the images were permanently emblazoned in his mind. Flashes of painful memories seared his consciousness like the flames from the fire stabbing at the darkness of the cave.

The day seemed like only yesterday. The Pathet Lao had come without warning early one morning. The Hmong were herded together in the center of the village and surrounded by enemy soldiers. The Communists publicly beheaded the tribal leaders before systematically executing all adult males with a gunshot to the head. The women and young girls were tied spread-eagled between two trees and raped repeatedly before being bayonetted to death. Lo Chang had never been able to silence the sound of the bloodcurdling screams echoing through his mind as the victims begged for death to come quickly.

The small children of the village, he one of many, were marched to a concentration camp on the Laotian border with North Vietnam. He grimaced as he recalled the beatings he received for no other reason than his ethnic background. The forced labor too was difficult to endure. He wasn't fed enough to remain strong. The worst part of the imprisonment, however, was the indoctrination class. The Communists sought to destroy his heart and soul by controlling his mind.

His father had taught him the ways of the jungle and how to survive on what the land offered. He knew he must escape or die trying. He waited and watched, and at last an opportunity for freedom came during the monsoon season when torrential rains caused massive flooding to the camp. One dark night, he was able to dig the soft, rain-soaked earth and slither his emaciated frame beneath the barbed wire fence. He put as much distance as possible between the camp and him before seeking shelter in a small cave just before dawn. Throughout the ensuing days and weeks, he regained his strength by feeding on snakes, fish, frogs, and fruit.

He trekked continuously westward until he came upon a Hmong village in the central highlands and was given shelter by the local tribesmen. There he learned to fight the Pathet Lao and their North Vietnamese comrades. Over the next decade, he participated in guerrilla warfare with his people against the enemy. When he reached the age of manhood, he took a beautiful young maiden named Thao Nhia as his bride. Their first prized possession, Lo Na, was born a year later. His sister, Lo Moua, was born the following year.

Reclining by the campfire, he smiled to himself as he remembered the early years of his marriage when he and his wife were nearly inseparable. And then he and his son were forced to leave the village to fight the enemy. The last ten years since then had been marked by loneliness and long periods of time in which he never knew if his wife and daughter back in the village were alive or dead.

As he glanced at his son's body nearby, he wondered when and how he would be able to tell his wife their son was gone. The loss would be terribly painful to accept, but not being present for his burial would magnify her anguish tremendously. Unfortunately this situation was all too common for the Hmong as the war against the Communists raged on.

He pulled out his knife and began sharpening it on a whetting stone he carried in his pack. In the morning, he would need to remove the bullets from Lo Na's chest. According to Hmong custom, even a single piece of metal could block the soul's journey. His son's soul must return first to the placental jacket, the place of birth, and then to heaven to ask for reincarnation.

With his knife sharpened, it was time to dull his mind. He took out a small, black piece of raw opium and placed it in the metal bowl of his thin bamboo pipe. He lit the opium and inhaled the pungent smoke deeply. The physical and emotional pain receded like the ebbing of the tide as water rushes out to the sea. Though he experienced no euphoria, the absence of pain was pleasure enough. He slept.

When he awoke, the chill of the predawn morning made his bones ache. The small fire had long ago died out, and the warmth of the sun wouldn't be felt for several hours. As he rose, he saw Lo Na's corpse and was shocked out of the drug-induced state brought on by the opium. Walking to a nearby stream, he drank the cool mountain water deeply, filled a large gourd with water, and returned to the cave to bathe his son's body.

As the first rays of light splintered the darkness on the west side of the mountain, he began the necessary burial preparations. After removing his son's clothing, he examined the two bullet holes marring Lo Na's chest. He rolled the body over and confirmed the bullets had not exited his son's back. With great care, he excised the two intact metal bullets lodged deep within the chest. He then washed his son's body and dressed him in the only fresh clothing available—a clean, rolled up shirt and a pair of pants made of hemp cloth dyed indigo that he had been carrying in his knapsack.

A small plateau was visible near the cave. It would serve as a good burial site. He dug a shallow grave there, returned to where he'd left his son, and dragged the litter holding Lo Na's body to the site. He gently lowered the corpse into the grave facing west, placed a small bottle of alcohol made from bamboo near the head, and covered the body with earth. Kneeling beside the grave, he sang "Showing the Way." The song was a Hmong initiation of the dead sung to help the soul on the journey to the afterlife. He then destroyed the litter and placed stones on top of his son's grave.

Under different circumstances, a thirteen-day mourning period would follow during which sacrifices would be made to show respect for the deceased. Lo Chang, however, had only one thing to offer now, and that sacrifice would become more difficult the longer he tarried. With the rites of passage to the afterlife completed, he needed to move on. He hoped the spirits would be appeased by the only sacrifice he could make—avenging the death of his one and only son. He had no other choice.

CHAPTER FOUR

D espite the pain racking Jake's body, exhaustion won out and he fell asleep. Too soon the hole was uncovered, and he was awakened by soldiers dousing him with a pail of water. He then was propelled up a bamboo ladder from the bottom of the pit by soldiers wielding AK-47s with bayonets. Other soldiers yanked on the rope around his neck from above. They forced him to walk a short distance to a nearby hut and deposited him on the dirt floor of the one-room building. Inside was a small bamboo table, a rickety chair, and a black-and-white picture of Uncle Ho on the wall behind the table. He had a good idea what was coming next.

As he sat on the dirt floor with his hands tied behind his back, he remembered what the instructors at survival school had said about how to survive an interrogation. "You're only obligated to give the enemy your name, rank, and serial number, according to the Geneva Convention. If you want to avoid torture and death, however, you'll need to give your interrogator something. Try to resist by giving false or misleading information when possible. Just remember, everyone can be broken, so don't die unnecessarily." He hoped his interrogator had read the same playbook.

The scar-faced man who had taken Donna's picture from him and then ordered him to be thrown into the pit came through the door and sat down on the bamboo stool behind the desk. He carefully placed all of Jake's belongings on the table, took out one of the Marlboro cigarettes, lit the end with the Zippo lighter, and inhaled deeply. As he exhaled, he leaned forward and blew the smoke directly into Jake's face. He then sat back and smiled smugly, enjoying the cigarette and the little game he was playing with his prisoner.

"No have American cigarette for long time," he said in broken English with a thick Asian accent. "You tell me things, I give cigarette. Maybe water. What name?"

"My name is Lemaster."

"What rank?"

"Sergeant."

"You fly B-52?"

"My name is Sergeant Jake Lemaster, serial number 372-62-5434."

"Who this?" he asked as he held up Donna's picture.

"My sister. Can I get a drink of water now?"

"Not sister. Maybe wife. I know you fly B-52. We have two more fly B-52."

Jake tried not to show surprise, but the man he dubbed "Scarface" could see the revelation rattled him.

Was he bluffing, or did he have Lieutenant Sizemore and Major Cash there too?

"My arms hurt, and I need water."

"What you do on B-52?"

"If you untie me and get me some water, I can answer questions better."

"You answer, I give water."

Jake thought back to when he was in basic training and had to choose what career field to pursue in the U. S. Air Force. An old sergeant told him that since he scored very high in electronics testing, he qualified to become what he called a "Defensive Fire Control Systems Operator." He said Jake's job would be putting out fires on an airplane by pulling circuit breakers. Only much later did Jake discover that the sergeant had given him a fancy title for a tail gunner on a B-52 bomber.

"I put out fires on the airplane."

"You not very good. Plane crash and burn," Scarface said as he laughed at his own joke.

"I answered your questions. Now can I be untied and have some water?"

Scarface snuffed out the cigarette and slowly rose from the stool. Jake wasn't sure if he was going to grant his requests or raise the stakes a bit. He called out to one of the soldiers, who came into the room and cut the ropes holding Jake's arms behind his back. The pain intensified for several minutes as circulation and feeling returned. Another soldier then came in and handed him a metal cup full of water, and he hastily gulped it down.

"How old you?" Scarface asked next.

"Nineteen," Jake said, clearly a lie, and yet apparently his answer was accepted as true. It was a minor victory, but one he desperately needed.

"Why you drop bomb? Good American protest war. Why no go school?"

"I'm not very smart."

That's a fairly honest statement or I wouldn't be in this situation.

Scarface brought out a piece of paper with writing on it that Jake couldn't make out. "Sign paper. I give food, water, cigarette."

It was obviously some sort of propaganda statement saying he had confessed to being a war criminal. Jake played along.

"I can't write. My hand is numb."

"Sign other hand."

"I can't write with that hand."

"You sign!" Scarface screamed and slammed his fist on the table.

When Jake didn't respond, Scarface called a guard in, and Jake's hands were again tied behind his back. As he was lifted roughly to his feet, he saw that the venom had returned to his enemy captor's eyes. Scarface gave a gruff command to the soldier. As Jake was being taken outside, Scarface said with confidence, "You sign paper soon."

The guard grabbed the rope around Jake's neck and dragged him to another, larger building with bamboo rafters and a thatch roof. Several more soldiers were there, and they untied his hands and then tied his wrists to a four-foot-long piece of bamboo placed beneath his armpits from behind. Then they tied ropes around the ends of the bamboo, threw the ropes over the rafters, and began hoisting him into the air as they pulled down on the ropes. When his feet were well above the ground, they tied off the ropes, leaving him suspended in midair.

It felt like his shoulders were dislocating. His two hundred pound frame hung like a carcass of butchered meat in the market. He cried out in agony like he'd never known before, wondering how long he could withstand the pain.

"Don't give in, Jake!" he heard from somewhere nearby.

Was that my imagination?

"We're no good to them if we're dead!"

It was not. The copilot's voice is coming from somewhere outside of the hut!

"Lieutenant Sizemore?" he shouted back.

A guard clubbed him in the head with the butt of a gun. He saw stars as blood flowed down his face. But deep inside of him something had been rekindled. He wasn't alone. At least one other from his plane had survived.

The vow he'd made to himself resurfaced in a mighty way. *Keep your focus on getting home to see your wife and baby.*

"We're gonna make it out of here, Jake!" his copilot shouted.

Jim Sizemore, held prisoner in an adjacent hut, also felt a renewed sense of hope for the first time since his capture. It was his duty not only to resist the enemy, but also to be a leader for the men in his command. He welcomed the new sense of responsibility that gave him a purpose beyond his own survival.

A soldier rushed out the door. A few seconds later, Jake heard yelling and then a dull thud like a man receiving a body blow with the butt of a gun. He listened but heard nothing more from his copilot.

A powerful new emotion swept over him. Anger welled up inside him for the first time since he'd been captured, and it felt good. He could use this anger to stoke the fuel of his resistance and his will to live. He would let it simmer inside him, dole it out a little at a time, and apply it to his pain, like massaging a soothing salve onto an open wound.

Lieutenant Sizemore's words echoed in his head. "We're no good to them if we're dead."

That makes sense, he thought. *They could have killed us at any time, but they haven't. We must've been captured by local Communist troops in Laos, who needed us for some reason. Would they keep us here in the jungle or take us to their North Vietnamese comrades?* Neither option appealed to him.

It was dark outside when he was cut down from the rafters. He had soiled himself, and the smell emanating from his flight suit was repulsive. The camp guards pushed him through the doorway of the thatch hut, where Scarface was waiting for the next round of interrogation to begin. He was smoking one of Jake's Marlboros and cradling Donna's picture in his hand. Jake was thrown to the dirt floor.

"Sign paper now," Scarface said as he shoved the propaganda document in front of Jake.

"How can I sign the paper when you have broken my arms?"

"Sign paper. Give food, water, cigarette. No more pain."

"How do I know you're telling the truth?"

Scarface barked out some orders, and a guard quickly freed Jake's hands and set a bowl of rice and a cup of water in front of him. He had difficulty even reaching out to pick up the cup, but he managed to get it to his parched lips and sip the much-needed liquid.

"Better when sign."

Scarface lit a cigarette, placed it in Jake's lips, and put a pen in his right hand. Jake took several long drags off the cigarette without using his hands and inhaled deeply. His right hand could not hold the pen, and it fell to the floor.

"I want to sign, but my hand won't work. Maybe tomorrow when my arms are better."

Scarface eyed him. He picked up Donna's picture and said, "Sign tomorrow, or no see wife." He said something to the guard, and then he left the room.

The guard motioned for Jake to eat the rice. As famished as he was, it was difficult to grasp the rice in his right hand and guide it into his mouth. He washed it down with water and finished the cigarette. The guard then motioned for him to stand up and exit the hut. He nudged him in the back with the muzzle of his gun and marched him to the hole in the center of the camp. A blow to the back propelled him into the pit once more. This time, however, the pit was left uncovered.

His body ached everywhere, but at least his hands were no longer tied behind his back. Gingerly he moved his arms and hands to get some circulation flowing again. Broken and alone in the pit, he reflected on the choices he'd made that had brought him here. *Maybe Scarface was right. I should be in school instead of fighting in this crazy war.*

Lying on his back at the bottom of the hole, he focused his eyes on the magnificent star-filled sky above. *What I wouldn't give to be camping in the Big Sky country of Montana right now.*

After a few minutes, the hole was covered, plunging him into complete darkness. In his mind, however, he could still see the endless expanse of the Montana night sky, brilliantly lit by billions of stars as he lay on his back in a sleeping bag in Blodgett Canyon, just as he had done many times before. That's where he'd found comfort and a sense of peace after his dad had died. And that's where he'd retreated to when Donna stopped answering his phone calls after the night he'd taken her to dinner at the Chinese restaurant, the night he first kissed her.

CHAPTER FIVE

The campfire popped and crackled as licks of flames sporadically stabbed the darkness but gave off a pleasing aroma of burning pine. To Jake it seemed a symphony of nature played in the background as the creatures in Blodgett Canyon sang their best to attract a mate for the new season. A brilliant full moon bathed the nearby mountain lake with light and cast ghostly shadows on the steep rock walls above. A gentle breeze flowed down the canyon from the west.

Jake's cousin Scott fried the brook trout they had caught earlier that afternoon while Jake sat near the fire and reflected on the important role this paradise played in his life. Blodgett Canyon had served as a sanctuary for him each year since his dad's death. The tranquility of the mountains in late spring brought a sense of peace and a renewal of his spirit that he found nowhere else. Scott and his brother Ken had made it their mission to expose him to the endless treasures of nature found in the Bitterroot Valley, an alluring area framed by the Rocky Mountains to the west and the Sapphire Mountains to the east.

It was late spring of 1969, at the end of his first year in college, and he'd made the sojourn to Montana once more. Scott, twenty-four years old by then, had agreed to join him for several days of hiking and fishing. He had gotten out of the Air Force two years before and was in college on the GI Bill. Ken, who was three years older than Jake, had followed in his brother Scott's footsteps. He was currently stationed at an Air Force base somewhere in northern Thailand.

"Well, as I see it, you're just not that good looking," Scott said. "If you'd groped me like that and said you couldn't live without me, I'd have run away too."

"Thanks a lot," Jake said. "I knew I could count on you for understanding."

During their hike into the canyon, Jake had shared with Scott about his relationship with Donna. He explained about the promising date and then Donna's subsequent refusal to see him again the next time he'd called her. Now Scott was ready to make sport of him and give him some feedback in his own callous way.

"Tell me again, Mister Jock, why an intelligent, beautiful girl with millions of dollars would want to get hooked up with you," he said as he flipped the fish over in the skillet. "And grab us a beer from the cooler. You can't get good beer like that east of the Mississippi."

Jake opened the cooler and took out two cans of ice-cold Coors and handed one to Scott.

"You mean besides my charm and wit?"

"Is that what I smelled? Keep going."

"Maybe the one thing I can offer her is something real. Real love, with no strings attached. She said she keeps her life secret because everyone treats her differently when they find out who she is. I won't do that."

"If Donna's father has been controlling her life so that she'll take over the family business, he's not likely to hand her over to a commoner. People like Donna, if they ever get married, usually end up with someone of influence who can add to their family fortune."

That part made sense to Jake. Donna's father was a very powerful man, and she seemed to be living by his rules. It concerned him that she'd said she never once considered doing anything else with her life except what her father wanted.

"You're probably right."

"It can't be that bad. A stud football player like you can surely get all the cheerleaders you want."

"I've never met anyone like Donna."

"Boy, you are in love. How old are you now?"

"Nineteen."

"My advice is to take it easy and enjoy life. You've got a lot of years ahead of you."

Scott put the trout from the pan directly onto two plates. He and Jake consumed the delicious catch and talked about old times from past visits to the canyon. As they did so, Jake chewed on Scott's advice. It tasted bitter, like the cod liver oil his mom had made him take every day growing up. They had another beer and then sacked out for the night in sleeping bags beneath the stars.

Jake lay on his back for a long time and gazed at the stars. He tried to imagine how it would feel to have Donna lying there beside him in that special place.

Someday, I'll fulfill my promise to show her the Bitterroot Valley.

In mid-August 1969, Jake returned to Grantham and immersed himself in football and his academic studies. His intention was to let nature take its course in regard to his relationship with Donna. He would not pursue her. If the opportunity to see her arose, however, he would certainly welcome it. To his surprise, he found the English Literature and Journalism courses even more enjoyable than he'd anticipated. On the social front, he dated a few girls occasionally, but his thoughts never strayed far from Donna.

As a sophomore, he won the starting quarterback position and was having a decent season by the time the homecoming game against archrival Hancock College arrived in mid-October. The football team was 4-1, and they were anxious to avenge last year's 31-0 drubbing at Hancock.

The day of the game was a picturesque fall day. The deep blue sky was dotted with cottony, white clouds being moved along slowly by a chilly wind from the north. Autumn leaves sporting various shades of crimson, yellow, and gold rustled in the breeze and made a sound to match the shaking of the cheerleaders' pom-poms. It was a perfect day for football.

During warm-up before the game, Jake scanned the stands as fans continued to file in and take seats on both sides of the field. To his surprise, he saw Donna sitting alone near the middle of the bleachers. His heart began to race. He was infused with a new purpose that transcended the immediate goal of winning the game.

Jake played that day with a passion previously unknown to him, and Grantham prevailed 28-7. After the game, fans stormed the field to celebrate the victory with the players. But when he looked for Donna, she was nowhere to be found. Later that evening, he called her telephone number and was relieved to hear her voice on the other end of the line.

"Hello."

"Excuse me, Miss, but I saw a somewhat shallow-appearing coed matching your description sitting in the stands at the football game today."

"Very cute. I'm amazed you could see me with those cheerleaders hanging all over you."

"Do I detect a touch of jealousy in your voice?"

"Don't flatter yourself. I was just studying the business side of sports for a class project."

"All the same, I'm glad you came to one of my games."

"You're actually pretty good."

"I owe it all to you. You were my inspiration. Why don't we go out for a pizza, and you can tell me what you learned about the business side of sports today."

"No strings attached?"

"No strings attached. I'll pick you up at eight o'clock."

"I'll be outside the dorm. See you then."

As he pulled up in front of Bethany Woods dorm, Donna walked toward the car. Her hair was pulled back in a ponytail, displaying her delicately chiseled features and her creamy smooth skin. Her yellow sweater and white pants were definitely stylish without being excessive. She was even more beautiful than he'd remembered.

He got out and made his way to the passenger side of the car. To his surprise, she gave him a light kiss on the cheek as he opened the car door for her. Simon and Garfunkel were singing "The Sound of Silence" as the tape played on the eight-track car stereo system.

"I had you pegged as more of a country and western music fan," she said as he jumped back into his Mustang and pulled away from the dorm.

"I should be offended by that remark," he said with feigned distress. "I like folk rock because the lyrics are like poetry set to music. They actually tell a story. As someone who likes to write stories, I can relate to this kind of music in a spiritual way. What kind of music do you like? Wait. Don't tell me. You have season tickets to the symphony."

"Now I'm offended. When I listen to popular music, which isn't very often, I prefer Peter, Paul and Mary."

"Excellent folk singers. We've got some common ground there."

They arrived at the pizza place and went inside. A good Saturday night crowd was there, including many from the football game enjoying a night out on the town. Donna and Jake were greeted warmly as they took a seat at a booth by the window. After ordering a pizza, they caught up on the events in their lives since the last time they'd spoken, nearly six months before.

"How're your classes going?" he asked. "Are you still looking to graduate after three years to work for your father's company?"

"Yes, although I've considered getting my master's degree in business administration. I'm not sure if I'll get it here at Grantham or at St. Louis University. How about you?"

"School's going okay. I'm really enjoying my classes this year."

"Congratulations on becoming the editor for the school newspaper. I've been following your weekly editorials. I enjoy them, but I'm never sure which side of an issue you're on."

"That's the goal of a true journalist. I try to be objective and allow the readers to make up their own minds rather than tell them how they should think about a particular issue. There's certainly a lot to write about. The world seems to be in a perpetual state of upheaval, with a new revolution every week."

"One revolution that hasn't taken place yet is women in the business world. That's one fight I intend to join."

"What are you talking about? There are a lot of women doing well in business."

"Leadership positions within the business world have traditionally belonged to men. Women typically have been relegated to less important roles with little or no chance of advancement beyond a certain level. Everyone knows it, despite the fact that it is rarely acknowledged. Even if a woman is more qualified than a man, nine times out of ten the man will be given a position of power within the corporate world instead of a woman."

"That sound's like a good topic for my next editorial. Are you going to burn your bra and denounce marriage like the feminists do?"

"Jake, I'm being serious. Women should be judged on their own merit, not on their gender."

"I agree, and I know the issue is one that deserves serious attention. So how do you feel about women who say that being a good wife and raising a family is the most important thing in life?"

"Every woman should have the right to live her life as she chooses. But personally, I think staying home with a bunch of kids would be a terrible waste of my education and the opportunity to bring about change in the business world for all women."

"So you don't see yourself getting married and having kids?"

"Maybe someday. There are a lot of things I want to accomplish first though. I know most girls my age are looking for a husband at college. That's not me."

Jake was shocked and disturbed over the conversation. The pizza arrived, changing the tone of the evening. They ate and made small talk about school life. And then it was time to take her back to Bethany Woods.

"Thanks for being a good listener. I do enjoy being with you," she said as they arrived.

"Then answer your phone once in a while. What're you doing over Christmas break?"

"I'm going to Switzerland with my family. Blanford Pharmaceuticals has a European plant near Geneva, and my father is going there for meetings."

"Yeah, I was considering a skiing trip in the Alps, but there are just too many tourists for my liking."

She laughed and grasped him by the neck with both hands. "You are so mean."

"Tell me the truth. You're going skiing with the other jet setters, aren't you?"

"I may try out the slopes while my father is busy with his meetings. My family has had a Swiss chalet near Interlaken for many years. This trip is one of the few things we still do as a family."

"Sounds great. You deserve to have some fun and take it easy for a while."

"Thanks—for everything."

She leaned in close and cradled his face in her delicate hands, pressing her lips to his. Her tongue playfully teased him as she moaned seductively. Then suddenly she broke off the embrace, hopped out of the car, and disappeared inside the dorm.

As he drove back to Grover Hall, he replayed in his mind everything she'd revealed about herself during their conversation. She was feminine and sexy beyond belief yet desirous of goals that most girls would never dream of. He admired her competitive spirit and her desire to help other women achieve a better quality of life. The downside, however, was that there may not be a future for them as a couple. It didn't lessen his desire for her.

He tried to reach her by phone in the coming weeks, but once again she did not answer or return his calls. Each time he listened to the song "I Am a Rock" by Simon and Garfunkel, he thought of her.

Like the lyrics say, she hides within her room, she touches no one, and no one touches her. She's made herself an island.

The springtime of 1970 was a turbulent time on college campuses across the country. Antiwar protests escalated as the Vietnam War dragged on with no discernible end in sight. After the shooting of students by Ohio National Guard troops at Kent State University, violent protests and destruction of property became rampant. Grantham was spared from major violence, but students were becoming more vocal against the U.S. government's policies regarding the ongoing draft and the continued presence of American soldiers in Southeast Asia.

The trip to Montana after his sophomore year in college was the worst trip he ever experienced in the Bitterroot Valley. Neither of his cousins was able to join him, so he trekked into Blodgett Canyon on his own. A late spring snowstorm unexpectedly dumped more than a foot of snow, so he had to hunker down in a tent for a few cold days before he could get back to the trailhead and then home. In retrospect, he told himself he should've seen it as an omen for what was to take place in the coming school year.

During the third game of the football season in 1970, his junior year, he sustained a badly sprained left knee as he was hit while running. The team doctor placed him on crutches for a week and then wouldn't allow him to practice for two more weeks. Derek McCall, the backup quarterback, took over the starting position and led the team to three straight victories. Jake had serious doubts about being able to win back his starting position. The injury had really slowed him down.

In class one day, a friend told him about a party taking place off campus that evening and invited him to come. He hadn't heard from Donna in almost a year. Steeped in self-pity, he decided to drown his sorrows at the party. A keg of beer was flowing freely when he arrived. Someone handed him a cup and filled it with Budweiser capped with an inch of bubbling white foam.

He couldn't remember how many times he refilled the cup that night, which was not a good sign. When he came to, he was lying face down on a scratchy, olive wool blanket on a cot, staring out through the iron bars of a jail cell. The local police chief informed him that he'd been arrested for driving while intoxicated the previous night. The police had taken the liberty of calling Coach Littrell, his college football coach, who was not pleased to have to bail him out of jail.

"You screwed up big time," Coach Littrell said as he drove him back to Grover Hall. "You know the team rules. I'll have to suspend you and take away your scholarship. I like you, but there's no way around this."

"Thanks for getting me out of jail, coach. I'm sorry I let you down."

The DWI cost Jake $110 in fines and a lot more after that. His scholarship was revoked at the end of the fall semester, leaving him with no means to stay in college. He still had a year and a half of school left in order to finish his journalism degree. More importantly, dropping out of college would make him eligible for the draft. Although he was not against doing his patriotic duty in the service of his country, joining the military was not an attractive idea for most college students in the early 1970s.

His stepfather, Mike, loaned him the money to pay the tuition and fees for one more semester of school. Even with that assistance, he would have to figure out what to do for his senior year. He took a job as a bartender at a local pub on campus just to earn some spending money and pay for meals. For the first time in his life, involvement with sports was not an option. He always knew his football career would end someday and he would need to get a job in the real world. The way it ended, however, left him feeling directionless, like a ship without an anchor, adrift at sea.

One day in late March of 1971, he ran into Donna on campus while walking to class. Her neatly coiffed hair adorned the shoulders of her light gray coat, and a pale blue scarf accented her crystal blue eyes. Her arms were crossed in front of her, clutching two textbooks and a notebook. Her face, however, was devoid of the winsome smile he'd once known. It had been replaced by a sad and forlorn look. It reminded him of the look Jake's mother had worn for years after his father died.

"Hey, stranger," he said. "It's good to see you."

"Hi, Jake."

"I'd thought about reporting you missing."

"I've been busy."

Her eyes seemed to be welling up with tears, so he asked, "Is something wrong?"

"It's personal," she said.

She hadn't confided the news about her mother's illness with anyone. In fact, she was still in denial that her mother had been diagnosed with a terminal illness. Her father had said it was better to carry on as though nothing had happened.

"I've never shared your secrets with anybody," he said.

Unexpected tears began streaming down her face as she tried to answer. Finally she said, "It's my mother. She has cancer."

He reached out and put his arms around her, and she began to sob into his coat.

"I'm sorry. When did this happen?"

"She was diagnosed in December, just before finals."

"I don't know what to say."

"The doctors say she only has months to live."

"I wish I'd known what you were going through. I could have at least been a shoulder to cry on for you."

"Thank you, Jake, for your kindness to me. I don't deserve it."

After regaining her composure, she decided to share more. It felt good to talk about the burden she had been carrying alone for so long.

"My father has the best doctors money can buy, but they all say there's nothing more to be done. She's had surgery and all the radiation treatments, but the cancer has spread to her lungs and brain. Chemotherapy is no longer an option. She's so thin and weak I hardly recognize her. I don't know what to do."

Jake knew nothing about cancer. As Donna revealed her dilemma, however, thoughts of his father's death and the agony he felt flooded his mind.

"I can be there when you need someone to talk to, someone to lean on," he said, remembering his loneliness after his father's passing.

"How's your dad handling it?"

"My father isn't used to losing at anything. He thinks she can still beat the cancer, even in the face of evidence to the contrary. To avoid dealing with the day-to-day situation, he's chosen to immerse himself in his work."

She glanced at her watch, clearly concerned about the time.

"Do you have time to sit and talk for a while longer?" he asked, not wanting the moment to end.

"No," she said, wiping away new tears. "I have to get to my next class."

She gave him a big hug, kissed him lightly on the cheek, and then hurried off, wiping the last of her tears from her eyes as she went.

He stood there watching her walk away and wondered if he'd ever see her again. He wanted to hold her, to comfort her, and to make her pain disappear. But she would have to free herself from her father's control before he could become the most important man in her life. Right now she had a more immediate crisis on her hands.

As spring semester wound down and summer break loomed ahead, it became exceedingly clear that he couldn't afford to stay in college. He was in debt to his stepfather, who was struggling to make ends meet in supporting the family back at home in Clarkston. Asking him for more money was not an option. With gas at twenty-five cents a gallon, he had to limit his driving by buying a dollar's worth whenever he could. Something had to change.

As he weighed his options, a plan began to materialize. The day classes ended, he took the necessary steps to begin a new phase of his life. Only one thing remained to be done. He needed to see Donna one more time.

CHAPTER SIX

As Jake knocked on Donna's dorm room door, a million thoughts raced through his mind. He had so many things he wanted to tell her, and yet he could sum up his feelings for her in just three words.

"Jake, what are you doing here?" she said as she opened the door.

"I just want to say good-bye. Can I come in?"

"Sure," she said as she cleared a spot on the bed for them to sit. "I apologize for this mess, but I've been preoccupied with getting ready for finals and graduation. I guess I'm a terrible housekeeper."

"How's your mom doing?"

"About the same. My father took her up to Mayo Clinic. Now she's back home on some new experimental cancer drugs."

"Are you holding up okay?"

"I've tried not to think about it too much. Fortunately I've been busy with my studies, and it's kept my mind occupied. Now that classes have ended, I'm going to spend as much time with my mother as I can. I'll be moving back to St. Louis next week and living at home to be near her. Are you heading out to Montana soon?"

"No, I won't be going this summer. I'm leaving for San Antonio, Texas, in a few weeks."

She looked puzzled. "What in the world are you going to San Antonio for?"

"I'm going to explore my career options in the Air Force."

"Why? You have one more year of school and then you'll have your degree."

"I lost my scholarship, and I can't afford to stay in school. My lottery number was low, so I would have been drafted soon anyway and forced to spend two years in the Army, probably as a foot soldier. My cousins in Montana told me enlisting was a good way to keep from getting sent to Vietnam. And when I get out of the service in four years, I'll have the GI Bill to pay for my schooling."

"Jake, I can loan you some money. You don't need to join the military."

"Thanks, but I've already enlisted. Maybe the Air Force will send me to Switzerland, and we can ski the Alps together."

"That's not funny. You'll probably end up in Southeast Asia. Now I'll be worried about you all the time."

He took her delicate hands in his, "That's the nicest thing you've ever said to me. I'm hoping you'll write and let me know how you're doing."

"I'll try. My MBA program at St. Louis University will be starting soon. And my father already has an office for me in the corporate headquarters."

"Cherish the time you have left with your mom."

"I will. I know she needs me."

He wanted to tell her that he needed her too, more than anything else in the world. He wanted to say that he couldn't imagine never seeing her again. He wanted to say, "I love you, Donna." But he knew it was not the time.

"If you'll give me your address, I'll write you once I get settled in basic training."

"What will you be doing in the Air Force?" she said as she wrote down her home address on a piece of notebook paper and handed it to him. "Will you be an officer?"

"No. You have to be a college graduate for that. I'll be given an assignment in a month or so. When I'm done with basic training in six weeks, they'll send me to another base for more training. I'll let you know where I'm stationed as soon as I find out."

"Don't expect me to send you a box of homemade chocolate chip cookies in a care package at Christmas time."

"Swiss chocolate will work. You can tell your European friends you're doing your part to support a poor soldier."

"You know, everyone in Switzerland is required to serve in the Army."

"I thought Switzerland was neutral and stayed out of wars."

"Maybe no one attacks because everyone there is trained and armed."

"Good point."

"Actually I won't be going to Switzerland next winter. If my mother is still alive, she won't be strong enough to manage the trip. And if she's gone, well, it won't be the same."

He wiped a tear from her eye and kissed her closed eyelids. The saltiness of her tears was like honey on his lips. He sensed no resistance from her.

"No one can ever take away the memories you have of your mother."

"Thanks. Talking with you always makes me feel better. I'm going to miss you."

"Promise me you'll call me if you need to talk. No strings attached."

"I know I've said this before, but I don't deserve you, Jake. You're the best friend I have, and yet I'm always pushing you away."

"Look, if you feel that bad, why not enlist with me?"

She laughed hard as she considered how preposterous that suggestion was. It was good to see her laugh again.

"Okay, forget that idea. Somehow I can't see you taking orders from some butch sergeant and living with fifty other women in a barracks."

"I wouldn't last a day. Seriously, don't ever change. You're the only person I can turn to when I'm hurting."

He pulled her to her feet and began slow dancing with her as he sang, "You just call out my name, and you know wherever I am, I'll come running to see you again."

She pulled him close and kissed him with a passion and a sense of urgency she hadn't displayed before. Running her hand through his hair, she whispered, "You've found my weakness."

"Bad singing?"

"James Taylor."

They both laughed and he pulled himself away reluctantly.

"I'll write you as soon as you send me a letter. I promise," she said.

And then he was gone. This time he was the one leaving.

Maybe my absence will make her heart grow fonder, he thought to himself as he exited the dorm. *Then again, maybe she'll forget about me when someone else comes along. I just hope he's not a James Taylor fan.*

Basic training for Jake was a lot like being at football camp. Sixty young men from all over the country got off the Air Force bus at Lackland Air Force Base in San Antonio, Texas, around midnight. They were met with a fusillade of obscenities spewing forth from the mouth of Tech Sergeant Goddard, who stated in no uncertain terms that the new recruits belonged to him for the next six weeks. Jake was finally in bed at 0300 hours, only to be awakened two hours later by Sergeant Goddard banging on a metal garbage can with a nightstick as he shouted, "Alright ladies, get your butts out of bed and downstairs in five minutes for a three-mile run."

At age twenty-one, and with three years of college behind him, he was one of the older enlistees in the squadron. When Sergeant Goddard got in his face and asked why he enlisted, he wanted to say he'd been inspired by George C. Scott's monologue at the beginning of the movie *Patton*. To avoid further harassment, however, he said, "To serve my country, sir!" He left out the part about losing his scholarship. And he failed to mention the part about having no money.

After the first week, he wrote a letter to Donna. He took the liberty of painting a vivid, somewhat humorous picture of boot camp and closed with, "Wish you were here!" He hoped she'd get a chuckle from that. He missed seeing her laugh.

Two weeks went by with no letters. Mail call was painful each day as he heard Sergeant Goddard call out the last names of soldiers in his squadron who'd received mail. He watched others eagerly rip open an envelope to get at the letter sent to them by a friend or a loved one. He was beginning to wonder if Donna had already forgotten him. Then one day Sergeant Goddard yelled out, "Lemaster."

He raised his hand and shouted, "Here, sir!"

Goddard flung the letter in his direction and proceeded to call out the names on other envelopes.

He recognized Donna's handwriting as he tore open the envelope and took out the letter inside. With some trepidation, he began reading.

Dear Jake,

I'm glad to see the Air Force hasn't altered your sense of humor. Your letter made me laugh so hard I nearly peed my pants. I miss you a lot more than I thought possible.

I've started my MBA program, and it's going well. The classes are given in the evening, so I'm at the office most days, where my father has me shadowing department managers to learn about all aspects of the pharmaceutical industry. The work is challenging, not so much from an intellectual standpoint, but from resistance I've received from the men I'm supposed to be learning from. I don't think they realize they are biting the hand that will one day be feeding them.

As for my mother, she is basically confined to her bed. She has very little strength to walk. Occasionally she'll sit in a chair and look out her bedroom window to see the beautiful garden she tended for many years. She had a seizure yesterday despite all of the medication the doctors have prescribed for her. All I could do was cry for help while she shook violently and turned blue. It was horrible. I thought she was going to die right in front of me while I stood by helplessly.

Father has hired a nurse to be with her twenty-four hours a day. He says I shouldn't spend so much time with her since there is nothing I can do to help the situation. But there are times when she is feeling a little better, and we talk for hours. She's told me so many things about our family I didn't know before. She also told me things about her life she says she has never shared with anyone else. You were right. These are precious times with her that I wouldn't trade for anything.

That's all for now. Write soon and let me know where you will be stationed next.

Love,
Donna

He read the letter over and over for the next few days. The tone seemed to be softer and more intimate than many of their conversations. Perhaps she was changing. Or perhaps it was easier and less threatening for her to share her true feelings when they were so far away from each other.

The following week, he received his assignment for the next four years. He was told he would be a "Defensive Fire Control Systems Operator." The sergeant in charge of career assignments said he would be "flying on a plane and putting out fires by pulling circuit breakers." He figured he could handle that.

A month later, he discovered his true job—tail gunner on a B-52 bomber. By then he had finished basic training and was in south Florida for a week of water survival training. There he parasailed for the first time as part of training and was taught how to survive in the ocean in the event he had to bail out of the airplane over water.

Next he was sent to SERE (Survival, Evasion, Resistance, and Escape) training at Fairchild Air Force Base in Spokane, Washington. During the month of intense training there, he learned how to perform a good PLF (parachute landing fall) without breaking his legs. He attended extensive lectures on how to build shelters, escape and evade the enemy, forage for food to survive off the land, and use the equipment in the survival kit. Fresh trout and Coors beer wouldn't be available where he would be going, he was told.

The most challenging part of survival training was the simulation POW camp. The trainees were taken out to a mock battlefield at night. Their objective was to make their way through the obstacles without being captured. In reality, however, everyone was captured and placed in a simulated concentration camp. The "captors" then subjected the trainees to treatment similar to what they could expect from the North Vietnamese if they were unfortunate enough to be in that situation.

Trainees were subjected to mild forms of torture—solitary confinement, interrogations, sleep deprivation, and being placed in positions of discomfort—and they were to utilize the survival techniques they'd been taught in the classroom. Jake thought he was prepared to survive off the land, but he didn't think life as a POW would suit him well. The number one take-home message at the end of the month was this: don't become a prisoner of war.

The six-month technical school for B-52 gunners at Castle Air Force Base near Merced, California, was next. It was scheduled to start in early September of 1971. The training would consist of three months of classroom work followed by three months of flight training. After that, he would be ready for combat, at least in theory.

Jake took a commercial flight from Spokane, Washington, to San Francisco, California, wearing his Air Force uniform proudly. The airport in San Francisco was teeming with Hare Krishna followers with shaved heads and saffron robes, dancing through the airport and chanting their mantra. An airport shuttle bus took him to the downtown Greyhound bus station on the corner of 7th and Market streets. As he waited for the dispatcher to announce the departure of the bus to Merced, several scruffy appearing hippies offered to sell him mescaline and LSD. Other less friendly, longhaired individuals taunted him with epithets including "baby killer" and "war monger."

The Air Force training was changing the way he thought about being an American. He was repulsed by their lack of understanding and respect for people wearing the uniform. At the same time, he was not certain if he agreed with all that the U.S. government was doing overseas. His response to the taunting was to say and do nothing. *I guess someone has to defend their freedom of speech so they can root for a Communist revolution,* he thought.

Once he settled into the barracks along the flight line on base, he wrote a letter to Donna to let her know where he'd be for the next six months. He guessed it would be a long time before he heard from her again.

He shared a room in the barracks with two other young gunners. Steve Abrams was a likeable eighteen-year-old from Louisiana who loved Cajun food, water skiing on Lake Charles, and Creedence Clearwater Revival's music. He was madly in love with his high school sweetheart, a pretty young girl named Sarah. The other roommate, Danny Burke, was a more introverted nineteen-year-old. Danny was from a rural town in Iowa, and like Jake, he too had lost an older brother to the war in January 1968. Unlike Jake, however, Danny had a more admirable reason for enlisting. He did it as an act of honoring his brother.

Jake purchased a small stereo system from the Base Exchange, or BX, to listen to music in the barracks. The FM station out of Fresno, KFYE, serenaded him and his roommates each morning with Rod Stewart singing the words of his hit tune, "Maggie May."

Rod is right. It is late September, and maybe I should be back at school. But that's no longer an option, he told himself.

In October he received a letter from Donna that gave him hope while simultaneously filling him with unbridled anxiety.

Sometimes getting what you ask for has unintended consequences, he thought.

Dear Jake,

It was good to hear from you again. Being stationed in California doesn't sound too bad after your POW camp experience in survival training. I'm sure you'll enjoy it even more when you start flying.

Grad school is still going well here. My work at Blanford Pharmaceuticals actually gives me a chance to apply some of what I'm learning in my MBA program and makes both endeavors more enjoyable.

My mother's condition has continued to deteriorate since I last wrote to you. I'm spending as much time with her as I can. Although it's difficult to watch her dying slowly, I enjoy our talks more and more all the time. I've told her all about you. I hope you don't mind. She is happy to know that I have someone special to talk to.

My mother would like to meet you while she still has the chance. She told me to invite you to come to our house for dinner sometime during the Christmas holidays and meet my father and her. It would mean a great deal to her, and to me, if you can do this. I need to see you again.

Write me soon. I miss you.

Love,
Donna

He'd already planned to fly home to Illinois to see his family during the two-week leave over the holidays. His intent was then to drive his car back to California, a leisurely trip of three to four days of steady driving, after he'd worn out his welcome in Clarkston. Logistically it would be no problem stopping in St. Louis for a visit with Donna and her parents. Logistics, however, were the least of his concerns.

The fact that Donna's mother had heard all about him and still wanted to meet him was a plus. She appeared to be his biggest ally in the battle to win Donna's affection. He liked her already. On the negative side of the ledger, he didn't think Douglas Kingston would be excited about allowing him inside the castle to court the heir to the family fortune. One thing he knew for certain. Mr. Kingston would be ready for him.

His follow-up letter to Donna said he was available to join her family for dinner over the holidays, and it would be an honor for him to meet her parents. He'd already purchased a Christmas present for Donna. Now he could give it to her in person.

CHAPTER SEVEN

Chicago's O'Hare airport was the busiest airport in the world, and the holiday season added to the air and ground traffic considerably. Fortunately for Jake, Carl Simpson, a friend from Clarkston, would be picking him up at the airport and driving him home. Carl had attended a junior college for two years, majoring in partying with a minor in agricultural science. He was helping his father farm a thousand acres of prime Illinois soil, all of which would someday belong to him.

The American Airlines pilot announced that the temperature in Chicago that day, December 23, was an unseasonably warm 40 degrees with clear skies and unlimited visibility. Jake surveyed the picturesque skyline of the city during descent. The nearly completed Sears Tower, soon to be the tallest building in the world, impressively anchored the south end of "The Loop." The iconic Hancock Center was prominently displayed on beautiful north Michigan Avenue. The Cubs had broken his heart in '69 when they lost the pennant to the Mets, but he looked in vain for Wrigley

Field anyway. He located Soldier Field and watched the heavy traffic flowing both ways on Lake Shore Drive as commuters made their way through the city.

Carl was waiting for him at the arrival gate. The two young men had become close friends while playing football together in high school. At six feet four inches tall and 230 pounds, Carl had been an animal on the offensive and defensive lines. Since then he'd gained a few pounds, and his crew cut had been replaced by near shoulder length black hair. His rugged face sported long side burns and a thick mustache. His ever-present smile, however, had not changed.

Greeting Jake with a bear hug that nearly broke his ribs, Carl said, "Welcome home, Colonel."

After catching his breath, Jake replied, "You must not be making any money farming. You can't even afford a haircut or a shave."

"You sound like my old man."

"It's good to see you. Thanks for offering to drive me home."

"No problem. Let's get your bags and head home before the rush hour traffic starts."

They retrieved Jake's baggage and began the one-and-a-half-hour drive to Clarkston, their hometown with a population of 10,000 residents. Like most communities in Illinois, Clarkston's economy was driven by agriculture and manufacturing. That time of year, the fields had long ago been harvested. As Jake gazed out the car window, he saw the fertile, black, Midwest soil that would lie dormant until spring planting season arrived once again. No irrigation was needed there, unlike the San Joaquin Valley where he'd been living the past three months.

Carl shifted through the gears of his orange and black 1968 Plymouth Roadrunner. On the car radio, WLS-AM was playing "Brown Sugar" by the Rolling Stones. His parents had given him the car as a gift when he'd graduated from high school. Jake knew Carl's parents had inherited a lot of land from both sides of the family and had added more acreage through the years. Carl's future was definitely secure—unlike Jake's.

The conversation started out easy enough.

"So how's military life?"

"I'm surviving."

"Are they going to send you to 'Nam?"

"No. But I'll probably end up in Thailand sometime next year if the war is still going on."

"David Browner just got home about a month ago. He was a gung-ho marine when he went in a few years ago. Now his hair's longer than mine, and he's joined the antiwar protesters."

"That seems to be happening a lot."

"What made you join up?"

"I lost my scholarship and didn't want to burden my mom and my stepdad."

Jake knew most people at home were unaware of how he'd lost his scholarship. The official explanation was a knee injury.

"You should've said something to me. I could've loaned you some money. Dad could've hired you to help us on the farm."

"Thanks, but I'm not a farmer. I'll finish my degree with the GI Bill when I'm discharged. Don't feel sorry for me. I'll be using your tax dollars." Then trying to change the subject, he asked, "Mind if I smoke?"

"Since when did you start smoking?"

"Drinking beer and smoking cigarettes seem to be a job requirement in the military. Are you still going out with Peggy?"

Jake lit a cigarette and listened as Carl gave him an update on his love life and the latest news about their friends and former classmates. It sounded like not much had changed in Clarkston the past few years. Carl would soon marry his sweetheart, Peggy Stanton, when she graduated from college the following summer with a degree in elementary education. The wedding date hadn't been set, but that was a mere formality.

With a wry grin, Carl pointed toward the glove box and said, "Open that up. I brought you a welcome home present."

The look on Carl's face gave no hint of what was inside the glove box, but he seemed quite proud of himself for springing the surprise. Jake had seen Carl's flair for gift giving in the past, and the recipients weren't always pleased. He once had taken a crap in a paper bag, lit it on fire, and deposited it on the chemistry teacher's doorstep.

"Gee, Carl, you shouldn't have gone to so much trouble."

"Go on, open it up."

Jake slowly opened the glove box, fully expecting something to jump out at him. Instead, what he saw was a plastic bag full of a green, leafy substance and some rolling papers. Carl had obviously rolled two joints in advance and placed them inside the bag as well.

"It's all yours. Light up one, and we'll celebrate."

To Jake it seemed that Carl had just deposited a bag of crap on Jake's doorstep, and now wanted him to set it on fire himself. Although he'd been around people smoking marijuana at college, he'd never tried it. Grantham was a small school, and drug use was not widespread. He didn't consider himself a prude, but alcohol had always seemed a more acceptable and legal way to cop a buzz.

"Carl, I'm not a lawyer, but I think this is illegal."

"Illegal, like a DWI you mean?"

"So you heard? I suppose everyone in Clarkston knows."

"Come on, man, don't be such a pansy. You must've gotten high at college."

"I've been at parties where people were smoking pot, but I've never tried it. Did you buy this in Clarkston?"

"I'm a farmer. I grow my own. This is some of my best home-grown stuff. I just plant a few rows in the middle of a cornfield, and I've got enough for my own stash and enough to turn on a few friends like you."

"Does your dad know about this?"

"Get real. He'd go crazy if he knew."

"I can't show up at home all spaced out from smoking dope. The people I've seen smoking marijuana were doing weird things, and their eyes were bloodshot and squinty."

"You need to loosen up a bit, dude. It'll just mellow you out some. I guarantee you'll enjoy it."

"What is this, a two-year supply?" *The Illinois State police would probably call it five to ten years at Joliet State Correctional Center*, he thought to himself.

"That's a pound of Illinois' finest. It'll usually last me about a month."

"Sorry, Carl. I appreciate the offer, but I have to pass." Closing the stash back inside the glove box, he asked, "So how are the Illini doing in basketball this year?"

As Carl told him about this year's team, his mind was racing to catch up with the changes he had seen in Carl since their high school days. Although he was very aware of the seismic shifts in society in general during the last decade, he somehow had miscalculated in thinking Clarkston would remain unscathed. Now he wondered what others surprises awaited him at home.

They entered Clarkston from the north, where the giant green dinosaur on the sign outside Mike's Sinclair station was clearly visible. Mike was under the hood of a customer's car, wiping oil from a dipstick to check the level. Carl honked, and Mike waved as they sped by. Next they came to the Dog N Suds drive-in restaurant, which was closed for the winter, and then drove past the high school football field. "Lots of memories there," Jake said.

At last they pulled up in front of a tri-level structure at 570 West Elm Street, and Jake said his good-bye and thanks to Carl. It was always strange for Jake to come to this house, Mike Chalmers' house, whenever he was back in town. Although Jake's mother had married Mike when Jake was fourteen, this place would never be his home, and Mike would never be his father. He liked Mike, and Mike had been very good to him, but they weren't what might be called close. Mike's financial help had raised Jake's admiration for his stepfather, but his recent troubles at school had probably lowered Mike's opinion of him.

His mother met him at the door with open arms. Mrs. Mike Chalmers' long black hair was curled and fell onto the shoulders of her lavender sweater. Her face was pretty, and the makeup she used sparingly highlighted her natural beauty. The sad look she had carried in the past was no longer evident. At forty-eight, she actually looked younger than when her husband died over ten years before.

"Welcome home, Jake! It's so good to see you again. Come on in, and make yourself at home. Mike's still at work, but he should be home for supper in about an hour. I made a pot roast for you."

"Thanks, Mom. You look great. Mike must be doing something right."

"That man was a gift from God. He treats me like a queen."

He and his mother sat on the couch in the living room. "How are you doing out there in California?"

"I enjoy living in California. My classroom work is done now, and the flight training starts in a few weeks."

"Have you had a chance to travel around much?"

"Not yet. I hope to see the ocean and the mountains after I drive my car back next week."

"Next week? I thought you had two weeks of leave?"

"I do. But I promised to stop in St. Louis and visit a friend on the way to California."

"It sounds like you have a girlfriend you haven't told me about. Am I right?"

"Maybe. It's a girl I went to college with at Grantham. Her mother is dying of breast cancer, and she asked me to stop by and meet her family while I was home."

"Oh, that's terrible. What's the girl's name?"

"Donna Kingston."

His mother searched her memory bank, slowly shook her head, and then said, "I don't recall you ever mentioning her name. Are you seriously involved with her?"

Confessing his feelings about a girl was something he hadn't done with his mother before. In the past, his friends were the main source of advice about how to deal with members of the opposite sex. The results spoke for themselves. It was time to get a woman's perspective.

"Actually, I think I'm in love with Donna. I met her in college during my freshman year. I've been working on my relationship with her for a couple of years."

"Does she know how you feel about her? Is that why you're going to meet her parents?"

He was surprised at his mother's questions, but he decided that in order to get her advice, he would have to tell her Donna's background. He spent the next ten minutes detailing all he knew of her family and their situation. He could tell by her serious expression that she wasn't anticipating the arrival of grandchildren from this relationship anytime soon.

Finally he asked, "What do you think?"

"I think this girl likes you. But she may have trouble giving and receiving love like most people. She's used to pleasing her father by being an overachiever. You're competing with him, and he's not going to like it."

"Should I go to her house like I planned?"

"You'll regret it the rest of your life if you don't. She needs to hear you say you love her. The rest will be up to her."

The conversation ended as Mike walked in. He shook Jake's hand firmly and said, "Good to see you. Glad you could join us for Christmas."

Mike Chalmers had always been a good man. But after his wife's death, he'd devoted himself to his church even more. Most people would've been angry and bitter toward the drunk driver who crossed the centerline and hit his wife's car head on. Mike, however, actually went to see the man in jail, prayed with him, and forgave him. Jake respected him for it, but he couldn't really understand it.

"Thanks, Mike. It's good to be here for the holidays. Where's Mary?"

Jake's mom headed to the kitchen, gave Mike a kiss, and said, "She went shopping with a friend from college, but she'll be home soon."

Mary was Mike's eighteen-year-old daughter who was now in her first year of college. She had a lot of unresolved anger from losing her mother and had given Mike a difficult time for several years. Jake's mother's presence in Mary's life had been good for both of them as they each dealt with the loss of a loved one. Unlike her father, Mary hadn't forgiven the man who'd taken her mother's life.

Mary and Jake lived under the same roof for a few years before he went to college, but they didn't really talk except in passing. Their age difference and circumstances in life had made the relationship awkward at best.

He heard a car pull up in front of the house, and then Mary opened the front door. As she entered, he could see she'd gained some weight since he'd last seen her the year before. Her long, straight, brown hair was held in place by a headband adorned with peace signs. She was wearing bellbottom jeans, a black turtleneck sweater, and sandals. A dingy blue jeans jacket rounded out her wardrobe.

Jake's mom greeted Mary first, "How did the shopping go?"

"It was a real drag. The mall was super crowded."

Jake rose to greet Mary, who flashed him a peace sign and said, "Hi." Without another word, she glided down the hall into her bedroom.

Jake's mother sensed his questions. She explained that Mary's rebelliousness had found a new home in the antiwar movement on the campus of her college. She said that she and Mike were praying that Mary would not get caught up in drugs and "other worldly vices."

Jake remained in the living room with Mike. Thirty minutes later, all four of them sat down together at the supper table for the first time in several years. After Mike closed the blessing with an amen, Mary asked Jake, "So how does it feel to be a trained killer?"

"Don't start this now, Mary," Jake's mother said. "Can't we just have a nice meal together?"

"I just want to know how this war pig can sleep at night with blood on his hands."

"You've been brainwashed by too much propaganda at school, Mary," Jake said. "The only things I've ever killed were pheasants and rabbits when I was hunting."

Mary had obviously been planning this frontal assault for quite some time, and she hadn't yet expended all of her ammunition. "When the students rise up and overthrow this imperialist government, you and your fellow tin soldiers will be tried as war criminals. Then you won't be so smug."

Mike's face turned a deep violet color. "Mary, you'll keep a civil tongue when speaking in this house."

"Jesus, what hypocrisy," she said. "Our government and its lackeys are butchering innocent people in Vietnam, and you're worried about how I talk."

"Don't take the Lord's name in vain, Mary," Jake's mother said.

"Why not? He forgot about me a long time ago."

Mary seemed to have fired her last prepared shot, so Jake seized the opening. "Actually, Mary, you have every right to voice your opinions about the war or any other matter you feel passionately about. As Americans, we all have a first amendment right to free speech. And as a journalist, I couldn't do my job without freedom of the press. In a Communist country, you would be shot or imprisoned for speaking out against the government the way you just did."

"That's just conservative Republican bull put out by the Nixon Administration."

"Personally I'm not a big believer in this war either. But Nixon didn't start the war. President Johnson had over a half million of our soldiers there a few years ago, and he was a liberal Democrat from Texas. Hopefully the war will be over soon, and then we can all move on with our lives."

Jake's mom jumped in, hoping to change the subject to something less contentious. "Mike and I are hoping we all can go to the Christmas Eve worship service at church tomorrow night at nine o'clock. It will be such a blessing to have us all together in church again."

"Oh, that's sounds really cool," said Mary sarcastically as she pushed away from the table and retreated into her bedroom.

"I apologize for the way she treated you," Mike said, obviously distressed by his daughter's behavior. "She's young and too impressionable."

"She didn't say anything I haven't heard before."

His mom wanted to steer the conversation in another direction. "I have some errands to run tomorrow, so you can make yourself at home. You can warm up some of this pot roast on the stove for lunch if you like. I'll be home around 4 p.m. Mike is closing the station early so we can have supper and get to the church by 8:30."

"That was a great meal, Mom," Jake said as he stood up from the table. "I'm going to do a little reading and then hit the sack. I'm exhausted from traveling all day. See you tomorrow, Mike."

"Good night," they both said in unison.

He went to sleep feeling like he had fallen into the rabbit hole in *Alice and Wonderland*. His redneck farmer friend was now growing marijuana, and his stepfather's daughter had accused him of committing war crimes.

Tomorrow should be fun.

When he woke up in the late morning, there was no sign of anyone else in the house. After showering and shaving, he grabbed a bowl of cereal for breakfast and made a cup of coffee. As he read the daily paper, he automatically lit a cigarette and inhaled deeply.

"You're in deep trouble now," said Mary as she strolled into the kitchen. "Dad doesn't allow anyone to smoke in this house."

He quickly held the cigarette under running water from the sink and then flushed the contraband down the toilet. "Sorry about that. I wasn't thinking."

"I'm sorry too. I came on a little strong last night. I guess I'm just freaked out by being back home."

To his surprise, she sat down across the table from him. For the next hour, they connected for the first time in their lives. Fate had taken a parent from each of them and then thrown them into a new, makeshift family not of their choosing. Neither had been reconciled to it. Although completely unforeseen, their morning conversation was a good start in the healing process between them. Jake hoped more healing would come that evening for him when he went to church for the first time in a long while.

As the family drove to the Clarkston Presbyterian Church that evening after dinner, memories of his father's funeral service came rushing back. The pastor had said, "The Lord giveth, and the Lord taketh away." As a child, Jake had seen his dad taken away, but he didn't know what the Lord had given him. Now eight years later, he was back in the same church. In the interim, the Lord also had taken his brother Greg. He was still waiting for the Lord to give him something.

Maybe God will show me tonight, he thought to himself with hope for the first time in a long time.

The church was crowded almost to capacity as they took their seats and exchanged greetings with those nearby. A number of his old classmates and their families were in attendance for this special service. He'd always gone to church as a youth, mainly because his parents had made him go. The life-changing event that some people experienced, however, had apparently passed him by.

The pastor talked about the significance of Christmas as the birth of Jesus Christ, the Son of God. He said that God loved everyone so much he sent his son to earth to live like a man and sacrifice his life so people could have their sins forgiven and live in heaven with him when they died. Jake had heard it all before, but the thought of someone sacrificing his life made sense to him now that he was in the Air Force facing a likely deployment to Southeast Asia. In spite of his unresolved anger over his father's and his brother's deaths, he was moved by the message.

He prayed silently and asked God not to give up on him. He prayed too that God would change Donna's heart so she would love him as much as he loved her. "Just give me that one thing, and I'll believe you really love me. If you're there, let me know."

Sitting next to him, Mary began sobbing uncontrollably and buried her face against his arm. At first he thought her tears were in response to the preacher's words. He was totally unprepared for what happened next.

"Please forgive me for being so hateful," she whispered into his ear. "I should have given this to you yesterday." She took something from her purse and handed it to him. It was an envelope with Donna's handwriting on it. "I wanted you to be as miserable as I am."

A flash of anger swept over him, but the remorse he saw on her face was genuine. Something had softened her heart. Putting his arm around her, he whispered, "I understand." He had to fight the urge to tear open the letter right there during the church service.

Mary continued sobbing, and her tears splattered the envelope in his hand. His mother leaned close and asked, "Is Mary okay?"

"She's all right. She's just dealing with a lot of emotions."

When the family arrived back home after the service, what happened next was a surprise to everyone.

"Thanks for holding me while I had a meltdown," Mary said to Jake. "I asked God tonight to forgive me for all the terrible thoughts I have and the way I mistreat people. I've been holding onto my anger for so long I didn't think it would ever be possible to change."

Mike heard what his daughter said and embraced her in his strong arms. "Mary, God knows the anger you've harbored, and it has been hurting you in many ways."

"I've tried to forgive, Dad, but it just seems impossible. I can't understand how you could forgive the man who took away Mom."

"It's humanly impossible to forgive others on our own. Only when we understand the depth of love Jesus has for us can we begin to forgive others."

"I want that. I'm so tired of being unhappy. I hid Jake's letter when it came in the mail a few days ago because I didn't want anyone else to be happy if I couldn't."

Jake had heard enough for the night and had much to think about. He gave Mary a hug, said goodnight respectfully to everyone, and then retreated to his room to read Donna's letter. He flipped on the bedroom light and sat on the edge of the bed as he ripped open the envelope. It had been several weeks since he'd heard from her, and he was hoping her mother's condition hadn't deteriorated to the point that a visit would no longer be possible. Anxiously he read the letter.

Merry Christmas, Jake!

I hope you're enjoying a relaxing time with your family during the Christmas season. My mother is really looking forward to your visit. Tuesday, December 28, seems to be the only time we can all get together. Can you come that afternoon to meet with my mother and then stay for dinner? My father will be working during the day, but he has said he wants to speak with you privately after dinner, man to man, of course.

I miss you so much. I hope you haven't forgotten me by now. My mother is barely holding on to life, and the prospect of your visit seems to give her a purpose to keep going. Actually, the thought of you coming soon has kept me going as well. Without you to talk to, the way we do, I don't think I could go on.

Something has happened to me these past few months as I've watched my mother dying. You know how much I used to have my heart set on becoming a recognized woman in the business world? Now, after seeing my fifty-year-old mother wasting away and hearing the regrets she has about the things she's left undone, I don't want to waste my life on things that can't bring me real joy. Mother read me a verse from the Bible that said there is nothing better for us than to be happy and do good while we live. That verse is just after chapter three of the Book of Ecclesiastes. You would recognize it because the Byrds used it in their hit song "Turn! Turn! Turn!" a few years ago.

Anyway, I guess what I'm trying to say is that I really like you, Jake. The whole time I was telling you I couldn't get involved with you, I knew it was a lie. It had already happened. Mother could see it whenever I talked about you.

She helped me understand what a mistake it would be to deny the feelings I have for you.

There, I've finally said it. I hope my confession doesn't scare you away!

I have included the directions to our house. It's a bit secluded, but I think you can find it on your own. Call me if you get lost!

Love,
Donna

P.S. Please tell your mother how much we appreciate her sharing you with us during the holidays. I hope I can one day meet your family.

He read the letter over and over to savor every word she'd said. God had given him exactly what he'd asked for in his prayer earlier. Yes, the Lord had taken away his father and brother, but now it seemed he was giving him someone new to love.

CHAPTER EIGHT

The three-and-a-half-hour drive from Clarkston to St. Louis gave Jake plenty of time to reflect on all that'd happened in the last few days. Mary's transformation following the Christmas Eve church service was nothing short of a miracle. She seemed at peace, and that had made everyone's Christmas much more enjoyable.

Jake was still trying to come to grips with his own miracle. The woman he'd desired for more than three years had suddenly opened her heart to him. Now he needed to see where that would lead.

He sensed a battle with Donna's father loomed just over the horizon. He wondered if she'd told her father what she'd shared with him about the change in her thoughts about her future. His guess was Mr. Douglas Kingston was going to honor his dying wife's request to meet with the poor peasant boy who'd captured his daughter's affection and then dispose of him as expeditiously as possible.

By early afternoon, he was nearing his destination. Donna's directions led him through the countryside to a rural highway that ran along a high brick wall surrounding a wooded estate off to the right. As he turned through the gated entrance and followed the half-mile long paved lane to the Kingston residence, he began to appreciate just how improbable it was for him to be there. Some of his friends back in Clarkston had nice homes, but nothing like what he was seeing directly in front of him.

The large, white, two-story mansion with antebellum architecture looked like a Georgian plantation house from the old south, or some sort of Greek temple that'd been transplanted to Missouri from the Acropolis high above the ancient city of Athens. Even on such a bleak wintry day, the house and the property were magnificent. He could only imagine how splendid it would look with all of the trees sporting their foliage and the garden in full bloom.

As gorgeous as the house was, nothing could compare to the beauty of the woman standing in the open doorway as he stopped the car in the circle drive in front. She was wearing a peach colored turtleneck sweater and stylish jeans. She wore no makeup, and her hair was pulled back in a ponytail. He could see she'd lost some weight and her face was slightly drawn, but her smile was as radiant as ever. He stepped out of the car, and she came running out to greet him. They embraced at the foot of the steps and released their pent up emotions with a long and passionate kiss.

"I'm so glad you're here. Come inside. It's freezing," she said as she took his hand at last and led him into the house.

"How's your mother doing?" he asked, shocked by the lavish interior.

"Not well, but she's anxious to finally meet you. I haven't seen her this excited in years."

"I hope I don't disappoint her."

"That'd be impossible."

Taking her delicate face in his hands, he said, "You know, you couldn't have given me a more perfect Christmas present than your letter. I'm not much into religion, but I asked God to change your heart so you would love me as much as I love you."

"That's the same thing my mother has been praying for!"

He kissed her again, softer and slower this time. A few tears of joy trickled down her face. The taste of her tears reminded him of the last time they were together.

Gently wiping the tears away, he said, "Remember, I know your weakness."

"Slow dancing?"

"James Taylor."

He took a wrapped present out of his backpack and handed it to her. "Merry Christmas."

"What'd you get me?"

"You'll have to open it to find out."

She hastily tore open the gift like a child on Christmas morning. The album cover read *Mud Slide Slim and the Blue Horizon.* A photo of James Taylor wearing a blue shirt and green pants held up by suspenders adorned it.

"This is fantastic. I love all of his music, especially our song, 'You've Got a Friend'."

"Our song, really? I must've heard that song a thousand times during basic training. It always reminded me of you."

"I'm so glad you are here. Mother's probably wondering where we are. Are you ready to meet her?"

Taking his coat, she led him to the grand staircase. Although he'd seen sick people before, he'd never seen anyone dying of cancer. To say he was apprehensive about meeting Donna's mother was an understatement. As they ascended the stairs and walked down the hallway toward her mother's room, his attention was drawn to a number of family photos decorating the walls on either side.

One photo in particular captivated him—that of a beautiful young brunette adorned in a wedding gown.

Donna followed his gaze. "Mother aged quite well until the last few years. The cancer has really taken a toll on her."

"I can see where you get your beauty."

"Thank you, Jake, but Mother's greatest beauty is inside her. It still remains. In fact, it shines even brighter now since her physical beauty has faded. She's taught me a lot about life and love during the past few months. You were right when you said I should cherish the time I have left with her. She's not gone yet, but I'm afraid she can't last much longer."

Donna gently knocked on the door to her mother's room. "Jake's here, Mother. Can we come in?"

From within the room a weak voice said, "Come in, dear."

Donna opened the door, revealing a lovely bedroom with a sitting area on one end with bay windows providing a view of the garden below. As she and Jake entered, he rested his eyes on a pale, gaunt ghost of a woman propped up in a hospital bed with a handful of white pillows around her. A colorful knitted cap covered her head, bald from the cancer treatments. She bore little resemblance to the young woman in the picture hanging in the hallway, but her eyes shone brightly as they fixed on him.

A large green metal cylinder stood next to the bed. It fed life-giving oxygen to the woman laboring to breathe through a long, thin, plastic tube. A middle-aged woman dressed in a white nursing uniform hovered over her, finishing the administering of the scheduled breathing treatment to her patient. "I'll leave you alone with your visitors now," Mrs. Billingsley said. "I'll be downstairs if you need me."

"So this is the young man who turned my daughter's world upside down," said Donna's mother as they approached. "I feel like I already know you from the letters Donna has shared with me."

"It's a pleasure to meet you, Mrs. Kingston."

"Donna, bring a chair over here next to the bed so Jake can sit down."

"That's all right, ma'am. I can stand."

"Nonsense. I want to spend some time talking with you, and I want you to feel at ease here. I know I look a fright, but today is really a good day for me."

Donna set a leather wingback chair next to the bed and placed her hand on Jake's shoulder, "I'm going to go and check on dinner while you two get to know each other."

Donna had shared very little of her feelings with him in the brief times they'd spent together at college. Like the ephemeral sight of a dolphin surfacing in the ocean at dawn, only unexpected glimpses of her inner workings had come to the surface and then were quickly submerged. He realized that he might now find out much more about the woman he loved through a brief conversation with her mother. Mrs. Kingston must've sensed his uneasiness as he watched Donna close the door behind her. With a faint smile she said, "You're safe with me, Jake. You and I are on the same team. You are a football player aren't you?"

"Yes, ma'am. Well, I was in college."

"Then you know what it means to be a good teammate, working together for the good of something bigger than yourself. In our case, we're working together to see that Donna lives a long and happy life. We both love her. I've seen the way she looks when she reads your letters and when she tells me about how supportive and encouraging you are to her. Unfortunately I won't be around to see her get married or to enjoy playing with my grandchildren."

"Donna said the doctors were hopeful the new chemotherapy treatments will make a difference."

"That's what doctors say when they can't face reality. I'm sure they're doing the best they can, but some things are beyond their control. This cancer is one of them."

She coughed long and hard for a good ten seconds and then wiped the thick, green secretions from her mouth with a tissue. Her breathing was raspy, and he could see even minor activity stressed her weakened body.

"Please excuse me. I'm not very ladylike. I don't have time for proper social graces under the circumstances. Tell me, what're your plans in regard to Donna?"

"I've had strong feelings for Donna since I met her in college. Nothing would make me happier than to spend the rest of my life with her. But until recently she was so driven to become a female business executive that she didn't allowed herself to consider being married and having a family."

"That's my husband's plan for her. It always has been since I was unable to bear him a son." Tears welled up in the corners of her eyes as she paused to catch her breath. "I prayed for God to give me a son, but it wasn't to be. After a few miscarriages, I gave up. Douglas couldn't accept it, so he turned his back on God. And he decided to take matters into his own hands by grooming Donna to be the son he never had. As you probably know, he's hell-bent on making her the future CEO of Blanford Pharmaceuticals."

Jake's mind raced with questions and what to say next. "How did you and your husband meet, if you don't mind my asking?"

A thin smile appeared as she recalled events long ago. "It was after the war, 1950 to be exact, and Douglas was working for my father as a chemist to develop new drugs for his company. We met at a company event. I was smitten with him."

"Really? I assumed he came from a high society family like, well, like you did."

"He'll never tell you his story, so I'd better do it for him. Douglas was born in 1920 in a small southern Illinois coal-mining town. His mother died of tuberculosis when he and his little brother Joe were still very young. His father worked long hours in the mines, so the boys had to fend for themselves most of the time. The Depression was hard on everyone, and they did what they could to survive—including working deep underground in those God-awful mines even before they were old enough to shave."

"Why do you say he would be reluctant to talk with me about his past?"

"Douglas would just as soon forget those times. His father was killed when the mines flooded in 1937. You may not know this, but the Ohio River flooded so severely that spring that towns and fields were under water at least fifty miles away. After his death, the boys worked in the mines until the war broke out in 1941."

"I saw a picture of someone in uniform in the hallway. Was that your husband?"

"Yes. He was a handsome man in uniform. He served as a corpsman in the Army for three years. He never talked much about what he went through in Europe—all the blood and guts and gore from the wounded soldiers he took care of. When he was released from the Army, he used the GI Bill to get his college degree at Grantham. Would you believe he almost made it into medical school?"

"What happened?"

"His brother Joe committed suicide. Joe had been a marine in the battles of the Pacific during the war. He couldn't get over the things he saw—and did—during those horrible years. One night he couldn't take it anymore. He blew his brains out with a handgun."

"I can see why your husband would rather not dwell on the past. He's had a lot of suffering to overcome."

"Douglas has worked hard to forget where he came from. It's as if he's been trying to change his past by achieving success. In some ways, I guess, he's accomplished his goal. But he can't undo the past. Rather than be proud of his heritage, he's chosen to sweep it under the rug, as they say."

"After your marriage, was he groomed to take over your father's business?"

"In a sense he was. But my father wouldn't have turned the company over to him just because he was family. He is smart and gifted, and my father could see that. I give Douglas a lot of credit for growing the company to where it is today; however, we've all paid a price for that success."

Jake shifted in his chair, sensing the difficult part of the conversation was about to begin.

"That's why I wanted to meet with you, Jake. My husband isn't a very kind man. I like to think he was at one time, but his heart has become calloused over the years, and he has turned his back on God. When I'm gone, Donna will be at his mercy unless you are there to love her and protect her. She doesn't yet realize how much she is going to need you.

"Douglas always taught her to be unemotional and business-like. I'm afraid I allowed him free reign in grooming her to develop her detached demeanor. I felt guilty for not being a good wife, and as a result, I wasn't a very good mother either. Only after I became ill did God give me the strength to speak the truth to her."

What he was hearing matched what Donna had written to him in her letters. Her mother was reaching out to her to help her find her own mind, her own future.

"Enough of that. Donna says you're going to be a journalist when you get out of the Air Force."

"Yes, ma'am. At least that's what I hope to do."

"I think you'll make a fine journalist. You're a very good listener. That's the first thing she told me about you after her first year at college. She said she could talk to you about anything and you always made her feel good about herself. Putting the needs of others ahead of your own is a Christ-like behavior. Are you a follower of Jesus?"

As he tried to formulate a response to Mrs. Kingston's question, he squirmed in the chair like an unprepared schoolboy asked to give a book report. Mrs. Kingston graciously broke the awkward silence.

"I understand. I didn't commit my life to Christ until a few years ago. If I had it all to do over again, however, I'd have given my life to Jesus when I was much younger. The physical and emotional pain we go through in life is so much harder to bear when we don't have God to turn to for peace and comfort. Trust me, you don't want to wait until you're in a crisis to seek God's help."

"To be honest, ma'am, I don't really know what to think about God or Jesus. I was mad at God for a long time after my dad and my brother died. I'm guessing Donna told you about both of them and my family—my mom, my stepdad, and my stepsister."

"She told me a little bit. You've had some rough circumstances to overcome too, Jake."

"Anyway, for the past several years, I just couldn't understand how God could take away my dad and then my brother. A few days ago, on Christmas Eve, I prayed for the first time in years. And I asked God to open up Donna's heart so she could love me as much as I love her. Almost immediately, my stepsister handed me a letter from Donna that said she needed me. Was that God?"

Without hesitation Mrs. Kingston smiled and said, "I believe it was. God loves you more than you can imagine, and he wants only the best for you and Donna. It fills me with joy to know that God answered your prayer so clearly. Donna and I have been reading the Bible together since she moved back home, and I can see how God has been changing her heart. She has learned from my experience that money and social status can't buy happiness. The world, however, will tell you otherwise. Don't believe the lie. Remember this conversation, and remind Donna when Douglas and others like him try to lead her or you astray."

She grimaced suddenly with pain and then was besieged with another bout of coughing, which turned her face beet red. She was unable to talk for more than a minute as she fought to regain her breath. When she composed herself, she reached out and took his hand in hers.

"God brought you and Donna together for a reason. Seek him, follow him faithfully, and you'll be blessed in ways you can't even imagine. Promise me if you two marry that you'll have lots of children so I can watch them from heaven as they grow and enjoy life."

Jake's mind was reeling from the intensity of the discussion and the surreal environment. He felt her cool, bony fingers gently squeezing his as her thumb lovingly stroked the back of his hand. Her eyes were locked onto his, and she pleaded with him to fulfill her dying request.

Had she made a similar request of Donna? She must've, or I wouldn't be sitting here with her today and having this talk, he thought. *What had Donna said to her mother about marriage and children? Having a family wasn't even on her radar screen the last time she talked to me about her plans for the future.*

Just then Donna returned. As she stood beside him and gently ran her fingers through his hair, he knew the answer. Turning to look at Mrs. Kingston, he said, "I promise."

"What kind of conspiracy are the two of you cooking up?"

A contented smile adorned Mrs. Kingston's face. "I was just telling Jake our family secrets."

Donna sat on the edge of her mother's bed. "I'm surprised you didn't run away."

"I didn't hear anything too scary."

"Wait until my father has his talk with you. Oh, by the way, he called and said we should have dinner without him. He's in a meeting."

Mrs. Kingston sighed heavily. "That's just like him. He knew how much I wanted him to meet Jake and spend time with him."

"Don't worry, Mother. He's coming home in time to meet Jake. I'll make sure he keeps his word."

"Jake, don't let him push you around," Mrs. Kingston said. "I love Douglas, but I have to warn you. He's used to being in control. He'll exploit any sign of weakness and use it to his advantage. That's a good trait to have in business. It's served him well in running my daddy's company all these years."

Donna squirmed a bit and said, "He's really not as evil as Mother makes him out to be."

The placid smile faded from Mrs. Kingston's face. "Never underestimate your father. He'll do anything to get what he wants. He's chosen not to serve God with all we've been given. He's only concerned with making money and satisfying the desires of the flesh."

"You look tired, Mother. Maybe we should let you rest now."

Donna stood and pulled Jake up beside her next to the bed. He sensed the conversation had become strained and was causing Mrs. Kingston a great deal of anxiety. Her color had worsened and her breathing was more labored.

"Thank you for allowing me to meet with you today, ma'am."

Mrs. Kingston smiled weakly. "Take good care of my girl. Remember your promise."

"Do you want me to bring you anything, Mother?"

"No. You and Jake need to spend some time together. Just let me get some sleep."

"I'll check on you in a little while then."

Donna and Jake walked downstairs and sat on the couch in silence as they tried to come to grips with their thoughts. Neither of them knew quite what to say. The short visit with Donna's mother had left Jake exhausted, so he could appreciate the toll the past few months had taken on Donna. Grasping her hand in his, he asked, "How are you holding up?"

She began sobbing, and he took her in his arms and tried to comfort her. The tears continued to flow. He had no idea how to comfort her through the emotional release, which she so desperately needed. When she regained her composure enough to speak, she said, "I'm sorry. I didn't mean to lose control like that."

"It's okay. You've been under a lot of stress. I'd be shocked if you didn't cry under the circumstances."

"My father has always said crying is a sign of weakness. He won't tolerate it."

"It's a sign of being human. If we don't acknowledge our emotions, we become dead inside."

"Maybe that's what happened to my father after Mother had health problems at a young age. He channeled all of his energy into the business and shut down his emotions at home."

"What did your mother mean when she said he was only concerned with making money and 'satisfying the desires of the flesh'?"

"Jake, this is very personal and confidential, of course. And I don't want it to affect your meeting with my father tonight, but it is a part of who he is that I am learning about. Until recently I had no clue. He was gone a lot when I was growing up, but I just thought he was working long hours at the office. Now I know better. Mother said he's had a number of affairs over the years. She knew what was going on, but she protected me from it. As a result, she said, she felt like she was dying a slow death long before the breast cancer happened."

Jake was not surprised. The more he learned about Douglas Kingston, the less he liked him. Part of him wanted to get out of there and head back to California without meeting this man who'd dominated Donna's life and heaped misery on her dying mother. If he left now, however, Mr. Kingston would win. He had to face Donna's father now or risk losing her forever.

"Donna, thank you for sharing what must be painful information for you," he said, trying not to show the anger that was building in him toward the man he was about to meet. "But let's not spend all of our time together talking about your father. I want to hear all about what you have been doing since we were last together."

The rest of the afternoon passed by slowly as the anticipated confrontation approached. Donna and Jake talked about their lives. Her two-year MBA program was going well despite the major distractions at home. At work she held the title of Vice President of Program Development, and she'd gained a good deal of knowledge about the family business. And the time with her mother had been life-changing for her, she told him. He shared about his growing understanding of what it meant to wear the uniform, to do something few college guys his age considered important in this time of antiwar protests.

Since Mr. Kingston wasn't joining them for dinner and Donna's mother took her meals in her room, they ate a quiet meal together in the dining room.

Mr. Kingston arrived home at eight o'clock as they were finishing the dinner cleanup. A knot developed in the pit of Jake's stomach when he heard footsteps from the garage into the kitchen. Donna gave him a quick kiss and said, "It'll be okay."

Douglas Kingston entered the kitchen and tossed his car keys in a porcelain dish on the counter. He appeared even more distinguished than Jake had imagined. At fifty-one years of age, he had an athletic physique and an air of nobility about him that commanded attention. Jake guessed he was about six feet tall and around a hundred eighty pounds. Streaks of gray accented his raven black hair, adding to his look of sophistication. But it was the eyes that made Jake's blood turn cold. Those intense, dark eyes penetrated his as he set his leather briefcase down on the counter.

"I apologize for not being here to dine with you two. My meeting ran longer than expected. Please forgive me."

Donna gave him a peck on the cheek and said, "That's all right. We enjoyed the time alone."

Mr. Kingston reached out his hand and said, "It's a pleasure to meet you, young man."

Jake felt the vice-like grip of his handshake. "Thank you, sir. I've heard a lot about you."

"I assure you, the rumors of my despicable character are greatly exaggerated. Did you have a chance to meet with Mrs. Kingston this afternoon?"

"Yes. She's quite a woman. I can see where Donna gets her compassion and love of life."

"That's an interesting comment. I'm afraid Donna has lost some of her focus since her mother's illness. She spends too much time listening to the regrets of a dying woman and not enough time working on her own future. Would you agree?"

"With all due respect, sir, I have to disagree. My dad died when I was ten years old, and I'd have given anything to have had time to spend with him like Donna's had with her mother recently."

A wry smile on Mr. Kingston's face seemed to declare he was ready for a battle he knew he would win. "What do you think your dad would have told you? Don't grow up to be a factory worker like me, son. Find some rich girl to marry, and you'll be set for life?"

The suddenness of the verbal assault stung Jake in an unforeseen way. The harsh words about his father struck him like a body blow and knocked him off balance. At that moment, Mr. Kingston could have finished him off by escorting him to the door of his castle and tossing him out into the night. His powerful ego would not be satisfied, however, until he had completely destroyed him in his daughter's presence.

"Father, that was rude and unfair," Donna said. "Jake is a guest in our home."

"You're right," he said, considering his next move. He would lead young Jake away like a lamb to the slaughter. "Come, Jake.

Join me for a drink in my study. I want to hear all about your life as a soldier."

Donna's eyes let Jake know now was the time. She turned back to finish the dishes. As Jake followed Douglas Kingston down the central hallway and into his study, he glanced back at Donna. He saw the tension in her face and understood how important it would be for him to hold his own against her father tonight. If they were to have a future together, she would need to know he was strong enough to protect, support, and provide for her when she left the sanctuary of her father's domain.

Mr. Kingston closed the large oak door to the study and said, "Have a seat. What can I get you to drink?"

Jake took a seat in a finely crafted leather chair facing a massive stone fireplace, above which hung a portrait of a distinguished, elderly man. The engraved plaque on the frame beneath the painting read, "Edward S. Blanford."

"Nothing for me, thanks," he said as Mr. Kingston walked to a wet bar in the corner of the room and poured a scotch and water for each of them.

Handing Jake the drink, he said, "Coach Littrell tells me you like your liquor."

The man had obviously done his homework. Jake should have known his tentacles could reach well beyond the city of St. Louis. For a man of wealth and influence, information was a valuable commodity.

"I made a mistake last year when I got drunk at a party. That won't happen again."

"Men usually get drunk when they're running away from something. What were you running from?"

"To be honest, sir, I was feeling sorry for myself after I got injured during football season. I tried to drown my sorrows in beer. I won't make that mistake again."

Standing in front of Jake, Douglas Kingston made the pronouncement Jake had been anticipating.

"I like your honesty. Now let me be straight with you. I allowed you into my home this one time to appease my wife and daughter. In the future, however, you are to stay away from Donna. She has a great future at Blanford Pharmaceuticals, and I won't allow you or anyone else to interfere with our plans. Do you understand me?"

"Are those your plans or Donna's?"

"They're one and the same. Donna will do as I say, especially when her mother is no longer filling her head with romantic ideas."

"If you truly love your daughter, shouldn't you allow her to decide what she wants to do with her life?"

"Allow her to marry an enlisted man in the United States Air Force? Allow her to throw away a career as one of the first female CEO's of a Fortune 500 company so she can live in government housing? I'm a man of considerable means, and I will not allow that to happen."

As Jake rose from the chair to stand face to face with Mr. Kingston, a somewhat humorous thought burst forth and caused him to sport a furtive smile of his own. "You just may have met your match, Mr. Kingston."

Bristled by that remark, he responded with venom. "I seriously doubt that. I eat people like you for lunch every single day."

"Oh, I wasn't talking about me, sir. I was talking about Donna."

His face flushed with anger as Jake nodded that the conversation was over, turned, and opened the door to the study. Without looking back, he made his way down the hall, where Donna was eagerly waiting for him in the living room. Standing at the open door of the study, Mr. Kingston let loose a tirade of profanity aimed at him but did not pursue him.

Not wanting to escalate the tensions, Jake told Donna it was best for him to say good-bye. She looked at him with bewilderment.

"What did you say to him? I've never known him to be so upset before!"

"I told him the truth," he said as he walked toward the front door. "If he truly loves you, he'll let you decide what you want to do with your life."

"That's what made him so angry?"

"Probably not."

"Then what was it?"

"I told him he'd finally met his match."

"You think you can best my father?"

"No, Donna. Only you can do that."

Taking her into his arms, he kissed her deeply, letting go of her only as he saw her father coming down the hallway to make sure Jake knew he was no longer welcome. She stood in the open doorway and watched as he drove away from the house and down the lane toward the gate. In the rearview mirror, he saw Mr. Kingston pull her back inside the house.

Tonight had been the opening salvo in the battle for her allegiance. He would faithfully do his part. The ultimate battle, however, was hers to win.

CHAPTER NINE

Jake pulled into a gas station on Route 66, heading southwest out of St. Louis. As the attendant filled his tank, he reached for the Christmas present wrapped in brightly colored paper lying on the front passenger seat of the car. The card on the package read, "Think of me every time you hear these songs. Love, Donna."

He ripped open the package and found an eight-track tape by Carole King entitled *Tapestry*. Several of the songs on the tape were familiar to him. The rest would be committed to memory during the next few days as he covered the two thousand miles separating him from Castle Air Force Base in California.

With a full tank of gas and a mind reeling from all that had happened that day, Jake was ready for the long drive ahead, and he was anxious to hear the tape he'd just received. He decided to put as much distance behind him as possible. The events of the day were weighing heavily on his mind. As he drove, he tried to make sense of everything that'd happened. Listening to Carole King's melodious voice, he reflected on the good hours he'd just shared with the woman he loved. The lyrics from the second song, "So Far

Away," resonated with him in a meaningful way. He longed to stay in one place, any place, if Donna were there with him. When the third song, "It's Too Late," played to the end, he hoped its message wasn't true for Donna and him.

The cross-country trip was a grueling journey to make alone. The solitude, however, afforded him sufficient time to recover from both a stressful reunion with his family and an even more taxing visit with Donna's. By the time he arrived at the barracks along the flight line at Castle Air Force Base, he was ready for the beginning of flight training.

Jake shared stories of family visits with his roommates, listened to theirs, and then found a secluded area to write Donna a letter. The next three months for him would literally fly by. He was scheduled for two or three eight-hour training missions each week. Donna would remain on a deathwatch while trying to carry on her studies and work at the same time. He hoped his visit hadn't made her life even more difficult to bear.

Two weeks passed by before he received a letter from her. As he opened it, he went over in his mind once more the possible scenarios that may have transpired between Donna and her father after he left their house. By now he could be a certified enemy of the Kingston family if she'd succumbed to the will of her father. In that case, the message he was about to read would be a short "Dear Jake letter." His hope, however, was that her love for him would prevail over the designs of her domineering father. He was greatly relieved after reading her opening sentence.

Hi Jake,

I guess it's customary for soldiers to lob a grenade and then run for the hills. Nice work, GI Jake! My father is still cursing your name. My mother made me tell her every detail of what you said to him. She just smiled and said, "I like that young man."

As for me, I had to endure a stern lecture from my father about how you were trying to take advantage of me. I told him I offered to give you money to stay in school last year but you wouldn't consider it. That news made him angry with me. Of course, nothing I could say would change his mind about you. So I just keep quiet and busy with school and work.

Mother's condition remains the same. She talks a lot about living to see her precious flowers bloom when spring comes. I hope she can last long enough to see it happen one more time. We continue to talk about my plans for the future after she is gone. I don't know what you promised her, but it seems to have given her a sense of peace she didn't have before.

When will you find out where you'll be stationed after your flight training is over? Maybe I can come and visit. You can show me a B-52 and that little hole in the back of the plane where you gunners live.

Your visit was a blessing for me. I miss you so much it makes my heart ache. I always thought I was strong enough on my own to handle whatever came my way. Mother's cancer has taught me different. Watching her die has made me realize how little control I really have over my life. Control, it seems, is just an illusion.

Well, that's enough babbling for now. Please keep the letters coming. I hope you don't mind me reading them to mother—or at least parts of them. She enjoys them almost as much as I do. I can't wait to see you again.

Love,
Donna

Jake aced the academic portion of the training, and the flight portion was going equally well. He requested to be stationed at Wright-Patterson AFB in Dayton, Ohio, after he completed training in late March. He hoped his request would be granted. He was already counting on being based as close to Donna as possible in hopes they could see each other often.

In early March, he received orders to report for permanent duty at Wright-Patterson AFB no later than April 7, 1972. He was ecstatic. It was all he could do to maintain his composure as he waited to pack up his bags and head back to the Midwest to be near her. He planned to stop in St. Louis in early April and see her as he made the 2,000-mile trek from California to Ohio. Donna told him during a phone call, however, it would be best if he didn't come. She promised she would try to get away for a short visit to see him when he was settled in Dayton. He must've heard Neil Young sing "Heart of Gold" a hundred times on the radio during that cross-country drive. Worse yet, he couldn't get the depressing tune for "A Horse with No Name" out of his head.

Meanwhile Donna's mother was barely clinging to life. She required narcotics more frequently to deal with increasing pain from the aggressive cancer. As she became less alert, Donna often sat next to her mother's bed and read the Bible aloud. The precious talks between them lessened as her mother's condition weakened.

Within a week after arriving at Wright-Patterson, Jake was flying training missions with his new crew. At the same time, thirty thousand North Vietnamese soldiers crossed the Demilitarized Zone, or DMZ, and invaded the northern provinces of South Vietnam. In response, President Nixon dispatched 124 B-52s from bases in the U.S. to Andersen AFB on the tiny Pacific island of Guam. Jake knew his chances of being deployed to Southeast Asia had just increased dramatically.

He and Donna continued to write at least once a week over the next few months. When he wasn't flying missions, he was pulling nuclear alert for a week at a time. Three B-52 bombers, each loaded with four thermonuclear hydrogen bombs, were parked right next to the alert facility at all times. The bomber crews were prepared to run out to the aircraft, take off, and strike pre-designated targets inside the Soviet Union in the event of an all-out war. He loved Slim Pickens in the movie "Dr. Strangelove," but there would be no riding an H-bomb to the ground if he could help it.

The best part of spending a week on nuclear alert was getting off on a Thursday morning with three and a half days before he had to report back to the base. Before leaving the alert facility one week, however, his aircraft commander, Captain Morgan, called the crew together to make an announcement. "I've just been informed that our orders for deployment to Southeast Asia have been cut. We leave here October 1. So if you want some time off before heading overseas, you'd better put in for leave now."

The news of the deployment wasn't a surprise. Jake already knew he and his crew were next in line to rotate to Southeast Asia from their base as one of the other crews returned home. The specific date of departure, however, lent a sense of urgency to his relationship with Donna. He needed to see her. There were things that needed to be said—not in a letter, but in person.

The news that Donna's mother had died came to him just before his last alert tour. Donna sent him a letter detailing the events surrounding her mother's death and burial. His initial reaction was one of relief, knowing Donna's mother would suffer no more. Admittedly he was a little hurt she'd not told him sooner, but she said she'd had her hands full helping with the funeral arrangements and dealing with her own grief.

A few days after the letter arrived, she called him. It was a Wednesday evening, and she said she wanted to visit him in Dayton for a few days. She said she needed to get away from St. Louis and clear her head after all that had happened recently. They hadn't seen each other for more than six months. It was time for them to be together.

He took heart in the knowledge that she hadn't forgotten about him after her mother's death and took the initiative to call. He smiled to himself as he remembered the time she told him they would both be old and gray if he waited for her to call him. Someday he would playfully remind her of that comment.

Donna was not smiling. She couldn't remember the last time she had. Her mood was somber as she drove her '71 Camaro east on I-70 from St. Louis to Dayton. The car was a gift from her father when she graduated from Grantham the previous year, and she was especially grateful to have it now. Her father was away on business, so he was unaware of this trip.

The last months of her mother's dreadful terminal illness had exacted a heavy toll on her, both physically and mentally. She desperately needed to escape the pall of death that hung over her like a raincloud. And a deep anger toward her father simmered just below the surface.

There was no denying the emotional need she had to be loved unconditionally. Her mother had filled that role, and now she was gone. Her father, she knew, wasn't capable of giving her the emotional love she needed. Even the allure of status and achievement appealed to her less than it once had even though she was still firmly committed to her education and future in business. But the emptiness—the massive void inside of her—had to be filled by something or someone.

Listening to James Taylor had always given her a sense of peace. The car's eight-track stereo played one of her favorites, "Fire and Rain." Lord knows she'd had plenty of both recently. The sunny days he sang about—none came to her mind. Lonely days—yes, too many to count. The thought of seeing the one she now knew she loved—that's what had sustained her. It had given her hope for the future.

At the point in the song when the lyrics talked about dreams and "flying machines" lying on the ground, she suddenly had a vision that terrified her. "Dear God, don't let that happen to Jake, to us." She pulled the eight-track cartridge from the tape player and drove the rest of the way with only her thoughts as fretful companions.

After finding her way through the streets of Dayton using the directions Jake had given her, she eased her car along the curb in front of a small but well kept Victorian home. She could see why Jake liked living there. It was a quiet neighborhood on a shaded street near the University of Dayton. He even had his own entrance to an apartment off the north side of the house. Her mood lifted at the thought of seeing him. A knock on the door heralded her arrival.

"Hi," she said when he opened the door. "I want you to know I've never done this before. I haven't dated much, let alone visited a guy's apartment. But I had to see you."

He took her in his arms and kissed her. "That's what they all say." Without another word, he brought her inside. "Make yourself at home. It's not much to look at, but the price is right."

He motioned for her to be seated on the couch and joined her. He had done his best to make his humble, one-bedroom apartment presentable. His short-term lease on the place, which was near the campus on the south side of the city, made it possible for him to leave without a problem when the time came. The college atmosphere of the location suited him better than living on base.

Donna had much to say to him, but one thing was on the top of her mind. "I'm sorry I didn't invite you to mother's funeral."

"Don't worry about it. I was on alert then anyway. Besides, your father would not have wanted me there."

"Mother was so happy to have met you. We talked about you every day until she . . . until she couldn't."

"How is your father?" he said, seeing her fight not to break down into tears. She was grateful for the change of subject.

"He's moved on. Mother was barely in the ground when he started hounding me to forget about her and throw myself into school and work. That's his answer for everything in life."

"He's not exactly a lovable sort, is he?"

"Oh, he can turn on the charm when it suits him. And I know he loves me in his own way. But *you* won't get any love from him. He's banned the use of two words in his house—Jake Lemaster."

He clutched his chest as if mortally wounded and rolled off the couch onto the floor. "Save me. Only a kiss from my princess will take away the pain."

She laughed for the first time since she'd arrived. It warmed his heart to see her smile again. As he pulled her down to the floor, she said, "I thought it was the princess who was supposed to be saved by a kiss from her prince."

"That's the old version." With his best Humphrey Bogart impression he said, "Show me your CEO moves, sweetheart."

Their kisses were sensual. As the tension left Donna's body, Jake felt her defenses fall. She was more passionate and vulnerable than ever before. They held each other and talked for nearly an hour. Being alone in each other's arms for so long was something he'd only imagined.

As the sun began to go down, early evening shadows crept into the room and danced across the wall. "Are you hungry?" he asked. "There's a Greek restaurant on campus that serves a mean gyro."

"Perfect. I haven't eaten anything all day."

They walked the three blocks to the campus along tree-lined streets as the love song from cicadas filled the hot evening air. During dinner, she told him more about her life since they'd last seen each other. She'd finished her first year of the MBA program without difficulty. At work she was now accepted, even respected, by many of the men who'd previously shunned her. The management changes she implemented as a result of her conversations with her mother and her schooling already were paying dividends in her business life.

Finally he had to ask. "Does your father know you're here with me?"

"No. He's in Europe on a business trip. We see each other in passing at the office, but he's rarely at home now. He prefers to have his secretary leave me notes on my desk with instructions for the day."

"Are you still enamored with becoming the CEO of Blanford Pharmaceuticals one day?"

"Yes and no. Before my mother's illness, my goals were to run the business as my father had planned for me. Mother coached me to focus on the people who work for the company and the consumers. I'm looking at the business from a whole new perspective. I'm sure my father won't approve when he becomes aware of some of the changes. His style of leadership has always been to maximize the profits, even at the expense of his employees."

"I'm glad you haven't adopted the 'I am woman, hear me roar' philosophy."

"Talk about a double standard! If a man in a position of authority yells and barks out orders, he's considered a strong leader. If a woman does it, everyone makes cat calls and says she must be on her period."

"I see your point."

"I'm figuring out how to be a strong leader without sacrificing my femininity."

"Let's go back to my place and work on that last part, your femininity."

She gave him a wry smile and led him out of the restaurant. It was the first time they'd ever been together when they weren't burdened by the concerns of school or work or family. It felt good to walk leisurely, hand in hand, back to the apartment.

"I have some news I need to share with you," he said at last. He hoped what he was about to say wouldn't dampen the mood.

"What news is that?"

"I've just received orders to go to Southeast Asia for six months."

She stopped walking and turned to face him. "When?"

"October 1."

"Do you have to go? Is there any way to get out of it?"

"The military gives orders. My superiors are not good at taking requests from lowly sergeants. Besides, I'm part of a crew, and I need to do my job."

"You're all I've got. I can't lose you too."

"You're not going to lose me. You'll be so busy at work and school you won't even miss me."

"Part of me wishes I could go there with you."

"Bob Hope is looking for some American beauties for his USO tour. Can you sing and dance for the troops?"

"I'm only interested in one soldier," she said, hugging him tightly as they resumed their homeward journey.

"I was hoping this stupid war would be over soon and you wouldn't have to go to Vietnam."

"Actually I'll be splitting my time between Thailand and Guam."

"It's all the same to me. You'll be halfway around the world, and I'll be worried about you the whole time you're gone."

"Nothing to worry about. I made a promise to your mother that I intend to keep," he said as they entered the apartment.

"Oh, really. Tell me what it is."

"It's classified. Top secret. I'd have to kill you if I told you."

"I'll have to pry it out of you then," she said as she kissed him.

"You'll have plenty of time for that tomorrow. Right now it's late. I only have a single bed, so I'll sleep on the couch and you can take my room."

"You're too big for the couch. I'll be fine out here."

"Are you sure?"

"Absolutely."

He gave her a blanket and a pillow and then kissed her good-night. "Let me know if you need anything else. I'll see you in the morning."

Although he was happier than he'd ever been, sleep eluded him as he tossed and turned fitfully in bed. Donna's presence in the next room tempted him greatly, but he wouldn't allow himself to take advantage of her. He was determined to let their relationship grow according to her timetable.

CHAPTER TEN

As the sunlight washed the bedroom early the next morning, the fragrant aroma of fried bacon awakened his senses. From the doorway, he saw Donna busily preparing breakfast. She looked more radiant than ever.

"Good morning," she said as he entered the small kitchenette.

"You look beautiful," he said, kissing the back of her neck and hugging her as she turned the bacon.

"I couldn't find another frying pan. I'm going to have to fry the eggs in the same pan with the bacon grease."

"That's just the way I like them."

The coffee had just stopped percolating, so he poured himself a cup and took a drink. It was rather strong, even for his taste.

"How is it? I don't drink coffee, so I guessed at how much to put in."

"It's perfect," he lied. "Do I have time to take a quick shower?"

"Sure. I'll have everything ready when you get out."

The events of the last twenty-four hours swirled through his brain while he showered, shaved, and dressed. He'd decided he couldn't tempt fate another night. He knew what had to be done. When he returned to the kitchen, she was sitting at the table, wiping a tear from her eye.

"What's wrong?" he asked, putting his arms around her.

"Well, I ruined the eggs and spilled bacon grease all over the stove. And I can't make coffee the way you like it. Is that enough?"

"It's okay. None of that matters."

"To be honest, I haven't been thinking very clearly since mother died. I've just felt so alone."

Now was the time he'd been anticipating. He knelt down in front of her and raised up her chin so their eyes met. Wiping a stray tear from her eyes, he said, "I'm in love with you. That will never change. Never."

"How do you know that? What if I can't make you happy?"

"I'm ready to take that risk if you'll have me. Donna Kingston, will you marry me?"

A gasp escaped from her quivering mouth, and she flung her arms around his neck. Pulling back, she looked him in the eyes. "Yes. I love you too, Jake. And I just hope I can be a good wife."

He kissed her and grabbed her hands. "Well, that part's settled, but I don't have a ring for you yet. My upcoming deployment moved up my timetable for proposing to you. We have some time this weekend to shop for an engagement ring and make some plans for a wedding when I return."

"Let's get married now, before you go."

Her response shocked him. "Now? I thought you'd want to wait until I got back from overseas."

"I know it seems sudden, but we've both been wanting to be together, really together, for a long time. I don't have a good reason to wait another six months or a year."

"What about wedding plans? Don't we have to send out announcements and decide where we're getting married?"

"My family and friends will understand. And we can plan a big reception when you return home. It will be great to show you off to them in full uniform."

"What about your father?"

"I don't think you want to ask my father for my hand in marriage."

"He's going to be furious."

"I'm willing to face his wrath."

"He'll disown you. And can you live like this?" he asked as he waved his hand around the cramped apartment.

"I can survive anywhere as long as we're together. Besides, mother left me a nest egg and her shares of stock in Blanford Pharmaceuticals. We can find another place to live that has more room."

"What about your MBA program?"

"I can finish my degree here at the University of Dayton while you're gone. By the time you get back, I'll be ready to graduate."

"Have you already checked this out? Can you transfer in time for the fall semester?"

"Well, I did call the business department at the university a few months ago just to see if a transfer was possible."

"A few months ago?"

"Mother and I had a few secrets of our own. She told me to be ready as soon as she was gone and to do whatever it took to be with you. I promised her I would."

"What about your dreams of becoming a CEO and helping other women in the business world?"

"I can still pursue my business aspirations, though probably not in the same manner I once thought. Anyway, Mother told me to trust God to provide for my future, and I'm learning to listen to her advice as well as my father's."

They talked for a while about their dreams for their life together and what the next six months to a year would look like. Donna assured him that marrying into her family would have some perks, like a trip to Switzerland some day to her family place there. Jake expressed his desire to have children one day, when their lives settled down. Donna agreed that it sounded good one day, but it was not something she would want for a few years at least. And then they talked about finances, his and hers. It would be rough at first. That discussion brought them back to the need to make plans for the wedding.

"You're sure about this? I don't want you to feel deprived because we didn't have a big wedding."

"My mother and father had a high society wedding. Look what it did for them. I don't need it. I just need you."

"I don't even know where to start. Do you?"

"A justice of the peace could marry us at the local courthouse, but I'd rather be married by a pastor in a church."

"I suppose I could call my parents and see if the pastor of their church in Clarkston could perform the ceremony."

"Oh, I'm sorry. I never even asked what your family would think."

"Mom and I had a few secrets too. She told me to go after you or regret it for the rest of my life. She may be surprised by the suddenness, but she'll understand and approve. Let me make a call and see what I can find out."

"What about the Air Force? Can you take time off now?"

"I think so. My pilot told the crew to request leave now before we head overseas. I'll call him after I talk with my mom."

Donna cleaned up the kitchen while he made the phone call to his mother. She was surprised but happy. She informed him that her pastor in Clarkston was on vacation for the next two weeks, and she didn't think a wedding ceremony with the visiting pastor could be arranged. She also let him know she wasn't thrilled with his recent letter about his impending deployment to Southeast Asia, especially as reports of the intensified fighting in Vietnam filled the news.

He assured her that he would keep her informed of their plans. After hanging up the phone, an idea came to him. He joined Donna in the kitchen.

"What would you think about getting married in Montana?"

"Montana?"

"Maybe my cousin can arrange a wedding for us out there. Everything in Montana is a lot less rigid, more spontaneous. They don't even have speed limits in most places."

"Well, you did promise to show me the Bitterroot Valley someday. It might be a great place for our honeymoon."

"If you can do some hiking, we can go up into Blodgett Canyon and spend a few days camping. I'll show you the place I've been going to since my dad died."

"That sounds great. What a beautiful honeymoon, just you and me, alone in the wilderness. I've dreamed of going there since you first told me about Montana."

"Let me give my cousin a call."

Scott thought Jake was insane, as usual. He did, however, promise to call his pastor and confirm that an impromptu wedding could be arranged. His wife, Molly, said she would help in getting everything together when he and Donna arrived in Montana. She said the only thing they'd need to get married in Montana was a certified copy of their birth certificates. Jake had his, but they needed to go back to St. Louis to get Donna's.

Jake's next call was to his pilot, Captain Morgan, who took the news in stride. He called the squadron commander and arranged for a ten-day leave for Jake effective immediately. Then he said he'd pay for the airline tickets to and from Montana as a wedding gift. Jake was overwhelmed. He said it wasn't necessary, but Captain Morgan insisted.

Calling the airport, Jake learned that a Northwest Airlines flight would be leaving St. Louis the next day at 2 p.m. and arriving in Missoula, Montana, at 6 p.m. local time. He booked two coach seats and phoned Scott with the travel plans. Scott said he and Molly would meet them at the airport when they arrived in Missoula.

Donna and Jake ate breakfast at the local IHOP restaurant and then bought wedding bands at a jewelry store downtown. She also picked out a modest diamond ring that didn't cost him a fortune. She knew he wouldn't allow her to pay for it, and she didn't want to stress his budget.

That evening he hastily packed what he thought they would need for the trip and they headed for St. Louis in his car. As they drove, the local deejay announced over the radio, "Now here's the number one song atop the hit parade this week, 'Too Late to Turn Back Now' by Cornelius Brothers and Sister Rose." It may not have been too late for Jake and Donna to turn back, but neither of them entertained the thought.

Arriving at Donna's house just before midnight, Jake's memories of his last visit there came flooding back. He was relieved that Mr. Kingston was in Europe on business.

"This time I'll be the one to sleep on the couch," he said as they entered the stately mansion.

"We have several spare bedrooms upstairs," she said.

"I'll be fine down here. Get some sleep, and I'll see you in the morning," he said, kissing her and shooing her off before she could object.

Long after Donna had retired to her room, he lay awake and pondered his circumstances. *Can she give all of this up in exchange for a life with me?*

The house was as grand as he'd remembered. Yet he was overwhelmed by its emptiness. He'd never thought a house could be sad, but this one seemed gloomier than any place he'd ever been. As he drifted off to sleep, he recalled a favorite saying of his mother's—a house isn't a home without people who love each other.

Yes. There's my answer. We're doing the right thing.

The next morning was rushed as Donna packed for their trip. Finding her birth certificate was the least of her concerns. Anticipation of their wedding night filled her mind. Shortly after noon, they left for the airport.

Scott and Molly were there to meet them as they walked off the plane in Missoula. Scott immediately embraced Donna and said, "You're not nearly as homely as Jake let on. And what is it you see in this jock?"

"Donna, meet Scott," Jake said.

"Don't pay any attention to his blather, Donna," Molly said. "Welcome to Montana."

"Don't worry, Jake's told me all about you, Scott. I'm sorry you suffered those head wounds when you were overseas."

"Head wounds? What head wounds?" Scott asked as Molly and Jake roared with laughter. "Very funny. I may postpone the wedding just to make you suffer."

"Molly, it's a pleasure to meet the woman who corralled this wild man since I saw him last," Jake said. "And thanks for helping us out on such quick notice."

Scott gave Jake a ferocious bear hug. Picking up the suitcases, he said, "Come on, young lovers. Let's get on the road. You've got a wedding to prepare for."

The evening air, crisp and dry, was a welcome change from the humid conditions Jake and Donna endured in the Midwest. The sun had just set behind the rugged, snow-capped peaks of the Rocky Mountains in the west as Scott and Molly led the way to their car. The Sapphire Mountain range, forming the eastern border of the Bitterroot Valley, was painted bluish-green with a faint purple hue. Donna was delighted, saying it was more beautiful than she had imagined.

They headed south on Highway 93, which followed the Bitterroot River, for the fifty-mile drive to Scott's home outside the town of Hamilton. As they approached the destination, Jake looked out the window to the right and saw the mouth of Blodgett Canyon fading in the twilight. He was looking forward to the honeymoon adventure into the wilderness separating Idaho from Montana.

"Here it is," Scott said as the car pulled into the circular driveway in front of the three-bedroom log cabin home he'd recently built. "Make yourselves at home."

After getting unpacked in her room, Donna went into the kitchen to talk with Molly. Scott and Jake sat outside and enjoyed a beer and a talk about what'd transpired since they'd been together.

"You've done well for yourself," Jake said. "Molly seems like a great woman."

"She's better than I deserve, that's for sure. I see why you fell for Donna. But I always remembered you saying she wasn't interested in getting married. What happened?"

"Her mother developed breast cancer. The ordeal changed Donna's perspectives on life."

"I'm sorry to hear about her mother. Is she going to make it?"

"She died a little over a week ago."

"Donna seems to be holding up pretty well."

"She was at her mother's side for more than a year, watching her die. In the process, her mother taught her about living, how to go about finding the things in her life that would make it most meaningful."

"What do you mean?"

"Donna's mother and father weren't very close in the last few years of their marriage. In fact, they were antagonists near the end. Donna's father was grooming Donna to take over his business. Her mother wanted more for her. Mrs. Kingston had a lot of regrets about how her life turned out. Her dying wish was for Donna to have a happier marriage than she had."

"How's ole Dad Kingston taking the news? As I recall from your call after you met him, he's not an admirer of yours."

"He doesn't know we're getting married. He's out of the country on a business trip."

"What! He's going to go crazy when he finds out he's lost his daughter."

"I know. We've already had one dramatic confrontation, so the next one is sure to be even more tense. I'll cross that bridge when I come to it."

"It's going to be a big one! I can only imagine."

"I haven't had time to tell you this yet, but I got my orders for Southeast Asia a few days ago. When Donna came for a visit, that's when I asked her to marry me. I was shocked when she said she wanted to get married right away and not inform him."

"Well, she knows him a lot better than you do. I'm sure she has her reasons."

Over dinner, Scott informed them that they'd meet with the pastor after the church service the following morning. The wedding ceremony would take place on Monday at the church. Jake said he would like to head up into Blodgett Canyon with Donna as soon as the ceremony was over. There was a nice camping spot he wanted to reach before the sun went down. Donna would finally experience the majesty of this wilderness, on their first night as husband and wife.

The sermon at church the next day was based on Scripture that said a man had to be born again in order to make it into heaven. Jake didn't really understand the concept, but he made a silent promise to God that he'd spend more time reading the Bible. He owed God that much after his prayer had been answered in regard to Donna.

The couple met with Pastor Granger after church and made plans to hold the wedding ceremony at the church at 10 a.m. the next morning. Molly then took Donna shopping in Missoula so she could buy a dress suitable for the occasion and other necessary items for the honeymoon.

Scott and Jake spent the afternoon assembling the supplies and gear Jake would need during the trek into Blodgett Canyon the next day. Scott had a new Winchester Model 94 30-30 hunting rifle and a 1911 0.45 caliber sidearm for Jake to carry along for protection. He said there'd been reports of bears and mountain lions sighted in the backcountry recently. Jake smiled to himself as he envisioned Douglas Kingston digesting the headlines of the *St. Louis Post-Dispatch* as it declared, "Sole heir to Blanford Pharmaceuticals fortune saved from bear attack on honeymoon adventure."

Donna and Jake had a good time with Scott and Molly, just relaxing and sharing some family stories that evening. Jake was pleased to see how well Donna had taken to Molly since she had said she didn't have any female friends to speak of. Hopefully it was a thing of the past.

The next morning, Jake and Donna went to the Ravalli County courthouse in Hamilton to obtain a marriage license. A short time later, they were married in a simple church service with Scott and Molly as their witnesses. Donna's face quivered with emotion and her eyes were moist with tears of joy as they exchanged wedding vows. Jake's mind was filled with images of their brief time together in college. As he held her hand in his, she gently stroked the back of his hand with her thumb just as her mother had done when he vowed to take care of Donna after she was gone. He was sure Mrs. Kingston was smiling down from heaven and nodding her approval of this holy union she'd helped arrange.

Scott dropped off Mr. and Mrs. Jake Lemaster at the Blodgett Canyon trailhead just after noon. The newlyweds said their goodbyes and agreed to meet him at the same spot four days hence. Minutes later, they were on the trail. Donna was immediately in awe of the picturesque granite cliffs forming the canyon walls as they hiked from a starting elevation of 4,000 feet. She'd done some hiking in the Alps over the years, so she handled the trek without difficulty.

As the sun began to cast long shadows, they reached the spot where Jake and Scott had bivouacked the summer after his first year in college. The couple set up camp, made a fire, and cooked their first meal together as husband and wife. Scott had provided a bottle of champagne for the occasion, so they made a toast to themselves and then one to Donna's mother.

That night they made love out under the clear night sky, filled with an endless canopy of stars in the heavens above. They did so without any fear or remorse—only tremendous freedom and joy. Later, while he listened to the sound of his wife's gentle breathing as she slept peacefully, he lay on his back and gazed into the infinite depths of space. He thanked God for creating this magnificent sanctuary that had restored his soul so many times before. He thought he heard God whisper a response. "You will need a sanctuary in the future. I will be with you and keep you safe."

CHAPTER ELEVEN

The echo of a horrific cry for help reached Jake's ears and jolted him awake. He could not comprehend the confusing sensory information assaulting his brain. The world seemed upside down, and it felt as if a hundred knife-like wounds had pierced his face and neck. Although he could not open his eyes, a ray of sunlight peeked through the slits of his eyelids. From somewhere nearby came the incongruous sound of laughter.

A splash of water rained down from above, and it eased the excruciating stinging and burning momentarily. Only then did he realize the scream he'd heard had come from him, from his own grotesquely swollen face. Regaining full consciousness, he remembered. The Pathet Lao soldiers had hung him upside down by the ankles, hands tied behind his back, over a nest of biting ants. Time seemed to stand still as the malicious tormentors repeatedly had lowered him onto the mound of ferocious ants protecting their home at his expense. It was all he could do to try to keep the ants from crawling inside his mouth and nose while still finding a way to breathe. Somehow he'd lost consciousness.

Sergeant Jake Lemaster and Lieutenant Jim Sizemore, apparently the only two survivors from the crash of their B-52, were war prisoners of a brutal man they called Scarface, a local Communist prison camp commander, and his minions. Between torturing sessions, they were moved from one location to another to avoid discovery by American search planes or any rescue attempt by friendly forces. Scarface had decided not to turn them over to the North Vietnamese. The good news was he had no plans to kill them. The bad news was he had no intention of ever letting them go.

After the two Americans had endured more than a month in captivity, Scarface announced there'd been a signing of a peace treaty between the United States and North Vietnam. He declared the event worthy of a celebration, and he called his men together in the middle of the compound, where a small wooden table and two rickety bamboo chairs were placed. On the table were two empty wooden bowls and two small metal spoons. He announced that the two prisoners would be given special treatment because of the peace treaty. It would be the first time Jake would be allowed to see Lieutenant Sizemore face-to-face since their ill-fated combat mission.

Scarface declared the day, January 27, 1973, a historic day in the lives of the heroic peoples of Vietnam and Laos. It was to be a holiday in remembrance of the victory over the American imperialists. As a gesture of goodwill toward his enemy, he said, the prisoners would have a delicious meal prepared by his men.

The two emaciated prisoners were brought out and seated at the table. Seeing each other at last was a feast for their spirits, but they remained silent. A soldier came forward and poured a steaming concoction into the bowls. Jake looked at Jim across the table and saw he too was puzzled.

Scarface encouraged the Americans to eat to regain their strength. The Communist troops looked on as Jim and Jake examined the contents of the bowls. The mixture contained rice and some sort of chopped up meat cooked in a brown broth. It looked as if a pale meatball was floating among the other ingredients. They exchanged a wary glance as they tasted the unappetizing soup. The meat was spongy and tough, and it had a rancid taste.

As Jake choked down the first mouthful, Jim saw his reaction and said, "We've got to eat or we'll die."

The soldiers laughed as the two prisoners struggled to finish the horrible food. Jake suspected some devious trick was being played on them, but they had no choice but to go along with their captors. They both gagged a few times before finally getting it all down.

Nausea gripped Jake's stomach. Scarface gave a command to one of his soldiers. The soldier disappeared behind a thatch hut and returned momentarily, leading a water buffalo by a rope tied around its neck. Dragging behind the animal was a litter carrying something covered with a canvas shroud.

Scarface clapped his hands and gave a mock salute. "You comrade make great sacrifice."

Scarface then nodded to the soldier, who removed the canvas, exposing Major Cash's decomposing body. His empty eye sockets teemed with maggots scurrying in and out of his skull. Jake vomited uncontrollably as his mind comprehended what he'd just eaten. The sound of Jim retching in unison with Jake filled Scarface with tremendous joy. Scarface's Communist soldiers also were given a lesson that day not to mess with their lunatic commander. It seemed Scarface held no loyalties to anyone save the devil.

For a brief instant, Jake begrudged Major Cash for being beyond the reach of any further persecution. Then, from deep within his soul, he summoned forth a measured dose of anger to counteract the self-pity he was feeling. Bitterness toward the enemy fed his will to survive and sustained the hope that he'd see his wife and child one day.

As the endless months of captivity wore on, Jake came to cherish the solitude of confinement that served as a brief respite from the agony of daily torment. Day after day, he was subjected to various forms of barbaric torture each time his captors pulled back the thatch mat covering his refuge. His physical strength waned from being fed just one small cup of putrid rice daily. As a further insult, he suffered from abdominal cramps and explosive bouts of watery diarrhea. The hole in which he was kept, some six feet in diameter, had turned into a revolting cesspool from which there was no escape.

Jake remembered his promise to God, that if Donna would love him, he would pray and spend time reading the Bible. So each day he prayed, "Dear God, give me the strength to survive."

I guess God got tired of waiting for me to come to him and fulfill my vow to him, he thought bitterly one night. *He certainly has my attention now. To be fair though, God did warn me on my wedding night,* he reminded himself. *I distinctly remember his whispered message to me under the starlit sky of Montana that some day I would need a sanctuary, and when it happened, he would be there to protect me.*

Interrogation was no longer a motive for the daily meetings with Scarface. Jake had no useful information to give him. What Scarface needed was the satisfaction of inflicting pain on someone. His eyes glowed with pleasure each time Jake cried out in pain or begged him to stop. He had an unquenchable desire to break his spirit and exert his will on the prisoner. Jake grew weaker physically each day, but he remembered his survival training and clung to his hope for the future, when he would be rescued and could return home.

Scarface often consumed alcohol made from fermented rice during the heat of the day. At those times, he was prone to fits of rage like the one Jake and Jim had just experienced. He would get so violent even his own men avoided him. He often threw things and broke whatever was near. Glass and clay pots were favorite objects of his anger.

One day Scarface found an area where Jake was particularly vulnerable to attack. As usual, he was bound by ropes and seated in a chair. In the middle of the daily torment time, Jake saw a six-foot-long snake slither into the room through a hole in the far wall of the hut. Scarface sensed his prisoner's anxiety as he watched the deadly viper explore the room. His eyes lit up with anticipation. He had found a new way to torment Jake.

Scarface shouted to one of his soldiers, who came into the room and skillfully captured the cobra without killing it. He gave the soldier some commands before turning his attention to Jake. "You no like snake. We play game today." His grotesque face was twisted into an evil smile as he called for the guards.

Jake was taken outside the hut with his hands still tied behind his back. His anxiety turned into downright terror. Despite years of experience exploring the wilderness of Montana, where rattlesnakes were common, he'd always had a fear of snakes. The guards led him to a large tree on the edge of the camp with a pit below it. The cobra was nowhere in sight.

Jake watched as Lieutenant Sizemore was brought out to the tree as well, and all the Communist soldiers assembled to enjoy the spectacle Scarface was directing. First Jim's hands were unbound, and then a long rope was tied around Jake's ankles. A soldier threw the other end of the rope over a tree branch so that it hung directly over the open pit.

Scarface looked into the pit and then drew back quickly. "Cobra angry. Good to face fear. Make stronger if you live," he said with a maniacal laugh. Turning to Lieutenant Sizemore, he said, "Sergeant no like snake. Up to you save him."

He spoke again, this time to two soldiers, who pulled down on the rope. Jake was heaved to the ground and then suspended upside down over the pit below. The grayish-green reptile coiled, and its hooded face waved menacingly as the soldiers slowly lowered Jake's head down to the edge of the pit. Sweat dripped from his face. The cobra lunged for his head. The soldiers yanked on the rope just in time and pulled him up out of striking distance.

"See how play game?" Scarface said to Lieutenant Sizemore. "Now you."

The soldiers handed him the rope. Jake's panicked eyes met Jim's. "I've got you," Jim said.

Jake watched the grimace on the lieutenant's face as he struggled to keep him from sliding down to certain death, knowing he had little strength left in him and would not be able to hold the rope long and keep Jake from sinking.

"Get mad, Jim. Don't let me die like this!" Jake yelled.

Beads of sweat popped out on the lieutenant's forehead as he struggled to keep Jake out of the pit. Scarface and the soldiers jabbered in Lao, laughed excitedly, and pointed in Jake's direction. After a short time, Jake saw Scarface lose his smile. It seemed he'd become impatient with the way his game was going. Without warning, Scarface swung and hit Jim in the stomach with his fist. Jim doubled over in pain, and Jake plunged downward toward the waiting viper.

Jake turned his head to the side and twisted his body away from the striking cobra as the free fall stopped suddenly. He felt something grab the pocket on the left shoulder sleeve of his flight suit and looked to see the snake recoil. Jim pulled hard on the rope and hauled him out of the pit. His heart was galloping so fast he thought he was going to pass out. Had he been bitten, or was it adrenaline coursing through his veins? Scarface grabbed him and looked for signs of snakebite on his face and neck. Seeing none, he pushed him away, causing him to twist and turn with the rope, still dangling above the pit.

"You conquer fear?" he asked Jake mockingly.

"Screw you!" Jake yelled.

"Sergeant have bad manners," Scarface said to Jim. "Not learn lesson."

Scarface thrust his knee viciously into Jim's unprotected groin, causing Jake to slide downward once more as Jim struggled to hold on. Jim's knees buckled, and he nearly fell to the ground. Jake plummeted until the slack in the rope became taut again, leaving him inches from the bottom. He heard the hissing of the snake as it shot past his left ear and the groans of Jim straining to drag him out of the pit once more.

Scarface looked Jake over for snakebite again. "You lucky. Lieutenant strong."

Jake looked at Jim and saw he was hurting after the fierce blows he'd taken. Fighting back would only make things worse for both of them.

"I've learned my lesson, sir," he said to Scarface. "I'm sorry I yelled at you. Thank you for helping me conquer my fear."

Scarface said something to his soldiers, and they took control of the rope and brought Jake to the ground beside the pit. Without warning, the commander then grabbed one of the Pathet Lao soldiers and threw him into the pit. Loud screams could be heard as the cobra bared its venomous fangs and bit the unfortunate soldier over and over. The frightened soldiers closest to Scarface were ordered to circle the pit and prevent him from escaping. They watched as the soldier struggled in vain to avoid his inevitable death and his breathing became labored as the venom paralyzed his muscles.

"You lucky," he said to Jake as he barked out more orders to his men. One of the guards fired his AK-47 into the pit, killing the cobra. Another pulled the dying man from the pit. Jake's hands and feet were then untied.

"No fear snake. Eat snake," Scarface said to him.

Jake was so thankful to be alive that the thought of eating the dead snake didn't phase him at all. He jumped into the hole, gathered up the body parts of the snake, and scrambled out again. He looked at his friend, who had slumped to the ground.

"Screw you?" Jim whispered, imitating Jake's earlier epithet. "What a thing to say to that monster. We're both lucky to be alive. And yes, my gonads are killing me."

"Sorry about that. I almost lost my head," Jake said, surprising himself that he could make a joke out of the ordeal the two of them had just endured.

"You owe me big time now, partner."

"I promise I'll let you win the next time we play hoops."

"I always win anyway. You're going to have to do better than that."

The lessons Jake had learned in survival training had kept him from sheer panic and appeased his captor. Scarface was content for the time being. He ordered the two prisoners to clean and cook the snake over a small fire being built by the soldiers. It tasted like an oily chicken, but it was the best meat they had eaten in a long time.

When they weren't being tortured or interrogated, Jim and Jake occasionally had a chance to see each other briefly. Typically it was as their captors led them to the river for bathing or placed them near each other in small bamboo cages above ground. The cages did not allow them to sit or kneel, so they were forced to stay in a squatting position for hours at a time. This form of confinement, however, afforded them the opportunity to boost each other's spirits with words of encouragement. The camaraderie made subsequent beatings by the guards a little more tolerable, at least for a while.

"Who won the NCAA tournament in 1960?" Jim asked one day as they spent time in the cages. "You can't miss this one if you live in Ohio."

"Ohio State," Jake said. "Jerry Lucas was the MVP, but I liked Havlichek."

"All right, wise guy. How about 1961?"

"Cincinnati beat Ohio State for the championship in '61 and '62."

"Those were too easy, all Ohio schools. Here's a tougher one. Who won the championship in 1963?"

"It had to be UCLA."

"Gotcha. It was the Loyal Ramblers from Chicago."

And so it went. The two airmen focused on keeping each other mentally sharp in spite of the utter hopelessness they frequently felt. They had to be careful, however, not to annoy the guards while they quietly carried on the banter.

One day Jake discovered a six-inch piece of broken bamboo in his cage that he was able to pry loose and hide in his flight suit. Once in the hole at night, he buried the bamboo to avoid detection. To use it in his escape, he would need to find a way to sharpen it into a lethal weapon.

An opportunity came one day as he was being taken to the river for bathing. He spotted a broken piece of glass embedded in the mud on the bank of the river. He purposely tripped and fell next to the glass and was able to conceal it in his flight suit as he removed his clothing to bathe. Back in the hole at night, he gradually fashioned a crude knife from the piece of bamboo. After that, he bided his time until an opportunity to escape presented itself.

For the first few weeks of captivity, small aircraft frequently could be heard flying near their position throughout the daylight hours, presumably still in search of the downed crewmembers. Then, for months following the peace accord, earth-shaking explosions from B-52 strikes became a commonplace event at any time of day or night. Apparently the U.S. Air Force had turned its full attention from the bombing of Vietnam to the interdiction of supplies flowing down the Ho Chi Minh Trail in Laos. Some of the B-52 raids were so close that the concussions from the bomb blasts would rupture the eardrums of enemy soldiers nearby. What a cruel irony it would be, Jake thought, to survive torture only to be killed by bombs dropped by one of his fellow B-52 aircrews.

Scarface's savage treatment of Jake and Jim increased with the ferocity of the B-52 attacks. He took pleasure in exacting retribution for the fear and chaos brought on by the bombing, as though Jim and Jake were personally responsible. Lieutenant Sizemore whispered to Jake after a particularly brutal interrogation session that they needed to make an effort to escape before they were killed during one. Dying a slow death from malnutrition and disease was the other likely scenario. They knew, if the war was indeed over, that American POWs held in North Vietnamese prison camps would soon be liberated and sent home. But as for them, they wondered who would even know they were alive.

The Pathet Lao soldiers gradually became lazier and more complacent the longer the prisoners were in their presence. The most recent hole they'd dug for Jake was no more than nine feet deep. Although he'd see about a dozen soldiers around the camp throughout the day, it seemed only one guard was on duty at night. It was time to take action.

One night, using the makeshift knife, Jake was able to carve out a few rough steps and handholds to climb out of the hole. Well after nightfall, he climbed up gingerly and peered out from under the mat covering the hole. There was enough moonlight to make out the silhouette of a lone soldier sitting on the ground next to a tree about fifty feet away. His chin was touching his chest, and he was motionless. An AK-47 rifle lay across his lap. All was quiet except for the high-pitched whine of mosquitos and the gurgling of the river nearby.

Jake knew his and Jim's only hope of escape depended on his ability to kill the guard silently without alerting the other soldiers. After that, he would need to free Lieutenant Sizemore, and the two of them then would have to exit the camp undetected before something foiled the plot. He no longer agonized about killing.

The months of hell he'd gone through in captivity had cured him of that. He was prepared to slit the throat of every one of his captors in order to get home. In fact, he was actually looking forward to it.

Crawling slowly from the hole with the makeshift knife held in his teeth, Jake slithered away from where the guard was positioned and made his way to the edge of the jungle surrounding the camp. After pausing for a moment to listen, he followed a narrow path around the perimeter of the camp until he was directly behind the spot where the guard slept.

Jake's heart was pulsating so hard he heard the whoosh of every heartbeat in his ears. As he crouched behind the tree and leaned forward with the knife in his right hand, he could hear the guard's slow, even breathing. Ever so carefully, he brought his left hand into position to cover the guard's mouth. Uncorking the pent up anger inside him, he plunged the knife into the guard's neck and viciously sawed back and forth. The feeling of warm blood cascading over his hands was a welcome sensation. The guard went limp. Jake quietly dragged the lifeless body into the jungle and covered it with palm branches.

Returning, his next move was to retrieve the guard's AK-47 and head to the pit where Lieutenant Sizemore was confined. He quietly removed the mat and saw Jim standing four feet below him. He held a finger to his lips to communicate the need for silence and thrust his other hand out to his friend. Jim reached up toward him and grabbed the extended right hand. Despite his weakened physical condition, Jim scrambled up the side of the hole and hoisted himself to the ground.

The two escapees embraced briefly and then hurried down a path heading west out of the camp. The feeling of exhilaration at being free again was intoxicating. Navigating through the jungle at night was treacherous, but they had to put as much distance as possible between the Pathet Lao and themselves before morning came. Concealment would be their ally then. Being recaptured would certainly lead to a fate worse than death. Jake was determined not to allow that to happen. They would not surrender without a fight.

When they had walked briskly for about fifteen minutes, they stopped to catch their breath and decide what to do next.

"Good to see you, sir," Jake said as he gasped for air. "Are you holding up all right?"

"I'm a lot better now. Thanks for saving my sorry butt. And just call me Jim from now on, will you? It's just you and me now, partner."

"Do you have any idea how we can get out of here?" Jake asked. He was hoping the copilot had a handle on where they were and which direction to travel to get safely back to Thailand.

"I think we're somewhere southeast of the Plain of Jars."

"The Plain of Jars?"

"It's kind of a plateau ringed by mountains. We targeted that region a dozen times before we bombed Hanoi. There're a lot of mountain tribesmen to the west of here helping the CIA run covert ops against the Communists. They might be able to help us."

"The CIA? I'm impressed. You really get around."

Jim chuckled. "Not really, but I did meet some of those crazy Air America pilots at the Officers Club at U-Tapao a while back. They told me they'd been flying missions here for years."

"So we head west then?"

"Scarface will probably expect us to head west and south toward the Thai border. We have to head west, but we might angle a bit to the north to throw him a curve. What do you think?"

"I'll feel better once we get up into the mountains and away from this oppressive jungle."

"I'll lead for a while," Jim said. "Let me know if you need to rest. We'll try to get to the north side of that mountain in the distance before sunup."

They set out for the destination with a renewed sense of optimism. A three-quarter moon illuminated the night sky and revealed the surrounding landscape in vivid detail. A ghostly veil of fog enveloped the summit of the mountain ahead and sent fingers of mist drifting slowly down the eastern slopes facing them. A cool breeze occasionally wafted toward the escapees from the west, providing some pleasant relief as it soothed their perspiring bodies.

The pace of the march was a mixed blessing. Although it felt good to exercise his body once again, the muscles of Jake's legs had atrophied significantly from lack of use during captivity. Cramps sporadically gripped his calves, especially as the terrain began to slant upward. He consoled himself with the fact he was now carrying a lot less weight. He must have shed about forty pounds in the last few months.

The Scarface diet was a heckuva way to lose weight, he told himself with a smile. *That's a good sign, Jake. Your morbid sense of humor is starting to return.*

After an hour or so, the two men came to a small river blocking their advance up the mountain. Jim motioned for Jake to follow him off the trail. Once hidden in a thicket of dense trees, he whispered, "We need water. Let's make sure it's safe to refresh ourselves here for a few minutes before we head out again. I'll go down first while you cover me."

With parched lips Jake said, "Don't drink it all."

Jim shot him a smile and then crept down to the edge of the river. His profile was clearly visible as he dipped his hands in the stream and drank repeatedly. There was no sign of enemy activity. Jake's tongue felt dry and pasty as he waited for his turn to savor the life-sustaining liquid. Jim poured several handfuls of water over his head, and then he retreated back into the thicket.

Jake handed the AK-47 to Jim and cautiously slinked down to the riverbank for his turn. The water was cool and invigorating to his senses. Although his thirst was great, his shrunken stomach had a limited intake. Dousing his head in the stream momentarily took his breath away and sent the head lice scurrying for cover.

What I wouldn't give for a bar of soap about now, he thought.

Quickly he rejoined Lieutenant Sizemore.

"How was it?" Jim asked.

"It's not Coors beer, but it'll have to do."

Jim gently slapped his arm, "You ready to take the point?"

"Let's rock and roll."

Jim handed him the AK-47 and fell in behind as they waded slowly across the river and scurried up the other side. The trail turned to the north and wound its way up the side of the mountain. The continual climb made the journey more strenuous due to their weakened condition. The cool mountain air, however, felt to Jake like a brisk autumn Montana day in late September.

As Jake distanced himself from the nightmarish ordeal he had endured, a feeling of euphoria set in. Thoughts of home re-emerged with the force of a submerged diver desperately gasping for air as he breaks the surface of the water. Captivity and torture had forced him to reduce his thoughts to mere survival. The freedom he now enjoyed, however tenuous, was more palpable and liberating than anything he had ever experienced. Until freedom had been lost, its true worth had gone unrecognized.

Pangs of guilt swept over him when he realized how little he'd thought about Donna lately. She'd always been there with him, of course, but he would not have wished for her to see the broken man he'd become as a result of the unrelenting torture his captors so cruelly handed out. So he'd kept her memory in a secret place where he could go for comfort when he was alone. Thoughts of her gave him little solace during times of physical torture. Only rage sustained him then.

It seemed his sister Mary had it right after all when she called him out on joining the Air Force. He was a killer now. The scary thing was, he felt no remorse for slitting the guard's throat. In fact, he'd enjoyed the rush it gave him. That was another sin he'd have to deal with someday. As for now, he'd kill again in a heartbeat to get back to civilization.

Without warning, the valley they'd escaped from erupted in a cacophony of explosions that threw him into the air against the rocky wall of the mountain. He turned to see Jim lying on his back, his hands covering his ears, as blood oozed from his nostrils. Jake's chest felt like it was going to collapse as the concussion from hundreds of exploding bombs assaulted his body. The mayhem went on for what seemed an eternity, but in reality was no more than a minute. Just as suddenly, all was once again quiet.

"So that's what a B-52 strike feels like on the ground," Jake said.

"If enemy soldiers were close behind us, they just got sent straight to hell," Jim said as he wiped the blood from his face.

"That would be too good for Scarface. You okay?"

"Yeah, I'll be fine. I think I'll put in for a Purple Heart though."

"We have a few more hours before the sun comes up. Let's keep moving and look for someplace to hide before daybreak. There're a lot of caves a little higher up that may serve us well."

"Roger that. A cave sounds mighty good about now."

Jake's legs were wobbly, and his balance was off a bit as they resumed the journey. He couldn't help but wonder how many people already had been vaporized by the bombs dropped every day by B-52s flying six miles above the earth. Army infantrymen and marines had told him stories of the sheer terror evoked by an attack like they'd just witnessed. Now he understood.

An amusing thought captured his fancy. *I don't think this is what Carole King was writing about when she sang about feeling the earth move under her feet and the sky tumbling down. Oh, Jake, you are one sick puppy.*

The men walked for at least an hour without encountering another soul. The first hint of daylight exposed a small, secluded cave carved out of the limestone cliff about a hundred yards above the trail. It would give them a place to hide while providing a good view of the trail below. Jake didn't want to be caught out in the open again. With so little firepower, they would have to rely on stealth.

"That cave should do nicely," he said to Jim. "I'll make sure it's vacant."

Jim hid alongside the trail while he scampered up the side of the mountain. The cave was indeed empty and large enough for both of them to find shelter in. He scanned the terrain below as Jim scaled the mountain. Midway between the cave and the trail, rocks gave way beneath Jim's feet and careened down the side of the mountain. It was a terrifying moment for both of them. Fortunately Jim did not follow the rocks down, and no enemy forces seemed to be alerted by the commotion.

"Sorry about that," Jim said as he pulled himself inside the cave. "You didn't see any snakes in here, did you?"

The effort at humor was thin, reminding him of that terrible day with the cobra. His retort was sarcasm.

"I tried to get you a room in the officer's quarters, but they were all full."

Jim laughed heartily as he stretched out on the cool floor of the cave. "Compared to the Scarface Inn, this place feels like heaven. I wasn't sure I'd ever get out of that camp alive."

"Hearing your voice that first day and knowing I wasn't alone kept me going," Jake said.

With eyes closed, Jim said, "My wife didn't want me to join the Air Force. She thought we both should get teaching jobs out of college and settle down in the suburbs of Chicago near her parents. According to her plans, we should've had two kids by now."

"So what happened?"

"I'd always wanted to be an airline pilot, and military experience seemed like the way to go. Shows you what I know."

"I'm going to be a father soon. Donna told me the day before our mission over Hanoi."

"Congratulations. I wish I had a cigar to give you."

"I'd settle for a steak and a beer."

"Will you take a rain check?"

"It's a deal."

"By the way. You look terrible. I think I could take you in a game of one-on-one now."

"In your dreams. I only let you win once in a while so you don't bring me up on insubordination charges."

It felt good to laugh and exchange barbs with Jim again. Jake knew his copilot was joking of course, but he was sure he did look disgusting. He hadn't shaved in over six months, and he was still wearing the same clothing he'd put on in the gunner's barracks before the last flight. His hair and beard had mobile creatures living in them, and their numbers had increased daily.

"Speaking of dreams, one of us should get some shut-eye while the other stands guard," Jim said. "We can make a plan after we've each had some rest."

"Sounds good," Jake said. "I'll keep an eye on things while you get some sleep. You older guys need more rest."

"We're going to make it out of this hellhole, Jake. We have to."

"Roger that, sir."

It didn't take long for Jim to doze off. The sun was beginning its daily arc across the sky as Jake scanned the valley below for any sign of a threat. Somewhere out there Scarface was probably crucifying his soldiers for letting his pet prisoners escape.

Better them than me.

He recalled the last time he'd been in a cave before his capture. The radio call to *Raven* had filled him with hope that rescue was imminent. How quickly things had changed for the worse. At least two people had died trying to save him. He needed to make sure their efforts were not in vain.

The temperature was cooler at that altitude, and the smell of rain was in the air. Cumulonimbus clouds passed overhead, hinting monsoon season may soon be approaching. The thought of rain reminded him of how thirsty he was. He and Jim were going to have to find food and water soon. Room service was out of the question, so he decided to take matters into his own hands.

He spotted a small river about a half a mile north of their position that looked accessible. Getting to the river and back could be hazardous without the cover of darkness, but it was worth the risk. He figured it would be best for him to go alone so Jim could escape if something went wrong.

With the AK-47 slung over his shoulder by the strap, he made his way cautiously down the side of the mountain and crossed the trail and followed a small path that meandered through the jungle toward the river. Along the way, he found some bananas and hastily devoured them. Fresh fruit was a delicacy he'd not tasted in a long time. Small purple berries were growing near the path as well. They tasted sweet and juicy. He pocketed a handful to share with Jim when he returned to the cave.

Suddenly the jungle came alive with the sound of rain splattering the leaves of palm trees all around him. While he'd been gorging himself, fog and rainclouds had descended from the mountain, obscuring the cave where he'd left Jim sleeping. He moved on, picking his way through dense vegetation, and quickly found himself on the bank of the river. Scanning the area, he saw no one. After setting the AK-47 down, he lay flat on his stomach and drank from the stream until he could hold no more.

Just as he moved to get up, the cold steel of a rifle muzzle pressed against his neck and a boot ground into the middle of his back. He looked at the AK-47 next to him and saw a boot firmly holding it to the ground.

How could this be happening again? Where are you, God? You said you'd take care of me and keep me safe. I can't handle any more torture. If you're really there, dear God, please help me now.

CHAPTER TWELVE

"No move," the man with the gun barked. He grabbed the AK-47 and flung it out of Jake's reach while keeping him face down on the ground.

Jake's mind raced to consider what options he had. *How stupid it was to come out of hiding in daylight. I could be safe in the cave right now and taking my turn getting some much needed sleep.*

"American?" the man asked.

The man is speaking English. Is he one of the villagers working with the CIA that Jim had spoken about? Probably not, since he's wearing military boots. Scarface spoke broken English, and other Pathet Lao soldiers did as well. Jake knew he couldn't pass for a local so he figured there was no point in lying.

"Yes, American."

"Where you get rifle?"

That question was rather tricky. A Communist soldier wouldn't think kindly of the honest answer. His fate, however, seemed already determined. He would soon be killed or imprisoned again, so he might as well enjoy the moment.

"I slashed the throat of the Pathet Lao holding it," he growled.

"Then we friends," the soldier said as he took his foot from Jake's back and removed the rifle from the nape of his neck.

In disbelief, Jake rolled over onto his back and slowly sat up to face the one who'd spared his life. There before him was a man barely five feet tall, outfitted in tattered jungle fatigues, holding an American-made M-16. His face was drawn and wrinkled, obviously Asian, but his arms were sinewy and powerful appearing.

"My name Lo Chang. Hmong warrior."

"My name is Jake Lemaster. I'm a B-52 tail gunner."

"B-52 crash there," he said as he turned and pointed southeast. "Communists kill one man."

"Yes, that was Major Cash."

"You have more?"

"One more," Jake said, holding up one finger and then pointing up toward the cave now visible in the distance.

Lo Chang walked over to the brush and picked up the AK-47 he'd tossed away and handed it to Jake. "Come. Not safe. Too many enemy."

"We need food and water."

Lo Chang quickly looked around. He took a machete from a sheath on his back and skillfully cut down a clump of bananas and some coconuts. He handed them to Jake.

"Must go to cave."

"Is it safe there?"

"Yes."

Jake followed as Lo Chang moved off at a quick pace while constantly looking left and right of the path for any sign of trouble ahead. The rain continued to come down in a steady drizzle, making the path slippery. For the first time since he'd been shot down, Jake felt confident of being rescued and making it home. On his own, or even with Jim's assistance, there was only a faint glimmer of hope. With Lo Chang, their chance of survival rose exponentially.

When the two arrived at the cave, Jim met them with a puzzled look on his face. "Where'd you go?"

Jake dropped the fruit on the ground and handed him a banana. "We needed food and water, so I went out shopping. Meet Lo Chang. He's a Hmong warrior I met down by the river."

As Jim shook hands with Lo Chang, Jake said, "Lo Chang, this is my pilot, Jim Sizemore."

Lo Chang nodded and looked around the cave before taking a seat on the ground. "Rain good," Lo Chang said. "Enemy stay inside." He skillfully cut a hole in the end of a coconut with his machete and handed one to Jim. He then repeated the process and handed one to Jake.

After consuming a banana and drinking some coconut water, Jim asked, "What happened out there? I thought you'd been captured."

"So did I," Jake said as he shared some of the purple berries with Jim. He recounted the story of his improbable introduction to Lo Chang as they refreshed themselves with more sweet coconut nectar.

"You're one lucky dude."

Although Jake laughed along with Jim, he knew he was neither brave nor lucky. He was intensely aware that God had answered his cry for help, and in a way he never could have imagined. For some reason, God had allowed a lot of bad things to happen to him. It was becoming increasing apparent, however, that he was there for him when he cried out for help.

The sound of thunder reverberated across the mountain, and the light rain turned into a torrential downpour. The sky turned dark gray, and the temperature fell to a point where Jake felt a slight chill inside the cave. The soothing sound of the rain numbed his tired body and mind. With a full belly and a new sense of security, he fell fast asleep.

When he awoke, it was dark outside. He was disoriented at first as to his whereabouts and what time of day it was. The sensation reminded him of times when he'd taken a nap after school as a child and woken up in the dark with no clue whether it was morning or night. Sitting upright, he saw Jim peering out the mouth of the cave at the torrent of rain coming down.

Lo Chang had made a small fire upon which he cooked a broth with some sort of leafy green vegetable in it. He motioned for Jake to join him. He cut a dry coconut in half, dipped the makeshift bowl into the broth, and handed it to him. "Drink," he said.

The slight bitterness of the broth was offset by the pleasing flavor of coconut. The steaming hot liquid quickly warmed his chilled body and soothed his aching muscles. It was the first warm thing he'd consumed in months.

Jim took a portion of the broth from Lo Chang's extended hand and settled against the side of the cave across from Jake. He smelled the vapor rising from the soup and sipped from the coconut shell. "Very good," he said as he nodded to Lo Chang.

As they drank the broth, Jake said to Jim, "Do you know anything about the Hmong?"

Jim shook his head and said, "Not really. The CIA guys didn't give me any details about who they were working with in Laos."

Lo Chang leaned forward suddenly and said, "You know CIA?"

"I talked to CIA pilots in Thailand," Jim said.

"Yes, CIA fly plane from Thailand. You know 'Cowboy'?"

Jim shook his head. "I don't know the pilots' names."

"CIA number one. Help Hmong fight Communists."

"Why do the Communists fight against the Hmong people?" Jake asked.

"Communists want Hmong land. Kill our people since I was boy. Hmong fight first with French. Now Hmong fight with Americans. Hmong always fight to be free and save our people. Viet Minh and Pathet Lao hate Hmong because they not kill us all."

Jake was curious what role Lo Chang played in the war effort. Had he just happened upon him by the river? Was there a Hmong village nearby? And more importantly, could he put them in touch with one of the CIA pilots and get them out of Laos?

"Where's your village?" Jake asked.

"Village no more. People go to mountains. Hide from Communists."

"Do you have a family?" Jim asked.

Lo Chang answered in a somber voice. "Have wife and daughter. No see long time. Only son. He die when B-52 crash."

An unexpected chill ran down Jake's spine when he heard Lo Chang's words. "What happened to your son?" he asked.

A pained expression gripped Lo Chang's face as he recalled the day of Lo Na's death. "B-52 crash at night. We go far to find men. Find one killed by Pathet Lao. See American plane shot down looking for men. Son goes on. Hear two gunshots. Find son dead."

As Lo Chang retold the tragic events of the day of their capture, his words reinforced what Jake already knew. Lo Chang had sent his son to save him, and he'd killed him.

"I'm sorry, Lo Chang," Jim said. "He must've been a very brave warrior."

"Very brave."

"I'm sorry too, Lo Chang," Jake said with tears welling up in his eyes.

Lo Chang fixed his eyes on Jake's and nodded slowly.

Jake sensed Lo Chang knew the truth when he saw how his story had affected him. The shame and remorse he'd felt through months of captivity came flooding back to him with a vengeance. How many nightmares had haunted his fretful sleep? How many days had he awakened to discover anew the fateful deed could not be undone? What would be served by saying more? Did he wish to relieve himself of the terrible guilt plaguing him by making this noble father relive the loss of his son? Did he have that right?

"I killed your son," Jake said as tears streamed down his pained face. "He was walking toward me saying something I couldn't understand. His face suddenly looked panicked, and he raised his rifle and pointed it right at me. I shot him twice in the chest. I didn't realize until I'd been captured that he had been aiming at the Pathet Lao soldiers coming up behind me."

A mournful expression devoured Lo Chang's weathered face. He remained silent for a long time as he remembered the day, the horror, and the hurried burial of his son. He asked himself again, as he'd done a thousand times since that terrible day, why he'd sent his son off alone. It was a mistake. He knew his son would still be alive if he'd made a different choice. His glazed eyes seemed to be searching for answers he knew would never come. The spirits would forever remind him that he had failed. Now, faced with his son's killer, he struggled with his choices.

"It is good my son die for American," he said at last.

At that moment, Jake felt something he could only describe as the beginning of forgiveness coming from Lo Chang. Lo Chang had every right to kill him for what he'd done. Instead, he was helping his son's killer regain his freedom. Inadvertently or not, Jake had robbed this man of one of the most precious relationships in his life. What could he offer in return for this man's sacrifice and help now? The only thing he could think of was pledge his life to find some way to help Lo Chang. Before he could speak again, Jim decided to redirect the conversation.

"Lo Chang, do you have a radio?"

"Radio no good."

"How do you communicate with other Hmong and with the CIA?"

"Go CIA base. We go in morning. Eat, sleep tonight."

Lo Chang pulled a crude pipe out of his knapsack and placed something black in the bowl. He lit the pipe and smoked from it before handing it to Jake. As their eyes met, an unspoken bond was made. Jake took this gesture as a sign of peace between them.

"What is this?" he asked Lo Chang.

"Opium."

The rush he felt from smoking the black substance gave him a profound sense of euphoria and well-being. All the aches and pains he'd suffered just disappeared as if a switch had been turned off.

Jim took the pipe and inhaled several times. "I haven't felt this good since I left home."

The three men passed the pipe around several times before the opium was used up. Jake's body felt like it was floating, and he had a feeling of inner peace he'd not known before. One demon had been exorcised—the killing of Lo Chang's son was no longer a secret that could eat away at his soul. As he gazed into the fire, he knew many more demons would need to be faced eventually. But for now, the opium overpowered them all.

In his dreams, Jake could see glimpses of Donna in a crowded place as he frantically tried to catch up with her. Every time he got close, she was suddenly out of reach. His body moved in slow motion. He tried to speak, but no words came from his mouth. Then someone grabbed his shoulder. An icy hand paralyzed him. To his horror, he saw it was Donna's father but with a jagged scar on his scowling face. He continued shaking Jake's shoulder and laughing as Jake lashed out to strike him.

"Wake up!" Jim said as he blocked the punch Jake threw at him. "We need to get moving."

"What a nightmare."

"Scarface?"

"Yeah, in spades."

"Me too. He's never very far away."

Lo Chang led them out into the darkness of the early morning. The rain mercifully had stopped during the night. The men relieved themselves and then headed west in search of friendly forces. Jake was groggy from the aftereffects of the opium, but at least he felt no pain. The purple berries still in his pocket gave him some nutrition and moistened his mouth as they marched on.

They stopped briefly to get a drink from a small river before sunup. The rain from the day before had caused it to swell nearly over its banks. Several hours later, they came to what remained of a Hmong village. The huts had all been destroyed, and human skeleton parts were scattered on the ground. No sign of life was present.

Lo Chang picked up the pace as the sun climbed higher in the sky. He seemed to be as eager to get to the safety of a friendly base as the Americans were. In the distance behind them, they heard the familiar rumbling of a B-52 strike, sounding to Jake like thunder rolling through the sky.

By the time long shadows grew in their wake, they'd covered a lot of ground. Lo Chang had moved them through his countryside with a sense of ownership, and he led them now to a well-concealed cave just before sunset. From the mouth of the cave, Jake watched the fading sun paint the western sky with shades of yellow, orange, blue, and purple.

That surreal image created by God would've taken Monet a million lifetimes to capture on canvas, he reflected as he sat down. *Some day, if I get out of here alive, I'm going to thank him properly for it.*

"Wait here," Lo Chang said. He disappeared into the gathering darkness, leaving the Americans to rest and come to grips with their good fortune.

"This guy seems to know his stuff," Jim said. "Let's hope the CIA hasn't left since the peace treaty was signed. It'd be a long walk to Thailand from here."

"Lo Chang could've killed me the day he found me," Jake said. "There's something special about him. It's almost like, like God brought him into our lives to lead us out of here."

"You getting religion now?"

Jim had never been a strong believer in God. He wasn't an atheist by any means. But church had always been a place he was required to go with his parents twice a year—Christmas and Easter. After his parents divorced, he saw no reason to continue the meaningless ritual.

"Maybe I am. He's the second person I've met that was able to forgive someone who killed a family member."

"Who's the other one?"

"My stepfather. He forgave the drunk driver who killed his wife."

"I'd never forgive any man who killed my wife or my son."

"Yeah, it's hard to comprehend. But having been on the receiving end, I'm glad Lo Chang forgave me. Can you believe what he said, that it was good his son died saving an American? "

"What you did was something that happened in the fog of war. I would've done the same thing if I'd been in your place. Maybe Lo Chang feels that way too."

"I owe him my life, several times over."

Lo Chang entered the cave. He was carrying some sort of rodent that looked like a large sewer rat. Holding it up proudly for their inspection, he said, "Meat for soup."

Jim and Jake exchanged a quick glance. Jim shrugged his shoulders. "That rat's relatives have been nipping at my butt for the past seven months. I guess it's time for some payback."

They watched as Lo Chang cleaned and dressed the animal and threw chunks of meat into the soup. He sprinkled in some sort of spice and stirred the concoction as it heated. With a small wooden spoon, he sampled his creation. Smiling, he declared, "Very good."

Lo Chang filled the coconut bowls and passed them around. Jake was surprised at how good the soup tasted. It had a bite due to the spice, but it gave him and his copilot protein they desperately needed to rebuild their weakened muscles. He had a second bowl for good measure and then ate a banana for dessert.

Jim patted his stomach and said, "That was definitely the best rat I've ever eaten."

Lo Chang beamed with satisfaction, and all three of them reclined against the inside walls of the cave. "Tomorrow see Hmong people. Many village in mountain."

"How long before we get to the CIA base?" Jim asked.

"Soon. Watch for plane."

"Sounds good to me. The sooner the better."

Lo Chang took out his pipe and dropped a piece of opium in the bowl. As he lit the intoxicating substance, Jake eagerly awaited the absence of pain it would bring.

After his turn with the pipe, Jim said, "Hey, Jake, now I know why Dorothy and her friends never made it out of the poppy field in the *Wizard of Oz*. I sure hope that good witch Glinda is looking out for us."

When it was at last Jake's turn and the smoke filled his lungs, he felt as though a fire had been lit in his brain, causing a warm rush to spread throughout his body. By the time the opium was spent, sleep beckoned him like the Sirens' song calling out to Ulysses. He found himself sailing into the dream world once more.

Vivid images of Donna and his mother filled his dreams during a night of fitful sleep. Their faces bore the same sorrowful expression of death as they stood side by side, gazing down into a deep, dark pit. As he hovered above them, he too looked down into the abyss and watched a disfigured man desperately try to cover the hole above. As the two women in his life turned and walked away, he understood it was him in the pit. A voice from somewhere said, "You are mine forever. I will never let you go." The evil presence of his tormentor filled him with horror. He screamed for help amid the suffocating feeling of a coffin lid closing tightly over his face.

CHAPTER THIRTEEN

When Jake awoke from the nightmare, Lo Chang was kneel-ing next to him with a hand clasped tightly over his mouth. "No yell," he said.

Jake was drenched in sweat and frantically tried to make sense of where he was. Mercifully the demonic spirit was no longer plagu-ing him.

"Go soon," Lo Chang said.

Jim was up and stretching his aching muscles in preparation for another day of painful travel. "Are you all right?"

"I'll be fine as long as I never sleep again."

"A hot bath and a nice soft bed would do wonders for me."

"I hear you."

The first light of dawn blushed the eastern sky as they exited the cave and drained their distended bladders before resuming the trek westward. Jakes body was slowly getting stronger each day from the walking. Lo Chang continually found fruits along the trail and fed the Americans liberally. It seemed the jungle was capable of yielding a bountiful feast to anyone with the ability to recognize its treasures.

By mid-morning the men had covered a lot of ground, so Lo Chang led them to a small stream surrounded by tall trees where they could take a break and rehydrate their perspiring bodies. He seemed to be a bit more anxious that morning, as if he could sense danger lurking nearby.

A sound of thunder broke the silence of the morning. Looking at the sky, Jake saw no evidence of ominous clouds on the horizon. A second roaring sound reverberated somewhere west of their present position. He turned toward Lo Chang with a puzzled look.

"Communist artillery," Lo Chang said.

"Who are they attacking?" Jim asked.

"Hmong village."

Jim and Jake fell in behind Lo Chang as he once more led the way, now down partially hidden trails winding through a valley between two sizable mountains. The distant sounds of artillery intensified in number and grew louder as they proceeded. Off to the left, they heard the unmistakable drone of an airplane engine approaching from the south at a rapid speed. A moment later, they spied a United States Air Force T-28 single-engine military trainer heading north through a light blue sky pockmarked with puffy white clouds.

"That is one gorgeous sight," Jim said. "We must be getting close to friendly forces."

Lo Chang pointed to the T-28. "Hmong pilot. Very brave. Bomb Communists."

"Hmong pilot?" Jim asked. "I didn't know there were Hmong pilots."

"Many Hmong pilot now. Fly Thailand many time every day."

The T-28 disappeared on the far side of the mountain to the north. The characteristic sound of antiaircraft artillery pounding the sky quickly followed. Several huge explosions rocked the ground just before the T-28 reappeared overhead and circled in preparation for a second bomb run on the enemy positions. This time the plane went into a steep dive as enemy ground fire erupted all around it.

"Go up mountain," Lo Chang said. "Village other side."

The T-28 made several more strafing runs with the nose-mounted machine gun before leaving the combat area to return to base for rearming. Heavy artillery and mortar fire continued at a feverish rate. This was no small firefight taking place. Two formidable armies were engaged in mortal combat not far away.

The sun was directly overhead when the men reached the summit of the mountain and cautiously began descending the northern slope. The sound of artillery had been supplanted by sporadic bursts from automatic weapons and small arms fire. Although it was easier going down the mountain, the fear of encountering Communist forces escalated dramatically the farther they went. The Americans' fate was dependent on the noble warrior who was rushing to the aid of his fellow Hmong tribesmen. He'd saved Jake's life and pardoned him for his transgressions. Jake owed him trust and allegiance.

Thick black smoke billowed from the village far below, obscuring any vision of what lay ahead. The men would need to get much closer to see if there were any Hmong survivors when the siege ended. Jake couldn't imagine how Lo Chang felt, not knowing if his wife and daughter were in that village. It was the equivalent of him fighting a war to protect his family, his home, and his way of life in Illinois or Ohio. Americans had been blessed not to have a war in their homeland for more than a hundred years. The Hmong hadn't been so fortunate.

Lo Chang found a rock outcropping sheltered by dense vegetation about a quarter of a mile away from what remained of the village. He motioned for the Americans to join him on the ground nearby. The smoke from burning thatch and bamboo huts had dissipated enough to afford the men a view of the tragedy unfolding below. Several hundred enemy soldiers were encamped in the open area where the village had previously stood. The soldiers wore the dark green uniforms and sandals typical of the Pathet Lao forces.

High-pitched screams from the other end of the clearing drew their attention to where a group of soldiers had clustered together. Several young Hmong women had been stripped naked, their hands and feet tied to stakes so they were spread eagle on the ground. The Pathet Lao soldiers were taking turns raping the women while their comrades cheered them on. The gruesome crime grew in scope as more and more women were brought forth and similarly abused despite their pleas for mercy.

One young girl had her clothes savagely torn from her body, revealing a protuberant abdomen characteristic of pregnancy. Several soldiers tied her spread eagle between two adjacent trees and viciously raped her. What happened next was the vilest thing Jake had ever seen a human being do to another. As she cried for help, one of the soldiers took his knife and began cutting open her abdomen. Undeterred by her unspeakable pain, the malevolent man fileted open her uterus, exposing the premature infant. He plucked the baby from its mother's womb and severed the umbilical cord with his knife. As the mother's life-giving blood drained from her, he held the limp infant in front of her as if taunting her.

A wave of nausea gripped Jake's stomach as the macabre scene unfolded. The image before him would stay with him all the days of his life. His mind envisioned Donna being cut open and his unborn child being brutally killed. He was filled with rage beyond what he'd experienced when dealing with his own suffering at the hands of Scarface.

Tears flowed down Lo Chang's cheeks as he witnessed the inhuman treatment of his people at the hands of his archenemy.

How many times had he witnessed such atrocities? Jake knew he must've been wondering if his wife and daughter had already met with a similar fate. He began to understand the depth of hatred Lo Chang harbored against the Communists.

"This isn't war. This is barbarism and genocide," Jim said. "It's pure evil."

"No one back home would ever believe you if you tried to tell what we just saw," Jake said. *And no journalist would willingly come here to report it,* he thought.

Jim tapped Lo Chang on the arm and signaled to him it was time to leave. Nothing could be gained by lingering. The three despondent men retraced the path up the mountain for a distance and then followed a trail leading westward. The journey was made in silence, their hearts heavy with grief and their minds burdened by the heinous crimes they'd witnessed.

Sleep tonight may be a mixed blessing, Jake thought. *New demons are waiting their turn to haunt my dreams.*

Darkening their mood even further, a steady downpour of rain commenced. Traveling became more difficult as the wet jungle vegetation made the footing treacherous. Just before nightfall, they arrived at a limestone cave. The rain intensified, the sound of thunder rumbled through the sky, but they once again had found a refuge.

As he'd done the night before, Lo Chang foraged for food while the Americans rested. When he returned with several small rodents and some fruit, he busied himself preparing a fire. Without looking up, he said, "Find CIA tomorrow. You go home."

Jim and Jake looked at each other, and a million thoughts rushed to the forefront of Jake's mind as he tried to come to grips with the idea of being rescued, of returning to the United States. He and Donna had only been married a few months before his deployment. So much had happened since then. He was no longer the same man. How could he be? Would she be able to love what he'd become? He wondered as well what could have transpired in her life during those long months with no word from him.

Will I ever be able to fit back into society? Will I be able to experience physical and emotional intimacy with Donna after all of the torment and torture I've endured? For so long, all touch has brought only tremendous pain. What if I can't love as I had before?

"This wasn't supposed to happen," Jake said. "I was just going to finish my enlistment and get on with my life with Donna."

Jim saw the fear in Jake's eyes. He too harbored some serious concerns about his own ability to reenter the life he'd left at home. Would his wife still be waiting for him? How could he ever make up to her for the pain she'd suffered because of him?

"I'm not sure I want to fly anymore," Jim said. "Maybe Lisa is right. Teaching school nine months out of the year doesn't sound too bad. If that'll make her happy, that's what I'll do."

"America forget Hmong," Lo Chang said. "Soldiers go home. Leave Hmong to die."

"What do you mean, Lo Chang?" Jim said.

"CIA tell Hmong no leave. Give gun, plane, training. Now CIA go home too."

Jake wanted to tell Lo Chang he was wrong, but he knew better than to lie. The truth was, America was tired of the Vietnam War. Worse yet, the American people knew nothing about the Hmong or the secret war that'd been waged in Laos for nearly a decade. Even he'd never heard of the Hmong until now in any of his military briefings.

"I'm a journalist, Lo Chang, or I soon will be. When I get back to America, I'll write stories about what I've seen here so the people will know about the Hmong. They'll know your people fought and died for American soldiers."

"Do you know what a journalist is?" Jim asked Lo Chang.

Lo Chang shook his head no.

"Do you read books or newspapers?" Jim asked.

"Hmong not read. Only fight."

"Even if you never hear about or read about it, I'll do my best to let the world know what the Communists have done to your people, what I saw them do to this village today," Jake said.

Lo Chang passed bowls of soup to Jim and Jake. "Happen every day. Need big book."

The three men ate the soup in silence and reflected on what had transpired and what lay ahead for each of them. A sense of excitement filled Jake with the thought of regaining his freedom the next day. Yet his enthusiasm was tempered by the realization that many innocent people would be murdered in the days to come because they valued freedom and resisted the Communist onslaught. The Hmong people had to fight or die. There was no other choice.

"You know, Jake, I thought Scarface had a monopoly on torture. But after what we saw today, I'd say what we went through was child's play in comparison."

"Colonel Nguyen Hue," Lo Chang said. "Man with scar on face."

"What? Do you know that monster?" Jake asked, *suddenly on high alert again. Could it be that Lo Chang knows our torturer?* "It was his soldiers that captured us after our plane crashed. We were treated like animals for I'm not sure how many months. If we hadn't escaped, he would've tortured us until we died."

"Hmong know him. Run camp for Pathet Lao. Many Hmong see. Some escape. Say evil spirit in man with scar on face."

"Is he Vietnamese?" Jim asked.

Lo Chang nodded. "Young officer fight French at Dien Bien Phu. Grenade blow off face, but no die. Evil spirits save him. Now use for pain and death."

"I've looked into his eyes, and I can tell you I saw pure evil in him," Jim said. "I've never sensed that in any other human being. If the whole Communist army is like him, God help us."

"I kill many Pathet Lao and Viet Minh," Lo Chang said. "Have picture wife, children. No like him."

"Where's the CIA base we're heading for?" Jim asked.

"Not far."

"I hope the CIA are still flying in and out of there."

"Yes. Many plane."

"The CIA pilots I met said they were flying C-123s out of Udorn almost daily," he said to Jake. "That's good news for us, partner."

"Isn't that the plane the Air Force uses to drop flares over the Ho Chi Minh Trail at night?"

"Yeah, but it's perfectly capable of hauling us back to Thailand," Jim said with a smile.

"I'll sit out on the wing if that's what it takes," Jake said.

As Lo Chang took out his pipe and placed a piece of opium in the bowl, Jim asked, "Lo Chang, how do you get your orders if you don't go to the base?"

"Sometime have radio. Sometime meet Hmong soldier in cave. Order always kill enemy. Know what to do."

The war Lo Chang fought was a very personal and daily struggle for survival. He'd obviously done his job well. He was still alive, and he'd already rescued Americans before now. He checked in with the base from time to time, but ultimately he alone was in control of his destiny. What he couldn't control at that point in time was the fate of his wife and daughter. He might spend the rest of his life searching and never find them.

"What is your plan for finding your wife and daughter?" Jake asked.

"Hmong people one family. Talk friend at base. Maybe one day friend see or hear something."

"I hope you find them soon," Jim said. "I personally can hardly wait to call my wife and tell her I'm on my way home."

"You have wife, children?"

"I have a wife," Jim said. "We don't have kids yet. Jake is the one with a baby on the way."

"You have children?" Lo Chang asked Jake.

As Jake pondered the question, a pervasive sense of uncertainty made him apprehensive. He had no clue when his baby was supposed to be born. For all he knew, Donna might be giving birth to their child at that very moment. Once again he felt guilty for not being by her side to share in the joy of her pregnancy. "My wife told me she was pregnant the day before we were shot down," he said. "I don't even know if I'm a father."

"Life bring much pain. Children bring much joy."

Lo Chang handed Jake the pipe and lit the opium as Jake inhaled the soporific drug. "You go home. Make many children."

Lo Chang's words were eerily similar to the plea Donna's mother had made to him. Finding his wife would be easy compared to the ordeal Lo Chang would have to go through to discover his wife's whereabouts. A simple phone call or two would locate Donna. The future size of their family? That was another matter. Jake took several hits off the pipe and then passed it to Jim. He watched his friend enjoy the tranquilizing effect of the narcotic.

"Maybe we can start up an opium den when we get home," Jim said. "What do you think? All we need is some good music and this stuff. We could make a fortune."

While the physical and mental pain melted away, Jake chuckled at Jim's absurd notion. In his mind, he could hear the sweet voice of Carole King singing the lyrics to the song "Home Again." The tune came to life as he found himself crooning its words.

When Jake finished singing, Jim said, "You could be shot for disturbing the peace with noise like that in a lot of states."

"I've got the music right here," Jake said as he drowsily tapped on his head. "They took a lot of things away from me, but they couldn't take away the music."

"That's good, because you didn't have that much in there to start with."

A bewildered Lo Chang looked on as Jim and Jake broke out in laughter that left them both in tears. The laughter was therapeutic to their broken souls. The opium was making Jake's situation tolerable for another night. Feeling right, however, would only come when he was home again.

Lo Chang took his turn with the pipe and passed it around again. Jake wondered how long it'd been since Lo Chang had shared a time of fellowship and merriment with his friends and family. Inhaling the potent smoke, it occurred to him that this moment might be as good as it would ever get for Lo Chang. Life was certainly not fair.

After the opium was depleted, Lo Chang said, "Sleep now. Leave in morning."

Sleep came easily as Jake focused on the image of Donna and him at home in the apartment. The fears he'd repressed during so many months of captivity often found an outlet in his dreams. That night the demons inexplicably gave him a reprieve. Instead of his usual dreams, he found himself sitting with his pilot, Captain Morgan, beside a beautiful lake on a sunny day. Captain Morgan's serene features made Jake desirous of whatever he possessed to cause such inner peace and tranquility.

"He's waiting for you, Jake."

"Who's waiting for me, sir?"

"The one who can heal your soul."

"No. It's too late for me. Why did he let such terrible things happen?"

"Why don't you ask him?"

"I don't think he'd like me after what I've done."

Captain Morgan got up and stood in front of him. "You've been forgiven. Now you need to learn how to forgive."

As he turned to leave, Jake said, "I have so much anger. I can't forgive the people who tortured me."

"He knows. Make the right choice."

CHAPTER FOURTEEN

The sound of Lo Chang stuffing gear into his knapsack awakened Jake from a pleasant slumber before sunrise the following morning. With the anticipation of freedom giving him renewed strength, he stretched his aching muscles and went outside the cave to drain his bladder. A cool breeze caressed his face as he splattered the rocks outside the cave with a powerful stream of urine. Stars twinkled brightly in the clear sky above.

Jim was still sleeping when he reentered the cave. He gently shook his shoulder and said, "Rise and shine. It's time to go home."

Jim looked around to orient himself before saying, "You ruined a perfectly good dream, sergeant."

"Sorry about that, sir. I thought you might want to join us."

"Go now. Find base," said Lo Chang.

A few minutes later, the two Americans were once again hiking through the jungle behind their Hmong ally, Lo Chang. They ate fruit as they followed a gradually climbing trail winding between two small mountains. Just after dawn, a steady drizzle of rain moistened the earth. Even the dark gray clouds rolling in from the southwest could not dampen their spirits. Barring any unforeseen circumstances, they were soon going to be liberated by their countrymen.

Somewhere around the middle of the day, Lo Chang suddenly held up his hand to signal them to stop. He motioned them to crouch down and stay silent while he listened intently to a commotion up ahead. Jake's heart raced as he envisioned the nightmare of being captured once again. He flicked the safety selector on the AK-47 to full automatic as sweat dripped from his forehead and stung his eyes.

After a few tense moments, Lo Chang relaxed. "Hmong people. Come."

Lo Chang ventured forward once again, this time in pursuit of his tribesmen headed to safety deeper in the mountains. Jake breathed a sigh of relief and moved the safety switch on the rifle to the safe position again. As they came upon the retreating throng, Lo Chang gave a warm greeting in his native tongue. Jake watched as the Hmong acknowledged Lo Chang and viewed the foreigners with a wary eye. Their looks of suspicion turned to friendly smiles as Lo Chang explained that they were B-52 airmen shot down, captured, and tortured by the Communists.

The humming of airplane engines became audible as the three men joined the Hmong people in the trek toward the base at Long Chieng. Ten minutes later, they saw a USAF C-123 transport plane overhead as it sliced through the broken clouds several thousand feet above them.

Jim turned to Jake. "There's our ride, partner."

Jagged purple mountain peaks jutted into the sky directly ahead. The C-123 disappeared on the far side of those mountains, and all was again quiet. Lo Chang pointed to where the plane had last been seen. "Base there."

Although the base was no more than a few miles away, the group still had to climb the mountain ahead before reaching their destination. From Jake's years of hiking experience in the mountains of Montana, he knew they had some rough going before this last leg of the journey was over. The adrenaline coursed through his veins, propelling him onward. Finally, after several hours of hard climbing, they reached the summit of the mountain. There below was a small dirt airstrip in a valley ringed by rugged mountains and limestone karsts. Wooden and thatch buildings were scattered about on either side of the single runway. Movement at the far side of the base caught Jake's attention. He watched in disbelief as the C-123 started its takeoff roll to the southeast. The plane was leaving without them!

Jim and Jake frantically waved their arms in the air and shouted as the C-123 leaped off the dirt runway, climbed above the mountains, and headed toward Thailand. The Hmong watched the two Americans curiously and then began the descent down the mountain to the base.

Lo Chang saw their disappointment and understood. "No problem. Plane come tomorrow."

"I told you to call the CIA and get reservations," Jake said.

Jim shrugged. "I guess we'll get to hear spook stories around the campfire tonight."

Some of the Hmong children had run ahead of the group and reached the base long before the two Americans. As a consequence, the whole village was there to meet them as they reached the perimeter of the base. Standing at the front of the pack was a middle-aged Caucasian man with a crew cut sporting a Dallas Cowboys football shirt.

Lo Chang pointed to the American. "Cowboy. Number one CIA."

"If you two are who I think you are, you must have quite a story to tell," the CIA agent said. "No bodies were ever found from your plane that went down, and there's been a lot of speculation that some of the airmen made it out alive and have been living out there in the jungle. More on that later. I'm Lieutenant Colonel Mark Watson, but you can call me Cowboy."

Jim assumed a military bearing and saluted the Colonel. "I'm First Lieutenant Jim Sizemore, and this is my tail gunner, Sergeant Jake Lemaster, sir. We survived the crash of Sapphire 3, our B-52."

"Sir," Jake said and saluted.

"At ease, gentlemen," Cowboy said as he shook their hands. "Welcome to my world."

"Thank you, sir," Jim said.

"Follow me," he said. He started them walking toward a nondescript wooden building near the airstrip.

"Did we miss a ride out of here a while ago?" Jim asked.

"In this weather, we're down to one flight each day. Don't worry, we'll get you out of here tomorrow. There'll be a lot of people wanting to talk with you back at your base in Thailand. First though, we'd better get you cleaned up and fed properly. You guys look like death warmed over."

Cowboy gave instructions to several Hmong women to prepare a hot bath and some food for his guests. They scurried away as the rest of the people followed the foreigners to the wooden building. He then ducked inside his makeshift headquarters and came out with a bottle of Scotch whisky and three small glasses. Setting them on a table near the door, he poured two fingers into each glass and handed one to Jim and one to Jake. Raising his glass, he proposed a toast.

"Here's to freedom. I expect you two will cherish it now more than ever before."

The Scotch burned as it hit Jake's empty stomach, and it made him a little dizzy. He looked around and realized Lo Chang was nowhere in sight.

He's probably asking about his wife and daughter. God, please help that brave man who sacrificed so much to bring me here today, he prayed silently.

"I'm anxious to hear all about your ordeal," Cowboy said. "While you're getting cleaned up, I'll make a radio call to headquarters at Udorn and have them contact your superiors at U-Tapao. I take it there were no more survivors?"

Jim shook his head. "No, sir."

"You guys are lucky to be alive. I've been here ten years, and I've seen lots of planes shot down. If the surviving pilots and crew-members aren't rescued in the first few hours, they are never found. There's probably some of our boys being held prisoner in the jungle that we'll never find."

Two Hmong women came back and indicated the bath water was ready. Cowboy went inside his living quarters and returned with two sets of civilian clothing for them to don when they'd finished bathing. He also handed a pair of scissors and a razor to Jim so they could cut off their lice-infested hair and beards. A crew cut was mighty appealing to Jake at the moment. He'd never been that dirty for so long in his whole life.

"Hold on a second," Cowboy said as he went back into his quarters and came out with a Polaroid camera. "You need to see how bad you guys look."

He took a number of pictures so they could each remember the historic occasion. When he presented the images to them, their expressions were shock and disbelief.

"I was feeling pretty good until I saw these pictures," Jake said.

"Is this how the CIA tortures people?" Jim asked.

"We'll take a few more after you're cleaned up and you look a lot better," Cowboy said. "You certainly can't look any worse."

The sun was setting behind the limestone karsts that formed the western border of the hidden valley when Jim and Jake rejoined Colonel Watson in his quarters. A spread of chicken, rice, and fruit adorned the small wooden table in the center of the room. The only light came from two large candles mounted on saucers on each end of the table. The orange-colored flames waved with the air currents set in motion as the three men sat down on empty ammo crates around the table. As his eyes adjusted to the dark, Jake saw a large rat dart for cover behind a sack of rice in the corner.

There'll be plenty of meat for soup in the camp tonight, he thought.

"Help yourselves, gentlemen," Cowboy said. "It's not much, but it's probably a lot better than you had with the enemy."

"Thank you, sir," Jim said as they feasted on the chicken.

Cowboy placed a can of Olympia beer in front of each of the men and said, "I apologize for the warm beer. Ice is hard to come by out here."

Jake popped the top on the beer and heard the familiar hissing of carbon dioxide being released. Under the circumstances, the room temperature beer was fantastic.

"What exactly are you doing out here, Colonel, or I guess I should say Cowboy?" Jim asked.

"If I give you the answer to that question, I'll have to kill you." He chuckled and then added, "Considering the sacrifice you've made for your country, I guess I can share a few secrets. The short answer is that the CIA has been conducting a war in Laos since before the official Vietnam conflict began."

"We've only been bombing Laos for the last year or so," Jim said. "You're saying the CIA has been here since 1964?"

"That's right. The North Vietnamese, with assistance from the Russians and the Chinese, have been trying to take control of this country since the mid-50s. The Eisenhower administration believed if Laos fell to the Communists, the rest of Southeast Asia would follow. That's what you know as the Domino Theory. The CIA was given the task of training and supplying indigenous forces to prevent the Communists from achieving their objective."

"Lo Chang told us the Hmong have been fighting the Communists since the end of World War II," Jake said.

"That's true. The Hmong are the reason Laos hasn't fallen yet. The North Vietnamese have had anywhere from fifty thousand to a hundred thousand regular army troops in this country fighting alongside the Pathet Lao for better than ten years now. No doubt our air strikes have slowed the commies down some. The Hmong soldiers, however, have done most of the fighting. They've been slugging it out in the trenches, day in and day out, for most of their lives. While the U.S. has been fighting to win a war between democracy and communism, the Hmong have been fighting for their survival."

"Yesterday we saw a T-28 bombing a Hmong village that'd been overrun by the Pathet Lao," Jim said. "Lo Chang said many Hmong pilots are flying T-28s now. Is that true?"

"It's true. For the first few years of the war, we used American and Thai pilots to conduct air strikes in support of the Hmong ground forces. That required a Hmong who could speak English to fly in the back seat of the T-28 and function as a forward air controller. The FAC would have to communicate with a Hmong radioman on the ground to coordinate the bombing. When Nixon started pulling American soldiers out of Vietnam, we saw the handwriting on the wall. It was just a matter of time before all Americans left Southeast Asia. So we trained a number of the elite Hmong soldiers to fly the T-28."

"Has the program been successful?" Jim asked.

"Beyond our wildest dreams. It took them a while to learn the nuances of flying, but the Hmong pilots are absolutely fearless. They're flying close combat support missions all day every day against heavy antiaircraft artillery and SAMs."

"Scarface told us a peace treaty was signed that ended the war," Jake said. "Are we still at war?"

"Who's Scarface?"

"He's the camp commander of the soldiers who captured us," Jake said. "Lo Chang said his name is Colonel Nguyen Hue. Months ago he made us watch as his men tied the corpse of our EW, Major Cash, to a water buffalo that dragged it around the camp. Scarface said we were celebrating a peace treaty."

"Sounds like a nice guy. The North Vietnamese did sign a peace treaty with the United States about five months ago. You guys in your B-52s played a major role in ending the war."

"What happened?" Jim asked. "We got hit by SAMs the first night of bombing Hanoi and crashed somewhere east of here."

"I remember. We tried to get rescue teams to you, but we were too late. The area you went down in wasn't exactly friendly territory."

"That's a fair statement," Jake said as he gulped his beer. "What did you mean when you said we played a major role in ending the war?"

"The B-52s bombed the heck out of Hanoi and Haiphong. After about two weeks, the North Vietnamese had had enough. A month later, the peace treaty was signed in Paris."

"How many other B-52s were shot down?" Jim asked.

"I think we lost fifteen, including yours, during the eleven days of bombing."

Jim shook his head. "Fifteen B-52s. That means at least ninety airmen went down."

"The ones we rescued here are already home. The crews shot down inside North Vietnam were sent to the Hanoi Hilton with all our other POWs. They made it back to the States about three months ago. As far as I know, you two are the only B-52 airmen unlucky enough to have been found by the Pathet Lao and lived to tell about it."

"So what happens to us now?" Jake asked.

"We'll get you on a C-123 tomorrow and fly you directly to SAC headquarters at U-Tapao. I've already notified them. You didn't tell me you were war heroes. The brass told me you shot down a MiG-21."

"Jake saved my butt a couple of times," Jim said.

"The real hero is Lieutenant Sizemore, sir," Jake said. "He managed to fly our crippled B-52 from Hanoi to wherever it was we crashed. I wouldn't be sitting here today but for his heroism under fire."

Colonel Watson got each of them another beer. "Then I guess I'm buying the beer tonight. Now cut out all the bullcrap, and tell me what really happened to the two of you."

Jake listened as Jim told the story of his capture by the Pathet Lao almost as soon as his parachute hit the ground. Amazingly Jim hadn't suffered any injuries from the SAMs that destroyed the plane and killed three of their crewmembers. He was taken to Scarface's camp a few hours before Jake's arrival there. As he told of his treatment in the prison camp, he showed an unusual sense of detachment. It was almost as if the pain and suffering of those agonizing months of captivity had never really taken place. Almost.

"How about you, sergeant?"

"Sir?"

"Do you have anything to add to what Lieutenant Sizemore said?"

Jake was silent for a moment, uncertain how or what to share.

How can I tell anyone what I've gone through besides someone who experienced it, someone who could believe my story? Jake thought. *Jim being there was what kept me going when everything else failed me. The camaraderie of our suffering gave me hope and a reason to survive. Yes, that and a deep hatred for Scarface.*

He decided to keep the focus on Jim.

"I remember Lieutenant Sizemore telling me we were going to make it out of there. Whenever I thought I'd reached my limit, I would remember those words."

"So how did you manage to escape?"

"Jake got us out," Jim said. "I think we'd have died soon if we hadn't escaped."

"Tell me about it, Jake."

Jake then told how he'd fashioned a knife out of bamboo and used it to get out of the pit. As he explained how he'd slit the guard's throat, a rush of adrenaline once again coursed through his veins. "I actually enjoyed ripping that man's throat open," he said.

"After what they did to you, I'd be surprised if you didn't take some pleasure in it," said Cowboy.

"When Jake pulled me out of that hole, I could have kissed him," Jim said.

"Son, I've got pictures here to prove neither one of you were worth kissing," Cowboy said. "How did you get hooked up with our Hmong friend?"

"By doing something stupid," Jake said. He told the story of how Lo Chang came upon him getting water while Jim was asleep in a cave. "I thought sure I'd been captured by the Communists a second time."

"Those are incredible stories, gentlemen. I'm sure you'll be re-telling them many times over the next few days."

"The guy that rescued us, Lo Chang, is looking for his wife and daughter," Jake said. "What're the chances of helping him find them?"

"Do you know what the Communists do to the women they capture? After what you went through, you can appreciate there are fates worse than death. I hope he finds his family, but the Hmong are fleeing their villages as the Communists advance. Most of them are hiding out in the mountains or have moved south toward the Thai border."

"If you have a pen and paper, I'd like to give Lo Chang my name and information to contact me in the States," Jake said. "I owe him big time. His son died trying to save me. And then Lo Chang risked his life getting me here. Maybe someday I can repay the favor."

Cowboy took a notebook and pen from the other room. "I appreciate your heart. The Hmong have become like family to me. I'll see he gets it."

"Can I ask you a question, Colonel?"

"Sure thing."

"If the war is over, why're we still fighting in Laos? We nearly got vaporized by a B-52 strike just after we escaped from Scarface's camp."

"The Paris Peace Treaty called for an end to the war in Vietnam. Period."

"I don't get it."

Cowboy thought for a moment before speaking. "Technically we've never been in Laos, if you get my drift. American combat troops never waged war on the ground in Laos. We used military and civilian advisors to assist the Hmong in their fight to remain free. We established radar sites to facilitate the accurate bombing of North Vietnam. We tried to stop the flow of soldiers and equipment on the Ho Chi Minh Trail into eastern Laos. This here was a secret war that had to be fought alongside the open conflict going on in Vietnam. You saw how Congress and the public went nuts when they found out we were in Cambodia in 1970. The Communists have used Laos and Cambodia for years, but we're not supposed to fight them here or there."

"So what you're telling me is that what's happening here is not really happening here, according to the reports that make it home to the press and the American public?" Jake said.

"Exactly. And why are we still fighting in Laos? I'd like to say we're fighting to win, but I can't. The truth is, our leaders are already looking for an exit strategy. The United States has a vested interest in Thailand, not Laos. Before long all these brave Hmong people who have fought for us will be left to fend for themselves. There'll be no exit strategy for them. They'll have to fight to the death against the Communist invasion."

CHAPTER FIFTEEN

Sleep came quickly for Jake and Jim on their last night in Laos. Colonel Watson allowed them to bunk in his quarters by sleeping on army blankets on the uneven dirt floor. Jake woke up with all of his fingers and toes intact the next morning, so he assumed the hut rat had become a casualty of war.

A breakfast of eggs, rice, and coffee was prepared for them. Jake had forgotten how much he enjoyed a morning cup of coffee. As he sipped the strong java, he recalled the potent mixture Donna had made for him before they were married. That seemed like a lifetime ago.

After they'd finished eating, Jim said, "Why do they call you Cowboy, Colonel?"

Colonel Watson pulled a pack of Winstons from his shirt pocket and offered one to Jim. "Smoke, lieutenant?"

"No thank you, sir. I have to stay in shape to kick Jake's tail in basketball when we get home."

Jake took a cigarette from the pack and said, "I'm trying to destroy my health to make things even."

Colonel Watson lit Jake's cigarette. "I like your spunk, gentlemen. You should think about joining the Company."

"The Company?" Jake said.

"The CIA. That's what the recruiter said to me at Texas Tech back in 1950. He said, 'You'd make a good Company man, Mr. Watson.' I grew up on a ranch in west Texas where the only thing more numerous than the oil wells was tumbleweed. The CIA promised me a life of adventure with little rewards, and it's pretty much been delivered."

"Were you ever married?" Jake asked.

"A couple of times. The Company doesn't discourage marriage, but it sure makes it difficult to sustain one. I've spent most of the last twenty years in Korea, Japan, Vietnam, Thailand, and Laos. It's not a lifestyle conducive to a good marriage. At least that's what my ex-wives said."

"I've been married for almost a year, and I was only with my wife for two of those months," Jake said.

"See there, you're already acting like a Company man."

"It wasn't by my design. I was deployed sixty days after my wedding. And then my wife told me she was pregnant the day before we got shot down. I hope to see my first child soon."

"Congratulations. I hope the Air Force takes good care of you after all you've been through. If they don't, and you're looking for a job, give me a call."

Jake laughed. "Are you in the phone book here?"

Colonel Watson smiled as he took out his pen and wrote his contact information on a piece of paper. "You can reach me by calling this number. Someone there always knows where I am."

A squawk from the radio interrupted their conversation. "Cowboy, Cowboy, this is the Lone Ranger," a deep voice said. "How do you read, over?"

"There's your taxi, gentlemen." He picked up the handheld microphone, pressed the switch, and said, "Roger, Lone Ranger. Cowboy reads you loud and clear."

"Roger, Cowboy. Please advise. Is field secure for pickup and delivery?"

"Field is secure."

"Roger. ETA is one-five minutes. Copy?"

"Cowboy copies. ETA is one-five minutes."

"Well, gentlemen. You have fifteen minutes to pack your bags."

Jim and Jake went outside to survey the base in broad daylight. Jake walked around the camp, hoping to say good-bye to Lo Chang. Although a large number of Hmong were living on the base, he couldn't find the brave warrior who had rescued him.

The C-123 could be heard for several minutes before it appeared over the purple mountains to the southeast of the base. The camouflaged plane painted tan, gray, and green descended rapidly to make a short-field landing on the crude dirt airstrip. It quickly taxied up in front of Colonel Watson's quarters as Hmong women and children lined the east side of the airstrip.

After the plane came to a stop and the engines shut down, the cargo door on the left side of the fuselage aft of the wing opened. Colonel Bill Smith, Wing Commander at U-Tapao, bounded down the steps and marched over to where Lieutenant Sizemore and Jake stood with Colonel Watson. Jim and Jake came to attention and saluted Colonel Smith, who returned the salute and then shook their hands vigorously. As CIA crew on the plane unloaded supplies, Captain Maynard emerged from the cargo door and explained that he was the flight surgeon who'd be making sure they were fit to fly.

After a cursory physical examination there on the airstrip, Captain Maynard announced that the two airmen were stable enough to make the flight to Thailand. It was good news to Jake, who felt ready to brandish his AK-47 and grab Colonel Smith as a hostage, if necessary, to secure his future. No doctor, or anyone else for that matter, was going to keep him from getting on that plane to freedom.

Colonel Smith exchanged greetings and updates with Cowboy while the pilots cranked up the engines for departure. "Time to go, men," he announced at last. "Let's get the heck out of Dodge."

As the prop wash from the engines gained strength, Cowboy shook Jake's hand. "Good luck. Remember my offer. Look me up sometime."

"Take good care of these people, sir," Jake said as he nodded toward the Hmong people watching. Then he turned and scrambled up the steps into the cargo bay of the C-123. Jim was right behind him, followed by Colonel Smith and Captain Maynard.

The crew chief quickly seated and strapped them in for the three-hour flight to U-Tapao. All crew and passengers then donned headsets so they could communicate during the flight despite the noisy environment inside the aircraft. The pilots in the cockpit turned and gave the passengers the thumbs up signal. They returned the motion in unison.

The aircraft taxied to the north end of the runway and started the takeoff roll. The jungle landscape raced by Jake's window on the left side as the plane lifted off the runway and then climbed out at a steep angle in order to clear the mountains ahead. Looking off to the east, Jake could see the dense mountain jungle that had held him captive for far too long. He remembered thinking during the mission over Hanoi that he would need to learn about the people down there someday. He had definitely gotten more than he had bargained for.

Everything seemed so peaceful from his vantage point, but he knew just how quickly evil could come. Somewhere down there was a madman masquerading as a commander so he could exact unspeakable suffering on his fellow human beings. Jake was certain nothing could ever even the score with Scarface. If the opportunity for revenge presented itself, however, he felt he would savor every moment.

When the plane reached a cruising altitude of 10,000 feet, Colonel Smith asked the pilots of the C-123 to switch their headsets to a private intercom channel. He then spoke to Jake and Jim. "I can't tell you how proud I am to have served with fine young airmen like you two. We lost a lot of good men in the Hanoi bombing missions during the eleven days of Linebacker II, including the other four members of your crew. Your country owes you a tremendous debt of gratitude for the sacrifices you've made. I thank you, men, for your service."

"What's our status, sir?" Jim asked. "Have our families been notified that we're alive?"

He shook his head. "Not yet. We have to get you guys fully checked out before we make any announcements. The medical people at the base will give you a thorough examination and treat any tropical diseases you may have picked up in captivity. I have to say, though, you look surprisingly good for being in a Laotian prison camp for more than six months."

Jim pulled out his Polaroid and handed it to the Colonel. "This photo was taken by Colonel Watson before we got cleaned up last night."

"I stand corrected. It's more like what I was expecting to find. The CIA cleaned you up pretty good."

"So once we're cleared medically, we can go back to the States?" Jake asked.

"I know you're both anxious to get home, but try to relax now and let us take care of what has to be done next. After the medical examination and treatment, the intelligence people will pick your brains about what happened during your last mission and your time as POWs. The information you give them may help us rescue others still missing in action."

"Sir, were we listed as missing in action?" Jim asked.

"I'm not sure what your families were told. I'll make some phone calls when we get to U-Tapao and see what I can find out."

"Sir, when can we call home and talk to our wives?" Jake asked.

"We'll get you an overseas call as soon as we can and home as quickly as we can thereafter. Remember, though, the Air Force has certain protocols to follow when repatriating our POWs. The immediate effects of the trauma you've suffered may be over. The long-term effects, however, may not show up right away. We'll need to make sure you're closely monitored even when you return home."

Captain Maynard, the flight surgeon, joined the conversation. "Your wives have suffered right along with you. Whether you were listed as KIA or MIA, they've feared the worst. We'll do everything we can to get word to them soon that you'll be coming home. We need to be prepared to answer all the questions they'll have."

"Sir, my wife was pregnant when I got shot down," Jake said. "Do you know if I'm a father yet?"

"No, I sure don't. Until we received a call from the CIA at Udorn last night, I'm afraid you guys weren't even on our radar screen. We hadn't written you off, but not many POWs escape their captors in Laos and live to tell about it."

After fifteen minutes, a call from the cockpit interrupted their conversation.

"Excuse me, Colonel Smith," said one of the CIA pilots on the intercom. "I'd like to welcome Lieutenant Sizemore and Sergeant Lemaster back to Thailand. You made it, gentlemen. Well done."

Jake looked out the cabin window and saw the mile-wide Mekong River separating Laos from Thailand directly beneath the aircraft. The murky river that snaked its way from the mountains of Tibet all the way to the South China Sea meandered out of sight in either direction. It was no longer a barrier blocking his return home. Some day soon he hoped to see the Mississippi River out the window of a plane taking him to his home in Dayton, Ohio. Only then would he know the nightmare was truly behind him.

"We made it!" Jim said as the two men clasped hands.

"You always said we would," Jake said. "I guess I'll have to start listening to you from now on."

"You got any brothers, Jake?"

"My only brother died in 'Nam in '65."

"Well, you've got one now."

"Thanks. That means a lot to me."

"I'm still gonna kick your butt in hoops though, brother or not."

An hour later, the plane landed at U-Tapao and the passengers and crew disembarked. Both CIA pilots shook hands with the grateful airmen. One said to Jake, "You must have made quite an impression on Cowboy. He told us to take good care of you. Here's how you can find me if you need anything while you're over here." He handed Jake a business card that read "The Lone Ranger Rides Again."

"Thank you for bringing us back here," Jake said, taking the card.

A staff car was waiting to whisk them away to the base hospital for the next step of their return, a battery of extensive medical tests. As they climbed in, Colonel Smith promised to move things along as fast as he could and let the men know what he found out about their families.

Their arrival apparently had been kept very quiet. The medical personnel attending to them were surprised to hear the two former POWs would be staying with them for a while. They were given orders to keep the men in the hospital until further notice and not to divulge their whereabouts to anyone.

"Colonel Smith, can you do me a favor?" Jake asked.

"I'll do my best."

Jake removed the magazine from his AK-47 and handed him the rifle and ammo clip. "Can you see that this weapon gets sent to Wright-Pat in Dayton, Ohio, for me?"

"I'll see that it gets done," he said and then saluted Jake and Jim.

The two returned POWs were put in a separate isolation area while initial tests were performed. Jake's weight was down from 200 pounds to 160. An IV was started, and fluids were administered intravenously to treat for dehydration. The blood work showed he was suffering from malaria and anemia. The stool specimens revealed the presence of intestinal parasites. The doctors had a field day standing next to his bed discussing Nematodes, Giardia, and other exotic diseases afflicting his body. Fortunately they found nothing that couldn't be cured with medications readily available to them.

Similar maladies were ravaging Jim's body. He had lost a total of thirty-two pounds from his six-foot frame. His spirits soared despite his ailments, and he reveled in the attention given him by the young American female nurses.

After the initial exam, Jake took the liberty of spending about a half hour in the steaming hot shower before shaving the hair from every part of his body, as instructed. When he finished, the nurse gave him a topical cream to apply to his skin to kill any remaining skin infection or fungal disease. Worn out, he collapsed on the bed in the air-conditioned room for a nap.

Sometime in mid-afternoon, a psychiatrist woke him and said he'd come "to examine the contents of your head." Jake appreciated the effort at humor and said he was already lying down, so he didn't need a couch. As the doctor asked him a barrage of questions to assess his condition, he thought of a book he'd read, the satirical novel *Catch-22*. He felt a bit like the character named Orr. If he told the psychiatrist he felt fine, the doc would think he was crazy and keep him locked up on some remote island. If he said he was crazy from being tortured, the doc would think he was sane and send him home.

The truth was, as he told the doc, he did feel fine. Was that normal? *What's normal,* he thought to himself, *for a guy who endured what I've been through these past six months?*

The psychiatrist left after about an hour. He didn't order Thorazine, so Jake assumed he must have passed the test. Fortunately the psychiatrist hadn't asked him how many people he'd killed or how many people were killed trying to save him. Those topics were not ones he was prepared to discuss at the moment.

That evening the hospital staff prepared the returning war heroes a nostalgic meal of cheeseburgers, fries, and a coke. After dinner Jim and Jake hung out in their hospital room and discussed what they hoped to do when they got back to Dayton. Another tour of duty was definitely not in Jake's future plans. The war in Southeast Asia was officially over, although there was no peace to be found except on the paper signed in Paris. A whole lot of bombing missions were still being flown each and every day.

By 2100 hours, Jim was already asleep. The nurses said goodnight to Jake, who was still awake, and dimmed the lights in the room. He was looking forward to a good night's sleep in a clean, comfortable bed for the first time in nearly seven months. The room was cool, so he pulled the sheets up around his chest. The gentle whirring sound of the air conditioner provided white noise that eased his transition into a twilight state.

Colonel Smith had informed him in the afternoon that Air Force officials in the States would be notifying Donna that evening that he was alive. He'd done the calculations. It was 8 a.m. in Dayton and 7 a.m. in St. Louis. In a matter of hours, Donna would receive the news he hoped she'd been waiting for.

I'd give anything to see the look on her face when she hears I'm alive after all these months, he thought as he drifted toward the land of nod. *Yes, sir. That would be quite a sight.*

PART II

Choices

CHAPTER SIXTEEN

Approaching downtown St. Louis from the west, the 630-foot tall Gateway Arch looked to Donna Kingston Lemaster like a stainless-steel rainbow in the brilliant early morning sunlight as she made the morning commute to the office. Today would be a new beginning—a coming-out party of sorts—as she left behind the pain associated with her husband's disappearance. She was eager to embrace her new role as CEO of Blanford Pharmaceuticals by chairing the executive board meeting for the first time. Her future seemed promising, yet something nagged at her and warned her of an impending crisis ahead. In the rearview mirror of her car, she observed ominously dark storm clouds rolling in, as if threatening to envelop her new life in darkness like the shroud of depression she had worn for so long. Hoping to lighten her mood, she turned on the car radio.

"Good morning. This is Natalie Hargrove, reporter at KMOX radio, The Voice of St. Louis, with the news on this Monday, July 23, 1973. The Senate Committee investigating the Watergate scandal, along with Special Prosecutor Archibald Cox, has ordered

President Richard Nixon to hand over a number of White House documents and oval office tapes. Rumors about the contents of the tapes have been growing since the discovery of a secret taping system surfaced during testimony recently by former presidential appointments secretary Alexander Butterfield. It is unclear whether the president plans to comply with the request.

"In sports, the St. Louis Cardinals defeated the Los Angeles Dodgers at Busch Stadium yesterday by a score of 5 to 4. Bernie Carbo went three for four with an RBI, while catcher Ted Simmons slammed a two-run homer to lead the way. Reggie Cleveland pitched six strong innings with Diego Segui picking up the win in relief.

"The weather forecast for the greater St. Louis area shows heavy thunderstorms on the horizon with a daytime high of 88 degrees and a low tonight of 72. KMOX time is now 8 a.m. Have a wonderful day."

"Have a wonderful day indeed," Donna said aloud to no one as she turned into her reserved parking space at the Blanford Pharmaceuticals administrative office. It had been more than seven months since her husband's plane had gone down somewhere in the jungles of Southeast Asia. After a brief time of mourning, everyone expected her to get over it and move on with her life. Outwardly she was able to pull off the charade. Inwardly, however, she was dying a new death each and every day.

"Good morning, Ms. Kingston," said Donna's secretary, Janie Powell, as she entered her office area. Janie was a bright twenty-year-old fresh out of college with an associate's degree in secretarial skills. She was exceedingly proud of her boss.

"Good morning," Donna said with a fake smile.

The nameplate on the office door next to the secretary's desk read "Ms. Donna Kingston, Director of Operations." *How quickly one could rise within an organization if one's father owned the company,* thought Donna.

Her lofty title had come with a high price tag. She would gladly forfeit it if she could have Jake back in her life.

Janie followed Donna into her office and placed a cup of coffee on the desk. "You have an executive meeting in the board room at 9 a.m. Is there anything else I can get for you?"

"No, thank you."

As Janie exited, Donna sipped the hot liquid and savored the bittersweet moment. The acerbic taste of the black coffee was something she still hadn't gotten used to, much like the dull ache in her heart. The delightful memories of drinking coffee every morning with her husband awakened her senses more than any stimulant could. A smile came to her face as she recalled what a mess she'd made of the breakfast she'd prepared for him that first morning in Dayton. Those were precious times they had shared before life became so complicated.

Tears moistened her eyes as she remembered her mother's death nearly a year ago. It seemed the people she had come to love most had been taken from her. How could God have allowed it to happen? She couldn't help but wonder at times like today if her father was right. Maybe God *had* cursed the Kingston family.

The buzz of the intercom interrupted her rumination. "Yes?"

"Excuse me, Ms. Kingston. Your father is on the phone. Shall I send it through to you?"

"Please do."

Her phone rang, and she picked up the call. "Good morning, Father. How is everything in Switzerland?"

"Good morning, Donna. We still have a few glitches in the manufacturing process for the new product line. I should finish my work here tomorrow, and then I'll be flying to Hong Kong for several days of meetings with the Chinese. Nixon has done us a huge favor by opening up some of the Chinese markets."

"You'd better take advantage of the opportunity while you can. Nixon's days are numbered. This scandal is going to bring him down."

"You may be right. Did you get my instructions for the executive meeting today?"

"I have them right here," she said as she picked up a document from the desk labeled *Important.*

"Make sure you play hardball with the labor unions. They're seeking too many concessions at a time when inflation is heating up. Tell them we'll have to start laying off workers if they demand higher wages."

"No problem. We can't absorb the escalating expense of higher raw materials and labor costs without our bottom line suffering."

"Exactly. Get Keating involved in the negotiations. He knows how to handle them."

"Anything else?"

"You're doing a fine job running the company for me. I always knew you would."

"Mother's been gone almost a year now."

There was an awkward silence before he said, "Keep your eye on the ball, Donna."

"I'll do my best."

"Everything worked out the way it should have. You see that now, don't you? This is what you were meant to do."

"Have a safe trip, and I'll see you when you get home," she said and then hung up the phone. His words haunted her as she looked out the window of the office while sipping her coffee. If he was right, why did she feel so empty? If this was her destiny, why had she felt so alive when she was with Jake and so dejected now? And she had to admit, it wasn't just her mother's and Jake's absences in her life. Something else was missing.

Turning her attention back to the desk, she picked up a framed picture of her mother. How she missed the time they had shared before her death and the priceless talks they'd had. Opening the bottom drawer of the desk, she took out the Bible her mother had given her before she died. Her mother had said the answers to all of life's problems could be found in it. Seven months ago, Donna would have believed her. That had been a time of unbridled joy and infinite promise as she and Jake were newlyweds. It had been the most precious time of her life.

Each day with Jake had been an exciting, new experience. The two months they shared before his overseas deployment, although much too short, were filled with times of laughter, friendship, and passionate lovemaking. She thought the brief interlude between his departure and subsequent return would pass quickly as she immersed herself in the task of finishing her MBA. Then something changed her life forever.

At first she thought the nausea was a consequence of the anxiety she felt after Jake left for Southeast Asia. Her menstrual cycles had never been regular, so the absence of a normal period did not alarm her at first. By the second month of symptoms, however, she shared her concern with the landlord, Mrs. Delaney, who had become a friend for her after Jake was deployed. A visit to the doctor confirmed the diagnosis. She was indeed with child.

Unconsciously she placed a hand on her lower abdomen where life once had grown inside of her. When she'd discovered she was pregnant, she couldn't wait to share the news with Jake. Although the pregnancy was not planned, she felt certain it was God's will for them. In a very short time, she had been transformed from a young, ambitious female businesswoman to an MBA graduate in line to become the next CEO and a wife preparing for motherhood. She remembered again how her mother had said to put her trust in the Lord in all circumstances. That once had seemed like good advice.

Jake's phone call to her before Christmas, after he arrived in Southeast Asia, allowed her to tell him he was going to be a father.

At the time, she didn't consider it might be the last time they would ever speak. He had been so excited he must have forgotten to tell her why he had called that day. It was only by reading the newspapers in the coming weeks that she learned of the terrible danger he was in. Even Betty Morgan, the wife of one of Jake's pilots, had no clue what her husband and Jake were going through.

The unexpected appearance of an Air Force officer and a chaplain at the apartment in early January brought Donna's world crashing down around her. The visitors said Jake's plane had been shot down, and there was no evidence of any survivors. Many more things were said, like statistics and probabilities of a POW returning even if he'd somehow managed to survive the crash. He would be listed officially as missing in action, the standard protocol, until remains were recovered. In her mind, however, they had pronounced him dead. They believed it too. She could see it in their eyes.

For a while, she met frequently with Betty Morgan and Jake's copilot's wife, Lisa Sizemore. The three of them tried to stay hopeful despite the lack of information given them by the Air Force officials. Then in late January, the Bomb Wing at Wright-Patterson held a special ceremony honoring Jake's crew after the Paris Peace Accord was signed. Donna was presented Jake's Silver Star and Distinguished Flying Cross medals earned during that last fateful mission over Hanoi. The three wives were told to keep the faith, but the ceremony seemed more like a funeral to them.

Donna braced herself for the inevitable visit from an Air Force official to declare the finality of her husband's death. In public she mindlessly carried on her studies and tried to continue the façade that she was a strong military wife. Privately she pleaded with God to bring Jake back home. She poured her heart out to God each night before crying herself to sleep. Still no answer came.

Eventually the emotional pain was replaced with apathy. There was some peace in not feeling anything, or at least in convincing herself it was so. It wasn't long, however, before apathy gave way to anger. The anger gradually grew in intensity and matured into fits of blinding rage. By opening herself up to be loved, she had become vulnerable to the indescribable pain and suffering associated with the loss of the one she loved.

Jake was the most frequent target of her ravings. None of this pain would have happened if he hadn't joined the military and gone off to fulfill his inane male duties in a country halfway around the world. Her mother was responsible as well as Jake, since she had urged Donna to marry Jake and have a life of her own, apart from Blanford Pharmaceuticals. She threw considerable fury her mother's way. But the most intense hatred she saved for the one who was supposed to love her most. God had obviously abandoned her—if, in fact, he had ever existed in her life. All the time she had spent reading the Bible seemed little more than a naïve, academic exercise.

The buzzing of the intercom jolted Donna back to the present. "Yes?"

"The staff is waiting for you in the boardroom, Ms. Kingston."

"I'll be right there."

She checked her appearance in the mirror. She had worn her hair in a tight bun since assuming a corporate leadership role in the company. The white blouse and black business attire suited her well. The stresses of the past year had aged her noticeably, but it was the least of her concerns. Most of the men she would be meeting with were twice her age and still considered her a child. Today it was time for her to establish herself as the new leader of Blanford Pharmaceuticals. She needed to make it clear that there was no more capable a person to run the company than her. If necessary, she was prepared to "kick ass and take names," as Jake used to say.

Her mother's advice hadn't been all bad. It had served her well when she began the leadership orientation program at Blanford. Her mother had schooled her that it was important to treat the employees with respect so they would want to achieve excellence in the workplace. That approach only went so far. Someone ultimately had to step forward and make the difficult and unpopular decisions for the good of the company and the shareholders. That obligation now rested squarely on her shoulders. It was a role she had been groomed for since she was a child by her father. With Jake and her mother gone, there was no longer any reason not to seize what was rightfully hers, by birth and by merit.

Jake had never discouraged her from pursuing the dream of being a top executive in the business world. On the contrary, he had been her biggest advocate. He and her father even may have reconciled one day. That eventuality would have made her the happiest woman in the world. But right now, for Donna, the two most important men in her life could not coexist without one playing the role of victor and the other the defeated.

"Good morning, gentlemen," she said as she quickly strode into the boardroom and assumed a seat at the head of the large, walnut, boat-shaped conference table. She politely nodded to the ten middle-aged men sitting around the table in black leather chairs as well as Janie, her secretary. A chorus of greetings reached her ears, including several that referred to her as Donna.

"First of all, let me say I realize it may be awkward for some of you to accept the fact that a young woman such as myself could run this Fortune 500 company effectively and efficiently. Let me assure you, that is exactly what I intend to do. I hope to have your unwavering support as I seek to make this company the envy of the pharmaceutical industry."

At Donna's request, Janie went over the minutes from the last meeting as the first order of business on the agenda. Donna read the eyes of each of the men to gauge their reaction to her introductory remarks. A few of the more senior men flashed a look of defiance—or reluctance to surrender, at the very least. Their responses were duly noted. Most of the others seemed to fall in line, realizing the gauntlet had been thrown down.

As Donna's father had warned, the topic of labor relations dominated the meeting. She listened patiently while the department heads voiced their opinions about how to handle the challenges they were facing. At appropriate times, she asked probing questions and then allowed them to try to come to a solution with the input of the group. In her judgment, their efforts were in vain.

"The bottom line, gentlemen, is that we cannot afford to allow our labor costs to rise any further at this time," she said at last.

"With all due respect, Donna, we can't alienate our unions," said Cole Chesterton, the personnel manager.

"The one person *you* can't afford to alienate is *me*, Mr. Chesterton. You will address me as Ms. Kingston from now on. Is that clear?"

He looked around the room for help, but none was forthcoming. "I understand, Ms. Kingston."

"Your point is well taken, sir. I have asked Mr. Keating, our attorney on the labor relations board, to address your concerns with the union leaders. If there is no further business at this time, gentlemen, let's get back to work."

She brought the meeting to a conclusion just after 10:30 a.m. To her surprise, some of the senior executives congratulated her for showing good leadership while chairing her first executive meeting. Ted Roberson, VP of marketing, said she was "a chip off of the old block." Considering the success her father had experienced running the company during his tenure, she took the words as a compliment. There was no doubt in her mind. Her passion for business had once again become the driving force in her life.

"Well done, Ms. Kingston," Janie said with a satisfied smile as Donna returned to the office.

"Thank you. I may have ruffled some feathers in there today, but I didn't hear any catcalls."

"The business world needs more women like you in leadership positions. This is the '70s, and it's high time women are recognized for accomplishments other than making babies."

Janie's last remark, although innocent in itself, pierced Donna's heart. The statement was one that she had shared with Jake while they were still in college, and it was something she still believed. Her recent pregnancy, however, had stirred emotions within her that she had never known before. Those emotions were now sealed off deep inside, like a hole in a wall is plastered over to keep something hidden.

"Would you like a second cup of coffee, Ms. Kingston?"

"That sounds good."

Janie brought her boss coffee and then closed the door and returned to her desk. As Donna reflected on the executive meeting, she felt a sudden rush of adrenaline sweep through her body. She now understood the intoxicating effect a position of power can yield to its owner. And she liked it. Another feeling was in the mix as well. It was subtler but no less powerful. Yes, that was it. It was rage.

After Jake disappeared, surges of anger had become a common occurrence. They often took her by surprise, as she typically used intellect, not emotion, to deal with life's problems. The emotion she engaged in internally was not responsive to the power of reason. She could not think her way out of the tremendous pain she was feeling at the loss of her husband. There was no logic in death.

A new war, she realized, had to be found before the anger devoured her. She would channel all of her energy into the business. She would attack the business world with the ferocity of a mother bear defending her cubs. This war was one she had been trained to win, and her decisions directly influenced the outcome of each and every battle.

The warm glow of victory repressed the anger when she was successful, but it never lasted. The rage was like a hungry beast that demanded to be fed each day. Could she control the rage and use it to her advantage without losing herself in the process? It remained to be seen. She had chosen the path her father had designed for her. It seemed to be her only choice.

The intercom buzzed, and Janie's voice said, "Ms. Kingston, you have two visitors here to see you."

"I don't have any scheduled appointments. Who is it?"

"Two Air Force officers."

So it has finally come at last, Donna told herself. *The Air Force is going to tell me what I've known for months. They'll say how sorry they are to inform me that Jake officially has been declared dead. "Please accept our condolences," they'll say.*

She had already steeled herself to receive the unpleasant news. "Show them in please," she said without emotion.

Donna stood up next to her desk as Janie escorted the two officers into her office. She recognized the captain from the visit in January.

"Gentlemen."

"Good morning, Ms. Kingston," the captain said. "Would you like to sit down before we talk?"

"No, thank you. Just say what you have to say and be done with it."

"Very well, ma'am. Your husband, Sergeant Jake Lemaster, is alive."

"He's wha—he's what?" she stammered as her knees buckled and everything turned black.

When she came to, she looked up to see the captain kneeling beside her, holding a wet paper towel to her forehead. "It's all right, Ms. Kingston. Your husband is going to be coming home soon."

"But how? I don't understand."

"I apologize for not knowing all of the details, ma'am. What we do know is that he was held as a POW in Laos after his plane crashed on its flight from Thailand to Vietnam. He and his copilot,

Lieutenant Sizemore, escaped recently and made it back to the base in Thailand. They're being checked out in a military hospital, but your husband seems to be fine, according to the information we've received."

"When will he be coming home? Can I talk to him?"

"We'll know more in a few days, ma'am. The Air Force has to make sure the returning POWs are completely stable before they are allowed to come home."

Her mind raced, and she felt sick at her stomach as she tried to digest the unanticipated news. Tears flowed from her eyes, and uncontrollable sobbing racked her body.

"I was sure you were going to tell me Jake was dead. After all this time, I'm ashamed to say I had given up hope of ever seeing him again."

"We understand, ma'am. Frankly we were shocked too."

"Have you told his mother yet? She's been a mess since he's been gone."

"Yes, ma'am. We're taking care of it."

"Does Lisa Sizemore know about Jim?"

"Two Air Force officers are telling her the good news as we speak."

"What about Captain Morgan? Did anyone else survive?"

The Captain shook his head. "We've confirmed that your husband and Lieutenant Sizemore are the only survivors."

"How tragic for the families."

"We're notifying the next of kin of all of the men who didn't make it. Can you sit up, ma'am?"

With assistance, she was able to sit up and drink a glass of water. So many questions were coming to mind, and no answers could be found for any of them.

"I'll be fine. What am I supposed to do next?"

"We'll be in touch with you each day, ma'am. I'll give you an update when we learn more from our people in Thailand. Until then, just be thankful your husband is coming home."

"Thank you, Captain."

He wrote down his name and base telephone number. "Don't hesitate to give me a call if you need anything."

"I won't," she said as she took the paper from his hand.

Janie showed the officers out as Donna regained her seat behind the desk and tried to come to grips with the fact that her world had once again turned upside down. So many convulsions had gripped her life in the past months. The anger and rage she had embraced recently should have given way to unimaginable joy, she thought. Instead, fear and shame cast a dark shadow.

"Janie. Get my father on the phone," she said over the intercom.

"Yes, Ms. Kingston."

As Janie called Mr. Kingston at the office in Switzerland, Donna was filled with dread about the conversation they were about to have. This battle would have no winners. She, her father, and Jake were all going to lose a part of themselves. She could hear her father's angry tirade now. Worse yet, she could hear the screams of a voice from within, crying to be set free from its bondage.

"I have Mr. Kingston on the line."

"Hello, Donna. Your secretary sounds upset. Is everything okay?"

"We have an issue to discuss, Father. Jake's alive."

CHAPTER SEVENTEEN

The sound of thunder reverberated through the office as Donna ended the phone conversation with her father. Rain suddenly pelted the window as flashes of lightning lit up the blackened sky. The overhead lights flickered momentarily and then went out as power to the building was interrupted by the storm.

"How fitting," she said aloud as she felt the new emotional storm sucking the life from her body. Sitting in the darkness in silence, she struggled to come to grips with the fact that Jake was alive. If he had been shot down over Hanoi, rescued, and sent home as a war hero, none of this would have happened. If she had known he was alive, she would not have run back to her father as she had. In retrospect, that was when her plans for her life had started to unravel.

She had called her father in late January from her home in Dayton, more than a month after receiving the news that Jake's plane had gone down. She wasn't sure whether he would even speak with her. She had chosen not to tell him she and Jake were married until months after the wedding when the topic could no longer be avoided. When she told him about Jake's plane being downed and his disappearance, he seemed genuinely concerned and also glad to hear from her. He was eager to offer his support, and he asked her to come to St. Louis to spend the weekend with him.

Thinking back now, she realized she should have known he would try once again to bring her under his control. But what else could she do? Without Jake, she was alone and extremely vulnerable. She felt she had no one else to turn to. All of the inner strength and self-confidence she had gained with Jake by her side had vanished.

Her father had graciously opened up his home to her in that time of need, even after she had spurned him in favor of a life with Jake. The words he spoke as he'd opened the door to greet her had filled her with remorse for hurting him. "Welcome home," he'd said as he hugged her tightly. "I thought I had lost you forever because of my selfishness. I won't ever let anything come between us again."

Painful as it was, Donna and her father had spent a lot of time that day discussing all that had happened since they had last seen each other. Mr. Kingston listened patiently as she recounted the details of her life with Jake. She'd never felt his fatherly love like she did that day as he allowed her to pour out her heart to him. By the end of their first day together, much of the anguish had evaporated. The most difficult issue, however, was yet to be revealed.

The following day, after a pleasant morning together, her father asked, "Why don't you come back to St. Louis and work at Blanford with me? We'll move forward together as though none of these unfortunate circumstances ever happened."

"I'm afraid it's not that easy, Father. There's another important piece of information I have to share with you. I'm pregnant."

His muted and pensive response surprised her. She had expected him to explode in an angry outburst. She had envisioned him saying how foolish she had been to take up with Jake and throw away a brilliant business career. She fully expected he would cast her aside at that moment. Instead he sat down in front of her and took her hands in his.

"Your life doesn't have to come to an end. There are ways to deal with a situation like this."

"What're you saying?"

"I'm saying women now have a choice whether to allow an unwanted pregnancy to ruin their lives. The United States Supreme Court legalized abortion just last week. I'm sure you've heard about Roe v. Wade. You have a right to decide what happens to your body and to your future."

"You're telling me to have my baby cut out of my womb?"

"That's one option. But there is another solution."

"I don't understand."

"Blanford Pharmaceuticals has been working on what we call an abortion pill, so to speak, at the plant in Switzerland. Women have been having abortions for thousands of years through unsafe means, but the law has prohibited legalized abortions in most countries because of Judeo-Christian values. Now the door is opening for women to have a safe medical procedure instead of risking their lives with back-alley butchers. Sometime soon, Blanford Pharmaceuticals will be able to offer women the option of aborting an unwanted pregnancy in the privacy of their own home."

"How is that an option for me?"

"Our scientists in Europe have been conducting clinical trials for several years now, and with good success."

"You're willing to put me at risk with something that hasn't been approved by the FDA yet?"

"I wouldn't offer it to you if I didn't have complete confidence in it. Just think about it. You and I could schedule a meeting with our people in Switzerland, you could take the drug, and then we could spend a few weeks vacationing at the chalet while you recovered. No one would ever have to know."

"It's too late for that. I told Jake he was going to be a father the day before his plane was shot down, and I'm guessing he told others. I told some of my friends in Dayton also."

He thought for a moment. "I think everyone would understand if you came back from Switzerland deeply saddened by a miscarriage brought on by the terrible loss of your husband."

"How could I lie about something as important as that? And how could I take my baby's life and then pretend nothing ever happened?"

"It's not really a baby until you hold it in your arms, Donna. Think about what I am offering. It would give you a chance to pursue your dreams of running the company. You can always have a family at some point in the future. At least give it some thought."

She did give it a lot of thought over the next week when she returned to school. In fact, it was all she could think about. On campus everyone was talking about the legalization of abortion and what a victory it was for women's rights. In the abstract, she was definitely in favor of a woman having the right to do with her body as she pleased. Being pregnant, however, had muddied the waters. The decision to take the life of her baby so she could pursue her dreams seemed selfish at best, criminal at worst.

Did the legalization of abortion somehow make it right? Her mother certainly wouldn't have thought so. She had said God hated all killing, especially the killing of innocent children. If that was so, why had God allowed her to get pregnant, knowing that she would be faced with raising a child on her own?

In the end, she just couldn't imagine having Jake's child without him there beside her. She decided her father was right. He had said she shouldn't suffer her whole life because of a few months of careless living. Although those words had pierced her, Donna was too weak to resist her father's plan.

I'll do it, she decided, telling herself it was a good choice, a fair choice for everyone, given the circumstances.

Mr. Kingston arranged for the two of them to take the corporate jet to Switzerland in mid-February. The trip was publicized as a working trip to meet with the executive leadership team at the Blanford plant outside of Geneva. He let the office know they would be staying for a two-week vacation following the conclusion of their business. Donna had no trouble convincing her professors she needed to take some time off to grieve the loss of her husband. The story of the fate of Jake's crew was well known in the Dayton community.

After arriving at the plant in Switzerland, Mr. Kingston introduced Donna to the current management team under the guise of her future role as CEO of Blanford Pharmaceuticals. They held several days of business meetings before retreating to the chalet in Grindelwald, near Interlaken. Donna had always loved the place. The rugged alpine peaks towered over the two-story stone and wood chalet where the Kingston family had enjoyed such wonderful vacations during Donna's childhood. Those unchanging mountains were the only constants in the maelstrom of her chaotic life at the time.

A torrent of memories overwhelmed her as she and her father walked into the chalet. The Blanford family had built this idyllic getaway some forty years before. For Donna, it was the first time she had been there without her mother. Her spirit seemed to permeate the surroundings despite her absence. Though the place was rarely used, her mother had refused her father's efforts to sell it several times over the years because she cherished the togetherness it had brought the family. Now it brought Donna only a sense of great loss.

Her father put his arm around her shoulder and kissed her forehead as she stood looking out the large living room window facing south toward the picturesque, snow-covered mountains.

She felt a great sense of urgency to make herself whole again. The only outward signs of pregnancy displayed by her changing body were a slight enlargement of her breasts and a small protrusion of her lower abdomen. Thankfully she had not felt any movement of the baby growing within her. Her single desire at the moment was to remain numb emotionally to what she was about to do. The quicker the crisis came to an end, the better.

"You're safe here," he said. "Everything will be better soon."

"I just want this nightmare to be over."

The moment had come, and her father was quick to seize it. "This is BG-1017," he said as he handed her a tan-colored pill the size of an aspirin. He had acquired the experimental drug from one of the lab research scientists, telling his staff the U.S. plant in St. Louis needed a sample to run independent quality control tests.

Under other circumstances, Donna would not have subjected her body to the use of an experimental drug. Desperate times, however, called for desperate measures.

"Is that all there is to it?" she said.

"You take that pill now, and then you take this pill tomorrow morning," he said while handing Donna a small yellow pill.

"What should I expect?"

"The scientists said most women experience contractions and bleeding similar to but certainly not as intense as a normal delivery. They say the first pill helps the lining of the uterus come loose. The second pill causes contractions and finishes the process."

The process. Yes, it is just a process after all. It's best to think of it that way, Donna told herself.

Aloud she said, "I didn't realize it was going to take two days."

Her father went to the kitchen, took a drinking glass from the cupboard, and filled it with water. "The sooner you get started, the sooner it will be behind you," he said as he handed her the glass of water.

She hesitated for an instant and then placed the tan pill on her tongue. She washed it down quickly with the glass of water.

Her father took the glass from her hand. "Do you want something to eat? I had the caretaker put some steaks in the freezer for us."

"I'm not hungry."

"How about a glass of wine?"

"Do you think it's all right to mix wine with the pill?"

"What harm can it do at this point? A few glasses of wine might do you a world of good."

As he opened a bottle of Barolo Giovanni Pippione vintage 1960, Donna sat down on the slate gray upholstered couch and surveyed the comfortable living room. The stone fireplace took up much of the wall facing her. She had warmed herself beside that fireplace many times after coming in from a long day of skiing. Her mother had taught her to roast marshmallows over the fire when she was five years old, but she had never understood how Donna could eat them when they were black and crunchy.

A chill ran through her body. She wondered if she would ever have a child that would one day have fond memories of her as a mother. What would she do if something went wrong with this plan and she ended up with a hysterectomy like her mother? What if she never married again? If she did, could she ever be fulfilled without experiencing motherhood? She had thought she could for many years before meeting Jake. Now she was no longer sure.

"Here you are," her father said as he handed her a glass of wine and took a seat next to her on the couch. He hoisted his glass in the air. "A toast to us."

The aroma of the Barolo reminded Donna of tar and roses while the tannin produced a slightly acidic taste that warmed her body as the nectar made its way from palate to stomach. Her father had always preferred fine Italian wines over the more heralded French spirits. He had taken her to the Piedmont region of northern Italy when she was a teenager to visit the scenic area where the unique nebbiolo grapes were grown. The hills and valleys around the town of La Morra were draped with lush vineyards that seemed to stretch to the horizon. They had made that amazing journey one summer while her mother visited an old friend in Paris. It was a time of innocence, a time when father and daughter had formed a special bond.

"What happened to us, Father?"

"What do you mean?"

"What went wrong? When I was a child, I always thought we had a happy family."

"We were as happy as most people, I guess."

"So what happened between you and mother that changed us?"

He swirled the wine in his glass and took a drink before answering. "Life is cruel, Donna. I think you see that now. I have always tried to protect you from being hurt, and I've been generally successful—that is, until recently."

"You still haven't told me what happened between you and Mother."

"What did she tell you during all those long talks you had when she was wasting away?"

"She said you turned your back on God after she was unable to bear you a son."

He snickered. "There is no God. You should know that by now. If there were an all-powerful, loving God like your mother believed in, she wouldn't have suffered the way she did. I couldn't pretend to have faith anymore after all of her miscarriages. Instead, I immersed myself in being successful in business. You would do well to follow the same path. The other way leads to tremendous pain."

"She said there were many other women in your life."

"What do you want to hear?"

"It's just you and me now, Father. I want to know the truth."

"Yes, there were other women in my life. All of the intimacy left our marriage after your mother's hysterectomy."

"You blame everything on the surgery?"

"There were other factors, of course, but your mother didn't enjoy making love after the surgery. It was like—like something died inside of her. So I coped with the situation in the only way I knew how."

"Which came first? The hysterectomy or your infidelity?"

"I don't see that it matters anymore which came first. If you're going to survive this ordeal, you need to stop looking back and stop trying to fix things that can't be repaired. I've been patient with you because I know you're hurting. But I won't lie to you. I never liked that—that boy you married. It wouldn't bother me at all if he were burning in hell. It would serve him right for taking you away from me."

His words stung her even as the wine numbed her, but she shot back one final comment. "You loathed Jake because he loved me more than life itself. If he is in hell for that, God help us both for what we're doing now."

"You should get some rest," he said, satisfied with the turn of the conversation. "I'll have dinner ready when you get up from your nap."

He rose and went into his office after refilling his glass with more wine. Donna headed upstairs.

Her bedroom in the chalet had always been a place of comfort. She loved the soft featherbed covered with thick patchwork quilts on cold winter nights. As she tucked herself under the covers, she wondered how her life could have spiraled out of control as it had, bringing her to this point. Her father was right. Life was cruel.

When she awoke, it was nearly 7 p.m. The familiar smell of burning pine in the fireplace reached her as she came down the stairs and entered the living room. Unexpectedly the crackling of the burning wood brought back memories of her honeymoon camping experience in the Bitterroot Valley.

Donna's father came in from the deck where he'd been grilling two ribeye steaks. "Did you get some rest?" he asked as he laid the platter with the steaks on the dining room table. "I hope you're hungry."

"Yes. I feel a lot better. I'm starving."

"Have a seat, and we'll get started," he said as he pulled a chair out for her at the table.

"I'm sorry I gave you a hard time earlier. My emotions have been unpredictable lately."

"No need to apologize. Let's put all of that behind us and make plans for the future."

The steak and salad he had prepared were delicious. The two of them made small talk during dinner and finished the bottle of Barolo they'd opened earlier with the meal. After dinner they washed the dishes and then retired to the living room.

"When we go home, I want you to come back to work at Blanford with me. There's no reason you shouldn't start running the company now."

"I admit, I like the idea. I'll have to see if I can finish my MBA in St. Louis rather than Dayton."

"That won't be a problem. I know the dean at the business school. I want you to get your feet wet as Director of Operations for six months while I spend time visiting our overseas offices. Then whenever you're ready to fly solo, I'll turn it all over to you."

"Do you think I'll be ready to assume control that soon?"

"You have the intelligence and soon all the education you need to do the job. What you lack is experience. And there's no way to get it without jumping in with both feet. The mental toughness you'll need is there. I've seen it. We just have to help you rediscover it."

"How do you think the executives at Blanford will react to having a young woman giving them orders?"

"That's up to you. First of all, you shouldn't care what they think. You'll be in charge, and they can adapt or find other jobs. If they perceive any weakness in you, they'll exploit it to their advantage. Business is like war. Never let the enemy find a chink in your armor."

"Who is the enemy?"

"Everyone is your enemy. If you want to be successful in this world, you need to take care of yourself and no one else because that's what we all do. People are basically selfish and self-centered. Somebody is going to benefit from every decision you make. Why shouldn't you be the winner?"

"Mother always told me to love my enemies."

His face flushed with anger. "That's the kind of garbage that will cause you to fail. Your mother was born with a silver spoon in her mouth. She never had to fight the daily battles I did to make her father's company what it is today. Forget everything she taught you. It will be difficult enough for you without trying to live your life according to a fairy tale. The Bible is for weak-minded people trying to find hope in this dog-eat-dog world."

"Are you happy, Father? It scares me to think I'll never be happy again."

"You make your own happiness. No one else can do that for you. I'm confident you will find happiness in business, just like I have. Maybe one day in the future you'll be the poster child for Blanford's new abortion pill."

A flash of anger and fear swept over her as she said, "Promise me you'll never mention this to anyone! I swear to God, I'll never speak to you again if you do!"

Smiling slyly he said, "Relax. Your secret is safe with me. I was only thinking what a great advertisement it would make for millions of young women to see the personal testimony of the CEO of Blanford Pharmaceuticals touting the benefits of our abortion pill."

"I'm serious," she said as she set her wine glass down on the coffee table in front of the couch.

"I understand. Anyway, the demand for our abortion pill won't need any sexy ad campaign to make us a fortune. There are already enough people selling the idea of abortion for us. We just need to hitch a ride on their wagon."

The antique wooden mantel clock above the fireplace had both hands on the ten. Donna was exhausted despite the afternoon nap she'd taken. "Good night," she said as she stood and headed for the stairs leading to her bedroom. "I'll see you in the morning."

"Good night, honey. You'll be your old self again soon."

As she stood in front of the mirror in the upstairs bathroom, she knew she would never be the same again. *No sense in waiting any longer for this little experiment to bear fruit,* she thought to herself. The second pill, the little yellow one she had just put in her mouth, would make sure of that. Her father had said she should take it tomorrow, but she saw no reason to wait. She had no idea how long the combined pills would take to abort her child, but the pain of prolonging the inevitable outcome was killing her.

Before getting into bed, she placed a large sanitary pad inside her underwear and slipped into a pair of old pajamas. As a precaution, she also placed a towel on the side of bed she would sleep on in case any excessive bleeding occurred during the night. The scientists had told her father the initial bleeding could happen within a few hours.

After all, she thought as she began to doze, *I've always wanted to be in the forefront of women's issues. Why should this circumstance be any different?*

Sleep came surprisingly easy that night. When the contractions in her lower abdomen awakened her, the alarm clock on the nightstand next to the bed told her it was 4 a.m. For a while she lay in bed as the contractions grew in strength and frequency. She tried to imagine what it would have been like to be in a hospital labor room with Jake by her side as she gave birth to their child.

When she felt a gush of liquid flowing into the pad between her legs, she got up slowly and went down the hall to the upstairs bathroom. The house was pitch dark, and the tiled hallway floor was cold on her bare feet. She flipped on the bathroom light and silently closed and locked the door. Her father's room was at the end of hall, and she didn't want to awaken him. This was something she had to do alone.

The contractions continued to intensify, and she felt a fullness in her vagina. She covered the floor with a towel and slipped off her pajama bottoms and underwear. The sanitary pad was soaked with blood. A sustained contraction gripped her and forced her to her knees. Inadvertently she let out a short scream. She felt her vagina empty, and warm fluid streamed down the insides of her legs.

Looking down on the towel beneath her, she saw it. The nearly transparent skin of the helpless thing, covered in blood and clear fluid, glistened under the light. It was so tiny—maybe four inches in length. And yet there was no denying it was a baby. Even through her tear-filled eyes, she could see all of the physical attributes of a perfectly formed human.

She carefully scooped up the lifeless being, thankful his eyes had not yet formed enough to gaze upon the one who had snuffed out his life. The son she would never know fit comfortably in the palm of her hand. Yes, it was a boy. She gently ran her fingers over his smooth, hairless body, taking note of his amazingly well-formed fingers and toes. Touching his delicate fingers, she regretted that her son would never throw a football the way his father had done so spectacularly. How had her life and his come to this point?

Contractions continued to rack her body. She sat on the towel on the floor and sobbed. The physical pain paled in comparison to the mental anguish plaguing her. She was only vaguely aware of the growing pool of blood accumulating on the bathroom floor. A knock on the bathroom door cut short her period of mourning. She realized she had awakened her father.

"Donna, are you all right in there?"

"Just a minute, Father," she said in a whisper.

Taking one last look at the baby, she knew what had to be done. She wrapped the tiny body—attached to the placenta by a small umbilical cord—in some toilet paper. She then quickly dropped it all into the toilet. She struggled to her feet and unlocked the bathroom door only after she had flushed the toilet and watched the water swirl around and around. The room began spinning, and she felt life draining from her body just as the remnants of her son were washed out of sight forever.

"Donna, wake up!" her father said as he shook her. He had opened the door just in time to catch her as she fainted. "My god, girl, you're going to bleed to death. What did you do?"

"It's the process," she said weakly. "I just completed the process."

CHAPTER EIGHTEEN

I t was a relief for Donna to get out of the city and drive down the open highway toward Jake's hometown of Clarkston, Illinois, after receiving the shocking news about him that day. She and Jake had visited his mother and stepfather after their marriage before returning to Dayton. She had spoken to Jake's mother by phone a few times after his disappearance, but the two of them had not communicated in nearly three months. Since then, so much had happened. All of their lives had been devastated in one way or another.

Mrs. Chalmers was sobbing with joy when Donna called her a few hours earlier. The Air Force officials had shared with her the good news of Jake's return at about the same time Donna had been told. She accepted Mrs. Chalmers's invitation to come and visit so the family could celebrate Jake's homecoming together. In truth, the reason for her visit was more calculated.

The three-hour drive from St. Louis to Clarkston gave Donna some time alone to reflect on the turbulent events that had tossed her emotions around since the news of Jake's rescue and return to the States. Her father had taken the news of Jake's homecoming rather well. He said they should carry on as usual with her running the company and see how things played out. After all, they didn't know what condition he would be in after his terrible ordeal. Her father even told her he had underestimated Jake's tenacity. It was about as close to a compliment as Jake would ever get from him.

As she made her way north through Illinois, an ambulance raced by with its lights flashing and sirens blaring. Her heart began pounding, and her palms were slick with sweat as she gripped the steering wheel tightly with both hands. The last time she'd been that close to an ambulance, she had nearly died. She had thought the process was complete that night in the bathroom, but it wasn't. And it was not supposed to involve surgery, but it did.

After finding her hemorrhaging in the bathroom in the early morning hours, her father called an ambulance. She was taken to a hospital in Interlaken for emergency treatment. Apparently some of the placenta was still inside her, causing the continued heavy bleeding after the baby had been aborted. The surgeon gave her a blood transfusion and then performed an emergency dilatation and curettage, commonly known as a D & C, to clean out the lining of her uterus.

For the record, her father told the doctor she had miscarried in the chalet as a result of extreme emotional stress due to her husband's death. Though he hadn't planned on having to take her to the hospital as part of the process, after the state of emergency passed, he felt things actually had worked out better than planned. A medical report now stated she'd miscarried. If she'd been alone when she took the pills that night, she wouldn't have survived the hemorrhage. Her report would've read DOA.

After returning to the United States, Donna announced to her friends in Dayton that she had miscarried while in Switzerland. No one seemed terribly surprised, considering the circumstances. Her professors also were very accommodating in allowing her to finish the last two months of her MBA program by correspondence. There was nothing to keep her in Dayton. She moved back to St. Louis to live with her father and began her new career with Blanford Pharmaceuticals.

In March she'd called Evelyn Chalmers, Jake's mother, to let her know where she was living. Evelyn was very kind and concerned about her welfare, and she promised to pray for her. She wished her the best as she pursued her business dreams once again and said she was certain Jake would be very proud of her. Donna did not tell her about the pregnancy.

As she parked the car now in front of the Chalmers' home in Clarkston, Evelyn rushed out of the front door to embrace her daughter-in-law. Tears of joy streaked her smiling face. "It's so good to see you again. Can you believe it? Our Jake is coming home!"

"I'm still in shock," Donna said as she returned Evelyn's hug. "Have you heard anything more from the Air Force about when we can talk to him?"

"No, all they've told us is that he is alive and he's doing better than they expected. Come on in the house. We have a lot of catching up to do."

Donna grabbed her overnight bag from the car and followed Mrs. Chalmers into the house. Evelyn looked good, considering the stress she had been under the past seven months. She was a bit thinner than when Donna had seen her a year ago, and dark circles had formed beneath her eyes. Her long, raven black hair was pulled back into a ponytail that highlighted her face, adorned with a winsome smile.

"I'll take that for you," Evelyn said as she reached for Donna's bag. "I'll put you in Jake's old room."

"Thanks. I'm going to use the bathroom and freshen up a bit."

Evelyn went down the hall and put the bag in Jake's bedroom as Donna entered the bathroom and closed the door behind her. The cold water she splashed on her face felt refreshing for an instant.

Unfortunately a slimy feeling of deceitfulness rapidly overtook her once again as she considered the mission she was on.

What was it my father had said? "Don't worry about what others think. Take care of yourself and make your own happiness. Everyone is your enemy."

She reflected now on the people who had become her family. Despite all that had occurred over the last year, Jake and his family were not the enemy. In fact, they had been victimized as severely as she had. It's what made her task so difficult.

These are good people. They are the only family I have left except for my father. And if he views everyone as the enemy, where does that leave me?

Nonetheless, a plan of action had been set in motion. She knew she had to do her part to avert a devastating crisis during this time of jubilation. In her time of weakness, she had unwittingly become a coconspirator to an act that had been a legal crime less than a year before.

I have to take ownership of some responsibility, the ultimate responsibility, for carrying out the abortion of the baby. My father may have planted the poisonous seeds and watered them, but I allowed the process to take place.

Although abortion was no longer illegal, the Chalmers would be deeply hurt if she told them the truth, that their only grandson had been deprived of a chance to live. Instead, she would have to tell Mrs. Chalmers about the "miscarriage." Even though Jake and his family would probably forgive her for what she'd done if she told them the truth, it didn't seem right to burden any of them with another distressing piece of news. At least that's how she justified what she was about to do.

"Would you like some iced tea?" Evelyn said as Donna entered the kitchen.

The kitchen was very clean and orderly with nothing out of place. It was obvious to Donna that Evelyn was a good housekeeper and took pride in her position as homemaker and mother.

"Yes, thank you."

Evelyn placed a glass of tea on the table. "Have a seat and tell me how you're doing."

She sat down, and Evelyn pulled up a chair next to her at the small rectangular wooden table. The bright yellow curtains covering the screened window near the table gently swayed in the pleasant breeze coming from the north. The round clock on the kitchen wall above the table read a few minutes before 4 p.m. Mike would not be home from work for another hour or so. That would be enough time to talk privately with Evelyn. After that, she would be Donna's advocate with the rest of the family.

"Well, I thought I was doing all right until today," she said. "The Air Force officials showed up in my office just after I had chaired my first board meeting."

"You look so professional," Evelyn said as she squeezed Donna's hand. "We're all so proud of what you're doing."

Touching her hair, Donna realized she was still dressed for the office. She removed the clip and shook out her hair.

"I was sure they were going to tell me Jake was dead. When they told me he was alive, I fainted. My thoughts and emotions are still running wild. I was in such a hurry to get here that I didn't even take time to change."

"It must have been terribly hard on you these past months, not knowing if you'd ever see Jake again."

"That's not the worst part. I'm so ashamed. I gave up on him. In my mind, I buried him and moved on with my life. I'll never forgive myself for that."

"Don't be too hard on yourself. After my first husband died, I was depressed for a year or more. There were times I could barely get out of bed. I even considered suicide for a while. My boys were pretty much on their own until I finally snapped out of it."

Evelyn's compassion eased her fears, and Donna could tell she was genuinely interested in her story. She had not felt this kind of love since her mother died.

"What happened to change things?" she asked.

"God brought Mike into my life. Someone in the church thought we might be able to console each other, as we were both grieving the loss of our mates. I had just about given up on God until then. Mike is such a better man than my first husband was. Don't get me wrong. I loved my first husband. But sometimes God removes something from your life in order to give you something better."

A feeling of rage swept over Donna at the mention of God. How was she to reconcile the turmoil in her life and be thankful for what had happened? There seemed to be no earthly reason for all the heartache she'd gone through.

"Honestly, Mrs. Chalmers, right now I'm angry with God for causing all this pain and suffering in our lives."

"I understand, sweetheart. You've been through a lot with the death of your mother and nearly losing your husband. It's easy to lose faith when bad things happen for no good reason. But God didn't cause Jake to get shot down. God loves him more than you or I can ever imagine."

"Then why would he allow it to happen?" Donna asked as tears began streaming down her face. "It makes no sense. I prayed constantly, and yet he gave me no answer."

"We all prayed for Jake. God did answer our prayers, but he did it in his own way and in his perfect timing."

"My father says people who believe in God are weak," Donna said as she wiped away the tears with a tissue. "He says you have to believe in yourself and rely on no one else. He told me to get on with life and pour all of my energy into business. That's how I've been coping lately."

"I'm sure your father loves you. He gave you advice based on what's worked for him, I suppose. Have you found happiness and contentment with your new life?"

"Not really. I do enjoy the work, but it's no substitute for the life I had with Jake."

"Everyone has a god, Donna, including those who say they don't. Some people worship their job, their possessions, money, or something else. It sounds like your father might have made himself his god. It's pretty common for successful business people."

"Mother and I read the Bible together when she was sick. It seemed like I was doing fine with God until my world fell apart."

Evelyn smiled to show her understanding. "That's when you need him the most."

"I need to confess something to you, Evelyn. There's something I haven't told you, and I'm afraid of what will happen when I have to tell Jake."

Evelyn's forehead furrowed, and her smile faded as she waited for what she was about to hear. "What is it?"

"The last time I spoke to Jake, the day before his plane was shot down, I told him I was pregnant. When I was in Switzerland on a business trip with my father in February, I—I had a miscarriage. Father called an ambulance and rushed me to a hospital, where I had a blood transfusion and surgery to stop the bleeding. The doctor said the miscarriage was probably brought on by the stress of Jake's situation."

Evelyn wrapped her arms around her. "I'm so sorry. No wonder you're worried and feeling depressed."

"Jake's going to be so disappointed when I tell him there's no baby," she said as she cried on Evelyn's shoulder. "I just know that's the first thing he's going to ask me when he calls, and I don't want to hurt him. After all he's been through, I don't want to cause him more pain. I feel like I've failed him."

"If I know Jake, he'll be more concerned about how you're doing. Sure he'll be disappointed, but he'll understand. After all, it wasn't your fault."

It seemed to Donna that Evelyn could sense the secret hidden deep inside of her. She had to avert her eyes to hide the guilt and shame she felt. The initial crisis, Jake's disappearance, had not been her fault. Her subsequent actions, however, had complicated matters in a far-reaching way that would negatively impact all of their lives. Instead of holding a newborn baby boy in her arms as her husband returned home, remorse and secrecy would be the offspring Donna would present him for what she'd done.

"I should've told you sooner."

"You can always call me. Sometimes it's helpful to share a burden like that with someone else. No one will ever be able to take the place of your mother, but I'd like to be there for you if you ever need someone to talk to."

"Thanks, Evelyn."

"For a minute there I thought you were going to tell me you'd found another man," she said and laughed. "That would have destroyed Jake."

"Oh, no. There's never been any other man in my life but Jake."

That statement was only partially true, and she could tell Evelyn knew it. Donna was certain that Jake had confided in his mother the complex relationship she had with her father. Her mother-in-law's intuition had allowed her to paint the portrait of Donna's life without ever meeting the other man. Nevertheless, she felt genuine love and acceptance from this woman she barely knew.

The loud ringing of the phone mounted on the kitchen wall interrupted their conversation.

"Hello," Evelyn said into the receiver. "Hi, honey. Yes, Donna's here. That'll be great. Okay. See you soon."

"I hope you don't mind eating some fresh corn on the cob and fried green tomatoes for supper. One of the local farmers gave Mike a big basket of sweet corn picked just a few hours ago."

"I've never eaten fried green tomatoes before."

"That's one of Jake's favorite meals during the summertime. He'll only eat tomatoes when they're fresh out of the garden."

"We had so little time together before he went overseas. There's so much we still need to learn about each other."

"God willing, you'll have a lifetime of happiness to spend together now."

"How's Mary doing?"

"She's fine. She's working as a phlebotomist at the local hospital this summer. You'll see her this evening after she gets off work."

Mike came home carrying a wooden crate full of sweet corn just after 5 p.m. He kissed Evelyn as he set the corn down on the kitchen counter.

"Hello, Donna," he said as he hugged her affectionately in a strong embrace. "It's good to see you again."

"Hi, Mike. Thanks for allowing me to visit."

"You're always welcome here. Excuse me for a few minutes ladies."

Mike went outside on the deck and shucked half a dozen ears of beautiful peaches and cream sweet corn. Donna saw him light some charcoal in the kettle grill and get some hamburger from the refrigerator. While he was working, Evelyn sliced up the green tomatoes and dipped them into a special batter she had prepared.

"I'll have to get that recipe from you so I can surprise Jake when he gets home," Donna said.

"Remind me to copy it down for you after supper. I'll give you my recipe for rhubarb cream pie too. That's always been his favorite dessert."

It was therapeutic for Donna to share a meal with Jake's parents. The conversation was upbeat as they anticipated the joyous occasion of Jake's return. After supper, Evelyn and Donna cleaned up the kitchen while Mike watched the CBS evening news with Walter Cronkite.

"I hope Jake finishes his degree in journalism when he's done with the service," Evelyn said. "That's always been his passion."

"There's no reason he can't get any job he wants after all he's been through."

"Will you be moving back to Dayton soon?"

"Mrs. Delaney, our landlord, has kept the apartment open for us. I left some of our things there when I moved back to St. Louis in March. I'll call her tomorrow when I get back to the office and let her know what's happened."

"You're leaving tomorrow?"

"Unfortunately, yes. Father is out of the country on business, so I need to be in the office until he gets back."

Mary came home from work a little after 7 p.m. "Hi, Donna," she said as she gave her a hug. "You must be on cloud nine with Jake coming home."

"Hi Mary. Honestly, it's just starting to become real. I had imagined this day for so long, and when it never came, I decided to stop torturing myself. Now I'm just waiting for a phone call so I can hear his voice again."

"Have you eaten, dear?" Evelyn asked Mary.

"Yeah, I ate something before I left the hospital."

Donna talked with Evelyn and Mary until about 9 p.m. It had been a long and difficult day, to say the least, beginning well with a full-fledged frontal assault in the business world. The nuclear explosion in her personal life, however, had sent her into damage control mode and left her emotionally exhausted. She said goodnight to the Chalmers family and retreated to the safety of Jake's bedroom.

Being alone in that room where the man she loved had grown up gave her a sense of comfort she'd not had in quite some time. As she looked around, she saw a large autographed poster of Ernie Banks on one wall. A menacing poster of Dick Butkus in full pads graced the opposite wall. Jake's high school letter jacket, adorned with row after row of medals from four sports, hung in the closet.

Her sleep that night was filled with vivid dreams, most of which she could not remember the next day. One, however, caused her to awaken in a panic. She dreamed she had walked into a board meeting at the office one day soon after Jake's return to find all of the Blanford executives reading the newspaper. There on the front page was her picture with a caption that read, "Blanford CEO aborts baby with new pill." In the dream, she tried to race home to get the newspaper before Jake could see it, but she could never reach the house. Everywhere she went, people were reading the newspaper headlines and staring at her. She tossed and turned fitfully the rest of the night until morning mercifully arrived.

In the morning, she showered and dressed early so she could get back to St. Louis as soon as possible. Mike had already left for work when she went to the kitchen for a cup of coffee. Evelyn was sitting at the table, reading the local newspaper.

"Good morning," Evelyn said. "Did you sleep well?"

"Nightmares are never very far off," Donna said as she sat down at the kitchen table.

"Would you like some breakfast?"

"No, thank you. I'm going to have a cup of coffee and then head back to St. Louis."

"I know you've gotten very involved in your family's business. There's nothing wrong with that. But please don't neglect your marriage. Jake is going to need you when he gets home."

"I'll do my best to take care of him."

"I hope you two can recapture the love you had for each other a year ago before any of this nastiness happened. It will take a lot of work. Both of you have been scarred emotionally. It isn't fair, but it happened. You can't change the past. All you can do now is move forward together as husband and wife."

"Do you think my work will be a problem for Jake?"

"I don't think so. But it may be a problem for you."

"I don't understand."

"I sense that your heart has been hardened by the specter of death swirling around you over the last year. Somewhere along the line, you seem to have lost that passion for life you had when I saw you last."

"How do I get that back?"

"Lasting happiness can only be found in a loving relationship like you have with Jake. If you try to find it in your work, you will be sorely disappointed. I'll be praying for you that you don't sacrifice your marriage for the sake of personal achievement in your career."

"I'm so confused right now. My father says we make our own happiness. He says the only way to be fulfilled in life is through achievement and success in business."

"Ask yourself what could have motivated him to say such a thing to you. If you want the kind of life he's had, then by all means go for it. But please realize that everything else in your life will suffer from the choices you will have to make to gain what he has."

"There has to be a way to have both. Men balance their time between commitments to work and family. Why can't women do the same thing?"

"I'm not saying it is impossible, just that it's a matter of priorities. If you keep your relationship with God first and family next, everything else will take care of itself. By the way, men haven't always succeeded in pulling off the balancing act you're looking for. It's why there are so many divorces and unhappy marriages these days."

Evelyn's words rang true as Donna thought of her mother's despair when her failed marriage left her feeling empty inside. Her father had made work and sexual liaisons with other women his main priorities in life. Bitterness and loneliness had littered the paths of their lives.

"Well, I'd better get going. Thank you for everything. I appreciate the words of wisdom. I know my mother would've agreed with what you've said."

Evelyn rose from the table and retrieved a piece of paper from the kitchen counter. "Oh, I almost forgot. Here are the recipes I promised you."

"Thank you. I'll call you when I hear from Jake."

Evelyn gave her a hug. "Good-bye. I'll be praying for you."

On the drive back to St. Louis, Donna reflected on the chasm between the two diametrically opposed worldviews she had experienced in the last few years. Before meeting Jake, she was quite comfortable in her father's narcissistic world. After experiencing the profound joy of selfless love in her marriage, however, her personal ambitions had lost some of their former appeal. Would she soon discover that her marriage had similarly lost its magic? No, she wouldn't let that happen. Evelyn had said it was a matter of priorities. She promised herself she would do everything she could to hold onto both her job and her marriage.

Back at the office just before noon, she greeted her secretary with energy. Janie was obviously pleased to see her in such a good mood.

"Ms. Kingston. I'm so glad you're back," she said, jumping up from her chair to offer her boss a big hug.

"Good morning," Donna said as she entered. "Is everything okay? You seem awfully anxious."

"I was worried about you after what happened yesterday. The fainting, I mean. Your father called a little while ago and asked me to contact him when you arrived. Shall I call him for you?"

"Give me about five minutes to get settled, and then place the call."

"Yes, ma'am. Can I get you some coffee?"

"Not right now," she said as she shut the door to her office.

My father isn't wasting any time checking up on me after my visit to see Jake's family. He's probably dying to know exactly when his nemesis is returning home to complicate his life. No doubt he wants to make sure I am still firmly under his control. To tell the truth, I'm wondering the same thing.

The intercom buzzed. "Mr. Kingston is on the line for you."

"Thank you, Janie."

"Hello, Father. Where are you today?"

"Hello, Donna. I'm at a meeting with some Chinese government officials here in Hong Kong. They're eager to make some of our products available in their marketplace of over one billion people. That would add a lot to our top line for years to come."

"I'm sure you'll convince them they can't live without us."

"How was your visit to Illinois yesterday?"

"The shock that Jake is alive has worn off now. The trip to visit his family gave me a lot of time to think."

"How did they receive the news about your—your unfortunate miscarriage?"

She wanted to tell him that she had bared her soul to Jake's family and they'd forgiven her. How cleansing it would've been to be free from the bondage.

"Jake's mother was very understanding. She hasn't spoken to him yet, but I told her about the baby. He still doesn't know, but I'll probably have to tell him when he calls and asks."

"That's good. Everything will work out fine. You'll see."

"When are you returning to St. Louis?"

"I'll be home by Friday if all goes well."

"Great. By the way, I'll be going to Dayton as soon as Jake gets home."

"Of course. You'll want to spend some time with your husband. Just make sure you keep your priorities straight."

"My husband is my number one priority right now."

"That was spoken like a loyal wife. You and I know better though, don't we?"

"Don't make me choose between you and Jake, Father."

He laughed wickedly. "When you sell your soul to the devil, you have no other choice."

PART III

Surrender

CHAPTER NINETEEN

The long flight home gave Jake plenty of time to reflect on his phone conversation with Donna earlier in the day. He should've seen it coming. He'd been so absorbed in his own battle to survive that he hadn't considered how severely she would be affected by his disappearance. Now he knew another life had been lost because of him. The others, the victims of war, burdened him with a sense of guilt. He hadn't kept track of the mounting body count. The loss of his unborn child, however, was more painful than he could ever have imagined.

The C-141 copilot came back to the cabin to announce that the plane was about three hundred miles from Dayton. As Jake looked out the left side of the aircraft, he saw the majestic Mississippi River carving out the border between Missouri and Illinois. The Gateway Arch glistened in the afternoon sun as it stood sentinel in downtown St. Louis. The sight reminded him of crossing high above the Mekong River separating Laos from Thailand. Crossing the Mekong had signified physical freedom for him from the nightmare of captivity.

I sure hope this river crossing brings me to a place and time for the emotional and spiritual healing I so desperately need, he thought.

As the wheels of the C-141 touched down on the runway at Wright-Patterson Air Force Base, Jim Sizemore shouted, "Home at last!"

The Air Force purposely had brought the two men home on a Saturday when there was minimum activity on the base. The reunion of the POWs with their wives was everyone's top priority. There would be plenty of time for interviews and briefings later.

Through the aircraft window, Jake could see Donna as the plane came to a stop in front of the base operations center. Her hair was pulled back in a ponytail, accentuating her delicate facial features. She wore a purple sleeveless blouse and tight white slacks. His heart quickened and his palms were moist with sweat. He was about to reunite with the woman he loved.

As he exited the plane, he saw her cover her mouth with both hands and begin to cry. She ran to greet him, and he threw his arms around her and hugged her so tightly he thought she might break in two.

"I thought I'd lost you forever," she cried as they kissed.

"You were the only thing that kept me going," he said. *She must never know the thoughts I entertained to keep myself alive in captivity,* he thought. "I had to make it home to be with you."

"Please forgive me. I wanted to be holding our baby in my arms when you came home."

"That was my fault. I should never have left you alone. I won't let that happen again. I promise."

They hugged and kissed as tears of joy washed away months of despair.

Squadron Commander Colonel Dempster interrupted the reunion to shake Jake's hand. "Welcome home, Sergeant. We're mighty proud of you. I want you to enjoy the weekend with your wife and then check in with me on Monday. You can call me at any hour if you need anything."

"Thank you, sir. Right now I have everything I need."

Wiping tears from her eyes, Donna said, "Let's go home."

It felt wonderful for Jake to get behind the wheel of his '65 Mustang and cruise south on Route 4 from the base to the apartment on the University of Dayton campus as he had done so many times before. What a great surprise that Donna had brought it to the airport for him instead of her own car. For a moment, he wondered if he had just awakened from a very bad dream. With his faithful wife sitting beside him, it was almost as though the nightmare of his time in Laos had never happened.

As he drove, Donna ran her hand across the stubble of hair on his head. "I've never seen your hair this short."

"You haven't seen anything yet. Wait 'til you see the rest of me."

"Let's get you home and out of that flight suit so I can do a thorough inspection. You've made me curious now."

After living in a filthy hole in the floor of the jungle for the past seven months, Jake thought the cramped apartment was luxurious by comparison. *Joni Mitchell had it right in "Big Yellow Taxi,"* he thought to himself. *We really don't know what we have until it's gone.*

While Donna was busy in the kitchen, he stripped off his clothes and stepped into the shower. The strong torrent of hot water washed away the agony of nine thousand miles of travel and rejuvenated his weary body. The smell of something delicious emanating from the oven in the kitchen was a powerful stimulant. His hunger for food, however, was overshadowed by a much stronger, more primal desire.

Donna was waiting for him as he came into the bedroom. "Oh, my," she said as she saw his hairless body.

"How do you like my clean-shaven look?"

"Very sexy."

The reunited husband and wife kissed long and deep as their bodies melded together in glorious rhythm. The months of intimacy they had been deprived of drove the passion and the energy of their frenzied lovemaking. Afterward they lay together, basking in the glow of their long-awaited reunion.

"I missed you so much," she said as she squeezed him tightly against her moist body. "I'm going to have to fatten you a bit. You've lost a lot of weight."

"I kept asking for seconds, but no one would listen."

She smacked him on the backside. "At least you kept your sense of humor. I hope you're hungry now, because I've planned a special meal for you. I'm going to make some fresh corn on the cob and fried green tomatoes for supper."

Later, as he finished the last of the food, he said, "That was fantastic. What's in the oven?"

"My secret weapon in case the tomatoes didn't turn out."

She served him a piece of warm rhubarb cream pie with vanilla ice cream on top. He hadn't eaten a home-cooked meal for a very long time. The pie was absolutely exquisite.

"Wow. That was better than anything my mother ever made for me."

"Speaking of your mother, we should try to visit your family soon. I know she's dying to see you."

"When I called her from Thailand, I told her I'd be busy for the first few days and then we'd drive up to Clarkston as soon as we could."

"What will the Air Force have for you to do now?"

"I'll need to tell them my future plans. I think you're going to like this part."

He explained to her the option he had been given to leave the Air Force early and go back to college on the GI Bill. She was ecstatic to say the least.

"That's perfect. I'm so happy you're going to get the chance to complete your degree in journalism. Have you thought about where to go to school?"

"It depends on your plans, I guess. I can get my degree anywhere. The more important question is, what do you want to do? Are you happy in your work at Blanford Pharmaceuticals?"

"I think I could be now that you're home. Like I told you when you called me from Thailand, I ran back to my father and my old plans when I thought I had nothing left. Without you, the only identity I had was my work. I wouldn't say I was happy at work, but it did fill the void in my life."

"Then I think you should keep doing what you're doing for the time being and see how things go over the next year while I'm finishing school. I suppose I could enroll at a university in St. Louis. We're going to have to find somewhere else to live besides your father's house though. I didn't escape one prison camp just to be thrown into another."

"Have you thought about going back to Grantham to finish your degree? We could rent a small home in the community for a year, and I could commute to my office in the city. It would only be about an hour's drive, and that's about what I'm doing now from my father's house."

"Actually I hadn't considered that option. It's not a bad idea. It would be easy for me to slip back into the school of journalism since I know all of the professors. Housing would be cheaper than in the city too."

"I like the idea of living in our own place in a small town. It would be romantic, almost like we were college sweethearts. Sometimes I wonder how things would have turned out if we'd gotten together sooner. Maybe we could have avoided all the bad things that happened to us this past year."

"We can't change what's in the past," he said as he reached out and took her hand in his. "All we can do is make the best of the life we have."

She hesitated for a few seconds. "You don't have to tell me what happened if you don't want to. The Air Force told me the kinds of things POWs go through. I just want you to know you can talk to me whenever you're ready."

"I'm going to be fine. How've you been holding up?"

She had told him about the miscarriage when they spoke by phone. He knew she'd been overwhelmed with feelings of sadness and guilt as a result of her terrible ordeal. Although he was grieving the death of their unborn child also, her loss was much more personal. She'd actually carried life within her, only to have it taken away.

Tears welled up in her eyes. "I tried hard to be strong. For the first month or so, I told myself you'd make it home alive. As time went on, it became harder to believe. I couldn't eat or sleep. All I did was cry."

"Don't beat yourself up. You did what anyone would do under the circumstances."

She rose from the table and went into the bedroom. He heard a drawer open and close, and then she returned with two objects in her hand.

"The Air Force held a special ceremony just after the peace treaty was signed. They presented me with these two medals for your heroism during the war."

She handed him the Silver Star and the Distinguished Flying Cross medals.

"I should've been so proud of you that day. But to me it felt like I was attending your funeral. After that, I lost all hope. That's when I turned to my father for help."

It distressed him to learn that she'd run back to her father when a crisis struck. On an intellectual level, he understood it.

She had no one else to turn to in her time of need. His pride was wounded, however, knowing that her father had once again played a prominent role in her life. He needed to find out just how deeply their lives had become intertwined.

"How is your father? I'm sure he was disappointed to hear I was still alive."

"You managed to surprise him. That's something not many people do. He said he underestimated your tenacity."

"I'm glad he helped you despite his feelings for me."

"After I lost the baby, I had nothing to look forward to. Then I saw TV coverage of the POWs from Vietnam returning home, and I was devastated all over again because you were not one of them. Looking back, I'm ashamed at how weak and selfish I was. I envied seeing wives greet their returning husbands and children rushing to embrace their fathers. I realized I was consumed by self-pity and anger, so I decided to immerse myself in the business and forget about everything else."

"The important thing is that we both survived this nightmare. Now we have the rest of our lives to spend together."

A feeling of exhaustion suddenly overtook him. His body was losing the battle against the effects of jet lag after the journey half way around the world.

"You look tired. Why don't you get some sleep, and we'll talk more tomorrow."

"Yeah, I could use some sleep."

She kissed him goodnight. "I'll have some coffee ready for you in the morning."

Sleep came quickly the first night at home in his own bed. Unfortunately sometime during the night, an old acquaintance came to haunt his dreams. He found himself in a deep dark pit, feverishly trying to carve out handholds and footholds with a makeshift knife. In the distance, he could hear a voice desperately calling for help. The more he worked, the deeper the hole became.

Then a menacing presence enveloped him, and an evil voice spoke. "You'll never be free. I'll always be here to torment you."

A bright light shined on his face and blinded him as he awoke suddenly from his dream. When he sat up, he saw Donna had opened the window shades, allowing the brilliant sunlight to wash the room with its warm glow.

"Good morning," she said as she sat down next to him on the bed and kissed him. "You must have been having a bad dream."

"Why's that?"

"You kept yelling, 'I'm coming, Jim.'"

"How's the coffee in this establishment?"

"I think you'll find it to your liking," she said as she went to the kitchen and brought him a cup of steaming hot java.

"What time is it?"

"It's ten o'clock. You slept almost fourteen hours straight."

"It looks like it's going to be a nice day," he said as he looked out the bedroom window. It was a great relief to put the recurring nightmare behind him and embrace the freedom of the new day.

After a relaxed and enjoyable weekend with Donna, Monday morning he went to the squadron to meet with Colonel Dempster. The Colonel said he was sorry to see him leave the Air Force, but he would make the appropriate phone calls to hasten his discharge. He also arranged for Jake to be on leave for the next two weeks until his discharge could be finalized.

"I have something to give you," Colonel Dempster said as he opened a metal locker in his office. He pulled out the AK-47 Jake had asked Colonel Williams to ship home for him. "I believe this is yours. Someday I'd like to hear the story of how you came by this weapon."

"Thank you, sir," he said as he took the rifle. "Maybe someday I'll be ready to tell it."

It was good to see a number of his gunner friends in the squadron again. Soon, however, he had to escape the awkward conversations. The wounds were still too fresh. It was time to move on.

Donna and Jake made the five-hour drive from Dayton to Clarkston on Tuesday. The leisurely trip gave them time to catch up on all that had happened in the world while he was gone. The Commander in Chief of the Armed Forces, President Nixon, was under siege by Congress and the news media for alleged nefarious activity. The breaking news had replaced the Vietnam War in the eyes of the media. He hoped he would get a chance to read about it in the newspapers or write about it in his journalism classes if the story didn't fade away too quickly.

Back in Clarkston, he was amazed at how it seemed nothing had changed in the sleepy little town since his last visit a year before. His world had been turned upside down, and yet life in his hometown had gone on seemingly unscathed by external events. He sensed his thoughts were full of self-pity and probably dead wrong. People there too had surely suffered from illness, injury, and other life-changing situations while he was a world away. The only difference was, their trials were dealt with in relative obscurity. His were high drama in comparison.

Jake's mother was waiting to greet them as they parked the car in front of the house. She was so excited to see him she couldn't stop crying and praising God. As for him, he was thankful God had not taken another son from her because of the war. She had suffered enough loss for one lifetime.

He told his mom that he and Donna had decided to move into a house near the Grantham campus if they could find something suitable before school started the following month. She was delighted to hear he was going to leave the military and finish his degree in journalism. She said everyone in the church, and most of the people in town, had been praying for him since he went to Southeast Asia last year.

"I ran into your friend Carl Simpson in the supermarket the other day," she said. "He said he wanted you to call him when you got home."

"How's he doing? Is he still farming?"

"He's been worried sick about you. Mike said he's been by the gas station to talk with him almost every day since your plane went down. He's even started going to church now that he's married."

"Married? When did that happen?"

"He and Peggy were married in April."

"It was just a matter of time, I guess. I'll give him a call after supper."

Sitting around the dinner table enjoying a delicious meal and great conversation with his family was truly an awesome experience. For the first time in at least a year, everyone had many things to be thankful for. After supper, Jake phoned Carl, who begged him to come out to the house for dinner the following night. Jake was actually looking forward to seeing his buddy again. His close circle of friends had shrunk considerably over the past few years, and he wanted to maintain contact with the few people who had known him when he was young and innocent. Maybe they could keep him grounded as he faced his new life.

CHAPTER TWENTY

The next day, Jake surveyed hundreds of acres of cornfields as he and Donna drove up the long gravel lane leading to Carl Simpson's house. Carl had built a very nice, three-bedroom brick ranch home a few years ago in anticipation of his marriage to Peggy Stanton. Several huge red machine sheds and barns containing hundreds of thousands of dollars worth of equipment surrounded the modern farmhouse. Carl stood in the driveway looking like the lord of a castle.

As Jake walked toward his friend, he noticed Carl's hair was much shorter and neater than the last time he'd seen him. His pork chop sideburns and bushy mustache were nicely trimmed as well. Peggy apparently had transformed her husband into a respectable, middle-class farmer and member of the Clarkston society.

"This is quite a spread here," Jake said as he reached out to shake Carl's extended hand.

"Those idiots shaved your head," Carl said as he pulled his friend close and gave him a big hug and a noogie. "And you're skinny as a rail. It's a good thing I butchered a cow for you. We're gonna feed you a big juicy steak tonight, partner."

"Carl, this is my wife, Donna."

Carl picked Donna up in the air and planted a big kiss on her lips. "I finally get to meet the crazy woman who tamed ole Jake."

Donna was flabbergasted by Carl's exuberant welcome. "It's good to meet you too," she stammered as he gently set her back down on the ground. "Jake's told me a lot about you."

"It's all a lie. Come on inside. I want you to meet my wife, Peggy."

Peggy was the daughter of another prominent farm family in the community. A good church-going girl, she'd been the salutatorian of her high school class and the president of the Future Homemakers of America. She went on to earn a bachelor's degree from Illinois State and was teaching English classes at the high school. From the looks of her ripening abdomen, she would soon be using her homemaking skills to raise Carl's offspring.

"Hi, Jake. Thank God you're safe," she said as she gave him a hug.

"You look great, Peggy. I hope this big ox is taking good care of you."

"You know Carl. He's a good provider," she said as she patted her ripening belly.

"Peggy, this is my wife, Donna."

"Hi, Peggy. It is a pleasure to meet you. When is your baby due?"

"Sometime in late September. We didn't do a very good job of planning. I'll have to take some time off during the fall semester at school. Fortunately we have two sets of grandparents close by who are eager to babysit their first grandchild."

Carl grabbed Jake by the arm. "Let's let the women get to know each other while I show you around the place."

"The baked potatoes will be ready in about an hour," Peggy said.

"I'll put the steaks on the grill soon," Carl said as he kissed his wife. "Let's go, Jake."

Carl led him out to one of the machine sheds and opened the door. "This is where I come to unwind," Carl said.

They entered a large, nicely furnished paneled room. A new stereo system with four large speakers pumped out loud FM music when Carl turned the receiver on.

"This room is bigger than my apartment," Jake said.

"You want a beer?"

"Sure."

Carl took two cans of Budweiser from a refrigerator in the corner of the room and handed one to Jake.

"Mom said you stopped by the Sinclair station a lot while I was gone."

"Yeah, I enjoy talking with your stepdad. I was freaking out when I heard you got shot down. He helped me see the big picture."

"The big picture?"

"Mike said we need to look at everything from God's perspective. He said God had a reason for allowing you to go through all that stuff."

"Well, if you figure it out, I hope you'll let me know. God and I aren't exactly on speaking terms right now."

"Mike said God allows us to go through tough times to make us stronger."

"Do I look stronger? You said I look like crap."

"I think Mike was talking about our faith being stronger. He said when his wife was killed by that drunk driver, he was angry and asked God why he allowed it to happen. When he finally realized nothing in this world happens that God doesn't allow, good and bad, he stopped asking why."

"So what good came from Mike losing his wife? That still doesn't make any sense."

"For one thing, he met your mom and became your stepdad. And he's helped a lot of people in Clarkston. He's even gotten me going to church again. Maybe God will use him to help you deal with the bad stuff in your life."

"You're a changed man, Carl."

"I'm working on it."

"I thought Peggy was the one who cleaned you up. I didn't realize you'd gotten religion too."

"I'm going to be a father, so I need to get my act together. I want my kids to be raised in the church."

"You sound like your old man."

"Having a baby will do that to you, I guess."

"The last thing Donna told me before the plane crash was that she was pregnant and I was going to be a father. The thought of coming home to be with my wife and my child kept me going when I wanted to give up. Then I came home only to find out God took my baby away. Donna had a miscarriage. I'm having trouble finding anything good coming out of this whole nightmare."

"I'm sorry. I didn't know Donna had been pregnant."

"She had the miscarriage sometime in February. I'm sure the stress brought on by my situation caused it."

"Maybe so, but women have miscarriages all the time. Bad things happen to good people every day."

"Now you sound like a philosopher."

Carl's comments stirred Jake's emotions and gave him a lot to think about. Mike had never pressured him to change his life or conform to the teachings of the church. He had always respected and admired him for the man he was and the way he loved his mother. Now he could see the positive influence he'd been on his best friend.

Maybe I need to consider asking Mike's advice on how to deal with the anger I'm feeling, he thought.

Carl displayed his cooking skills by serving up four large T-bone steaks that had been marinated and grilled to perfection. No Laotian rodent Jake could remember eating had tasted that good.

The rest of the evening went surprisingly well. Donna and Peggy hit it off like they were old friends. They talked nonstop about everything from living in a small town to the women's lib movement. Unlike Carl, Peggy was more in tune with world events. She was an avid reader of anything in print.

Donna and Jake said good-bye to Carl and Peggy at 9 p.m. and were back to his parents' home twenty minutes later. His mom was watching TV in the living room when they walked into the house. Mike had already gone to bed, since he was up every morning at 5 a.m. so he could open the station by 6 a.m. After a few minutes of conversation, Donna said she was exhausted and was going to bed. Jake kissed her goodnight and said he'd see her in the morning.

"I'm glad you had a nice time with Carl and Peggy tonight," his mom said. "I don't think they have many friends to run around with here in Clarkston."

"Carl's changed since I saw him last."

"Well, he's a married man now with a child on the way. It's time he grew up."

"Apparently his conversations with Mike have had a big impact on his life."

"Mike doesn't really tell me what they talk about. But I'm glad it's been helpful to Carl."

"He said Mike's helped a lot of people here in town."

"God seems to bring hurting people to Mike. He has a gift for helping people through difficult times in their lives."

"He's just an ordinary guy. How does that work?"

"In one respect, he is just an ordinary man. But God often takes ordinary people and uses them for extraordinary purposes. Mike went through a terrible time after his wife died. Fortunately he stopped fighting with God and started believing everything that happens to us is according to God's purposes. That's when God began to use him to help others."

"What other kind of troubles did he have? All I ever heard was how special he was for forgiving the guy who killed his wife."

"Why don't you ask him?"

"We've hardly ever talked. He's a nice guy, but I don't think he'd ever open up to me."

"Mike's not one to interfere in someone else's business. But if you initiate the conversation, I'm sure he'll tell you whatever you want to know. He's a very good listener."

"He's probably busy at work all day. I hate to bother him."

"Nonsense. He goes to lunch every day at noon while Kenny minds the station. I'm sure he'd love to have you join him. I'll tell him when he gets up in the morning. Trust me. Mike will be honored that you want to spend some time with him."

Donna was already fast asleep when Jake came to bed. Sleep eluded him for quite some time as his mind replayed the events of the day. He was already having second thoughts about talking with Mike.

Spilling my guts to my stepfather may not be such a bright idea, he thought.

Just as he was about to drift off to sleep, he heard Donna sobbing and mumbling something in her sleep. He sat up and leaned over her as she tossed her head from side to side and whimpered.

"The yellow pill did it," she said several times. "The process is complete. I'm sorry. I'm sorry. Please forgive me."

He didn't know whether to wake her or just leave her alone. He had never seen her talk in her sleep before. She appeared to be having a nightmare, most likely about the miscarriage. He figured they had both acquired some demons that were hard to shake.

The next day, Mike was waiting for him in a corner booth as Jake opened the door to The Country Kitchen restaurant just before noon. The local place on Main Street, owned and operated by Glen and Marge Custer, was a favorite dining spot for most of the lunch crowd. They could get a decent meal of roast beef, mashed potatoes and gravy, corn, and a roll for just a dollar. A cup of coffee cost ten cents, and Marge never let a cup get empty.

"Have a seat," Mike said as he shook Jake's hand.

"Hello, Jake," Marge said as she walked over to the booth. "What'll you boys have today?"

"I'll have a cheeseburger, fries, and a chocolate milk shake," he said.

"You need some fattening up. I'll have Glen make it a double cheeseburger. How about you, Mike?"

"I'll have the lunch special. Coffee to drink, please."

"Coming right up," Marge said as she poured Mike's coffee and then strode behind the counter, barking out the orders to her husband, who was doing the cooking.

"Thanks for taking the time to meet with me. I know you're busy at work," Jake said.

"What's on your mind?"

"Carl said you've really helped him. He seems a lot more mature than the last time I saw him."

"He's like the rest of us, a work in progress."

"Something Carl told me last night has me puzzled. He told me you said God allowed me to suffer as part of his master plan. That really makes me mad. I mean, what kind of a God would allow me to be tortured the way I was? Nothing good can come from that."

"Go on."

"The only thing that kept me alive was the desire to see Donna again and hold my baby in my arms. I'm angry that God took the baby from me on top of everything else I had to endure. I don't understand it. How can losing my child serve any useful purpose?"

"Those are good questions. Why do you think these things happened to you?"

"I don't know. I guess I was just unlucky."

"Everyone goes through difficult times. The only question is, how will we respond when a crisis hits? Right now you're reacting the way I did when my wife was killed. I almost ended up in prison."

"Prison? What did you do to deserve prison?"

"I was so mad at the world I wanted to kill somebody. One night I went to a tavern to drown my sorrows. Some poor soul at the other end of the bar was having a good time with some friends, and I resented it. So I picked up a glass ashtray off the bar and threw it at the guy as hard as I could."

"Did you hit him?"

"Right square in the middle of the forehead. I thought I'd killed him. His forehead split open, and blood went everywhere. By the grace of God, he just ended up with some stitches and a concussion. But he pressed charges against me."

"How did you keep from going to jail?"

"I pleaded no contest to aggravated assault. The judge let me off with probation as long as I went to counseling and stayed out of trouble. Everybody knew what I'd gone through with my wife, so they cut me some slack. That's when I started to heal. If I'd remained angry and bitter, I'd probably have been dead by now."

"So how did you get through it? All I'm feeling right now is rage."

"Forgiveness. I had to ask God to forgive me for my lack of faith. Then I had to forgive the man who took the life of the woman I loved."

"I don't think I'll ever be able to forgive the monster who tortured me."

"None of this makes sense if you don't believe in God. You're angry with God, so you must believe he exists, right?"

"I guess so. But every time I think He's given me something good, he just takes something else away."

"Maybe your perception of God is flawed. God doesn't exist to make us happy. He's our creator, and we exist to worship him. It would be pretty naïve to think we know more than the one who created us. Don't you think?"

"That still doesn't explain why this loving God would allow us to suffer so much pain."

"Maybe God allows us to experience pain and suffering to get our attention, and to make us better people. He wants a close relationship with us, and we tend to ignore him until something bad happens. Then we expect him to rescue us so we can go back to living our lives without him."

Mike's words pierced Jake's heart. He recalled all the times he'd promised God he would spend more time praying and reading the Bible if God would answer his prayers. How many times during the long months of captivity had he begged God to let him return home to his wife? God answered his prayers, albeit not in the manner or timing he would have preferred. In return, he had given God his anger instead of love.

"I'm guilty of crying out to God for help too, like you said, and then ignoring him. But forget about me. Why does he let good people suffer if they're doing all the right things?"

"Sometimes he allows us to suffer so we can be helpful to others when they go through a crisis. It may not be apparent now, but he may be preparing you to help others in a way you haven't considered."

Could this be the answer I'm looking for? Jake asked himself. *Did God allow me to crash into the Laotian jungle to experience some of the pain and suffering the Hmong people had been subjected to for so many years? Has he given me a mandate to use my journalistic skills to tell the world of the atrocities taking place at the hands of the Communists? One thing is certain. God showed me a world I never would have seen had the plane returned successfully to Thailand.*

"Here you go, gentlemen," Marge said as she laid the food on the table. "Can I get anything else for you?"

"I think we're good," Mike said.

After she left, Mike said, "Mind if I say grace?"

"No, go ahead."

Jake bowed his head as Mike prayed, and then the two men made small talk during the rest of the lunchtime. The whole time, Jake's mind was racing as he tried to sort out the feeling of excitement that had come over him. Mike had tapped into something, and he was eager to explore it further.

After finishing the food, Jake said, "Let's say I'm beginning to understand why God allowed me to suffer what I did. If I accept the idea, can I still do what he wants without forgiving the people who tortured me? Can I harness the rage I feel toward them and use it as a motivating force?"

Mike smiled. "It doesn't work that way. And frankly, you'll be miserable unless you let go of that rage you're carrying around. Most people who live with unresolved anger turn to alcohol, drugs, or other unhealthy ways of dealing with their self-destructive emotions."

"So how do I get from here to there? What you're asking seems impossible."

"It is impossible from a human perspective. You can't do it on your own."

"Then what's the answer?"

"Have you ever committed a sin?"

Thoughts of the people he had killed flashed through his mind. "Of course. Hasn't everybody?"

"Yes, everyone who has ever lived has sinned. Because of our sin, we are separated from God, and there is nothing we can do on our own to make things right with him. He sent his son, Jesus, into the world as a sacrifice for our sins so we could have our sins forgiven. From the conversation we've had, it sounds like God has been trying to get your attention so you'll get right with him. That can't happen, however, until you give your life to Jesus."

"How do I do that?"

"Confess your sins to God, and ask him for forgiveness. Then ask Jesus to be your Lord and Savior. All your sins will be forgiven because they've been paid for through the death of Jesus on the cross. But here's the catch. Jesus said if we want God to forgive our sins, we have to forgive those who have sinned against us."

"It doesn't make sense. Scarface, the guy who tortured me for six months, gets to go on torturing people, and I'm just supposed to forget what he did to me?"

"He's still torturing you, Jake. As long as you hold onto your rage, this Scarface is living rent free inside your head. You won't forget what's happened, but you have to forgive him so the torture can end."

Jake looked around the restaurant as he contemplated what Mike had said about forgiveness. Much of the lunch crowd already had left, and the people who remained were absorbed in their own conversations. Mike was not a priest or a pastor, but Jake felt an overwhelming urge to confess to him the thing that he was most ashamed of, the thing that he didn't think God could forgive him for.

Leaning forward with his hands tightly clasped on the table he said, "I killed a young, innocent boy. If I can't even forgive myself, how is God going to forgive me?"

"What happened?"

"After I got shot down in Laos, I was running down a trail in the jungle when someone came toward me carrying an automatic weapon. He was trying to tell me something in a foreign language. Then suddenly he raised his weapon and pointed it in my direction, so I put two bullets in his chest. Things happened so fast I didn't realize how young he was. His face still haunts me."

"It sounds like you did what anyone would do in that situation. It was kill or be killed."

"That's just it. He wasn't trying to kill me. He was trying to save me. I shot the poor kid for trying to save me."

"How can you be sure?"

"After we escaped from the POW camp, I was captured by a Hmong warrior named Lo Chang. Fortunately the Hmong were on our side fighting against the Communists. He and his son were trying to rescue the survivors of my crew after our B-52 got shot down. They had split up to cover more ground and find us before the Communists did. Lo Chang said he heard two gunshots and then found his dead son lying on the trail. The Communists had come up behind me and captured me immediately. We were gone by the time Lo Chang reached the scene. Don't you see? The kid was aiming his rifle at the enemy, and I—I killed him."

"Did you tell this Lo Chang you killed his son?"

"I had to. The guilt was tearing me apart."

"What did he say when you told him?"

"He said it was good that his son died saving an American. And then he helped me get to the base so I could be rescued and brought back here. That's what makes it so painful. I owe Lo Chang my life for saving me and for forgiving me for killing his son."

Mike leaned forward and smiled. "God sent his one and only son into the world to save us, and we killed him two thousand years ago. He would have every right to wipe us all off the face of the earth. Instead, he forgives us and offers us a new life here on earth plus an eternal life with him in heaven one day."

"I'm afraid I'm ignorant when it comes to the Bible."

"Give it time. You've been through a lot. Take some time to pray and ask God to heal you. You seem to be okay physically, but your spirit has been wounded. Jesus is the answer. You'll find him if you look for him."

"Thanks for listening, Mike."

"One thing I want you to do is stop beating yourself up. This Lo Chang has forgiven you, and God is willing to forgive you too. You need to forgive yourself as well. You're human, just like the rest of us. We all make mistakes."

As Jake drove back to the house, Mike's words brought back memories of the dream he had of Captain Morgan coming to him. It couldn't be a coincidence. Captain Morgan had said almost the same words Mike had spoken. "You've been forgiven, Jake. Now you need to learn how to forgive."

CHAPTER TWENTY-ONE

Once he was back home in Dayton, Jake called the Dean of the School of Journalism at Grantham and secured an endorsement from him to be allowed to start senior year classes in the fall semester. Donna talked to a realtor, who secured a three-bedroom house for them to rent close to the campus. They made plans to travel to Grantham as soon as his discharge was completed. Donna would return to work as soon as she had the house fixed up the way she wanted it. Jake's only requirement was no ten-foot deep holes in the backyard.

As they enjoyed a quiet night at home in their apartment, Donna said, "What did you and Mike talk about the other day?"

"Carl said something that upset me, and I had to get Mike's take on it."

"What did Carl say?"

"He said Mike told him everything that happened to me was part of God's plan."

"That sounds like my mother talking. Why would God allow you, allow us, to suffer so much?"

"I think I'm beginning to understand that part. Bad things happen in life to everyone. It's part of living. Both of us know that, and because we do, we can relate to each other in a new, deeper way. In other words, it would be difficult for you and me to help each other and anyone else through a crisis if we'd never experienced one."

"You gave me good advice when my mother was dying. The loss of your father and brother certainly prepared you to help me. But I don't see how your POW experience can benefit anybody."

"A lot of things that happened to me over there I'm not sure I'll ever be able to share with you. But I think you need to hear this story."

She took his hand in hers. "I'm listening."

"I killed a young boy. He couldn't have been more than thirteen or fourteen years old."

"What happened?"

"He was coming toward me down a trail in the jungle as I was trying to get rescued the morning after we got shot down. He was trying to tell me something in his own language. Suddenly he raised his rifle and pointed it right at me, so I shot him twice in the chest."

"He would've killed you. You were just protecting yourself."

"That's what I thought at the time. But the kid was a Hmong soldier trying to save me from the Communists. He was pointing his weapon at the enemy coming up behind me when I killed him."

"How did you find out who he was?"

"After Jim and I escaped from the POW camp, we hid in the jungle. I managed to get myself captured again, but this time it wasn't the Communists who found me. It was a Hmong warrior named Lo Chang."

"Who're these Hmong soldiers?"

"They're a tribal people who've been helping the CIA prevent the Communists from taking over Laos. The Hmong may be the only true friends we have over there."

"So did this Lo Chang know the boy you killed?"

"He heard the shots. He came to the scene after the enemy captured me and took me to the POW camp. He found his son dead there on the trail."

She was silent for a moment as she tried to digest the information he'd shared with her. "How did he know it was his son you killed?"

"That's the most amazing part of the whole story. After he rescued Jim and me, he told us how he and his son had tried to find us before the Communists did. When he described finding his dead son on the trail, I knew what'd happened. I told him I was the one who killed his boy."

"What did he say?"

"He forgave me. He told me it was good that his son died saving an American. That's what's eating me up inside. Lo Chang forgave me for killing his son, and yet I can't forgive the barbarians who tortured me for seven months. Mike said God is willing to forgive me for everything I've done if I forgive others for what they've done to me. I can't even forgive myself right now, let alone others."

"It all seems so senseless. I still don't see how God could use that experience to help anyone."

"As we were making our way to a secret CIA base in the mountains of Laos, I witnessed the Communists slaughter a whole village of Hmong people. They decapitated some of the men and shot the rest. Then they raped the women before killing them too."

"That's horrible."

"Lo Chang said the Hmong have been victimized like that by the Communists since the end of World War II. As I watched the Hmong people, our allies, being butchered, I told myself if I made it home alive, I would use my journalism skills to tell the world about those crimes against humanity. Unless people know about the atrocities, the Communists will continue to kill or imprison all the Hmong, especially now that we're not there to support them."

"So you are saying you now think God wants you to help the Hmong people? Why can't this Lo Chang and other people tell the world what's happening to the Hmong people?"

"Most of the Hmong are illiterate. They're very intelligent and proud people, but most of them have little or no education. Right now the media doesn't know about our country's involvement in the fighting in Laos. Maybe I'm being naïve, but when the news finally breaks, somebody's going to tell the story of these people. I think that someone needs to be me."

"Did Lo Chang ask you to do it?"

"No, he wouldn't do that. He told me to go home and have a lot of children."

"He sounds like a good man. What will become of him?"

"He doesn't have any choice but to keep fighting the Communists. He hasn't seen his wife and daughter in more than a year. They may even be dead by now. I feel like I owe him my life. I could've died so many times over there. God must have kept me alive for a reason."

As Donna listened to his incredible confession, a tremendous desire to share her own sin arose within her. Long-suppressed images of their unborn child, their aborted son, burst out of captivity from deep within her subconscious mind. How good it would feel, she thought, to be free of that dreadful secret once and for all. Surely he would understand.

"I need to confess something to you too." She paused for a moment before saying slowly, "I killed someone too."

Her statement caught him off guard. It was obvious from her demeanor that she wasn't joking, and yet he couldn't believe his wife would purposely hurt anyone. Words escaped him as he waited for her to explain.

"I killed *you*, Jake, and buried you when I lost hope. I'm so ashamed I gave up on you. And then in my grief, I ended up losing our baby. Now a part of me, a part of us, is gone forever. Please forgive me."

"Nothing you could ever do would make me stop loving you," he said as he kissed her. "You scared me for a minute. I knew you weren't capable of murder, but I wasn't sure what you were going to say."

"You'd be surprised how crazy I got when I thought you were out of my life forever. I was capable of more than you can imagine."

The moment had come and gone. She had failed to confess her sin. The wall she'd built inside of her, hiding the truth, was re-sealed. After a long pause, she spoke again, changing the subject.

"I think you should do it. I think you should finish your degree and write about the Hmong and try to help them."

"You are an amazing woman," he said as he kissed her. "There's only one thing you could have said that would've made me happier."

"What's that?"

"Honey, I killed my father."

"Oh, you are so cruel, Jake Lemaster!" she said as she tickled him until he had tears of joy in his eyes.

He felt a renewed sense of freedom after sharing some of his inner thoughts and fears with her. Opening his soul to the light of day had chased away at least a few of the demons plaguing him. His new life was starting to take shape. He was gaining a new perspective on his past with the help of his family. He wasn't ready to forgive Scarface yet, but he was beginning to appreciate that God may not be as hateful or indifferent as he had made him out to be. Maybe there was hope for him after all.

The next day, as Donna and Jake drove up in front of their new home, memories of their freshman year on the Grantham campus came rushing back to him. It was hard to believe they had met in English class just five years before as innocent, young undergrad students. So many unforeseen events had sought to derail their relationship since then. Now, having weathered a few storms, they were ready to enjoy all the promises marriage had to offer.

"It's even more perfect than I'd imagined," Donna said as she viewed the rental home for the first time.

The realtor had said an English professor who was on a one-year sabbatical in Europe owned the house. The two-story wooden structure had been built in the 1930s and just recently remodeled. Jake was surprised to see it was better than advertised. A white picket fence surrounded a well-manicured yard that sported a dozen mature maple and oak trees. The house was painted a light yellow color with white trim. The black doors and window shutters provided a pleasing contrast.

"It's definitely a step up from Grover Hall," Jake said.

She opened the gate in the fence and quickly walked onto the shaded front porch. He knew from their conversation during the drive from Dayton that she was eager to begin organizing her new nest. The house was furnished, so only minor alterations would have to be made to accommodate their needs. Compared to the tiny apartment in Dayton, this house was a mansion.

Mr. Kingston had graciously offered to buy Donna and Jake a house rather than have them rent one. Jake was sure he was still having trouble with the idea of his daughter living in what he would consider a hovel. In reality, however, he would have been equally distressed with his daughter living with him anywhere, even if it were the Taj Mahal or Buckingham Palace. It was something he'd have to deal with. And there was no way he was going to accept charity from Mr. Douglas Kingston. Donna thanked him but said they would not accept his offer.

Within a week, Donna had arranged everything to her satisfaction. Jake could sense she was getting anxious to return to work. She spent more and more time on the phone talking to her father.

He kept busy meeting with his professors and preparing for the first day of class the following week.

The couple quickly settled into a comfortable routine with Donna leaving for work each weekday around 7 a.m. and returning home around 6 p.m. Jake's classes were all bunched together in the middle of the day on Mondays, Wednesdays, and Fridays, leaving him with a lot of time off to study and work on getting into better physical condition. He began jogging a few miles every morning and lifting weights three times a week at the fitness center on campus. His sleep improved dramatically as his body got back in shape. Even the nightmares became less frequent.

Academic achievement had never been his strong suit. Since spending a semester at Scarface University, however, he viewed the opportunity to learn from a whole new perspective. He looked forward to attending classes, and he studied harder than he ever had. While most of his classmates moaned and groaned about how hard their lives were, he felt like he was on permanent vacation in comparison to his time in Laos.

As he left the house to jog early one morning in late September, he saw a black van parked across the street. The sun had not yet come up, so he wasn't able to see if anyone was in the vehicle. After stretching, he began the usual morning jog around the lake on campus. When he returned home thirty minutes later, the sun was shining and the van was no longer in sight.

Someone is watching us. I'm going to have to find out who it is and why.

He took a shower and grabbed some breakfast before gathering up his notebooks and heading to class. The paper he'd just written described the genocide he'd seen taking place in Laos no more than two months before. Although the Watergate scandal dominated the news, he thought the secret war the Hmong were fighting against the Communists in Laos was even more newsworthy. Whether the professor would agree with him remained to be seen.

A week later, on Saturday, October 6, the world was on the brink of a nuclear holocaust while Donna and Jake were enjoying a leisurely day at home with plans to join some friends at the Grantham football game that afternoon. That evening they were shocked to hear on the news that Syria and Egypt, with support from other Arab nations, had launched a surprise attack on Israel on Yom Kippur, the holiest day of the Jewish calendar. It was no secret the Russians were providing arms and technical support to the Arabs as they once again sought to wipe the nation of Israel from the face of the earth. Jake's former B-52 crewmembers still enlisted were on high alert to launch a nuclear strike against the Soviet Union if the war continued to spiral out of control. No threat as extreme as this one had faced the world since the Cuban Missile Crisis more than a decade before.

Ten days later, the oil-producing countries in the Middle East unexpectedly raised the price of oil by nearly 20 percent and began cutting the production and export of oil to the United States. Panic set in as gas stations quickly ran out of gas to sell to their customers. Long lines of cars formed at the gas pumps, and angry and frightened people tried to keep their vehicles operating so they could maintain the necessary activities of their lives.

Donna decided to stay at a hotel near her office during the two-week period while the oil embargo was going on. Although Jake worried about her, he felt better knowing she wasn't out on the highway looking for gas, as reports of violence at gas stations were hitting the news. Talk of gas rationing and price controls fueled the anxiety spreading through the country like a plague. A commodity that'd always been taken for granted suddenly had become much more expensive and scarce.

To Jake's chagrin, the Vietnam War had become a relic of the past, one no one wanted to reexamine. The paper he wrote about the plight of the Hmong had failed to resonate with his journalism professor. He told Jake the report was structurally sound, but it failed to capture his imagination the way an article about current events such as Watergate or the Arab-Israeli conflict would.

Jake learned a valuable lesson from that demoralizing experience. Apparently the American psyche was so wounded by the decade-long Indochina war that any further examination of the subject at the time was too painful to endure. The Hmong, who'd recently been abandoned by the American government, would have to continue to fight for their lives in anonymity for a while longer.

One evening in mid-October, he returned home from a workout at the fitness center after dark. Donna was still staying in St. Louis throughout the workweek, so he had plenty of time to himself. As he walked onto the front porch, once again he saw a black van, this time parked across the street a half block away. Something about that van made the hair on the back of his neck stand up.

As he unlocked the front door, he felt a strong urge to grab the AK-47 from the bedroom closet and see who was out there. Once inside the house, he entered the closet and pulled down on the string to turn on the bare overhead light bulb. The AK-47 was gone. Frantically he rummaged through the closet and then the bedroom, but there was no trace of his automatic weapon. Donna hated the rifle, so he was sure she hadn't touched it. *Someone must have broken in and stolen it. But how?*

As he walked into the living room, he had the sickening feeling he wasn't alone. From a chair in the corner, he heard a gruff voice. "This is a mighty fine weapon you've got here, Sergeant."

His heart was slamming his chest as he heard the intruder chamber a round. He tried quickly to assess the unexpected threat.

Someone who knew him was now in possession of the assault rifle, and the intruder's eyes had apparently adapted to the darkness of the room. He hadn't attacked him despite the advantage he held, so he must not be a thief. *What could he want from me?*

Suddenly the lamp next to the chair came on, revealing a well-built, middle-aged man with a crew cut, wearing a black leather jacket and a pair of thin black gloves. The stern-faced stranger was holding the AK-47 across his lap.

"You've got to hand it to the Commies," he said. "This is the best assault rifle ever made."

"I'm glad you like it," Jake said. "Now would you mind telling me who you are and what you're doing in my house?"

"The M-16 that I carried in 'Nam would jam if I urinated within ten feet of it. But you could carry the AK-47 in the rain all day, drop it in the mud, and it would just keep right on firing."

"Who did you say you're working for?"

"Relax. We're on the same side here."

"And which side is that?"

"We have a mutual acquaintance who asked me to check up on you."

"I'm touched," Jake said sarcastically. "Who's this friend of ours?"

"Cowboy. He warned me you were full of spit and vinegar. I guess that's what kept you alive for seven months in a Laotian POW camp."

"Cowboy? You know Colonel Watson?"

"Mark and I have been working for the same company for the past few years," the man said as he cleared the round in the chamber of the AK-47, ejected the ammo magazine, and handed the rifle to Jake.

"So you're with the CIA?"

"Let's just say I'm an independent contractor hired by the government to keep our country safe," he said as he lit up a cigarette.

"I was a member of an elite Special Forces long-range reconnaissance unit before Cowboy recruited me."

"I'm out of the military now. What do you want from me?"

"You made quite an impression on Cowboy. He has a great eye for talent, and he thinks you'd make a good Company man."

"I've heard that line before. I think it's the same one that snagged Cowboy. I'm afraid you've got the wrong guy this time. I'm planning to finish my degree in journalism, get a job, and enjoy some time with my wife."

"That's exactly what we want you to do. Go to school and keep writing those papers about the Hmong nobody will ever pay any attention to."

"How'd you know what I wrote?"

"It's a shame what's happening. Tens of thousands of Hmong have given their lives to help America fight the Communists over the last decade, and now we're just going to turn our backs on them."

"What are you trying to tell me? You just said nobody is going to pay any attention to what I write."

"There're other ways you can help. We can use journalism as a legitimate cover so you can gather more useful information. Maybe you'll even get a chance to get your hands dirty. I hear you're looking to even the score with some madman over there."

Images of the massacre of the Hmong village flooded Jake's mind as he contemplated the offer. He couldn't give up trying to help the Hmong just because one college professor wasn't interested in what he'd written. And what about Lo Chang? He owed Lo Chang his life. As for Scarface, getting revenge on him somehow would be an added bonus.

"What kind of information are you looking for?"

"Now that we've pulled out of South Vietnam and Laos, the North Vietnamese are planning to stage a massive invasion of both countries. When they do, the Hmong will be exterminated. The

Communists will kill them or put them in concentration camps. We've even heard the Soviets may use chemical weapons on the ones that won't surrender."

"Can't you get the Hmong out of Laos before it happens?"

"We're working on setting up some refugee camps in northern Thailand. But it's a logistical nightmare getting a hundred thousand people from the mountains of Laos to the camps across the Mekong River. And, oh by the way, the Thais are not too excited about the idea. That's where you can help us."

"I don't follow."

"When the Communists start their invasion, we'll need someone to let the world know what's taking place. Your objective reporting, with our help, of course, can rally the international community to stop the genocide and aid the Hmong."

"Why me? I'm not a spook."

"Mark seems to think you're up to the challenge."

"How would it work?"

"Let us take care of the details. When the time comes, we'll get you a job as a freelance journalist with a reputable organization that will dispatch you to Thailand to cover the unfolding story. Cowboy will be your contact on the ground over there. We'll provide you with everything you need."

"What am I supposed to tell my wife?"

"Tell her anything but the truth. Tell her you've been offered the chance of a lifetime to help a noble group of people who saved your butt. That's something she'll be able to understand."

"If I agree to do this, it'll be a one-time commitment."

"The world is full of crises. The Communists are taking over Indochina, and the Middle East is coming apart at the seams. The Arabs finally have discovered how to use oil as a weapon against us, and they'll be blackmailing us with it for the next fifty years. There's another story for you. I guarantee you'll never run out of things to write about if you work for the Company."

"Right. I'm sure the CIA is going to let me write my own material."

"Well, there may be some editing before it gets published."

"That's a nice way of saying the CIA will censor my material to meet their own needs. No thanks. I'm done after I help the Hmong."

"No problem. Let's just focus on the task at hand. I'll keep you informed of how things are unfolding in Laos. Until then, just enjoy that adorable CEO wife of yours and keep a low profile."

"Give my regards to Cowboy. Ask him if Lo Chang ever found his wife and daughter and let me know what he says. He'll know what I'm talking about."

"I'll do that," he said as he rose from the chair and began walking toward the front door. "You have a lot going for you. A war hero with a rich wife can do about anything he puts his mind to. Just wait until the press hears your story. You'll be famous. With the right backing, you might even have a career in politics. How does Senator Lemaster sound?"

"You guys are really something. You break into my house, con me into working for the CIA, and then promise me a future in the U.S. Senate. What else do you have to offer?"

"A chance to make a difference in this stinking world. Trust me, you'll never be satisfied writing a gossip column for some two-bit newspaper that only a few people ever read. And I can't see you staying at home baking cookies while your wife runs one of the biggest pharmaceutical corporations in the world. So, you do the math. I think you'll see the Company is where you're meant to be."

"Thanks for the advice, mister. What did you say your name was?"

"Cobra," he said. "You can just call me Cobra."

A chill ran down Jake's spine as he watched the CIA agent slither out into the darkness and drive away in the black van. The last cobra he'd encountered nearly took his life. This man's keen analysis of his inner workings now pierced him like the sharp fangs of a deadly viper. It wounded him to admit the man was right. When he weighed all his options, he could see the truth. He really had no other choice.

CHAPTER TWENTY-TWO

A few months before graduation, Jake started getting anxious about what he was going to do next if Cobra didn't show up soon. Donna was already pressing him to start applying for jobs at the major newspapers in the St. Louis area. To appease her, he did send out résumés to several organizations locally. Deep down inside, however, he was hoping an overseas assignment was in his future.

Donna surprised him with the perfect graduation gift—tickets to a Cubs game at Wrigley Field. She was planning to take him to Chicago the first weekend in May when the Cubs were scheduled to host the Cincinnati Reds on a Friday afternoon. The baseball season was young, and the Cubs, at least in theory, still had a chance to win the World Series. It would be an ideal getaway weekend.

On a Monday morning in late April, shortly after Donna left the house for work, he went out for his usual run. Classes were over, so he had the whole day to relax and enjoy a good workout. The stillness of the cool morning air felt refreshing as he jogged the first quarter mile down Cherry Street toward the campus lake. Suddenly he heard a vehicle coming up quickly from behind. When he turned around, he saw a black van no more than ten feet away and closing fast. He jumped to the side of the road as Cobra pulled up alongside and swung open the passenger door.

"Get in," he said.

"What took you so long?"

Cobra took a small package from the glove box and handed it to Jake. "Congratulations on your upcoming graduation."

He opened the plain brown wrapping paper and examined its contents. On top was a plastic I.D. card with his picture on it. The card identified him as an international reporter with Global Correspondents Incorporated. The second item was an American passport with a photo of him taken just before he had gone to Southeast Asia. The last item was an open-ended, round trip airline ticket between Washington, D.C., and St. Louis.

"Have you talked to Cowboy?"

"He said he could use your help now that you're properly educated."

"I've never heard of Global Correspondents Incorporated. My wife's not stupid. She'll want to know whom I'm working for. Is this a legitimate company?"

"Of course. It employs a number of freelance journalists like you."

"So whom do I report to?"

"Here in the States, you deal only with me. When you get to Southeast Asia, you deal only with Cowboy. The less you know, the better, just in case anything goes wrong, if you know what I mean."

Jake knew exactly what he meant.

"We need to have you come to headquarters before you go overseas."

"When do I need to be there?"

"The sooner the better. The situation in Laos is deteriorating."

"I'm supposed to be a journalist. My cover will only be believable if my work is printed in newspapers."

"Leave the details to me. You write about whatever you want, and send the articles to me. I'll see they get printed. Just give me a call when you book your flight, and I'll meet you at the airport in D.C."

Cobra stopped the van near the campus lake. Jake felt the urge to ask him one more thing—if he could whack his father-in-law as a favor. Instead he just said, "You got it, boss."

"Keep this meeting to yourself. You're in the big leagues now."

Later that day, the mailman delivered a letter from Global Correspondents Incorporated just as Cobra had promised. The invitation for a job interview looked very official, and it said a former military colleague had recommended Jake for the position. He hid the fake credentials and airline tickets so Donna would not become suspicious. She had encouraged him to seek a career in journalism and to write about the plight of the Hmong. She would not be pleased, however, to learn the new job required a return to the place that had been the source of so much pain and suffering for both of them.

Donna pulled into the driveway just after 6 p.m. He gave her a hug and a kiss as she entered the front door.

"Something smells good. What did you make for supper?"

"There was an old raccoon in the back yard today. It grilled up real well. I think you're going to like it."

"Very funny. It looks like pork chops to me."

"Yeah, but it tastes like chicken."

"You're in a good mood today," she said as they sat down to eat.

"I got a job offer."

"That's great. Who's it with?"

"Global Correspondents Incorporated. They're based in Washington, D.C. They cover the international scene. Perfect for me after all that happened to me over there in Southeast Asia."

"I've never heard of them before. What do you know about them?"

He handed her the letter and allowed her time to read it before answering.

"They employ freelance journalists. I get to write what I want and submit it to the office, and they'll get it printed in newspapers around the world."

"That sounds good. I'm not so sure I like the global part though. It sounds like travel may be involved."

"I'll find out when I go there for an interview. Maybe I can book a flight next week after we get back from Chicago."

"I was hoping you'd say the *St. Louis Post-Dispatch* had offered you a position. Now that you're done with college, we need to find a place to live closer to the city. I'm getting tired of the long commute, and we're spending a fortune on gas."

The young couple always found discussions about finances rather difficult. Jake's pride frequently got in the way, as he was uncomfortable using Donna's money to live on. She had offered to buy a house in the St. Louis area using some of the money she'd inherited from her mother. Maybe it was time he swallowed his pride.

"You're right. You deserve a new house near the city. I'll live wherever you want as long as it's not with your father."

"Are you serious?"

"Absolutely. I want you to be happy. And I can work anywhere."

"I'll have a realtor start looking tomorrow."

"What do you think about seeing Jim and Lisa Sizemore while we're in Chicago this weekend? I have not been in touch very much with him since our return from Thailand. Maybe we could get together if they're available."

"That's a great idea. Why don't you give him a call while I clean up the dishes."

Before talking with his old lieutenant buddy on the phone, he turned on the nineteen-inch color TV set in the living room. President Nixon was scheduled to give a televised address to the nation that night to explain the release of edited transcripts of the secret White House tapes. Congress already had started drafting articles of impeachment against him, so the Nixon administration was in full damage control mode. Donna came in from the kitchen to catch the end of the news.

"Do you think he'll survive this Watergate scandal?" she asked.

"I find it hard to believe he didn't know what his people were doing. And if he didn't know, it's even worse news."

Jake made the call. Jim was surprised to hear from him and excited to know his friend would be in Chicago in a few days. He was teaching math at a local high school while Lisa taught fifth grade at an elementary school in the Naperville area. The big news was that his wife was seven months pregnant. It would be their first child. They had no special plans for the weekend, so Jake and Donna arranged to stay with them Friday night after the Cubs game.

"Something like this would be nice for us," Donna said as they parked the car in front of Jim's house.

Jim and Lisa's home was located in a new subdivision in the suburb of Naperville, thirty miles southwest of Chicago. The small farming community of only ten thousand residents in 1960 had seen its population triple in the previous fourteen years as Chicagoans flocked to the suburbs to escape the city. Since Jim and Lisa had both grown up in nearby Downers Grove, they had a lot of family close to their home. Relatives would come in handy when their new baby was born, as Lisa was planning to continue teaching.

"I could definitely live here," Jake said.

The two-story brick home sat on a nicely landscaped, one-acre lot. With over 3,300 square feet and four bedrooms, it had plenty of room for Jim and Lisa to grow their family.

"Hello, Jake," Jim said as he greeted him at the door. "It's good to see you again."

"You've done well for yourself, professor," Jake said as he gave Jim a hug.

"Hello, Donna," Jim said. He embraced her and then ushered them both into the house.

"Where's the expectant mother?" Donna asked.

"Lisa's in the kitchen working on dinner. She had a parent-teacher conference after school today, so she's running a little behind."

"I'll give her a hand while you boys catch up."

"So you were a part of a historic event today," Jim said to Jake.

"How's that?"

"The Cubs won a baseball game. That doesn't happen very often."

"Very funny. Your White Sox aren't exactly tearing up the league either. The last time I looked, they had a losing record too."

"Can I get you a beer?"

"I thought you'd never ask."

Jim pulled two cans of Budweiser from the refrigerator and then offered to show Jake around the house. They talked about all that had happened since they had gotten back to the States nearly a year before. Jim seemed to be quite content with his new life as a teacher and a soon-to-be father. His decision to leave the military and return to the Chicago area had certainly made Lisa happy.

"So what're you going to do now that you've finished college?" he asked.

"I've sent out my résumé to several newspapers in the St. Louis area, and I've had some job offers. I'll probably make a decision in the next few weeks. Donna's anxious to move closer to St. Louis where she works. So we'll probably be moving there soon."

After seeing the house, Jim led Jake through the garage to a level driveway complete with a regulation height basketball goal. "Are you ready to get your butt kicked, Sergeant?" he said with a cocky grin.

"You've gotten old and fat since we last did this. I don't want you to get hurt."

Jim grabbed a basketball and threw it at Jake as he said, "Bring it on, baby. Bring it on."

Jim was carrying two hundred pounds on his six-foot frame and did not appear to be in good physical condition. The workout regimen Jake had faithfully adhered to the past year gave him a decided advantage in the game of one-on-one. Nonetheless, Jim's competitive spirit kept the bruising contest close. Jake finally prevailed by a score of 15- 12 after a hard-fought game. Fortunately neither man broke any bones or lost any teeth.

"Consider that your graduation present," Jim said as they each grabbed another beer and headed outside. "I let you win that one."

"You always were a dreamer."

Jim took a swig and then asked, "Do you ever have problems sleeping? I mean, like nightmares, ones where you wake up in a sweat and don't know where you are? I do all the time. I can't seem to shake it."

It was the first time Jim had brought up anything related to their dreadful past. The seriousness in his voice told Jake he was having some trouble he needed to share.

"Yeah, I know what you mean. The dreams are not as frequent now, but they're still just as creepy. Sometimes I think I need to see a shrink and get help for them."

"That might not be a bad idea. I'm afraid I'm going to hurt Lisa. One night I woke up from a nightmare, and I was choking her. It scared her half to death. In my dream, I had my hands around Scarface's throat. No matter how hard I squeezed, he just looked at me with those evil eyes and smiled."

Jake took a long drink of beer. "I've been told I'm supposed to forgive that devil for everything he did to us. Can you believe that? I just don't see how I'll ever get that done."

"Lisa has begged me to see a psychiatrist. I think she's worried I might hurt the baby or something. I'm probably drinking too much beer too. But it helps me get to sleep."

"I've been running and lifting weights to deal with the stress. It seems to take the edge off. If I miss more than a day though, I'm a basket case."

"Maybe I just need to get off my butt and start working out. I can't let you beat me again. The next time you see me, I'll be in better shape."

Lisa came outside. "Time to eat, boys. I hope you're hungry."

After dinner the conversation turned to hopes and plans for the future. Jim and Lisa said they were settled into a routine that would carry them through the next thirty years as schoolteachers. Donna said she was fulfilling her dream of becoming a CEO for Blanford Pharmaceuticals. Jake was silent.

What will my future look like? Jake thought. *Best not to mention Cowboy, Cobra, or the CIA.*

CHAPTER TWENTY-THREE

As the American Airlines jet descended over the nation's capital for a landing at Washington National Airport, it was difficult for Jake to imagine the magnificent piece of real estate below once was an uninhabitable swamp just two hundred years before. From his vantage point, he could see the beautiful white marble of the Lincoln Memorial with its reflecting pool pointing eastward toward the Washington Monument. The world's tallest obelisk was built to commemorate George Washington, the commander in chief of the Continental Army, and the first president of the United States. Just a half mile to the north stood the White House, where the thirty-seventh president, Richard Nixon, temporarily resided. It was a safe bet there would be no monument built to immortalize his achievements while serving as leader of the free world.

Cobra was waiting for him at the airport when he arrived. The CIA agent was seated in the terminal reading a copy of the *Washington Post* as he approached. The front-page headline read, "Formal Hearings Begin on Nixon Impeachment."

"What's in the sports section?" Jake said.

"The only sport in this town is dirty politics. Let's get out of here."

He led Jake out to the curb, where he'd parked the familiar black van in a spot reserved for government vehicles. As Cobra drove, he told Jake the House Judiciary Committee was beginning hearings to draft articles of impeachment for President Nixon. Apparently the CIA was under scrutiny as well because Nixon had used the Agency to pressure the FBI to slow their investigation into the Watergate scandal.

"How will Nixon's problems affect the CIA?"

"We're getting hit from all sides right now. Congress and the press are attacking us for our involvement in covert ops against antiwar protesters a few years ago. They're even rehashing the Bay of Pigs fiasco that took place in 1961. And we're being implicated in this Watergate mess too. I miss the good old days when I was just a field agent matching wits with the Russians and the East Germans. At least I knew who my enemies were."

After a short drive, they passed a security gate marking the entrance to the CIA Headquarters in Langley, Virginia. Cobra parked the van in a numbered spot and motioned for Jake to follow him as he exited the vehicle.

"We need to get you processed before you officially start working for the Agency."

As they walked up to the front of the massive building, Jake stopped to read an inscription carved into the stone wall. It said, "And Ye Shall Know the Truth and the Truth Shall Make You Free, John 8:32."

"Allen Dulles was the Director of the CIA when this building opened," Cobra said. "He was the son of a Presbyterian minister."

Jake was struck by the irony of what Cobra had told him about the CIA being investigated for illegal activities. The truth would indeed set someone free. In that case, however, it was the American people who would benefit from the curtailment of some of the oppressive acts of its own government.

Jake spent the rest of the day prepping for his upcoming clandestine activities with the Agency. Since he previously had held top secret clearance as a B-52 crewmember in the Air Force, the government had a large file on him already. Now they wanted to make sure his time spent in captivity with the Communists in Laos had not turned him into a double agent. He passed a polygraph test and endured several intense interviews that seemed to satisfy the concerns of the Agency as to his loyalties to the United States of America. At the end of the day, which included signing a new oath of secrecy, he was a bit disappointed when he didn't receive a secret decoder ring.

"What have you heard from Cowboy?" he asked Cobra at one point.

"He's in northern Thailand now, setting up a refugee camp at a place called Nam Phong. The Pathet Lao are just across the Mekong River in Vientiane, the Laotian capital, where they're stirring up anti-American protests, so we've pulled all of our people out of the country. Cowboy's just waiting for the invasion. When it comes, he'll have a flood of refugees to deal with."

"What happens after I finish here?"

"We want you to hang around Washington for a while and write articles about current events. We need to build your cover as a journalist before we put you in the field. Besides, it will be a chance of a lifetime for you to write what's going on here. Nixon's presidency won't survive the summer."

"I need to call home and tell my wife I'm now officially an employee of Global Correspondents. She isn't thrilled with the idea of me being gone a lot."

"Tell her we're going to put you to work covering Watergate. That should make her happy."

When he called Donna later that evening, she wasn't exactly pleased with the news. She was, however, excited to hear he would be covering the most newsworthy topic of the last few years. He told her he would call her in a day or two to let her know when he would return home.

In the meantime, Donna found a beautiful brick home in a quaint neighborhood of Clayton that captured her heart. It was an older, four-bedroom home that had been recently remodeled. In early June, they moved into the suburb just a few miles west of downtown St. Louis.

Jake spent the summer months flying to Washington, D.C., every Monday and returning to St. Louis every Friday. With the help of some leaked information from Cobra, he was able to break a story or two before the rest of the media. The early success and a bit of recognition appeased Donna and simultaneously built his cover.

On July 24, 1974, the Supreme Court ordered President Nixon to turn over all secret White House tapes to Special Prosecutor Leon Jaworski. Nixon complied with the request on July 30, two days after the House Judiciary Committee passed the first of three articles of impeachment, charging him with obstruction of justice. With no political support left in Congress, he had no choice but to become the first U.S. president to resign from office. On Thursday, August 8, he addressed the nation from the Oval Office at 9:01 p.m. His speech was broadcast live on radio and television. The next day he was gone.

Vice President Gerald Ford became the 38th president of the United States just before noon on August 9. He had been an All-American football player in college at the University of Michigan, so Jake enjoyed writing several articles about his life before he entered the political arena. By all accounts, he seemed to be an honorable man thrust into the leadership role of the country at an extremely difficult time. His integrity came into question, however, when he granted former President Nixon an unconditional pardon on September 8, just one month after his resignation.

The following weekend, Donna suggested she and Jake go for a walk in Shaw Park near their home to enjoy the gorgeous late summer weather. The deep blue sky on Saturday afternoon was graced with swirls of wispy white clouds that glowed in the sun like iridescent raiment fit for an angel. The majestic trees towering overhead still retained their full complement of leaves, barely beginning to turn colors. Just as the cool breeze rustling through the trees hinted at the change of seasons to come, Jake sensed something in Donna's temperament hinting at an upcoming change in their lives.

"It's nice to have you home with me," she said as they walked along holding hands. "It seems like you're gone all the time since you took that job in Washington."

"It won't last forever. I'm building up a résumé that should get me a better job closer to home in the future. The exposure I've gotten because of the Watergate scandal has already started to pay dividends."

"I wish you'd talk to the editor at the *St. Louis Post-Dispatch*. He's an old friend of my father's."

"I don't want any charity from your father. I can get a good job on my own merit. Besides, now is the time for me to be paying my dues and traveling before we have a family."

"You're just as stubborn as he is. I'm tired of coming home to an empty house every night. Something has to change."

The urgency in her words made him stop. He led her to a picnic table isolated among the trees a good distance from the path.

"Let's sit down and talk. I know I've been gone a lot. I just assumed you were keeping busy with your job too. What's got you so upset?"

"I'm pregnant," she said as her eyes filled with tears.

A mixture of competing emotions swept over him as he looked intently at his wife's face. The normally joyous announcement was fraught with anxiety as they both tried to come to grips with the implications of the new status.

"That's great," he said as he kissed her and held her close. "When did you find out?"

"I went to the doctor Wednesday. He told me I was about six weeks pregnant."

"You don't seem very happy. Are you worried about having another miscarriage?"

"I'm worried about everything. My mother had a number of miscarriages that essentially ruined her marriage. I don't want that to happen to us."

"We're going to grow old and gray together, whether we have ten kids or none. We've been through too much to let anything else in life tear us apart."

"I feel like I'm caught between two completely different worlds, and I don't know how I'm going to reconcile them. I thoroughly enjoy my life in the business world when I'm at work. But seeing all our friends with babies has filled me with a desire to be a mother too. And I thought if I were pregnant, you would be eager to be at home with me more."

"We can get someone to help with the baby if you want to keep working after the pregnancy is over. I promise I'll be there for you and do whatever I can to support you. If necessary, I'll just quit and find another job."

"I'm sorry for being so sad at a time when we should be happy, but I felt so alone the first time I was pregnant. I think I'm also afraid I'm not going to be a good mother."

"You're going to be a great mother."

"Will you go with me to my next doctor's appointment? I want you to meet the obstetrician."

"Absolutely. Just let me know when it is, and I'll be there with you."

"I love you," she said as she hugged him tightly. "Don't ever forget that."

On the morning of September 17, 1974, Jake was sent in by the CIA to cover a meeting of the Senate Foreign Relations Committee in which a resolution was introduced to establish a Select Committee on Intelligence Policy. It seemed there was great concern that the CIA had interfered in foreign elections and had negatively affected U.S. foreign policy. A number of senators were pushing for intensive congressional oversight of the CIA in order to preserve democracy. In short, the Agency was taking flak again.

As Cobra entered the chamber, Jake assumed he was there to hear what the Agency would be up against in Congress. Normally he just read Jake's articles and submitted them to one or more of the local newspapers. But there seemed to be an added sense of urgency to his gait that morning. He sat down beside Jake and whispered into his ear.

"Janie, your wife's secretary, just called and said she needs to speak with you right away."

"Did she say what it was about?"

"She just said it was important. You can use the phone in the press office across the hall."

Jake hurried out of the chambers and entered the small office reserved for members of the press. It was empty. He quickly dialed Donna's office phone number. As he waited for someone to answer, he tried to convince himself whatever was going on was not a crisis. Instincts, however, told him something different.

"Blanford Pharmaceuticals, Ms. Kingston's office," Janie said.

"Janie, this is Donna's husband. Were you trying to reach me?"

"Yes, sir. Ms. Kingston asked me to call you and tell you to come home right away."

"Where is she? What's wrong?"

"She started bleeding when she arrived at the office a little while ago. Her father took her to Barnes Hospital. I think she may be having a miscarriage."

"My God," Jake said as his worst fears were realized. It couldn't be happening twice. "I'm heading to the airport now."

Cobra was waiting for him in the hall. "What's going on?"

"My wife's having a miscarriage. I need to get home."

"Let me make a call," Cobra said as he pulled Jack back into the pressroom and picked up the phone.

Jake listened as Cobra explained the situation to someone at CIA headquarters. Meanwhile, he was beating himself up for not being by Donna's side. He was also more than a little angry with God for allowing yet another painful crisis to burden their lives.

"Come on," Cobra said as he hung up the phone. "We'll get you home quicker with an Agency plane."

As they drove to the airport, Jake told Cobra about Donna's previous miscarriage and her recent announcement that she was pregnant. Cobra listened patiently while he shared with him his feelings of guilt about not being there for her.

After a lengthy period of silence, Cobra said, "Maybe it's for the best."

"What's that supposed to mean?"

"Better it happen now than when you're in Southeast Asia."

He was right, of course. Jake had wondered how he was going to finesse a trip to Thailand and get back home before the baby was born. Much like Donna, he was trying to navigate two parallel worlds and not doing justice to either. It seemed unseen forces beyond their control were driving their lives off a cliff.

One of the Agency's Lear jets was waiting on the tarmac of the airport when they arrived. Two pilots in civilian clothes were cranking up the engines as Cobra brought the van to a halt by the open passenger door.

"Take whatever time you need," he said. "Just give me a call and let me know how things are going."

"Thanks," Jake said as he jumped out of the van and scrambled into the plane.

The Lear was airborne within minutes, he was left to contemplate what he would find when he arrived in St. Louis in less than two hours. He wasn't looking forward to seeing Douglas Kingston, especially under the circumstances. Although he knew miscarriages were a common occurrence, he couldn't help but worry that Donna had somehow inherited a problem from her mother that would prevent her from ever having children. If it were true, how would it affect their marriage? He found himself praying to God to take care of Donna and to help him understand why this crisis was happening.

As he prayed, he tried to see the "big picture" his stepdad Mike had talked about. If God wanted him to help the Hmong, he would have to prepare him to serve and clear a path for him to get to Southeast Asia soon. Cobra basically had said the same thing, albeit much less eloquently. Mike didn't say it would be easy. He said to trust God to provide everything needed to do his will. Right now, Jake was powerless to do much else.

When the plane finally touched down in St. Louis, he called Janie from a pay phone in the airport to see if she had any new information about Donna's condition. She told him Donna had been treated and released from the hospital and was now on her way home. Mr. Kingston had told her to tell him when he called that Donna did indeed suffer another miscarriage.

When he arrived home, Mr. Kingston's Mercedes was the only car parked in the driveway. He quickly parked the Mustang and ran into the house. Donna's father was waiting for him in the living room.

"Where's Donna? Is she okay?"

"She'll survive, no thanks to you."

Jake ran past him and headed upstairs to the bedroom. There was no point in causing a confrontation now. All he wanted to do was make sure she was all right. To his dismay, she was in bed sobbing when he entered.

"I'm so sorry," she said as he held her and gave her a kiss.

"It's okay. What happened, honey?"

"I started cramping this morning on my way to work. By the time I arrived at the office, I was bleeding heavily. Janie called my father, and he took me to the Emergency Room. The doctor examined me and said I'd lost the baby."

"It's not your fault. I'm sorry I wasn't home to take care of you. How do you feel?"

"I'm a little tired, but I'll be fine. The cramps are gone, and the bleeding has slowed down."

From the bedroom, he could hear the front door close. A moment later, Mr. Kingston's car started. Guilt wracked his senses. Twice now he had failed to be there to take care of Donna when she'd needed him most.

"I suppose I should have thanked your father for taking care of you."

"It would mean a lot to me if you would. The constant tension between you two is driving me crazy."

The thought of apologizing to that smug man made him nauseated.

He's probably gloating over his good fortune to be there for his daughter again in her time of crisis while I was away. He may already have tried to use it to drive a wedge between Donna and me. In her weakened state, she was no match for her father's cunning. It was time to give him a call.

"All right. I'll do it for you. Do you need anything?"

"Just some sleep. They gave me a sedative at the hospital and those pills to take."

The label on the small brown medicine bottle she pointed to told him she had been prescribed Valium. He handed her a pill and a glass of water.

"Take one of these. It'll help you sleep."

She swallowed the pill and laid her head back on the pillow. He kissed her on the forehead as she closed her eyes. She looked fragile lying there under the covers like a child awakened from a bad dream.

How quickly the tragedies of life can humble a person, he thought, *whether that person is a CEO of a major corporation or a gas station attendant. No question about it. Life is not fair.*

CHAPTER TWENTY-FOUR

One thing the instructors at survival school had stressed to Jake was to trust your instincts. When things around you just didn't seem quite right, trust your gut feelings rather than rely on what your senses told you. Emotions often clouded one's vision, like a dense fog rolling in off the ocean, and blinded you to the perils that lay ahead. It's where Jake found himself at the moment. The fog had silently enveloped him, leaving him no choice but to continue down the path he was on.

Fueled by pangs of guilt, he called Donna's father to thank him for taking care of her in his absence. Mr. Kingston was much more gracious than expected, especially considering his comment to Jake a few hours before. He caught Jake off guard when he asked him to come over to the house so they could bury the hatchet. In Jake's zeal to appease his wife, he accepted the invitation.

Maybe God will use the crisis to bring about something good for all of us, he thought. *Then again, maybe Mr. Kingston intends to bury the hatchet in me.*

As he drove up the lane to the Kingston mansion, he felt the hair on the back of his neck stand up. The last time he'd had that feeling was when his home had been infiltrated by the menacing presence of man called Cobra. This time Jake felt himself being drawn into the lair of a deadly serpent, an evil man with the character to deceive and the power to destroy. Douglas Kingston didn't play by the rules of civilized people. He made the rules.

"Ah, hello," Mr. Kingston said as he answered the door. "I wasn't sure you'd show up."

There was the opening salvo in the barrage of lies to come. Everything that man did was meticulously calculated, leaving nothing to chance. He knew Jake was obligated to accept his invitation as a favor to Donna and as a show of respect for his help. Refusing would've been perceived as an act of cowardice. Despite Jake's loathing for the man, Mr. Kingston had left him no choice but to meet with him face-to-face, and on his terms.

"I want to thank you for taking care of Donna," Jake said as he stepped through the door and into the main hallway.

"What did you expect?" he said as Jake followed him into his study.

Jake watched him go to the wet bar and pour whisky into two glasses. Walking toward Jake, he extended one to his guest as he said, "As a loving father, I couldn't turn my back on my daughter when she needed help, especially with you out running around God knows where."

For a second, Jake had a flashback to the time when Scarface had tried to entice him to sign a confession with promises of cigarettes or a drink of water. He wasn't going to allow Mr. Kingston to gain the upper hand in the interrogation by tempting him with alcohol.

"None for me, thanks. Actually I was covering a Senate Foreign Relations Committee meeting when I received Janie's call."

As he set one of the glasses down next to Jake, Mr. Kingston chose another angle, saying, "I don't understand you. Why would you take a job that requires you to be away from your beautiful wife? It's almost like you're living a—a double life."

Although the man had access to a wealth of information through his network of contacts, he couldn't possibly know about Jake's involvement with the CIA.

"I'm paying my dues working for Global Correspondents so I can land a good job locally after I build my résumé."

"Let me help you, for Donna's sake if not for yours. I can get you on at the *Post-Dispatch* with one phone call."

"I appreciate the offer, but I'll make my own breaks."

"What is it the Bible says, 'Pride goes before destruction, a haughty spirit before a fall'? Your pride is hurting my daughter, and I won't stand by and watch her suffer. I've had to clean up the messes you've made twice, and I don't like it."

"You know my job had nothing to do with Donna's miscarriage. I could just as easily have been at work in St. Louis and the outcome would still have been the same."

"Donna needs you at home. Frankly I don't know what she sees in you. But somehow you've managed to turn a strong-willed, independent woman into a sniveling little girl who depends on you for her happiness. I'm prepared to offer you a job at Blanford Pharmaceuticals. You'll be handsomely paid for directing our public relations department. And you can be home every night with your wife. You won't find a better offer than that."

"I'm not for sale. You can't buy me off."

"Every man has his price. What's yours?"

"Careful now. Remember, I'm a reporter. I may quote you on that."

"Don't get smart with me, you arrogant little weasel!" he hissed as his eyes burned with hatred. "I'll have you covering dogsled races at the North Pole before you know what hit you."

Another flashback struck Jake. He recalled how Scarface had lashed out at him in a fury of rage when he'd refused to follow commands.

It's always just a matter of time before the self-declared good guy reveals his true nature and morphs into a demonic creature right before your eyes.

"I think it's time for me to go," Jake said as he rose from the chair to leave. "I came here to thank you for helping Donna through her two miscarriages, and I've done it."

"Two miscarriages? Is that what she told you? Oh, dear. You poor naïve boy."

"What're you talking about?"

Mr. Kingston's face displayed a self-satisfied smirk as Jake acknowledged the wound he'd inflicted. With premeditated precision, his words had sliced his son-in-law like the razor sharp blade of a sword. Jake watched him slowly walk to the bar and refill his drink while he left his prey to ponder what he would say next.

"I suppose Donna was trying to protect you by hiding the truth," he said smoothly.

Jake's rising anger ebbed as a moment of self-doubt shook the foundation of his being like the seismic tremor of an earthquake. What had he missed? Had Donna lied to him, as her father now alleged? As his mind scrambled to make sense of the purported deception, he felt himself being sucked deeper into the vortex of the sinister trap that had been set.

"Since you've always been so concerned for my welfare, why don't you tell me the truth."

"That's another myth, you know. The truth doesn't always set you free, especially in this case."

A chill ran down Jake's spine as he heard the reference to the biblical verse displayed outside the CIA Headquarters building. Had he somehow underestimated this guy? Could he have connections with the Agency, or was his comment merely a coincidence?

"I thought men like you made your own truth."

Mr. Kingston smiled confidently. "We usually do. But sometimes even the most powerful men are faced with situations they can't control. That's what happened to me when Donna's mother suffered a number of painful miscarriages. I wanted a son so desperately I cried out to God time and again. And what did He give me in return? A barren wife and a lost marriage."

"That's when you essentially discarded your wife and tried to create your own son by destroying your daughter's life."

Mr. Kingston seemed oblivious to the comment as he savored the deathblow he was about to deliver. "You have to admire the irony, here," he said with a fiendish laugh. "I would have done anything to have a son, and God turned his back on me. You, on the other hand, had a son, and your wife flushed him down the toilet. Can you imagine that? Your adorable little wife disposed of your son like a piece of excrement and sent him swirling through the bowels of the Swiss sewer system. How beautiful is that?"

As Mr. Kingston continued a devilish laugh, Jake snapped. His tightly clenched right fist struck the madman squarely on the jaw and sent him flying through the air. By the time his body hit the hardwood floor, Jake was on top of him with both hands around his neck. He choked him so hard his face turned blue and his dazed eyes began to bulge outward. In the fit of rage, he could almost see a hideous scar distorting one side of his face.

From somewhere within the room, the incessant ringing of a phone sounded. The noise jolted Jake back to his senses, and he quickly released the stranglehold on Mr. Kingston. He was relieved to see the man's color begin to return to normal as he gasped for air. While the phone continued ringing, Jake considered his next move. There was nothing further to be gained by staying any longer.

As Jake exited the house through the front door, a raspy voice spouted obscenities and threats to destroy his life. The tires of his car squealed in reply. He sped away from the house and raced down the lane leading to the open gate at the entrance to the Kingston property. With emotions churning, he turned right and headed away from the city, where the most critical and defining confrontation of his life awaited. Until the fog of emotion dissipated, he would not be able to see clearly which path to follow. He needed time to process the grisly information he had just received.

He drove aimlessly into the darkened countryside, trying to make sense of what Mr. Kingston had said. The only way Donna could have had the baby in Switzerland and disposed of it in such a callous manner was if she'd had an abortion. If she'd had an abortion at a medical facility, she wouldn't have been the one to discard the baby. She must have terminated the pregnancy herself while she was at her family's chalet.

The more he thought about it, the more it made sense. Something went wrong, causing her to nearly bleed to death, so she had to be taken to a hospital for surgery. But how did an abortion take place? Who was involved? He couldn't envision his wife sticking a coat hanger inside her womb and scraping the baby out herself, as he'd heard some desperate women did. Somehow her father had to be part of the revolting deed.

Douglas Kingston had certainly proven himself to be a heartless creature. Jake had no trouble picturing him prying the baby from Donna's womb while simultaneously cursing God and laughing at the thought of Jake not being there. Taking the life of their son would have been the perfect way for him to exact revenge on him for stealing the heart of his daughter. For that scenario to have played out, however, Donna would have had to have been a willing accomplice. There had to be another explanation.

He found himself driving down a narrow blacktopped road with fields of mature brown-husked corn on both sides. Except for a pole light illuminating the barnyard of a farm house a mile away, the early autumn night was as black as his mood. He stopped the car and put it in park, feeling isolated and alone. The disorientation that gripped him was like the feeling he'd had as a kid running wildly through a cornfield, unable to find a way out of the maze he was in. It seemed he once again had been thrust into the pit, where new demons joined their comrades in tormenting him.

Opening the car door, he felt the chill of the brisk wind out of the north that rustled through the dry husks of corn all around. There, standing in the middle of the road, he let out a bloodcurdling cry, shook his fists at the sky, and implored God to tell him why his life was being torn apart. When no answer was forthcoming, he sank to his knees and wept like a child. He was no stranger to pain—the Communists had made sure of that. This agony, however, was infinitely worse because it came from the actions of someone who'd said she loved him.

When the venting of his emotions subsided, he began to pray. A flood of memories came back to him in response. He tried to recall the advice of those people he had known who seemed to have a relationship with God. Mike had said Jesus would forgive his sins and give him a new life if he asked him to. He had heard the same message over and over, and yet he'd done nothing. Something had to change.

With his life in total chaos, he had nothing to lose and everything to gain. On his knees in the middle of that deserted country road, he cried out to God for help in a way he'd never done before. He confessed his sins—and they were many—and asked Jesus to show him the way out of the hell he was in. As he asked Jesus to be his Lord and Savior, it seemed as if a heavy weight was lifted from his shoulders. A sense of peace such as he'd never known suddenly permeated his soul and filled him with hope to deal with whatever lay ahead.

The thick fog shrouding his mind began to recede as he prayed for God's direction in dealing with the crisis at hand. One word, forgiveness, echoed through his mind so loudly it could not be ignored. Forgiveness was the path he needed to follow. Captain

Morgan had told him in a dream that he'd been forgiven, and he must learn how to forgive. What better way to show his love for Donna than to forgive her for what she'd done?

It was nearly midnight when he returned home. The house was dark, and Donna was sound asleep in the bedroom. There was no indication she had any idea what had happened at her father's house a few hours before. He watched her peaceful, rhythmic breathing for a moment and then gently kissed her forehead.

Sitting in a chair in a corner of the bedroom, he allowed his eyes to adjust to the darkness in the room. Over time, he was able to see the silhouette of his wife nearby. As he allowed his mind to adjust to the new reality, he began to understand how they'd arrived at that critical juncture. Donna had hinted at how difficult it had been for her to be alone during the first pregnancy. Now he caught a glimpse of the desperation she must have felt.

She had been living for more than a year with a grave secret only she and her father knew. He had no doubt the man had used that information to blackmail her so she would remain under his control. Today, in his desire to destroy Jake and turn him against Donna, Mr. Kingston couldn't eschew the opportunity to skewer him with the abhorrent revelation of the abortion. It was a mistake. His arrogance would be his undoing.

No fairy-tale ending could come to the unfolding drama. No kiss from a prince could magically undo all the wrongs that had been perpetrated. He, however, could liberate his wife from bondage by bringing the dirty secret out into the open. Only then would she truly be free.

When he awoke, the room was beginning to turn gray with the first hint of daylight showing through the bedroom windows. His neck was stiff, and his right hand felt swollen as he stretched his tired muscles. Donna was still sleeping soundly. He needed to clear the sleep from his head before she awoke.

After he made a fresh pot of coffee, he went outside to get the morning newspaper from the front sidewalk. Fortunately no SWAT team was waiting to ambush him. He was equally relieved to find the front-page headlines said nothing about the death of one Douglas Kingston. It wouldn't have surprised him, though, if he'd broken the man's jaw or knocked a few teeth loose. The image of Douglas Kingston with his jaw wired shut brought a smile to his face.

After drinking a cup of coffee, he showered and shaved, all the while pondering how to confront Donna. By the time he was dressed, she was awake and had headed to the kitchen for coffee. He found her there. She looked a little groggy as she sat at the kitchen table.

"Good morning," he said as he poured another cup of java and sat down next to her. "Feeling better?"

"I think so," she said as she yawned. "I'm still trying to wake up."

"That Valium really knocked you out. You slept like a log."

"No cramping," she said as she mentally assessed herself. "Now it's just like being on my period."

"You'll feel better after some coffee and a shower."

"Did you talk to my father?"

"Yeah, I did."

"How'd it go?"

"I think I made quite an impression on him."

"Knowing your sense of humor, I'm not sure what that means."

"I'll fill you in on all the sordid details after you wake up. Why don't you get cleaned up while I fix some breakfast."

"That's sounds good. I'm hungry."

During breakfast he listened as she walked him through the unpleasant experience she had just endured. He could see the emotional pain on her face as she shared her fears. Physical scars left a visible reminder of an associated trauma, but the pain faded. Emotional scars were invisible and more insidious, and they could eat away at the fabric of one's being. Love and compassion seemed to be the only antidotes.

"I'm afraid I'm going to suffer the same fate as my mother. I've had two miscarriages already."

He stiffened at the comment but resisted the urge to pull away. Instead he said, "Do you know how much I love you?" as he reached out and took her hand in his.

"I think so. Why do you ask?"

"Because you're the most important person in my life. There's nothing you could ever do that I wouldn't forgive you for. I may not understand or agree with everything you do, but I will always forgive you."

"Why are you telling me this?"

"Because your father told me about our son."

Her face went pale, and she tried to pull her hand away as the shock of his statement struck her.

"I don't know what you're talking about."

"Donna, please. It's okay. I forgive you."

"You can't believe anything he says. He hates you and would love to see us torn apart by his lies," she said, still attempting to hold onto her own.

"I know. That's why we have to face this crisis together and get him out of our lives once and for all. I'm sure he thought I'd leave you when I heard about your abortion."

"You know about the—about that?" she said as tears welled up in her eyes.

"He told me all about it."

A faraway look came into her eyes as she struggled to give birth to the truth about the fateful actions that had led to the abortion.

"Father said I would be wasting my life by raising a baby all alone," she said after a long pause. "He told me our company was developing an abortion pill at the plant in Geneva, Switzerland."

"The yellow pill."

"How did you know?"

"You've been talking in your sleep about the yellow pill completing the process."

Tears rolled down her cheeks. "It happened in the middle of the night. He was so tiny. I held him in the palm of my hand."

He wrapped his arms around her as she sobbed uncontrollably. The depth of her emotional pain was evident in the shaking of her body as she expelled at last the demons that had tormented her for so long.

With a quivering voice she said, "How can you forgive me for killing our baby? I don't deserve to be forgiven after what I've done."

"You were alone and vulnerable. How could I not forgive you? I love you more than anything in the world."

She buried her face against his chest as she wept for several minutes. When she had exhausted her tears, she sat up in the chair and shook her head slowly, mournfully, from side to side. She searched for answers.

"How do we get beyond this? Even if you've forgiven me, I can't forgive myself."

"It takes time. I'm still working on forgiving myself for the bad things I've done too."

"I can't understand how you can be so at peace and I'm such a mess."

"I did something last night that changed my life. I'll tell you about it after we finish talking about what happened to you."

"You didn't kill my father, did you?"

"It was close. He wounded me so deeply I wanted to die."

"Mother warned me something terrible would happen if I let him tell me what to do. I knew it was wrong to have an abortion, and yet I selfishly justified it so I could take control of my life. Instead I gave my father tremendous power over me."

"I think we can appreciate that control is an illusion. We've both seen our lives turned upside down in a fraction of a second by unforeseen circumstances."

"So what did you do last night that changed your life?"

"I surrendered. I'm not used to giving up, but this time I did."

"I don't understand."

"I found a secluded place, and I cried out to God for help. I remembered Mike saying Jesus had already paid for my sins, and all I had to do was surrender my life to him. So I asked God for forgiveness and turned my life over to Jesus. I know it sounds corny, but like Mike did, I decided to stop fighting with God and try to follow him instead."

"Mother used to say the same thing. She said she made the same choice. So what happened?"

"It was weird. As soon as I asked God to forgive me for my sins and I told him I wanted Jesus to be in charge of my life from now on, the feeling of hopelessness and despair went away. I can't explain it, but that's what happened."

"I'm happy for you, Jake. Maybe someday I'll find the peace that you have. I don't think I'll ever be able to forgive my father for all of the terrible things he's done and convinced me to do though. And I don't see how I can forgive myself for what happened to our baby."

"Mike says we have to forgive others if we want God to forgive us. He didn't put a time limit on it. So let's hate dear old Dad for a while before we start working on the forgiveness part for him. Agreed?"

"Agreed. And thank you for being so supportive and under-standing. You've always treated me better than I deserve."

"That's the same thing I told God," he said.

PART IV

Forgiveness

CHAPTER TWENTY-FIVE

The dreary gray sky that characterized the onset of the winter season in the Midwest cast a pall over Jake's mood in early November. As reports from Cowboy described the worsening political and military situation in Laos, he felt a sense of urgency to help the Hmong. Time was running out for them to make an orderly exit across the Mekong River into the primitive refugee camps being established in several areas of northern Thailand. The world was oblivious to the impending genocide.

At home Donna and Jake were still adjusting to a new normal. She was still running Blanford Pharmaceuticals, but she'd cut off all direct contact with her father. Any business matters between the two of them went through her secretary. Her somber mood lessened as she and Jake worked through the complicated issues of their lives that had led to her abortion. One thing was certain. Neither was ready to talk about having a baby anytime soon.

The nightmares that frequently disrupted Jake's sleep added new actors to the eerie cast. Images of Scarface became interchangeable with Douglas Kingston. Visions of the Hmong in their present suffering joined his dreams as well. Occasionally he found it necessary to take one of Donna's Valium to help him get to sleep. Whenever he did so, he told himself John Lennon must have faced a similar dilemma. After all, his song, "Whatever Gets You Thru the Night," had hit number one on the billboard charts.

The request from Cowboy to come to Thailand finally came in the spring of 1975. Cobra handed him an envelope with the brief message. He was to report to the Nam Phong refugee camp in northeastern Thailand as soon as possible.

"Your plane tickets to Bangkok via Los Angeles are in the envelope," Cobra said. "You'll be met by one of our people at the Don Muang airport, and he'll fly you up to Nam Phong. Cowboy will meet you at the camp."

Jake called Donna from the hotel in Washington, D.C., that night. She had tolerated his absence the past year well, especially after the recent crisis had passed. Her reaction to the news of his sudden travel to Southeast Asia, however, was not as kind. Despite his assurance that the assignment would be short-lived, she remained adamantly opposed to the plan. He was glad he hadn't gone home to break the news to her in person.

At home in St. Louis, alone, Donna cried for nearly an hour after she hung up the phone. Jake's decision to return to Southeast Asia against her wishes drove her crazy. She couldn't understand why he was so willing to risk his life—and their marriage—trying somehow to rectify the wrongs of the past. It couldn't be done.

In the midst of her anger and self-pity, she realized the answer to that question. She'd seen how deeply he'd been affected by his war experiences. In fact, she too was still at war—with herself. Although he had so lovingly forgiven her for aborting their child, she'd still not found a way to forgive herself. He had to try. She understood. Finally she acquiesced. He could go with her blessing.

⊶✛✛⊷

When the door of the TWA jet opened at the airport in Bangkok, the stifling heat and humidity enveloped Jake like steam from a sauna. He'd almost forgotten what the tropical climate was like. After claiming his baggage and clearing Thai Customs, he made his way to the military side of the airfield. Several C-123s were parked on the tarmac in front of the terminal building. Standing next to one of them was a man he recognized, even without his black mask.

"Well, if it isn't the Lone Ranger," he said as he shook the hand of the CIA pilot who had flown him out of Laos almost two years ago. "I never thought I'd see you again."

"There aren't many of us left over here now. You look a lot better than the last time I saw you."

"Are you the one taking me to Nam Phong?"

"I'm the one. Throw your gear on board, and we'll head out. You get to be my copilot today."

During the one-hour flight from Bangkok to Nam Phong, Lone Ranger filled him in on the deteriorating situation on the ground in Laos. He said the Pathet Lao had recently seized control of the Lao government in the capital of Vientiane, rounded up those who opposed communism, and placed them in the reeducation camps located throughout the country. Those who resisted had either fled into the mountains or they'd been shot. Thousands of Hmong had sought refuge at the camp in Thailand. But the majority, more than a hundred thousand people, still fought the Communists in the remote mountain regions in Laos.

The paved runway at Nam Phong finally came into view five miles out as the plane descended through the dense air laden with moisture. Jake could see thousands of wooden barracks and tents scattered for miles around the base on both sides of the runway. Lone Ranger said Nam Phong had once been a Thai military base used by Thai and U.S. forces during the Vietnam War. Now the only tenants on the base were Hmong refugees and a handful of aid workers from government agencies and nonprofit organizations.

Cowboy was sitting in a dark olive-green U.S. Army jeep at the end of the runway. His suntanned face was dotted with beads of sweat that fell regularly onto his red-and-white Texas Tech T-shirt like melted candle wax dripping onto a table. The ubiquitous smile that had graced his face two years ago was absent. In its place was a look of deep consternation.

"Good luck," Lone Ranger said as he brought the engines back to idle. "I'll still be in country for a while. Give me a call if you need me."

Jake exited the aircraft and approached the jeep.

"Welcome back," Cowboy said without a smile. "I was hoping you'd join us."

"Thank you, sir. I hope I'm not too late to help."

The men shook hands and then loaded Jake's gear into the back of the jeep. Jake noticed that Colonel Watson had aged considerably. Although he'd been in his mid-forties when they first met, he'd had tremendous energy and enthusiasm. Now he looked old and haggard. The stress of his clandestine work appeared to have finally caught up with him.

"We need all the help we can get," he told Jake as he drove the jeep down a taxiway toward the wooden headquarters building. "The refugees who have escaped Laos tell us the genocide has already started. Now that the dry season has arrived, the North Vietnamese will invade both Laos and South Vietnam in a final push to topple both countries. We can't stop them this time. We can't even give the Hmong ammunition or medical supplies. They're on their own."

"How many people are living in this camp?"

"Somewhere around five thousand, give or take a thousand. Most of them are women and children. They're packed into those small barracks like sardines. We're short on everything—food, water, bedding, clothing, medical supplies, and staff. The sad part is it's only going to get worse."

"You warned me this was going to happen when we were together two years ago. I know how much you love these people. It must be hard watching this human tragedy unfold and not being able to stop it."

"That's why I brought you here. You understand, because you feel their pain too. Maybe you can make a difference in some of the lives here by writing about what you see and know from your past."

"So far everything I've written about the Hmong has been buried by the CIA. The Agency has really been taking heat from Congress and the press for all the scandals that have become public in the last few years. The last thing the Agency wants is for someone to start looking into the covert war its people conducted in Laos for ten years."

"Forget about the Vietnam War. Write some human-interest stories documenting the atrocities the Communists are committing against the refugees and their families right now. I'll get you an interpreter to work with. Show me your work, and I guarantee we'll get something published."

Cowboy stopped the jeep in front of a long, low, wooden structure with a corrugated tin roof. A framed picture of a man riding a bucking bronco hung on the door.

"Is that you?" Jake asked as they walked through the door into Cowboy's office.

"That was me when I was your age. I wasn't half bad at riding back then."

Cowboy took a bottle of Chivas Regal from a cabinet behind his desk and poured them each a drink and offered up a toast.

"To the fiercest fighters, the most loyal friends, and the most proud people I know. May the sacrifice of the Hmong never be forgotten."

The Scotch burned as it hit Jake's empty stomach. He relished this time of communion with a fellow warrior who had given many years of his life for a noble cause he believed in. Unfortunately the government he worked for had moved on to the next theater of operations. Southeast Asia, like Cowboy, was now passé.

"You'll be sharing this building with me. Throw your gear in the room off to the right, and then I'll show you around the camp."

As they walked through the camp, the stench from human waste assaulted Jake's sense of smell. There was obviously a major problem with sanitation that would lead to widespread disease if not quickly addressed. He quickly learned that although some running water was available, it was not sufficient to meet the needs of the burgeoning refugee population. As a result, the Hmong were using contaminated water from nearby streams for drinking and cooking.

"Where do you get food and water for these people?"

"Our government sent someone from USAID to work with the Thai government to bring in rice, fruits, vegetables, and water. The problem is that truckloads of new refugees are arriving every day. The Thai military pick them up after they cross the Mekong River and transport them here so they aren't taking up residence in Thailand. Now we have the Thai military guarding this camp to make sure the Hmong don't leave."

"So the Hmong have been driven out of their own country only to be penned up like animals in a foreign country."

"That pretty much sums it up. You can't blame the Thais, I guess. The Hmong will go out and hunt for food if they're not controlled. Then you'll have local Thai farmers whizzed off because their chickens and water buffalo are ending up roasting on a stick over a fire in this camp."

"I remember being that hungry. What's going to happen to the refugees? They can't just stay here forever."

"Nobody is happy with this situation. The Hmong are suffering here, and their leaders are starting to complain. And the Thais aren't pleased that the U.S. government has dumped this mess in their lap. Ultimately we hope to resettle the Hmong in countries around the world that will allow them to emigrate. That's one way you can help the Hmong. Make the world aware of their plight so others will welcome them into their countries one day."

By the time they'd finished a tour of the camp, Jake was exhausted. The 95-degree heat and 75 percent humidity had left him feeling weak and dehydrated. Unpleasant memories of the seven months of captivity began to seep into his consciousness as the reality of what he was doing sank in.

What made me think I could help these people? he thought. *Was I as naïve about that as I've been about everything else?*

Just then he saw a group of children playing a game of stickball with a large ball of heavy yarn. One of the children had only one arm. Another boy hobbled along on a makeshift crutch—in lieu of his absent lower left leg. Their radiant smiles declared the innocent joy of youth that somehow could not be suppressed despite the appalling conditions they found themselves in. In that moment, he knew that God had him in the right place.

"Their resiliency is amazing, isn't it?" said a pleasant female voice nearby.

He turned to see an attractive brunette dressed in blue surgical scrubs. She too was observing the children at play. A stethoscope was draped casually around her neck. She looked American—perhaps in her early 30s.

"We amputated that one's leg below the knee a few days ago. Landmine." The words came out with such matter-of-factness that she may as well have said the sun had come up that day.

"We?"

"My husband and I."

"You're a doctor?"

"Carol Mattingly, M.D.," she said as she reached out to shake his hand. "Pediatrician. My husband, Bill, is a surgeon."

"Jake Lemaster."

"What's your role in this god-forsaken place?"

"I'm a journalist. Just arrived."

"That still doesn't explain why you're here. The war is over. Haven't you heard?"

Jake appreciated her sentiments. No other American journalists were within a hundred miles of that place. Which is exactly why he had to be.

"Try telling that to the Hmong. Are you and your husband here with a relief agency?"

"We tried that route, through our church's denominational medical mission organization. The staff said they had no need for more missionaries in Thailand. Can you believe it? So we decided to come on our own."

"How long have you been here?"

"Almost a month, but it seems more like a year."

"Are there are any other doctors here?"

"There are a few nurses, but no other doctors."

He couldn't imagine the emotional and physical stress Carol and her husband must be under as the only doctors caring for the burgeoning refugee population in the camp.

Maybe I should get their stories on paper as well, he thought.

"I'm hoping to make the world aware of the plight of the Hmong. Maybe I could talk with you and your husband sometime. I'd like to get your perspective on what's happening here."

She looked at him suspiciously. "So what's your connection to the Hmong? It can't just be a story because nobody's interested in these people. Not even our own government."

"Let's just say I owe the Hmong a huge debt of gratitude."

"Are you always this cryptic?"

"Only with the people I like," he said and smiled.

"Then I'll take that as a compliment. You should come by the clinic and meet my husband. I think you two might have a lot in common. We open at 8 a.m. every day."

"Where's the clinic?" he asked as the doctor turned and walked away.

She smiled and called over her shoulder, "Didn't the CIA teach you how to gather information?"

CHAPTER TWENTY-SIX

C owboy treated Jake to a dinner of white rice mixed with eggs, chicken, and chopped up vegetables seasoned with pieces of ground Thai peppers. Fortunately there was plenty of ice-cold Olympia beer to ease the burning in his mouth and to make him forget he had vowed never again to eat rice. After the meal, Cowboy offered him a cigarette, which he took reluctantly. He had quit smoking when he returned home from Laos nearly two years ago.

As he lit the cigarette, he asked Cowboy, "Did you ever see Lo Chang again after I left?"

"Yes. He was with a group of soldiers defending the base at Long Chieng. The North Vietnamese were pounding that place with heavy artillery day and night so I had to pull out. The CIA frowns on having one of its own captured and vilified in front of the whole world. I haven't seen him since then."

"Do you know if he ever found his wife and daughter?"

"You still haven't forgiven yourself for killing his son, eh?"

"Could you if you were in my situation?"

"Probably not. That's what makes us different. Men like you and me can't just walk away when we see an injustice."

"The only way I can move on with my life is by helping Lo Chang find his family."

"How do you plan on accomplishing this quest of yours? The Hmong are scattered all over Laos, and they aren't exactly looking to be found. Do you even know what his wife and daughter look like?"

"I know it's a long shot, but I've got to try. I don't know what they look like, but Lo Chang did give me their names—Thao Nhia and Lo Moua."

"Well at least we have something to work with. There's a group of Hmong recording the names of everyone coming into the camp when they first arrive. That's where you need to start. Go down to the office near the front gate tomorrow, and check the logs to see if their names are on it. I'll send one of my best interpreters with you."

"Thanks. Next question. What can you tell me about the two American doctors here?"

"Nice folks, and from what I can tell they're good doctors. They apparently felt motivated by their faith to serve the Hmong."

"I met the woman, Carol, a while ago. She invited me to the clinic."

"By all means, check it out. You'll get a real education working with them."

"Where can I find the clinic?"

"It's near the front gate. I'll have someone point it out when you go there in the morning to check the log."

The next morning Jake awoke to the sound of hundreds of crying children expressing their discomfort from pervasive hunger and disease. The clanking of metal pots and pans signaled the start of the day's cooking with whatever food was available. Children chatted with each other as they carried jugs of water from the well to their shelter. In the distance, the sound of a woman wailing gave notice that death had visited the camp during the night.

He grabbed a cup of coffee and stepped outside the headquarters just as Cowboy walked up with a young man.

"Jake, this is Vue Pao. He's going to be working with you as an interpreter. I've explained to him what your mission here is."

"Hello, Mr. Jake."

"Vue Pao was an interpreter who flew along with American pilots during bombing missions in Laos before we started using Hmong pilots. He talked to the Hmong spotters on the ground and told our guys where to drop their ordnance. His English is good, and he's very reliable. I have some work to do, so I'll let you two have at it."

Jake spent the first day in camp going over the list of names of the refugees with Vue Pao. There was no one named Lo Chang, Thao Nhia, or Lo Moua on the camp registry. Vue Pao talked to the people registering the new Hmong coming into camp everyday and asked them to notify him immediately if anyone with those names arrived. With that done, Vue Pao introduced him to some refugees he knew that were anxious to tell their stories.

The central part in all of the stories Jake heard from the female refugees was similar. Their fathers, brothers, and husbands had gone off to fight the Communists, leaving them to take care of their families and villages the best they could. The men would come home for a visit when there was a lull in the fighting, usually during the monsoon season. When the dry season came around, the men would return to the battlefield, leaving their pregnant wives alone once again. For most of the refugees, it was the only life they had ever known.

One young woman's story was so shocking that he wouldn't have believed it if he hadn't witnessed something similar. She had been taken prisoner by the Pathet Lao when her village was destroyed.

The Communists used her as a sex slave until she became pregnant and gave birth to a child in the concentration camp. They planned to use her, and other Hmong women, as breeding machines for their new regime. She managed to escape with her baby and make her way into Thailand less than a month before Jake arrived at the camp.

After being in the camp for nearly a week and gathering stories, Jake decided it was time to visit the medical clinic. A long line of patients had already assembled outside the front door of the building as he arrived shortly after 8 a.m. He immediately appreciated what a precious commodity a female pediatrician like Carol was for the camp. Most of the patients waiting to be seen were women—many holding a sick child in one arm as they breast-fed another infant.

Dr. Carol Mattingly saw him come through the front door and went over to greet him.

"I didn't think you were going to make it."

"Sorry. There's a lot of work to do here."

"Tell me about it," she said as she glanced around the noisy waiting area. "Let's go find Bill. He's anxious to meet you."

"Nice place," he said as they went down a corridor with small exam rooms on both sides.

"The Americans and the Thais built this clinic when there were thousands of troops stationed here. Fortunately we found the building intact. We even have a decent operating room for Bill to use. The bad news is that medications and equipment are in short supply."

They passed through a courtyard in the center of the medical complex and then entered another wing of the building.

"This is our hospital ward," she said.

Jake looked around the dimly lit room. It was poorly ventilated, and the nauseating smell of feces, vomit, and sweat permeated the air. Rows of beds were lined up side by side with no curtains to provide any privacy. Many patients shared their beds with multiple family members.

"I guess a private room is out of the question."

Carol gave him a sardonic look and said, "We have room for about thirty patients. As you can see, there's no place for modesty here."

At the far end of the ward stood a tall, thin man with a receding hairline. He was holding a clipboard and examining the information it held. He wore surgical garb and looked at least ten years older than Jake.

In his mind, Jake wondered, *What does this guy have in common with me?*

"This is the young man I was telling you about," Carol said as she sidled up next to her husband. "Bill, meet Jake Lemaster."

"Pleased to meet you, Doc," Jake said as he shook Bill's hand. Although Bill had the delicate hands of a surgeon, his grip was strong and firm. Something else about him struck Jake. It was the way Bill seemed to penetrate him with eyes that were at once both confident and yet humble.

"Likewise," Bill said. "Glad to have you join us. What do you think we should do here?" he asked Jake as he turned toward the young woman lying in the bed before them.

Jake was no stranger to blood and guts, especially his own, but he was definitely out of his element in that primitive Third World hospital. He felt like a young medical student making rounds with Marcus Welby, M.D. The patient was in the latter stage of pregnancy, but beyond that, he had no clue what her problem was.

"I think we'd better call a doctor."

Bill and Carol laughed as they shared a furtive look.

"A wise choice," Bill said. "This young lady has been in labor for nearly twenty-four hours. Her pelvis is too small to allow the baby to deliver. So I'm going to perform a C-section as soon as she gets prepped for the operation. Care to assist me in surgery? I can always use an extra pair of hands."

"I have to get started in the clinic," Carol said to her husband. "Call me when you're ready to deliver the baby."

She turned and headed toward the wing of the building that housed the clinic. Jake watched her go, wondering what he would do next.

"You're going to cut her open?"

"If I don't, she and the baby will die."

Bill thought he saw Jake turn a little green around the gills, so he led him away from the hospital ward, saying, "Let's go have a cup of coffee in my office."

As Bill heated some water on a hotplate, Jake took a chair across from the doctor's desk. With great difficulty, he tried to banish the dreadful image of the Pathet Lao soldier he had seen savagely carving a baby from its mother's womb.

"Carol told me you're a journalist?"

"That's right. I've been working for a company called Global Correspondents for the past year or so. That's how I ended up here."

Bill dropped a teaspoon of Folger's instant coffee into a cup and added some hot water. He stirred the mixture as steam rose from the cup and then handed it to Jake. After repeating the process for himself, he plopped down in a chair behind the desk.

"Carol said you were somehow indebted to the Hmong. Is that the real reason you're here?"

Jake had a feeling Bill knew more than he was letting on. Had Cowboy already told the doctors about his past?

"What has Cowboy told you?"

Bill smiled as he took a sip of coffee. "He said you were shot down over Laos, and a Hmong tribesman rescued you after you spent seven months in a POW camp."

"You've got good sources, Doc. What else did he say?"

"That you're someone who feels the pain of the Hmong people and wants to help."

"Tell me something. Your wife said you and I have a lot in common. What was she referring to exactly—apart from our good looks, of course?"

Bill took another drink and then set his coffee cup on top of the desk before replying. "I was in Vietnam in the early '60s working for Army Intelligence."

"There's an oxymoron for you."

Bill laughed as he recalled the crucial time period of his early life. "My job was flying aboard an EC-130 gathering electronic intercepts as we flew over the Ho Chi Minh trail in eastern Laos. Remember, this was around '63 or '64, before we actually called it a war. Well, one day we were hit with heavy AAA fire and went down."

Jake's palms were wet with sweat as he listened to Bill's story. Memories of his fateful crash came flooding back with a vengeance.

"Everyone aboard was killed except me." Bill's face registered a pained expression, and his eyes seemed distant as he relived the tragic event. "Somehow—I still don't understand it—I was spared. It doesn't seem fair. Eleven other men lost their lives that day while I walked away unscathed."

Bill took another drink of his coffee before continuing. "Fortunately for me, a group of Hmong tribesmen rescued me before the Viet Cong or Pathet Lao could get their hands on me. If it hadn't been for the Hmong, I'd either be dead or rotting away in some hellhole in the jungle."

"So how did you go from that nightmare to becoming a doctor?"

"After my ordeal, I made a vow to myself and God that I'd use the rest of my life to help others rather than waste the life I'd been given. It was the least I could do, considering the blessings

I'd received. So after I left the army, I took the college courses I needed to prepare for the Medical College Admissions Test. Four years of med school and five years of surgical residency later, and here I am."

"I guess we are kindred spirits. I'm trying to do something useful with my life too."

"If you can get the world to help these people, you will have succeeded. But it's going to be an uphill battle."

"You're right about that."

A petite Filipino nurse poked her head through the door of the office. "We're ready for you, doctor."

"I'll be right there. Want to join me?"

"Doc, I saw something once that has haunted me ever since. The Pathet Lao had destroyed a Hmong village, and they were raping the women. One of the soldiers cut open a pregnant woman's womb and killed her baby—while she was still alive."

"No wonder you became woozy when I asked you to assist. I think this is just what you need to wipe that bad memory out of your mind once and for all. Our patient will be fully awake but won't feel any pain. We're going to place a beautiful baby in her arms."

"She's going to be awake for surgery?"

He chuckled. "Don't worry. We use spinal anesthesia for most procedures here. Come on, we'll do this together."

With a mixture of excitement and trepidation, Jake followed Bill to the surgery area. Bill found him some scrubs and then walked him through the rigorous hand-washing ritual before entering the surgery suite. The nurse, who had been well trained by Bill, had already administered epidural anesthesia to the patient. A Hmong interpreter stood in the corner.

Bill draped sterile sheets over the patient and then said, "Go to the opposite side of the table and face me, Jake." Once he was positioned, Bill said, "I never operate without saying a prayer first."

Bill called the interpreter over to the table and then began to pray. The interpreter translated the prayer for the Hmong woman, who listened attentively. Jake was in awe of the whole experience. Cowboy had been right. He was getting a real education. After the prayer ended, Bill sent one of the nurses to let Carol know her services would be needed in the next few minutes.

"All right, here we go," he announced to the team.

Bill had briefed Jake already on the major elements of the surgical procedure, telling him his main tasks were to observe and to hold retractors when requested. Jake was convinced his first duty was to refrain from passing out and taking a nosedive into the patient's uterus. As he watched, he was impressed with Bill's precision and speed. When the patient's abdominal cavity was opened, he looked at the patient's face. She was staring toward the ceiling without any hint of discomfort.

Carol entered the room and took up a position next to her husband, saying, "How're we doing?"

"We'll have a baby for you in just a second."

Carol looked across the table at Jake. Her eyes were twinkling with excitement above her mask. "Ready for your first delivery, Dr. Lemaster?"

Jake beamed with pride as he watched Bill make a generous incision in the uterus. A gush of clear amniotic fluid poured out of the womb while the nurse worked the suction to keep the surgical field clear. Bill then reached inside the uterus and plucked out a well-developed baby still attached to the uterus by the umbilical cord.

"It's a boy," he said.

Bill quickly held up the baby for the mother to see and then handed the infant to Carol. She dried the infant, suctioned its mouth and nose, clamped and cut the cord, and then performed a rapid assessment of the baby's heart and lungs. When she was satisfied the infant was stable, she wrapped the newborn in a cloth and placed him on the mother's chest.

Jake had to fight back tears. He was overwhelmed by the whole experience of seeing new life brought forth. The sound of the infant crying was like music to his ears. And the look of pleasure on the mother's face as she held her new son was priceless.

"How're you doing over there, Jake?" Bill asked.

"That was amazing."

"You did well too, Dr. Lemaster. Let's close up here, and then we'll get you signed up for medical school."

Jake was thankful he hadn't passed up the opportunity to witness the surgery and exorcise some demons in the process.

*And who know*s, he thought. *If journalism isn't my calling, maybe...*

After that initial medical experience with Dr. Mattingly, Jake frequented the clinic whenever he wasn't busy with other projects. He was able to see patients with the docs and assist Bill in surgery many more times. The number of Hmong with traumatic wounds continued to mount as the flood of refugees increased daily.

For nearly a month, he recorded the tragic accounts of the lives of the Hmong refugees and passed the articles along to Cowboy. Although most of the reports were rejected by the CIA, a few of the children's stories found their way into newspapers in the US and abroad. Unfortunately the press was preoccupied with the North Vietnamese invasion of South Vietnam, and America was looking for some closure to that infamous war. By the end of April, the Communists had captured Saigon. The death knell signaled the end of the Vietnam War and the beginning of the end for the Hmong warriors who remained in Laos.

CHAPTER TWENTY-SEVEN

With the month of May came frequent thunderstorms that drenched the camp with heavy rain and turned the red clay soil into a muddy quagmire. A constant stream of refugees continued to pour into the overcrowded camp. Tensions rose like ominous storm clouds as living conditions in the camp deteriorated. For the first time, a number of able-bodied men were seen among the refugees seeking shelter from the Communist storm sweeping through Laos. The arrival of some Hmong warriors portended much worse things to come.

Storm clouds were also brewing on the home front as Donna became increasingly impatient with Jake's activities abroad. He tried to convince her that his presence there was needed and he would return home as soon as the job was done. Her anger was mitigated only somewhat because she had read some of the heart-wrenching stories he'd written about the Hmong children. He knew he couldn't keep up the charade much longer without further damaging his marriage. Something had to give.

One day as he was having a cup of coffee with Cowboy in the headquarters building, the sound of a loud commotion erupted in the camp. They went outside to try and assess what had caused the disturbance. When they arrived at the scene, they saw a crowd of Hmong surrounding two men lying on the ground. Vue Pao joined Cowboy and Jake as they picked a way through the angry mob. Cowboy needed to find out who these men were and what they had done in order to quell the trouble before it got out of hand.

As they reached the center of the crowd, the shouting died down. Several Hmong warriors holding machetes stepped forward.

"Ask them what's going on here," Cowboy said to Vue Pao.

He listened as Vue Pao questioned the Hmong guarding the prisoners. The warriors spoke angrily and pointed toward the two men on the ground as the crowd once again joined in the ruckus. Several women kicked the prisoners and spat on them.

"These men are Pathet Lao spies," Vue Pao said. "Some of our women say they were raped and tortured by them in a concentration camp near Vang Vieng."

"Tie them up and bring them to my office before these people tear them apart," Cowboy ordered.

When the prisoners had been deposited in the headquarters building, Cowboy told Vue Pao to have the Hmong warriors construct some cages to hold the captives in. He also asked the Hmong people to allow him to interrogate the prisoners to find out how they came to the camp and what their purpose was. The angry mob reluctantly dissipated as Vue Pao begged the people to return to their shelters so the Thai guards would not become alarmed.

"What are you going to do with them?" Jake asked.

"We need to find out why they're here and if there are more of them among us. You can join me if you like."

Jake had once fantasized about torturing the enemy as they had done to him. Now that the opportunity had arisen, he was conflicted. Could he find pleasure in watching someone suffer as he had?

Cowboy ordered the Hmong warriors to take one of the captives and place him in a crude bamboo cage they had constructed nearby. When it was done, he removed the bag from the other prisoner's head and told Vue Pao to ask him his name and what he was doing there.

Vue Pao spoke to the prisoner in Lao and then to Cowboy. "He say his name is Dao Sayavong. He was told to spy on Hmong in camp and take information back to Laos."

"Ask him how long he's been here and how he got in the camp."

Vue Pao repeated Cowboy's questions and then shared the answers. "He say they come two day ago with refugees. They give names of Hmong held in concentration camp at Vang Vieng. He say he just soldier. Other prisoner, Tong Fu, is in charge."

"Ask him if he raped the Hmong women at Vang Vieng."

The frightened prisoner shook his head yes and told Vue Pao all Pathet Lao were forced to rape the women or be killed themselves. By that time, the young man was crying profusely and begging for mercy.

"Tell him we will spare him if he tells us all about the concentration camp at Vang Vieng."

The relieved prisoner told Vue Pao there were about fifty Hmong prisoners, mostly women and children, at the concentration camp. He said only ten Pathet Lao guards controlled the camp while most of the soldiers were laying siege to the base at Long Chieng. He said he wanted to stay in Thailand and seek asylum rather than return to his evil commander.

The hair on the back of Jake's neck stood up as soon as he heard those words.

"Ask him who his commander is," Jake said.

He listened as Vue Pao questioned the prisoner. His blood ran cold as he heard the devil's name proclaimed.

"He say commander is Colonel Nguyen Hue."

"Ask him if his commander has a big scar on the left side of his face."

The prisoner quickly shook his head yes as Vue Pao posed the question.

"Tell him I will consider his request for asylum if he fully cooperates with us," Cowboy said.

The prisoner's relief was evident as he gave a wan smile in response to the information spoken. Cowboy patted him on the back and then placed the bag back over his head.

"Give him some rice and water, and then stick him in a cage. Then bring me that other prisoner."

Cowboy offered Jake a cigarette and said, "It's a little easier being on this side of the table, eh?"

He lit Jake's cigarette and then joined him in a smoke as they waited for the purported leader of this little spy ring to be brought in.

"What do you have planned for the next prisoner?"

"I want to see if the first guy's story checks out. But the next one may be a tougher nut to crack. You may get to play the bad cop on this one."

Two Hmong warriors entered the room with the second prisoner. They shoved him down roughly on the chair and bound him tightly to it. When the warriors left, Cowboy took the bag from the man's head.

As Jake studied the prisoner's face, he had the feeling he'd seen him before. It had been nearly two years since his captivity, but he was sure this guy was one of the guards at the last camp he had been held in before he escaped.

"Ask him the same questions as we did the other guy," Cowboy said.

Vue Pao did as he was instructed, but the prisoner refused to speak and stared straight ahead at the wall.

"Tell him Dao Sayavong told us all about their plans."

When Vue Pao spoke, the prisoner flinched almost imperceptibly but remained silent.

"Tell him we know he is the real spy, and we will hang him unless he cooperates."

Vue Pao translated the threat, but again there was no response.

"Do you still have that nasty Polaroid picture you took of me right after I arrived at Long Chieng?" Jake asked Cowboy.

"Are you feeling nostalgic all of a sudden?"

"Can you get it for me?"

Cowboy went into the other room and returned a moment later with the Polaroid. Jake pulled up a chair and sat down right in front of the prisoner so the man could look him in the eyes.

"Do you know me?"

He watched the prisoner closely as Vue Pao translated. The man fixed his attention on the American and slowly shook his head no.

"Well, I certainly remember you. You were the one that tied a rope around my ankles and hoisted me into the air above a pit with a cobra in it." Jake then showed him the Polaroid picture.

As Vue Pao translated Jake's words and he looked at the picture, the prisoner's eyes got big. "Sergeant Lemaster?"

"I thought you'd remember me. It's okay. I know you're only doing what Commander Scarface wants you to do. Is he still at Vang Vieng?"

Tong Fu nodded yes after the translation. He then told Vue Pao that Colonel Hue had ordered him to carry out this mission.

"How many prisoners are in the camp?" Cowboy asked.

"He say forty or fifty," said Vue Pao.

"How many guards are at the camp?"

"He say sometime ten, sometime more."

Cowboy looked at Jake and said, "Anything else you want to know?"

"Ask him if he raped those Hmong women."

Tong Fu nodded yes and answered.

"He say all Communists rape the enemy's women," Vue Pao said. "Colonel Hue insist."

"I have no further questions," Cowboy said. "Vue, tell the Hmong to feed this guy and give him water before they cage him."

"Just a minute," Jake said. "There's something I want to do first."

"You want to rough him up a little? Maybe get some payback?"

"Tell the prisoner what I'm about to say, Vue."

Vue nodded his head as he waited.

"Tong Fu, I know Colonel Hue made you do those terrible things to me. I could see the fear in your eyes when you hurt me. You only did evil things because you were afraid Colonel Hue would hurt you if you didn't. He would've thrown you into the pit with the cobra if you disobeyed him."

As Vue translated Jake's words, he saw tears form in Tong Fu's eyes, and his lip began to quiver. He was certain that the man was recalling that day, when Colonel Hue cast one of his own men into the pit to die.

"I forgive you," Jake said as he placed a hand on Tong Fu's shoulder.

When the prisoner heard those words translated in his own language, he began to weep. Jake squeezed his shoulder gently as his sobbing intensified.

After a moment the prisoner spoke and Vue translated.

"Colonel Hue hate everyone. We all afraid of him. But he hate you most of all. He keep picture of you wife in pocket and pull out everyday. He become crazy and scream you name and curse you for getting away. He blame us and beat us for it. He is evil."

"Yes, he's an evil man. But you're not like him," Jake said.

331

A genuine look of remorse came across the prisoner's face. Vue translated his next words.

"I am sorry for what I did to you."

After the prisoner was led away, Cowboy said, "I said you could be the bad cop, not the good cop."

"That wasn't planned."

"It's a harsh world we live in. Sometimes we have to be as mean as our enemy if we want to survive."

"I suppose. But if we're not careful, we'll become as evil as they are. Besides, if I hadn't forgiven him, I would have remained angry and bitter. Some of that poison just melted away."

"You must've gotten religion."

"Something like that. Where is Vang Vieng?"

"It's about a hundred miles due north of Vientiane. We built a secret landing strip called Lima Site 6 a few miles outside of town."

"That's only about a 30-minute flight. Is the runway still operational?"

"It's operational, but the Communists own that whole region now. What's on your mind?"

"I don't know. I interviewed a young woman a while back who told me she was used as a sex slave at a concentration camp. Her story jives with what these two prisoners just said about Vang Vieng. I think I need to ask her some more questions."

Later that day, Vue and Jake found the woman crowded into a corner of a barracks with her baby. She was sharing the living space with ten other people. After Jake reintroduced himself, he had Vue ask her if she'd been imprisoned in Vang Vieng. When she said she had, he told Vue to ask her if she remembered seeing a woman named Thao Nhia and her daughter Lo Moua were there. A surge of adrenaline shot through his veins as the woman nodded her head yes and talked excitedly with Vue Pao.

"She say she know Thao Nhia and her daughter. She travel with them from mountains in north when they captured. She say they still in camp when she escape."

"Ask her the same questions we asked the two prisoners earlier."

His heart was pounding as he considered the amazing good fortune to have located Lo Chang's family. He listened patiently as the woman spoke to Vue about the concentration camp.

"She say same information. She say man with scar on face is devil."

That night Jake had some trouble sleeping as he tried to figure out how to rescue Lo Chang's family. A plan was slowly taking shape in his mind, but there were still a lot of unknowns. He would need the help of a number of people to carry out such a bold operation on enemy soil.

The next day, as Vue Pao and Jake were interviewing some new refugees, a woman knocked on the door of the barracks and asked to speak to Vue. When she was done talking, Vue had a big smile on his face.

"What was that all about?"

"I have very good news. A Hmong warrior named Lo Chang has just arrived."

"Where is he?" Jake asked as he stood up and headed out the door.

Vue apologized to the woman they were interviewing and followed him outside. "At main gate."

When Jake reached the main gate, he saw Lo Chang standing in a line of refugees, waiting to be assigned to a living space in the camp. He looked much older. Jake ran up to him and hugged him as the other refugees looked on in amazement.

"It's good to see you, my friend."

"You come back. Why you come back?"

"I have good news for you. I know where your wife and daughter are."

"Where?"

"They're being held in a concentration camp at Vang Vieng. Come with me. You can stay in my room if you don't mind sleeping on the floor."

Jake had Vue tell the registrar that Lo Chang was bunking with him, and then they headed to the headquarters building. Cowboy was sitting in his office when the men walked in.

"Look who just showed up!" Jake said.

Cowboy stood up and shook hands with Lo Chang. "It's been a long time. I'm glad you made it out of Long Chieng alive."

Lo Chang nodded and said, "Many Hmong die there. I come here when Communists take base. Think maybe family come Thailand."

"How are things in Laos?" Cowboy asked.

"Very bad. Too many Communists. We have no weapons, no bullets, no food."

"I do have one piece of good news," Jake said. "I know where Lo Chang's wife and daughter are."

"That is good news," Cowboy said as he grabbed three beers from the refrigerator and passed one to Lo Chang and one to Jake. He motioned for them to sit down at the table as he popped open his beer and took a big swig. "Where are they?"

"Vang Vieng. I talked to a woman who was imprisoned there with them before she escaped. She also confirmed all the information the prisoners told us."

Cowboy whistled. "Things are starting to get interesting. Lo Chang, do you know the area around Vang Vieng?"

"Yes. Communist camp five kilometer north of town."

Cowboy took out a CIA map of Laos and found Lima Site 6 located about four kilometers west of the town. He pointed to the map.

"That would put the camp about five or six kilometers from our airstrip. Could we walk from the airstrip to the camp without going over mountains or rivers?"

"No mountain. Small river with bridge here," Lo Chang said as he pointed to the map.

"Do you think Lone Ranger would fly us in there and take us out after we freed the Hmong prisoners?" Jake asked.

"It's possible," Cowboy said. "He's as frustrated as I am watching the Communists run roughshod over these people. How do you plan on taking the camp? We don't exactly have overwhelming firepower."

"I'll be the bait to draw Scarface out of the camp with some of his soldiers. While he's focused on me, the Hmong warriors can kill the camp guards, free the prisoners, and get them to the airstrip."

"I don't like the sound of that. How're you going to bait this crazy man?"

"You heard Tong Fu say Scarface hates me more than anything in the world. He won't be able to resist trying to capture me again when he knows I'm so close."

"How's he going to know you're there?"

Jake pulled the Polaroid picture out of his pocket. "We send Tong Fu back to him with this picture and tell him I'm waiting for him to come to me."

"Where are you going to meet him?"

"I haven't figured that out yet. Lo Chang, is there somewhere between the airstrip and the camp I could hide until Scarface comes to meet me?"

"Old French rubber plantation near camp."

Cowboy thought for a moment and then said, "He'll be suspecting some sort of ambush. What makes you think he won't just shoot you?"

"I know this man. He loved to torture me. He could have killed me anytime, but he didn't. He needed to hurt me to transfer some of his pain to someone else."

"You still haven't told me how you'll get away."

"We can put a sniper in the plantation building. He can take out the bad guys when it's time."

Cowboy was quiet for a moment as he considered the bold plan. "This would be a rogue mission that no one outside of our group could ever know about. If something goes wrong, you'll likely die at the hands of Scarface. The CIA won't send in the cavalry to rescue you."

"I'm willing to take that risk."

"Let's sleep on it," Cowboy said. "If you can find enough Hmong warriors, I'll see if Lone Ranger is willing to take you in there."

"Thanks. It would mean a lot to me."

"Don't let your personal feelings cloud your judgment, son. I know you want to repay a debt, but I don't want to see you lose your life over it."

"A boy lost his life for me, Colonel. The way I see it, I have to atone for his death. I really have no other choice."

CHAPTER TWENTY-EIGHT

The next morning, Jake awoke just before sunrise when a rooster crowed loudly somewhere within the confines of the camp. Lo Chang was already outside the headquarters building assembling his small army of a dozen Hmong soldiers for the upcoming raid. In the next room, Jake could hear Cowboy talking to Lone Ranger on the radio. Before his feet touched the floor, Jake said a silent prayer asking God to keep them safe during the mission to free Lo Chang's family and the other Hmong tribesmen. Today he was going to face the enemy and end the nightmares once and for all.

After making plans for the assault the previous night, he had recalled what Lo Chang said about the Pathet Lao he'd killed. He said most of them were just normal people with families who were merely following the orders of their commanders. That's what Jake had heard from the two prisoners, Dao Sayavong and Tong Fu. They were just pawns in this crazy war. Unlike the insane tyrant they had been forced to follow, they didn't have killers' eyes.

He had spoken last evening with the two Lao prisoners and told them the plan he hoped to carry out with their assistance. As he explained their roles in the expedition, he watched their reactions closely. They expressed some fear and hesitancy to return to Laos until he assured them they would be brought back to Thailand after the mission was accomplished. Although there was a possibility the Lao prisoners could once again fall under the spell of their evil master, he told them it was a chance they had to take. They would be covered by a sniper, he said, just in case.

"Lone Ranger will be here in an hour," Cowboy said, drinking a morning cup of coffee.

"Do you remember Lieutenant Jim Sizemore?" Jake asked.

"Sure. Whatever happened to him?"

"He's teaching school near Chicago. If anything goes wrong today—if I don't make it back—have the Agency contact Jim and have him notify my wife. I don't want some government official breaking the news to her."

Cowboy nodded. "I'll have some ice cold beer waiting for you when you get back."

Lo Chang's men were ready when Jake exited the headquarters building. Cowboy had ordered them to be equipped with enough weapons and ammunition to start a war. The Hmong were anxious to get back into the fight, especially when their efforts would win the release of many women and children.

"Can you speak Lao?" Jake asked Lo Chang.

"Yes."

"I want you to translate for me as I talk to the Pathet Lao prisoners."

Lo Chang followed him to where the prisoners were being held. Jake asked them if they were still willing to help, and they both answered affirmatively. He had Lo Chang arrange for them to be fed as the group waited for the plane to arrive.

"Do you think these two prisoners can be trusted to carry out the assignment we've given them?" he asked Lo Chang.

"Never trust Communists. We protect you."

Soon the droning of the C-123 engines could be heard reverberating through the air as the raiding party waited near the airstrip for its arrival. After landing, the aircraft taxied to the far end of the runway. Jake was relieved to see Lone Ranger had found a copilot for the hazardous flight. There was some comfort in knowing both pilots were veterans of combat who had made the journey into Laos thousands of times before. The invaders would need all the help they could get.

As a precaution, the Pathet Lao prisoners had been bound and blindfolded after finishing their meal. Jake and Cowboy did not want them to know how many warriors were involved in the operation in case they decided to compromise the secret mission. The two were strategically placed between the Hmong warriors on the aircraft. Communication was kept to a minimum by using hand signals. Jake knew the element of surprise would be on his side initially. Unlike the tides of the ocean, however, the tides of war could not be predicted with certainty by consulting well-established charts. He was counting heavily on divine intervention.

A heavy mist partially obscured the jungle below as the plane lifted off and began a steep ascent to altitude. Within a few minutes, he could see the reddish-brown waters of the mile-wide Mekong River directly below. A knot gripped his stomach. He was facing the reality of returning to the country where he'd been imprisoned for what had seemed like an eternity. He wanted to see that river only one more time—when he crossed it heading back into Thailand in a few hours.

He looked at the watch on his left wrist and saw the time was 0730 hours. The CIA had given him the special watch during training the previous year. For the first time, he pressed the stop-watch feature and saw the watch face briefly illuminate.

Let's hope this high-tech piece of equipment functions as advertised.

During the half-hour flight, the Hmong warriors remained stern-faced yet at ease on the eve of the upcoming battle. For them it was just another day in their endless struggle to survive. They had faced the enemy many times before, but rarely with a chance to rescue so many of their own people. For Lo Chang, however, this mission was unique. He had been searching in vain for his family for several years. Now his quest was nearing an end. His wife and daughter were somewhere nearby, and their lives depended on the success of the hastily prepared plan that had been adopted.

The aircraft began to descend toward the jungle canopy below as the pilots aimed for a narrow dirt runway a few miles in the distance. Jake could see the town of Vang Vieng off to the right. The plane banked steeply to skirt the populated areas. Further to the north, a gleam of sunlight reflected off the tin roof of a long structure surrounded by a courtyard of open ground. According to the information provided by Lo Chang, that place was the concentration camp. From Jake's vantage point, the trek on foot from the airstrip to the camp did not look difficult.

As soon as the plane landed and shut down the engines, the Hmong leaped into action. They quickly opened the cargo door of the aircraft and exited the plane to take up defensive positions in case the enemy was waiting. Seeing no immediate threat, Lo Chang hurried off toward the concentration camp with eight of his fellow Hmong warriors. They would lay siege as soon as Scarface had taken the bait. Two Hmong soldiers would be left behind to guard the pilots and the aircraft. One soldier, handpicked by Lo Chang, would act as Jake's bodyguard.

Jake waited several minutes before removing the blindfolds from the prisoners and exiting the plane. His bodyguard then led the prisoners down a path toward the destination several miles northeast of their present position. Jake brought up the rear of the small formation. The trail took them through a large rubber plantation extending for several miles in either direction. The untended rubber trees were a vestige of the French colonial era and later, of the Japanese during World War II. After a march lasting nearly thirty minutes, the group arrived at a dilapidated, two-story, stone plantation building that would serve as the rendezvous point with Scarface. It was time to set the plan in action.

Jake untied the prisoners and handed Tong Fu the picture of him taken by Cowboy right after his escape from Scarface. It was the Jake the madman would remember. He shook hands with Dao and Tong Fu and then watched as the two men hurried away toward the concentration camp. Jake positioned himself against a low cement retaining wall that ran around the plantation. His Hmong bodyguard had picked out a spot on the second floor of the plantation building where he had a clear view of the area with an open field of fire.

For a moment, he imagined Scarface and Douglas Kingston walking side by side as they made their way toward him. He was thankful he was dealing with only one demon at a time. Within a few minutes, the Hmong soldier guarding him indicated there were three people coming down the trail. Then Jake saw him.

Scarface was approaching armed with an AK-47 and flanked by a soldier on each side. All three had their weapons trained on him. He could see that the soldier to the left of Scarface was Tong Fu. Dao was nowhere in sight. The other soldier appeared large and menacing, glaring at Jake from a distance. The only one smiling was Scarface. Jake wondered what had happened to Dao and if something had gone wrong with the plan. He was about to find out.

"Sergeant Lemaster," snarled Scarface. "You come back to see old friend, yes?"

"Yes, I came back to tell you I have no hard feelings for the way you treated me. A war was going on, and you were just doing your job."

"War still going on. My job never end."

Scarface then barked out an order, and the stern soldier came forward to frisk Jake for a weapon. Finding none, he took the wristwatch from Jake's left arm and handed it to Scarface.

"You can have the watch. Now how about giving me something in return? You have my wife's picture, and I want it back."

Scarface put the watch onto his left wrist and admired it as he said, "You know time? I think time to show how much I miss you."

The soldier came forward again and held Jake's arms behind his back as Tong Fu kept his rifle pointed at Jake. Scarface leaned his own rifle against a tree and took Donna's picture from his left front shirt pocket. Slowly he approached and held the picture in front of Jake's face. He kissed the photo gently and then put it back in his pocket.

"I make love you wife every day. Every time make love to Hmong woman, I think of you wife. Now I think she belong to me."

Without warning, Scarface sucker punched Jake in the abdomen and knocked him to the ground with a chop to the side of the neck. The henchman dragged Jake to his feet as Scarface hit him several more times until Jake was gasping for air. The evil look had returned to Scarface's eyes, and his face was once again hideously contorted. This was the madman he had known and hated.

"You've gotten old," Jake said as he stood in front of the assailant. "You don't hit like you used to."

"I think you dream about me. Like I dream of you wife."

Scarface pummeled Jake's body with forceful blows, one after another, until he had to catch his own breath from the intoxicating pleasure of transferring pain to his captive. Jake's face was swollen and bleeding. He desperately tried to suck in air despite the excruciating pain from his bruised ribs crying out with each breath.

Hang in there, Jake, he encouraged himself. *Give it time. Just a little longer.*

He spit some blood onto the ground and spoke to his enemy. "Why don't you try fighting Hmong soldiers like a real man instead of torturing women and children?"

Scarface spit into Jake's face. "What you know of war? I fight French when only boy. Look what I get," he said as he pointed to his own face.

"Yeah, you're right. That's a face even your own mother couldn't love."

The madman's eyes flashed with anger. Then he laughed as he took a knife from the leather sheath attached to his belt and waved it in front of Jake's face. "I make mistake last time. Too nice. This time I give you scar. No more pretty face for you."

As Scarface approached him with the stiletto, he suddenly began screaming and shaking his left arm. Jake could see vapors rising from the skin on his forearm where the watch was firmly clasped into place. Scarface dropped the knife and tried desperately to take the watch off as he continued wailing loudly with pain.

Seeing his opportunity, Jake threw his head back violently, slamming it into the face of the soldier holding him, and wrenching free from his grasp as the startled man fell to the ground. Jake reached for the stiletto lying in the dirt, but the henchman recovered before he could grasp it. He aimed his AK-47 directly at Jake. There was a brief burst of fire, and then Jake saw the soldier's head explode like an overripe melon. The 7.65mm rounds from Tong Fu's weapon had found their mark just in time. Jake's eyes met Tong Fu's as the Lao soldier nodded to him.

An instant later, a single rifle shot sounded from the rubber plantation. It was from the sniper assigned to protect Jake who had misunderstood what had just happened and reacted to protect Jake.

"No!" Jake yelled as he watched Tong Fu's left chest spew blood, penetrated by the sniper's M-16 round. Tong Fu collapsed to the ground. Frothy red blood poured from his sucking chest wound. Jake rushed to his side, keeping one eye on Scarface, who continued to writhe in pain nearby.

Gripping Tong Fu's hand, he said, "Thank you, my friend."

The dying man smiled weakly as dark red blood flowed from the corner of his mouth. The unmistakable look of death overtook him.

Scarface writhed in agony as the flesh of his left forearm was being burned away. The concentrated sulfuric acid released from the high-tech CIA wristwatch had done its job just in time. Jake had activated it carefully in the plane so the toxic chemical would be released five minutes after the watch was removed from his wrist. James Bond would have been proud.

As Jake picked up Tong Fu's AK-47, he heard several short bursts of fire from automatic weapons coming from the direction of the concentration camp. He checked the weapon to make sure a round was chambered and then approached the whimpering man lying in the dirt. For the first time, he saw not a monster but a frightened human being. If he was to be free of the evil man's power over his life, there was only one thing left to do.

Scarface looked at the American standing over him and begged, "Kill me. Kill me."

"Colonel Hue, I forgive you for what you've done. God will be the one to judge you, not me." With those words came the release he had longed for, waited for since he'd first been told forgiveness was his only choice.

He took Donna's picture from Scarface's pocket and then turned his back on his one-time enemy to make his way to the concentration camp. Before he had taken a dozen steps, a maniacal laugh from behind him stopped him in his tracks. When he turned

344

around, he saw Scarface sitting up and facing him. Although the flesh continued to melt from his left forearm, he no longer seemed to notice.

"You never be free from me, Lemaster. You belong to me."

Scarface's appearance in that moment became no longer human but satanic. And his voice, its voice, no longer had any hint of an Asian accent. Jake reflexively fingered the trigger of his weapon.

"That's right, Lemaster. Pull the trigger. Send this miserable wretch to hell. Do it! Just like that innocent Hmong boy you killed."

The thing before him was wracked with spasms of hideous laughter as it gained its feet and headed toward him. Jake's first impulse was to shoot before it was too close. But that's exactly what it said it wanted. If he took orders from that thing—whatever it was—he would belong to it.

"Do it! Do it just like that pretty wife of yours flushed your son into the bowels of hell!" the evil voice that had taken over Scarface's body said.

Jake's finger tightened on the trigger as he fought to make sense of the supernatural warfare in which he found himself. Shaking his head slowly from side to side, he said, "You don't own me anymore. I belong to someone more powerful than you. I belong to Jesus now."

When he said the word *Jesus,* the demonic being that had overtaken Scarface's body convulsed as though it had been electrocuted. Thick, white, foamy spittle oozed from the corners of its mouth as Scarface's hand reached out to take hold of him.

The next sound was the report of a rifle, and Jake watched as Scarface lunged forward onto the ground. As he turned around, he saw the Hmong warrior who'd fired his weapon walk up and stand over the lifeless body of Scarface. His bodyguard nodded, as if satisfied with his efforts, and then began walking toward the camp.

Judgment day can come pretty damn fast, was all Jake could think at the moment.

≈+ +≈

Lo Chang and his warriors had reached their destination—the Pathet Lao concentration camp outside Vang Vieng to free its prisoners. Only three sentries guarded the gates of the compound, so the fight would be an easy one.

When they heard gunfire from the direction of the rubber plantation, they quickly took out the Communist guards and stormed the compound. Several more Pathet Lao soldiers appeared from within the bamboo and wooden structures scattered inside the walls of the camp. The Hmong warriors rapidly mowed them down with a hail of bullets.

The camp was then eerily quiet. Lo Chang and his warriors fanned out through the camp to search for their tribesmen being held captive. From somewhere within one of the wooden structures, the high-pitched cry of a young infant pierced the silence.

Lo Chang hurried to the building where the sound seemed to emanate from, all the while staying alert to the possibility of more Communist soldiers hiding within the camp. As he reached for the wooden door, he was filled with hope for the first time in many years. His wife and daughter must be there.

A burst of automatic weapon fire erupted from the building off to his right. He saw a Pathet Lao soldier exiting the building, his AK-47 spraying a pattern of bullets that splintered the wooden structure before him. Crouching reflexively, he fired. The enemy soldier fell to his knees. His eviscerated bowel spilled on the earth all around him. Lo Chang then fired a single shot to the head, nearly decapitating the man and ending his life.

The crying from within the building had intensified, and several new voices had joined the chorus during the violent encounter.

Keeping his weapon at the ready, Lo Chang threw open the door and leaped inside. Huddled in the far corner of the room was a group of Hmong women and children, maybe a dozen or more. He could see the expression of fear in their eyes change to hope as they recognized what had just taken place. His heart sank. His wife and daughter were not there.

Lo Chang spoke to the Hmong women and escorted them out of the building. As he reentered the open area of the compound, it was then that he saw them. There walking among another group of captives were his wife and daughter!

Thao Nhia was a shadow of her former self, so thin a strong wind could have knocked her over. But to Lo Chang's eyes, she was as beautiful as when he had made her his bride. The pain in her eyes pierced his heart. He would not allow his thoughts to dwell on what the enemy had done to her. Lo Moua, his precious daughter, walked next to her mother. Lo Chang saw that she had not yet become a woman. He hoped she had been spared from the unspeakable horrors the Communists routinely inflicted on the Hmong women. Although she was still a child, her sorrowful eyes told him the atrocities of the war had taken a heavy toll on her life as well.

Slinging his weapon over his shoulder, he rushed to his wife and daughter. Thao Nhia initially shrank back in fear as someone grabbed her shoulder from behind. When she realized who had touched her, she threw her arms around her husband and wept with joy. Lo Chang embraced his wife with one arm and his child with the other. Tears flowed down his face as he thanked the spirits for reuniting him with his family.

"Come, we must go quickly," he said to his wife and daughter. The three of them rejoined the cadre of liberated people heading away from the camp.

Before Jake could reach the camp, he saw a large group of women and children coming down the trail toward him. Hmong warriors were protecting the freed prisoners on all sides as the group retreated in the direction of the waiting aircraft. Near the back of the pack was Lo Chang with a woman and young girl by his side. Jake guessed the truth. It was his friend's wife and daughter. When Lo Chang saw him, a smile graced his face. Jake quickly joined the group alongside Lo Chang and his family.

One of the Hmong warriors had been sent ahead of the group to tell the pilots to have the plane ready to take off as soon as the group arrived at the airstrip. Jake picked up a small child struggling to keep up and walked along beside Lo Chang and his family. By the time the group reached the airstrip, the pilots had the engines running. They boarded quickly, taking their place on the cargo bay floor. Within minutes, the plane began its takeoff roll down the dirt runway.

The aircraft climbed to cruising altitude slower than before because of the weight of the passengers. Within fifteen minutes, however, the plane passed over the Mekong River and entered Thai airspace. Many women were smiling through tears of joy, barely grasping the reality of their newfound freedom. Others remained expressionless, locked in misery from the horrors they had been subjected to in captivity.

Cowboy was waiting for Jake as he exited the plane. "What took you so long?" he asked as he handed him a cold beer.

"I had to spend some time with an old friend."

"Some friend," he said as he looked at his battered face. "Good work, son. You've saved the lives of a lot of people today."

"Let's hope this isn't the only future these people can look forward to."

CHAPTER TWENTY-NINE

The refugee camp at Nam Phong was filled with shouts of joy and a renewed sense of hope that day as the freed Hmong celebrated a small victory in their life-and-death battle against their Communist adversaries. Jake watched the tearful reunion with a sense of pride and satisfaction, knowing he had played a small part in liberating those people. At the same time, he knew that much work remained to be done before the Hmong would truly be free.

A profound feeling of weariness draped itself over him like a lead overcoat. It was as if he had traveled forever and had reached the end of an arduous journey. But what had he actually accomplished? If he were brutally honest with himself, he would admit that selfish motives had driven him to that place. Yes, some good had come from his actions. And he'd had a chance to speak words of forgiveness to Scarface before the Hmong warrior had killed him. But he still felt he would never be able to do enough to be vindicated for the transgressions of his past.

"You look like you just got run over by a truck," his doctor friend Bill said as he approached and stood next to Jake.

He had spent a lot of time talking with Bill about God during the hours they were together in the clinic. He valued Bill's wisdom and spiritual guidance—both of which he desperately needed at the moment.

"I've been a fool, Bill. I thought life would magically be wonderful after I took care of some of the things that have plagued me for so long. Instead I feel like all I've done is neglect my wife as I chased an unattainable goal."

"Change your goal, Jake. The Christian life is a marathon. We have to follow Jesus every day, not just until we reach some personal objective of ours. The plumb line for our lives doesn't change. If it did, we'd continually be thrown off balance every time a new crisis came along. And believe me, one will. For now, celebrate one milestone."

"I don't know how you do it. So many of these people, your patients, will die in spite of everything you do for them. Don't get me wrong. I think you're a great doctor. But how do you deal with it when you can't heal someone?"

"I remember the prophetic words I heard long ago. Their message goes something like this: Oftentimes we live our lives in chains, never knowing we have the key."

"Did Jesus say that?"

"No, they're lyrics from a song by the Eagles," Bill said as he laughed and poked Jake in the ribs.

"I'm beginning to wonder about you, Doc."

"Actually Jesus did have a lot to say about that subject, and his words are in the Bible. My point is that it's not my job to heal everyone. It's humanly impossible, and I could never live up to that standard. Jesus is the Great Physician—the ultimate healer— and he was the key that freed me from the chains that held me captive. Only when I allow him to work in me and through me can I truly be of service to anyone. Yes, God expects me to show up prepared to serve every day, but the results of my work are in his domain. Does that make sense?"

Jake pondered Bill's explanation and tried to apply it to his own situation. "I guess you're saying I need to do what I can to help the Hmong and leave the results to God."

"Exactly. And now there's something else you need to take care of."

"What's that?"

"Your wife. The Bible says to love God above everything and everyone in the world. As a husband, your next priority is your wife. No matter what you accomplish for the Hmong, you are sinning against God if you neglect the woman he gave you to spend your life with. You have to get home and make things right with her, and when the CIA lets you, tell her the truth about why you are here."

Bill's words pierced Jake's heart. The words he had spoken resonated within him. There was no denying it. His obsession to help the Hmong had compromised his marriage long enough. It was time to go home.

"How much do I owe you for this visit?"

"This one's free. Go home, Jake. And if you ever need a reference for medical school, give me a call."

"Sounds like a plan," he said as he shook Bill's hand. "If you'll excuse me, I need to call my wife and tell her I'm coming home."

A few moments later, Jake sat impatiently in Cowboy's office as he waited for the overseas call to go through. A pervasive sense of guilt held him hostage. He had been so obsessed with trying to right the wrong of accidentally killing Lo Na that he had neglected the one person who loved him most.

"Hello," a distant female voice said at last.

"Hi, honey," Jake said. "How are you?"

"Lonely."

"I'm ready to come home now, if you'll still have me."

"Did you finish what you had to do?"

"Yeah. Listen, I owe you a huge apology for not being there for you."

"When are you coming home?"

"I should be there in a few days."

"Promise?"

"I promise."

"I'm counting on you, Jake. I'm tired of being alone. I need you here."

"I need you, too, honey. More than I ever realized."

"Your family is worried about you. I've spent some time with them while you've been gone. You owe them an explanation too."

"I'll do my best to make things right with everyone. Will you help me?"

"I'm here for you, Jake. But it's going to take some work to get our lives back on track."

"I'll do whatever it takes to make you happy."

"Try staying home for a while."

"You got it. See you soon."

Later that day, after the new refugees had been processed into the camp, Lo Chang sought out Jake to introduce his wife and daughter.

"My wife say thank you for saving Hmong today."

"Tell her you saved my life several years ago. I'm happy to see your family together again."

Lo Chang's wife nodded politely and then stepped away to tend to her daughter.

"Hmong soldier say Colonel Hue dead. You go home now?"

"Yes, very soon. Lo Chang, have you thought about coming to live in America? I know a place where there are beautiful mountains like in your homeland."

"We have no home now. But America? Maybe easier live on moon."

Jake laughed. And yet he understood Lo Chang's difficulty in imagining how he and his family might be able to start a new life in America. "I'll see what I can do to help. Cowboy will know how to get hold of me."

Lo Chang held out his hand. "Thank you. You always be my friend."

As Jake watched him walk away to join his family, he realized all the pain and suffering he'd gone through had been worth it.

Mike must be right. Maybe God does allow bad things to happen to us so we can be prepared to help others when they need it most.

That night at dinner, Jake told Cowboy it was time for him to go home to his wife. It had been nearly two months since he and Donna had been together. From the phone conversation with her earlier, he could tell she was losing patience. She was happy he was safe and had been able to help others, but she was definitely feeling neglected. He had pleaded guilty and promised to make it up to her soon.

"You deserve a break. I'll make a call tonight and get you a ticket home."

"I'll keep writing stories if you pass along the information you want people to know. By the way, can you help get Lo Chang and his family into the States?"

"Where're they going to go? They'll be like fish out of water in America without someone to help them get settled."

"If you get them to America, I'll take care of the rest."

"I'll see what I can do. Of course, you'll owe me for it."

"I was afraid you'd say that."

CHAPTER THIRTY

As Donna and Jake strolled hand in hand through Shaw Park after dinner, the dogwood trees were resplendent with color. A gentle, warm breeze kissed their cheeks and awakened their olfactory senses to the pleasing scents of a variety of blooming flowers. It was the springtime of their lives once again.

"How much did you miss me?" Donna asked.

"More than you'll ever know," Jake said.

"What exactly were you doing over there all that time?"

He pulled a well-worn picture from a shirt pocket. "I had to get your picture back."

She looked at her college picture. "There's a good story behind this wrinkled old photo. Tell it to me."

"The guy who tortured me for seven months took it from me when I was captured. I wanted it back."

"This guy was in the refugee camp?"

"No, he had his own camp."

"And you went there to see him and he just gave you back the picture?"

"Let's say he was dying to give it back."

"Now you're scaring me. I'm not sure I want to hear the rest of the story. You know how I feel about killing people."

"I didn't kill anyone, Donna. In fact, I forgave several of the men who tortured me."

"Have you ever thought of getting some counseling, Jake? It might help you after all you've been through."

"Do you think I need it?"

"Yes, I do."

"Then I'll do it if it makes you happy."

"You need to do it for yourself, honey. If you get your past squared away, then our life together will be better. Does that make sense?"

"It makes perfect sense."

"I spent some time with Mike while you were gone. He helped me work through some issues. He's the one who suggested counseling, for both of us. He said it really helped him after his wife died."

"Could we do it together, as a couple?"

"Well, I've already started seeing a counselor on my own. But I think we need to get some marriage counseling also."

"I'll start looking for someone tomorrow."

"Here's where you can start," she said as she handed him a business card with a name, address, and phone number on it. "My counselor said this guy is really good. He's a Vietnam vet himself."

"You've done your homework," he said as he took the card and pocketed it.

"I just want us to be a normal couple, Jake. Is that too much to ask?"

"No, it's not. And I think it's time for me to see about getting a job at the *Post-Dispatch*."

"Are you serious? I'll have my father call the editor tonight."

"He'll do that even after I almost killed him?"

"He told me about that night, what transpired between the two of you. He even admitted to me it was wrong for him to be the one to tell you about the abortion."

"Have you two reconciled your differences?"

"We're working on it. Considering you are the major point of contention between us, I'd say we're learning to coexist."

"I suppose this means I'll have to forgive him. He was so easy to hate."

She poked him in the ribs. "Do it for me. He's still family."

About that time a young couple came by, pushing an infant in a stroller. Jake saw the way Donna looked longingly at the baby.

"Something on your mind?" he asked as their eyes met.

"I think it's time. I think God wants us to have a child."

The Scripture verse from the devotional they had read that morning came back to him as he studied his wife's face. It was Jeremiah 29:11. "For I know the plans I have for you," declares the LORD, "plans to prosper you and not to harm you, plans to give you hope and a future."

Their lives reflected the choices they each had made, for better or for worse. The paths they had taken, separately and together, had been strewn with much pain and sorrow, often of their own making. For far too long, they had heeded the lie whispered to them by the great deceiver who said, "There is no other choice." But by the grace of God, their future was secure. Both of them, in their own time, had made the most significant choice of their lives.

Jake had come to believe God's timing was always perfect. Caressing Donna's face in his hands, he said simply, "Let's go home."

EPILOGUE
ONE YEAR LATER

July 1976

Lo Chang stepped off the Northwest Airlines 737 jet and entered the Missoula airport followed closely by his wife and daughter. A complex mixture of emotions raged within him as he realized he had reached the end of an improbable journey. He was grateful to his American friends, Jake and Cowboy, who had made it possible for him and his family to begin a new life in America. And yet he felt a profound sadness as well. So many of his Hmong tribesmen were still dying in the mountains of Laos or languishing in refugee camps in Thailand.

Jake saw the anxiety etched on Lo Chang's face as he and his family set foot in their new homeland. The memory of his initial encounter with Lo Chang in the jungle of Laos three years before made him smile.

Who would have ever believed it would turn out like this.

"There they are," he said to Donna.

She smiled and waved her right hand to the people who had come to be such an important part of her husband's life. Two-month-old baby Grace nestled comfortably in her left arm, oblivious to the momentous occasion taking place.

"They look frightened, Jake."

"It'll take time for them to adjust to a life of freedom. And they have a lot to learn about our culture."

He knew the Hmong he was about to greet had never experienced a life where they could live without the continuous threat of a relentless enemy who thought they were a subhuman species. But he was confident they would adapt to their new environment. After all, they were survivors.

"He looks like an outdoorsman to me," Scott said.

Scott, Jake's cousin from Montana, had been instrumental in finding a suitable house for Lo Chang's family in Hamilton and in procuring Lo Chang a job with a local logging company. He was there along with Jake and Donna to meet the family. Donna had insisted on buying the house Scott found with a portion of her inheritance money and turning it over to Lo Chang when he arrived there. She and Jake had devoted their lives to God and to each other, and they both felt blessed beyond belief. With the birth of their baby daughter a few months before, the wonders of motherhood had healed some of Donna's deep emotional wounds of the past. Although she still ran Blanford Pharmaceuticals, her priorities had definitely been rearranged.

"Welcome to America!" Jake said as he shook Lo Chang's hand.

"Cowboy say tell Jake hello."

"He's still there?"

"He very busy. Communists use poison gas from plane to kill Hmong now. Too many people go to Thailand."

"I'm sorry to hear that, but nothing surprises me anymore."

Jake had continued writing articles about the atrocities taking place in Laos after returning to St. Louis the year before. His *Post-Dispatch* employer failed to share his concern for the extermination of a people group on the other side of the world. To say he had lost his enthusiasm for journalism was an understatement. That, and his medical experiences with Drs. Carol and Bill Mattingly, had ignited a desire in him to pursue a career in medicine. Maybe then he could make a bigger difference in the lives of the most needy, like Bill was doing.

He greeted Lo Chang's wife and daughter and introduced them to Donna and Scott.

"My wife is waiting for us at the house," Scott said. "I hope you're hungry because she's cooking up a moose for supper."

Lo Chang looked puzzled and asked Jake, "What is moose?"

Jake laughed. "Don't believe anything this guy says."

As they walked outside, he watched Lo Chang drink in the majestic beauty of the mountains—his new home.

Lo Chang turned to him and said, "Dr. Bill tell me about God you worship in America. He say God sent his son to die for people so people may live. This God must be good. You must tell me more."

A huge smile broke out on Jake's face. "I'd love to. Let's get you home."

ACKNOWLEDGMENTS

This story is a tribute to the many aircrew members who served our country so valiantly during the Vietnam War. As a former B-52 tail gunner of that era, I was compelled to share what the crews went through in the perilous sky over Hanoi. Their courage and valor should never be forgotten.

My wife, Becky, was my biggest cheerleader throughout the nearly two-year project. She kept me on track with precious words of support even as I was sequestered in my room writing for many hours at a time. You are truly the love of my life, dear.

I am deeply indebted to my fantastic editor, Karen Roberts. She guided me through the many edits and rewrites with just the right mixture of honesty and encouragement. Thank you, Karen. I couldn't have done it without you.

Major General Rick Sherlock (U.S. Army Retired) came to my aid by providing valuable input to improve the story. Despite his duties as President and CEO of the Association of Air Medical Services, Rick graciously volunteered his time as he did on my previous book, *Answering The Call*.

Reverend Patrick Smith has taught me a great deal about how to live in the world as a man of faith. His insights sharpened the storyline tremendously. Thank you, Pat, for your extensive feedback, your wisdom, and your friendship.

Dr. Jim Turner, my ER colleague, enthusiastically backed this endeavor and added sage advice.

Sherry Minton helped me see the story from a woman's perspective. Her keen observations were instrumental in rounding out the characters.

Much of what I learned about the plight of the Hmong people was gleaned from the excellent book *Tragic Mountains,* written by Jane Hamilton-Merritt. Jane, a big thanks to you as well.

ABOUT THE AUTHOR

James Richard Milstead served in the USAF (1971-1975) as a B-52 tail gunner. He flew 59 combat missions from air bases in Thailand and Guam during the Vietnam War.

After completing four years of military service, Milstead attended Southern Illinois University where he received his undergraduate degree in Physiology in 1979 and his medical degree from the SIU School of Medicine in 1982. Dr. Milstead works as an emergency physician and lives with his wife, Becky, in Frankfort, Indiana. He and his wife have three children and seven grandchildren. He has been involved in short-term Christian mission work around the world for more than twenty years. He is Chairman of the Board of Directors of Hope in the Harvest Missions International, a non-profit organization working in Liberia to promote agricultural and personal transformation.

Dr. Milstead is the author of Answering The Call: The Story Of Grace On Wings, The Nation's Only Charity Air Ambulance. The book was published in 2013 by Xulon Press and received a Christian Writer's Award. He has served as Medical Director for the ministry of Grace on Wings since its inception in 2006.

www.ingramcontent.com/pod-product-compliance
Lightning Source LLC
Chambersburg PA
CBHW070754280626
47162CB00016B/282